WILL LOVE HEAL THE DEEPEST OF WOUNDS?

WHISPERED PRAYERS

of a girl

ALEX GRAYSON

Whispered Prayers Of A Girl

Copyright © 2017 by Alex Grayson.

Chapter One

Gwendolyn

"IT'S SUCH A SHAME WHAT HAPPENED."

"*They say it left him a bit... unhinged.*"

"*Well, I can't really say I'm surprised. I bet it would leave you a bit rattled too.*"

"*Not to mention the scars. You know he has to remember what happened every time he sees them.*"

"*That's why he only comes to town once every couple of months.*"

"*It's such a shame, and a waste.*"

I put the can of cherry filling in my shopping cart and peek around the corner of the shelf. Three old ladies are at the end of the next aisle over, same position as me—sneaking around the end of their own shelves—whispering behind their hands. With the three of them in the way, I can't see who they're talking about. I step out further to try to get a look, but all I see is the backside of a man wearing a black-and-gray plaid shirt rounding the corner several aisles over.

I shake my head, putting the whispers and my curiosity behind me. It's not my business to know what or who they're talking about. The last thing I want is to get caught up in rumors.

I walk the aisles, glad to know this small market has all the ingredients I need for my mom's cherry-apple pie recipe. Coming from a big city and having anything and everything just a few miles away, you'd think we'd have a hard time adjusting, but it's been just the opposite. The town may be small, but it has all the essentials we need to live.

Simple is why we moved here. Simple is what we need. Simple is hopefully what will make us all happy again.

And the people have been absolutely amazing and very supportive, too.

I glance down at my watch, surprised to see I've been gone for a couple hours already. Mrs. Tanner has been great the few times I've needed to run errands and the kids didn't want to come with me, but I refuse to take advantage of her.

I grab a bag each of Starbursts and York Peppermint Patties, the kids' favorites, at the end of the checkout lane, then start unloading my cart.

"Hey there, Gwen. How're you today?" the clerk asks while sliding items under the scanner.

I smile at the older man. "I'm doing good, Jeremy, thank you. How's Mrs. Peggy doing?"

"She's doing better. Her hip's still sore from the fall, but she's almost as good as new."

"That's good to hear." I grab a loaded paper bag and put it my cart. "She needs to be careful going up and down those steps."

"I've told her that. And as much as she hates to admit it, she's going on eighty. She's refused a ramp up until now, but I've told her she has no choice in the matter anymore. My son, Benny, is coming over next week to help me build one."

Last week, while I was leaving the school, which happens to be right across the street from the market, I saw Jeremy rushing to his car. The next day, the talk around town was that his mother fell

WHISPERED PRAYERS OF A GIRL

while walking up the steps to her house. She was lucky to only have received a sore hip and a couple bruises.

"How are the kids liking their holiday?" Jeremy asks.

I blow a few strands of hair out of my face. "Loving it, actually. Especially Daniel." I laugh. "It gives him more time on the video game. I have to really watch his time on the thing or he'd never get off."

He nods and chuckles. "Bring them to the house next week. Mom's been asking about them."

I smile. "I will."

Jeremy and his mom, Mrs. Peggy, have been wonderful since we've moved to Catalina's Valley, Cat's Valley to the ones who live here, a little over three months ago. Jeremy was my correspondent when I was looking for a place to rent. Since the teacher I replaced at the school was moving as well, her rented house became available, which happens to be owned by Mrs. Peggy. Over coffee one day, Mrs. Peggy told me Jeremy's only left her house once to go live on his own. It was twenty years ago when he met and married the love of his life, only for her to die a year later from a sudden aneurysm. She had just given birth to Benny six months prior. He moved back home to grieve and never left.

"That's going to be $68.17," he says, pulling me from my thoughts.

I whip my purse up on the belt and dig around inside for my wallet. I slide my phone, a package of tissues, a small bottle of hand sanitizer, and a nail grooming case to the side, but can't find the darn thing.

I grimace when I remember I left it on the counter at home when I paid my phone bill earlier this morning.

"Damn it," I mutter. "I'm so sorry, Jeremy. My wallet is still on the counter at home. Can I leave and come right back with it?"

"That's fine. I'll just push your cart to the side and—"

"Tack it on to mine," a deep voice says from behind me.

I look at Jeremy, shocked by the generous offer. He's not looking at me though, but at the person standing behind me. I turn to thank the stranger, but the words get stuck in my throat as soon as I see him. He's the man the old ladies were talking about. I know it from the shirt he's wearing.

He doesn't look at me as he puts his items on the belt. All I can see is the left side of his face. He has dark brown hair, slightly longer on the top, and his lower face is covered with bristly hair. It's not long, but definitely longer than just a few days' worth of growth. He has to be over six feet, and I can tell by the bulges in his forearms that he's ripped with muscles. I feel so tiny compared to him.

I turn to Jeremy, who looks just as surprised as me, then back to the man.

"I appreciate the offer, but you don't need to do that, Mr...." I trail off, hoping he'll supply his name. When he doesn't, I continue, undeterred. "I don't live far from here. It'll only take me a few minutes."

"No," he grunts, still not looking at me. I lift my brows at the short reply.

"Sir—" I try again.

"I don't have time to wait for him to cancel the order."

I let out a sigh and nod to Jeremy. Grabbing a small notepad and pen from my purse, I turn back to the stranger.

"What's your address so I can mail you a check?"

"No need," he replies.

"Sir, I'd feel more comfortable paying you back. Please."

I barely hold back my gasp when he drops a big bag of rice on the belt and turns toward me. The entire right side of his face is covered in scars. The beard hasn't grown back properly because of the scarring on that side. It's in patches, leaving some of the brutal-looking flesh visible. It starts from his neck and goes up his cheek and stops at his temple, missing his lips and eye. It looks like burn marks. Regardless of the scars, he's very good-looking. I glance down and see he also has them on his right arm. I don't know this man or what happened to him, but my heart hurts regardless.

"Not to mention the scars. You know he has to remember what happened every time he sees them." The words of one of the old ladies come back to me.

Whatever happened was tragic.

His black eyes penetrate me as he scowls. I swallow nervously, not because of his physical features, but due to the agitated vibes coming from him. I get the sense that feeling is one he usually emits.

"They say it left him a bit... unhinged."

I force my feet to stay in place and my eyes to focus on his and not the devastating scars marring his otherwise handsome face. His scowl deepens until the corners of his eyes crinkle. I decide to just give in. If he's kind enough to offer, then I'll accept. But the next time I see him, I'll pay him back.

"Thank you." I reach my hand out to him. "I'm Gwendolyn, but people call me Gwen."

He doesn't take it, just looks down at it for a second, then turns away and starts putting more items on the belt, dismissing me. When I look at Jeremy, he's ringing up the stranger's items. He looks at me for a moment and gives me a sad smile.

"Thank you, Jeremy," I say, walking to my shopping cart. "Tell your mom I hope her hip gets better."

"Will do, Gwen. Stay safe heading home."

I smile, nod, and with one last look at the man, I turn and push my cart between the sliding doors to my SUV, feeling strangely odd after the encounter with the man with the scars. While it was very nice for him to pay for my purchases, even if it was because he was impatient to be done himself, it was still something you don't see every day. Normal people would have huffed and puffed as the clerk cancelled the order.

When he looked at me with his dark gaze, I not only saw irritation, but also a deep-seated agony. Something so stark, I swear I almost felt the pain from it.

I slip my gloves and hat on when a gust of icy wind blows. Flurries flutter back and forth, leaving a light dusting of white on vehicles. This is the second snowfall since we've been here. Although we're used to the snow, I've heard that winters here in Colorado can be quite harsh. Much different than Indianapolis.

I come to a stop and lift the hatch on the back of my Range Rover. I'm putting in the last bag when something has me lifting my head and looking to the side. I watch as the scarred man walks his own cart over to an older model blue pickup truck. He stops, deposits the bags in the back, throws a tarp over them, then pushes the cart back to the front of the store. Although I know he has to feel my eyes on him, he doesn't look my way. I'm stuck in place as he gets inside his truck, pulls out of the space, and takes off down the road.

It's none of my business, of course, but I can't help the curiosity that plagues me as I watch him turn the corner out of sight.

What happened to him? Is what one of the old ladies said true? Is he unhinged? What memories were they talking about?

I wipe the thoughts away and climb inside my warm truck.

Stop it, Gwen, I scold myself. *It's not your business. You have your own life you have to worry about.*

Starting my truck, I pull away from the market and head back to Mrs. Tanner's house and my two kids.

"HEY, MRS. TANNER," I BLURT when the older woman opens the door. "I'm so sorry I took so long. It took longer than I thought it would at the post office."

She smiles and ushers me inside. "Bah! Don't you worry, Gwen dear, you know it's no problem."

I follow as she walks toward the kitchen. Mrs. Tanner was the first person I met when we moved to town. She's the secretary at the elementary school where I teach, and took an immediate liking to the kids.

"How were they?" I ask, slipping my keys into my pocket.

"They were right as rain. Just like they always are."

She pushes open the kitchen door, and my eyes immediately light on the two little redheads sitting at the table. I walk up to Daniel first and bend his head back so I can kiss his forehead.

"Hey, kiddo."

"Hey, Mom," he replies, his bright green eyes staring up at me as he smiles, showing two canine teeth missing.

"That looks good, Daniel. You can hang it on the fridge when we get home."

"This one is for Mrs. Tanner. She said her kids are too old to color pictures for her fridge anymore, so I figured I could color one for her instead."

I look up at Mrs. Tanner and see her smiling at Daniel. My eyes drop back to him.

"Well, that's awfully sweet of you. I bet she'd love that."

"It'll bring color back to my fridge."

I ruffle his hair before moving on to the silent girl in the next seat over.

"Hey, sweetie." I bend and place a kiss on top of Kelsey's head. She looks up at me and offers me a small smile with sad eyes, then continues her crossword puzzle. For being only eight years old, she's extremely good at them.

Whereas Daniel is open and talkative, Kelsey is the complete opposite. Unfortunately, her low-key response is normal for her. She's very reserved and quiet. For a little over two years, since her father died, she's only ever spoken twice. Once was when she begged me to bring Will back at his funeral, and the other time was a year ago when I had the flu. She quietly asked me if I was going to die as well. It broke my heart when those words left her lips. Not only because of what she asked, but also because I had prayed so hard for her to get better, for her to feel comfortable enough to talk again, for God to bring my little girl back, and when she finally spoke, her voice was more beautiful than I had remembered. I couldn't enjoy it though, because I knew she was terrified she was going to lose another parent.

Although she's only spoken to me those two times, I still hear her every night when she thinks only God is listening. One day, three weeks after Will's funeral, I was walking by her room when I heard something. I was about to go in and check on her, when her soft words stopped me. Peeking in through the small crack, I saw my little girl kneeling in the middle of the bed, her hands clasped tightly in prayer and her eyes closed. Her whispers, begging God to bring back her daddy, had me choking back a cry and holding on to the doorframe to keep from falling to my knees. Every night since then, I've listened to her whispered prayers. It tears me up inside that she doesn't come to me, and I know her heart only breaks more and more every day that her prayers are unanswered, but I'm glad she at least feels comfortable enough to talk to someone.

She has what therapists call selective mutism. It's when someone voluntarily stops speaking for whatever reason. In Kelsey's case, it was the traumatic event of finding her father dead on her bedroom floor after he went upstairs to get her favorite toy. At twenty-eight, he had a heart attack from an unknown blocked coronary artery. It was a freak occurrence that the doctors say only happen in about 5 percent of young men that have heart attacks. For it to happen to Will, someone who's never had heart problems in the past, and has no family history of heart attacks, the chances were even lower.

When Kelsey found him in her room, he was already dead. She was six at the time. The experience left her traumatized. There's really nothing the doctors can do for her. She's been to several therapists, went through multiple sessions without success, and they've all told me the only thing I can do is be her mom and care for her. To show her my love and give her emotional support. That it's up to Kelsey if she wants to be heard again. I just hope one day she will. They've also informed me that this may be permanent, but I refuse to believe that. Those prayers give me hope that my girl isn't totally lost.

I love both my children more than anything in the world. I loved my husband too. It's been a little over two years that he's been gone, and every day I grieve for him. I grieve because I lost the man I love, I grieve for my children who will never grow to know him more than they already do, and I grieve for my husband, who will never see his children grow up.

We moved to Colorado because I felt we needed a change. Although I was taking them away from the place they were born and where memories of their father were, I still felt they needed a new setting, a new start. Kelsey wasn't getting better, and my own grief was debilitating. It wasn't healthy for any of us. Daniel still remembers his father and misses him, but he was so young at the time, he wasn't as affected by his death as Kelsey and I were and still are. That's both a blessing and a curse for Daniel. While I'm glad his pain isn't as harsh as mine and Kelsey's, it still hurts to know that his memories of Will will more than likely fade away over time, until there's nothing left except for what I tell him, and pictures.

"Would you like a cup of coffee before you leave, dear?" Mrs. Tanner asks, snapping me out of my thoughts.

I brush my hands down Kelsey's hair and smile over at Mrs. Tanner. "Thank you for the offer, but I've got groceries in the truck. They'll probably be fine, but I want to get started on Mrs. Myers' pie that I'm taking out to her tomorrow."

She pulls something from the fridge and sets it on the stove before turning back to me.

"You best be careful going out tomorrow, Gwen. They say there's a snowstorm coming in tomorrow afternoon," she informs me.

I watch as Kelsey puts down an answer on the crossword puzzle. It's a word I can't even pronounce, let alone know the meaning. She may not talk, and keeps to herself, but that hasn't stopped her from being one of the smartest kids I've ever encountered. She's always been that way though, even before Will passed away.

"I'll be careful. I plan on going over early in the morning. We'll be back before the storm hits." I turn to Daniel. "Hey, kiddo, go make sure you have everything in your bag."

"Okay, Mom."

He gets up from the table with the picture and carries it over to the fridge, where he hangs it by a rectangular magnet. Stepping back, he admires his work.

"It definitely makes your fridge look more colorful," he says nonchalantly.

Mrs. Tanner laughs. "That it does, Daniel boy. But you should know, now that you've started putting your pictures up there, you're going to have to color me more. I want my fridge filled with them."

He looks over at her and grins toothily. "I'll color you one every time I come over."

Mrs. Tanner watches as he walks away to gather his things. "That boy is special."

I smile in return. "He is." I look over at Kelsey. "They both are."

I grab the cups the kids were using and take them to the sink to rinse.

"School's out for the next few weeks. Any plans for the holidays yet?" Mrs. Tanner asks.

I put the cups in the dishwasher, then walk over to gather Daniel's crayons.

"Nope. I think we're going to just stay here. Will's parents are in California with their daughter, Sophia, for Christmas, and, well... both my parents are gone."

Her smile turns sad as she walks over to me and lays a hand on my arm. "Why don't you three come here for Christmas dinner? My two kids, Kenneth and Bethany, will be here with both their families for a few days. Sara is Kelsey's age and Cody is Daniel's. Might be nice for them to have kids their age to hang out with."

I look down and flip the lid closed on the crayon box. It's the holidays that are always the hardest. This will be the third Christmas we'll have without Will. It was always his favorite holiday, so it was a big deal for our family. The house, inside and out, was always decorated to the max. All the shelves were filled with nativity scenes, all the doorways had lights and garland, the tree was loaded with ornaments. Per Will's request, and much to the kids' delight, we always had some type of Christmas snack the whole month of December. Christmas Eve everyone got a pajama set and got to open one Christmas present to tide us over until the next morning. It was our tradition. I've tried to stick with that tradition, to bring the holiday to life for the kids, but it's just not the same without him.

I look back up at Mrs. Tanner and offer a smile. Maybe being with more people will help distract the kids, and they'll be able to enjoy the holiday like they are meant to.

"Can we do it the day before Christmas Eve? Emma, my best friend, will be in town and we're supposed to have Christmas with her grandmother."

"Absolutely. The kids will be here all of Christmas week."

"Then we'd love to. But I insist on bringing something."

Her answering smile makes her seem ten years younger. "You bring whatever you want. As long as you and those two precious kids are here, I'll be happy."

"Thank you, Mrs. Tanner. We'd be honored to spend Christmas with you and your family."

She reaches up and pats my cheek. "Gwen, dear, how many times do I have to tell you to call me Ruth before you actually start calling me that?"

I laugh. "I don't know. Probably many more times."

"Well, since you'll be spending the holiday with me, I insist that you start."

I smile and scoop up the coloring book and crayons. "I promise I'll try to remember."

I walk around the table to Kelsey, just as Daniel comes back in the room with his book bag slung over his small shoulder.

I squat down beside Kelsey. "Hey, honey. You ready to go? You can help me make Mrs. Myers' pie if you want when we get home."

She looks at me, and I want to cry when her lips stay closed. She

11

gives me a small nod, but that's all. I know she'll help with the pie. She's a very good child, always doing what I ask without complaint. Sometimes I wish she would throw a tantrum. At least she would be showing some form of emotion. But then I feel terrible for thinking that way, because no matter how Kelsey acts, she'll always be perfect in my eyes.

I lean over and kiss her cheek before standing. She immediately gets up, her crossword book in hand, and stands beside me. I reach out and grab her hand. It may be odd for a mother to want to hold their eight-year-old daughter's hand when they are simply walking to the truck, but I steal as much attention as I can from Kelsey, and that includes holding her hand, kissing her head or cheek, hugging her as often as I can—anything I can get. I'm deprived of her voice, if I can help it, I won't be deprived of anything else.

I thank Ruth once more as she holds the door open for us, promising to stop by in the next few days to have dinner.

Chapter Two

Alexander

I PULL MY OLD FORD truck up to the cabin and cut the engine. Grabbing an armload of groceries, I carry them up the steps, then wrestle the key into the lock and kicking the door open with my boot once I managed to unlock it. I set the bags down and go out for the rest. I'll get the horse feed and few other items that go in the barn later.

Gigi, my black lab mix, trots behind me to the kitchen. Once I set the bags down, I pat the top of her jet-black head.

"Hey, girl. How're the pups?" I ask as she walks beside me into the kitchen.

Knowing what she's looking for, I grab a can of dog food from the pantry, pull the tab, and pour the chunky meat into her bowl. She runs ahead of me as I carry the bowl to the door leading to the huge utility room where her pups are. She slips through the doggy door right before I pull the door open. She immediately goes to check on her sleeping pups in the big dog bed across the room, sniffing them and nudging them with her nose, then comes back as

I'm setting the bowl down. She gives it a quick sniff, checking the smell of dinner, before diving in.

"Let me know when you're ready to go out, girl," I tell her. She doesn't acknowledge me, just continues to devour her food like she's starving, when she just ate a few hours ago. Her pups are taking all her nutrients and leaving her with hardly any.

I run my fingers through her hair a couple times, before walking back out of the room and closing the door behind me. I unload the groceries, then put a pot full of water on the stove to start boiling for the chicken. Grabbing another pot, I add more water and set that down on the stove for the rice.

Chicken and rice. One of the simplest meals, but one of the best.

By the time I'm done, Gigi's back from eating, waiting for me at the door. I grab my gloves off the counter where I discarded them before putting away the groceries, then we both walk outside.

The snow's coming down a bit more than it was before. The ground is already covered in a thin layer of white, but this time tomorrow, it'll be at least a couple feet deep, if not more. The snowstorm that's due is supposed to be a harsh one and last for several days. That's why I was in town a couple weeks earlier than normal. The road out here tends to be rough for days after a snowstorm, and I'd rather have everything I need just in case. I did most of the chores this morning that needed doing before the storm, but there are a few things that still need tending to.

As Gigi and I walk across the yard to the barn, I make sure to keep my eyes forward and not look at the half-built house. It's been sitting there abandoned for four years. I've been meaning to tear the thing down, but I just can't yet. It hurts to look at it, but the pain at the thought of destroying it is much worse. I've been trying to build up the courage; I just don't have enough yet.

Gigi barks and takes off in front of me. I chuckle as she chases a rabbit. It must sense the bad weather that's coming and is out foraging for food before being forced to stay in its hole. The rabbit takes off with Gigi after it. She stops after several feet, does her business, then takes off in another direction.

After watching her for a couple of minutes, I get to work on making sure the horses have enough hay and water and everything is secure against the heavy winds that are coming. Luckily, the temperature isn't supposed to be too bad, only the mid-twenties, so I don't have to worry about the horses being too cold since they'll be away from the winds.

I stop long enough to let Gigi in when she starts barking at the back door to the house, then continue the few things I have left. Bandit, the male Arabian I've been working at breaking in, snorts at me as I walk by. I flip him off because I'm pissed at him right now. My damn backside still hurts from him throwing me yesterday.

"Don't you snort at me, you big bastard," I say, baring my teeth with a forced smile. Horses may seem like mindless animals to some, but they're actually pretty smart. They're very watchful creatures and can sense moods.

Bandit's been one of the most stubborn horses I've come across since I started training them eight years ago. Ordinarily, it takes me anywhere from three to eight weeks to train the horses that are brought here, but Bandit's being ornery and doesn't take kindly to someone being on his back. Hell, he doesn't even like it if someone looks at him. I've had him for nine weeks already and have gotten hardly anywhere with him. He's solid black, a very pretty horse, but very moody. He's also purebred and cost the owners a fortune, which means they're being very patient. However, I don't see that lasting much longer if I don't make any more headway with him.

I grab a couple of apples out of a basket, stuff one in my back pocket, then approach the white-and-brown mustang. Bella came to me three years ago to be trained. A few weeks into training, the young girl the owners bought her for fell from another horse and broke her neck. She's now paralyzed from the neck down. Understandably, they no longer needed Bella to be trained for their daughter, so I bought her from them. Unlike Bandit, Bella is very gentle and docile. I put her next to him for a reason, hoping he'll see my interaction with her.

"Hey, girl." She neighs softly and nudges the hand holding the apple, not trying to take it, but letting me know she knows it's there. "I'll take you for a ride as soon as the bad weather passes."

I hold the apple up in my palm, and she crunches down on it. I run my hand down her neck, murmuring quiet words to her. Bandit snorts beside me, and although I don't acknowledge him, I do watch him out of my peripheral vision. His dark head is pointed our way, watching me interact with Bella.

I talk quietly with Bella for several minutes, ignoring the beast beside me, before finally turning to him. His black eyes watch me as I approach his stall, and he tosses his head back a couple times. When I reach out to place my hand on the side of his neck, he snorts loudly and kicks out a hoof.

"No need to get all pissy on me, Bandit," I tell him, keeping my voice calm. He snorts again and turns his head to the side to avoid my hand when I place it on his neck. "Shh... calm down, boy. It's alright."

He lifts his head, dislodging my hand, and takes a step back. I pull the other apple out of my pocket, and he eyes it with interest.

"You want it?" I ask, holding it up. "You have to take it from my hand."

I hold my breath with anticipation as he bends his head and sniffs the apple. His warm breath floats over my hand as I hold real still, not wanting to spook him. He nudges it a couple times, snorts, then knocks the damn apple out of my hand. I narrow my eyes at him when he lifts his head and looks me right in the eye. If horses could smirk, I have no doubt this damn animal would be right now.

"You little shit," I mutter.

He just snorts and turns away, going over to his hay and munching on it, telling me with his actions to fuck off. I bend and pick up the apple, putting it back in the basket. As frustrating as Bandit's been to train, I'm enjoying the challenge he's giving me. It's kept me distracted from thinking of other things. Things I don't like thinking about.

I walk back to the house once I'm finished in the barn. Gigi meets me with a soft bark, then heads back through the doggy door to be with her pups. After checking on the chicken on the stove, I make quick work of the buttons of my shirt as I walk down the hallway to my bedroom. This cabin may be small to some people, but it's perfect for me. Once upon a time, I had plans to build a big house and fill it with laughter, but not any longer. That ship has sailed, crashed, burned, then sunk.

I toss my shirt on the floor in front of my dresser, then take off my pants, leaving them in the same pile. In the bathroom, I turn on the shower to let it warm up. Turning away, I catch sight of my reflection in the mirror. Normally I try to stay away from mirrors. Not because the scars are hideous and I hate looking at them, but because of the memories that come with seeing them. I don't turn away this time. I stand there and force myself to look at them, and the memories immediately assault me.

A woman's laughter and soft smiles.
The screech of tires.
High-pitched screams of fear.
Deep screams of pain.
Innocent wails, then silence.
My own pain gripping me.
My vision fading to black as my life dies before me.

I look at the snarled and twisted skin on my arm and side. I was awake when the heat of the flames hit me. I was conscious when my flesh started to melt. But that's not what I remember when I see my scars. What I remember is what I almost had. I remember not being strong enough to save them. I remember the screams and the broken pleas.

I grip the sink in front of me and hunch over, dropping my head, no longer able to look at myself. It's been four years, but it feels like it was last week.

I turn without looking back at my reflection and get into the shower. The warm water hits my chest first, and it feels good. I relax my head back and blow out a deep breath. I wash away the dirt from the day, then get out and dry myself. Walking naked into my bedroom, I grab a pair of gray jogging pants and slip them on.

While the pot of rice is cooking, I chop up the cooked chicken, then throw it in the pot. I make both Gigi and myself a bowl and set hers on the floor in the kitchen. I carry mine into the living room, where I catch the last quarter of the Broncos game.

After, I put the leftovers away. That's another good thing about chicken and rice. Leftovers.

I let Gigi out once more and throw a couple logs in the fireplace before locking up the house. It's only nine thirty, but I'm exhausted from the extra work I've done today. I take off my jogging pants and put them on the end of the bed, and stretch out naked on the bed, my hands going behind my head.

An unbidden image of the woman from the grocery store comes to mind. *Gwen*. She had hair the color of brown sugar and eyes the color of a cloudless sky. Had I been a normal man, I would have admired her beauty, but I'm not normal and beautiful women are wasted on me.

I have no fucking idea why I offered to pay for her groceries. I told her I couldn't wait for Jeremy to cancel the order, but it was a lie. It wouldn't have taken him more than a minute or two. Actually, I do know why I did what I did. I saw some of the items that were rung up and overheard parts of her and Jeremy's conversation. She has kids. The thought of her dragging her kids out in this weather didn't sit well with me. They should be warm and safe in their home.

I wasn't trying to be rude or an ass when she asked for my name, but I have no desire to be her friend. I just wanted her gone so I could finish with my shit and leave. I hate going to town, and I only do it when I have to. The looks and whispers I get piss me off, and it takes iron will to keep my mouth shut.

She tried to hide it, but I saw the look on her face and heard her breath hitch when she saw my scars. I'm not sure why, but I didn't like the thought of her seeing my fucked-up face and being disgusted. I don't know why I gave a damn, but I did.

I push the thoughts of the brunette away and roll to my side. My eyelids drift closed and it's not long before the exhaustion from today pulls me into a deep sleep.

———

THE NEXT MORNING, I WAKE to fat snowflakes falling. It's not bad yet, but in the distance I can see the dark snow clouds heading this way. The forecast said to expect at least a foot later today and another couple of feet over the next few days.

Most people dread the heavy snowfall, but not me. I love Colorado weather, especially the winters when the snow will come down for days. It may be cold as shit, but it's still beautiful to be around. I like the thought of having a nice warm house to go to after work, walking in and smelling the logs burning in the fire.

After I get dressed, Gigi's waiting at the door to be let out. While I wait on her to finish her business, I make a pot of coffee and stir the fireplace back to life and throw on a couple more logs. I stomp my boots on and walk out back to grab an armful of logs from the back porch. Everything is covered in white, and it looks gorgeous. I've lived in Colorado my entire life, and I never get tired of looking at a freshly dumped snowfall.

Gigi comes bounding around the corner, her coat covered in snow. She stops just long enough to root her nose in the snow until it disappears, then flicks her head up, throwing snow in the air. I whistle and she makes a mad dash for the porch, stopping once she's on the steps to shake.

"Get your goofy ass in the house." I chuckle and snap my fingers.

I follow her inside and unload the logs beside the fireplace. I walk back to the kitchen, the smell of brewed coffee leading me. I'm just pouring a cup when my phone rings. I snatch it off the counter, then groan when I see my mom's name.

My mother is a good, loving woman, but there are times I just can't handle her. She worries, and I love that about her; I just wish she'd know when to leave shit alone. I know she means well, she's a mother after all, but her asking how I'm doing every time we talk, knowing she's referring to my emotional state, isn't something I want or need. All it does is remind me of what I try so fucking hard to forget. It's bad enough I see them every time I look in the mirror, I don't need them thrown in my face.

For almost a year after the accident, she hovered over me like a mother hen. It's just me and my younger sister, so when one of her kids is hurting, I know she hurts as well. Dad had to finally drag her out of my house when he saw she wasn't helping at all, but hindering my mental healing. Before the accident, they were supposed to move to Tennessee where my sister Christa lives, but the accident put the move on hold. Luckily, after realizing what my mother was doing, my father eventually convinced her to go forward with the move. I miss my family, but I'm glad they aren't so close anymore.

I hit Ignore and set the phone back down on the counter. I know I'm being a dick, and I do feel guilty, but I just can't talk to her right now. I'll call her back later or something.

I down the rest of my coffee and head back outside to check on the horses and to haul in another load of wood. My cabin doesn't have central heat and air, so I depend on the fireplace for all the heat. I like it that way.

Once I'm done, I refill my coffee and head outside to sit on the porch. It's fucking freezing outside, but it's beautiful and peaceful. I sit on the wicker chair with my feet up on the railing and look out over the field of white and the snow-covered mountains. I inherited this place from my grandparents ten years ago. My grandfather used to breed horses for a living, before he got too old. I'd come over every day after school when I was younger and help him around the place.

My grandma passed away twelve years ago, and my grandfather was never the same. He always told me the place was mine once he was gone. He knew of my desire to work with horses.

The snow is coming down in huge flakes now and it's halfway up the tires of my truck. Something catches my attention, and I try to focus on it. My feet clunk to the porch, and I get up from my seat. Walking to the railing, I squint. Something's off in the distance, but I can't tell what it is with the heavy snowfall. I set my mug down on the railing and walk off the porch. I've gotten about fifty yards when I realize it's a vehicle.

"Sonofabitch," I mutter. This is the only road out this way for miles. The vehicle looks to be at an angle, indicating they're more than likely stuck in a ditch.

I'm half tempted to leave them out there—it's fucking stupid to be out driving in this weather—but with how fast the snow is coming down and the dropping temperatures, they'll likely freeze to death.

I stomp back to the house, cursing under my breath the entire way. Helping some idiot is the last thing I want to be doing right now. I like my solitude out here, and except for the people I have to deal with regarding the horses I train, I try to avoid them as much as possible.

I swipe my keys from the hook just inside the door and grab a bigger coat from the closet, along with some thick gloves.

"Stay here. I'll be back," I tell Gigi, who's sitting at the door watching me.

I start the truck to let it warm up while I brush snow off the windshield and windows, then put the chains on my tires. Living in this area, it's pretty much required you have four-wheel drive, or you better bet your ass some time or another you'll get stuck. Like the idiots right now on the road that runs along the front of my land.

It takes me ten minutes to clear my truck enough to drive and for my windshield to defrost. The truck is toasty warm when I climb inside and go rescue some ass who's ruining my relaxing day.

Chapter Three

Gwendolyn

"THANK YOU FOR BREAKFAST, Mrs. Myers." I lean down and hug the tiny woman.

"It's the least I can do, Gwen. You really didn't have to drive all the way out here to bring me a pie."

I smile. "I wanted to. You've been so nice to me, and you're the reason I'm even here."

Mrs. Myers is the grandmother of my best friend, Emma, back in Indianapolis. One day Emma was on the phone with her grandmother, who she mentioned one of the elementary school's teachers where she lived was moving away and the school board needed a replacement. It was fate, because just that day before I had told Emma that the kids and I needed a fresh start.

She pats my hand and holds out a container with leftover stew to take home. "We're glad to have you here in Cat's Valley." She puts her hand on top of Daniel's head and ruffles his hair. "It's been a delight getting to know these two."

Kelsey is stoic as she slips on her coat, staring off across the room. I hand her her gloves and watch as she robotically slips them on. Mrs. Myers walks over to her, gently grabs her cheeks, lifts her face, and kisses her forehead. Kelsey doesn't respond in the slightest, just stares up at the older lady.

"You both be good for your momma, and I'll see you at Christmas," she tells both the kids.

"Will you have something for us?" Daniel asks, bold as you please.

"Really, Daniel?" I scold. "You don't ask questions like that."

Mrs. Myers cackles. "He's fine." She pinches one of his cheeks. "You, sir, will just have to wait and see." She turns to me. "Emma's already chomping at the bit to get here."

I hand Kelsey the container of stew to hold while I slip on my gloves. I pull my keys from my pocket, then take back the container.

"I'm excited to see her. I miss her so much."

Emma's been my friend since high school, and I've never gone this long without seeing her. We talk almost daily, but it's not the same.

I make sure both kids are bundled up tight before saying goodbye to Mrs. Myers. When I pull open the door, I'm shocked to see how much snow is on the ground and how hard it's still coming down. When we got here a couple hours ago, there was only about six to eight inches on the ground. Now, my truck has a layer of snow at least four or five inches thick. The heavy snowfall wasn't supposed to start until later this afternoon.

"Oh dear," Mrs. Myers says beside me. "I'm so sorry for keeping you so long. Will you be okay driving in this?"

I turn to look at both kids, not liking the idea, but knowing I'll have to in order to get home. "Yeah. I've got a four-wheel drive, and I've driven in snow before."

She looks worried as she twists her hands together, and I reach over and grab them. "Don't worry. We'll be fine." I offer a smile.

"Make sure you call me once you get home, or I'll worry."

"Will do."

I leave the kids in the house while I warm up the truck and

brush the snow off the windows and windshield. After saying our goodbyes, we load up. I'm used to driving in the snow, but it still makes me nervous, especially when it's coming down so thick. The roads are covered, so I ride down the middle since the lines are no longer visible anyway. I drive slow and grip the steering wheel tightly. When we come across the stretch of road that declines for two miles, I become anxious. Luckily, we make it down the hill without any problems. The relief doesn't last long though.

We've been driving for about twenty minutes and are coming around a curve when all of a sudden, something about the size of a dog with a gray fluffy tail runs across the road. I know better than to do it in this type of weather, and I realize my mistake right away, but my first reaction is to hit the brakes to avoid hitting the animal. The back end of my truck fishtails around until we're almost sliding sideways down the road. I vaguely hear Daniel yelling, but I'm concentrating on trying to straighten out the truck

It's a fruitless effort, as seconds later, we come to a jerky stop with the front end in a shallow ditch. I immediately turn to the kids.

"Are you both okay?" I ask, looking over Daniel, who's shaken but otherwise unharmed. My eyes go to Kelsey next and see no visible injuries. Her eyes are wide with fright and the look makes me sick to my stomach. "Kelsey?" Her gaze swings to mine. I reach back and grab her shaking hand. "Are you okay, baby?" She doesn't respond right away, just looks around wildly, and fear spikes through me. Finally, her eyes meet mine and she gives me a small nod. I blow out a relieved breath that neither are hurt.

I turn back around and take stock of our surroundings. The snow is coming down so hard that it's already starting to cover the windshield, blocking my view. I look out the windows and see nothing. Turning, I look out the back window, and don't see anything there either.

I turn the key, hoping by some miracle I can get us out of here. My truck may be four-wheel drive, but I highly doubt I'll be able to back us out of the position we're in. We're at too much of an angle and the snow is too thick. It's worth a shot, though.

I silently curse when it won't even turn over. I pull my phone from my purse to call Jeremy, and panic sets in when I find I have no signal. I look up when the interior of the truck starts to dim. The snow is covering the windshield fast, and I can already feel the temperature dropping.

I look back at the kids. "Keep on your jackets, hats, and gloves. I'm going to step outside a minute, okay?"

"I'm scared, Mom," Daniel says. He's always been my strong boy, so for him to show fear now means he's really scared.

I get up on my knees and lean over the seat. Grabbing his cheeks, I make him look at me. "Listen to me. Everything is okay. I'm just going to step outside for a minute. I'm not getting a signal on my phone inside the truck because of the snow covering it. I'm going to call Jeremy and he'll come help us."

He looks at me for several seconds, then he nods. I lean over more and kiss his forehead. I move to Kelsey next. She still looks frightened. "Watch over your brother while I'm outside, okay?"

She nods, and I kiss her forehead as well. Sitting back in the front seat, I pull my gloves and hat back on. It won't do much good without the engine going, and the heat won't last long, but I turn the key in the ignition and warmth blasts out of the vents. Grabbing my phone, I quickly get out of the truck and slam the door closed to keep in as much heat as I can. Looking down at my phone, I still have no signal, which isn't really a surprise. Although I detest lying to my kids, I wasn't exactly truthful to Daniel. The chance of getting a signal outside the car is slim to none in this weather. The wind and snow are probably blocking any signal.

I climb the small hill from the ditch and walk out to the middle of the road. I turn in circles, trying to locate a house, or some form of nearby living. The snow is coming down so heavy that it's hard to keep my eyes open to see through it. I shield my eyes with my hand, but it's no use, I see not one damn house around.

Crap. What in the hell am I going to do?

I walk back to the truck and quickly get inside. It's warmer than it is outside, but when I turn to face the kids, they already have puffs of white coming out of their mouths when they breathe. I kill the engine; the air coming out of the vents is no longer warm in the slightest.

"Mom," Daniel says, his voice quivering. "What are we going to do?"

I take a minute to answer him, because... well, I have no damn clue what I'm going to do. Obviously I can't tell the kids that though. I'm the adult, and am supposed to have plans for everything. Helplessness and fear slither in when I realize how dire our situation is. This stretch of road is long and a good distance away from town. The few times I've been out this way, I've only seen a couple of cars, and the chance of one driving by now in this weather is pretty damn slim.

What in the hell am I going to do? Think, Gwen!

"Mom?"

I look back at Daniel and force a smile. I need time to figure out a plan.

"For now, you and your sister are going to come up front with me." I point to the back. "Grab the blanket in the back and climb up here."

They both unbuckle, and while Daniel grabs the blanket, Kelsey climbs over the seat. I lift the console once Daniel has climbed up front as well. He sits in the middle, while Kelsey sits on the other side of him.

"Scoot closer together." They do so, and I put the blanket over all three of our laps. I always have a blanket in the back of my Range Rover. It stems from growing up in the north. My parents always told me it's never a bad thing to be prepared. A look at the windshield shows it's covered completely, and the window on my side is three quarters of the way. Kelsey's window only has a thin layer because of the way the wind is blowing.

"Are we going to be okay?" Daniel asks, and I look down at him, then over at Kelsey.

"We're going to be just fine. Someone is going to come by soon and see us." I ruffle his hair, acting as though I'm not worried, while I silently start to freak out inside. My options are very limited. I can either leave them in the car while I go look for a house, hope another car comes this way and spots us, or bring them with me. I don't like any of those options.

I jump when I hear a loud thump on the window. When I look over some of the snow has slid off the window, and I see someone standing there. Both relief and fear mix together at seeing the person. On one hand, I'm relieved that someone has already found us and we won't freeze to death, but on the other, I have no idea who it is. For all I know, it could be a serial killer. I don't really have a choice though. It's either take the chance and hope I'm not putting my kids in even more danger by opening the door, or ignore the person and hope someone else will find us before we freeze. I opt for decision number one, because the chances of a serial killer looking for victims outside in this weather are low.

I look back at the kids. "See, I told you." I smile.

I take a deep breath, say a silent prayer, and turn the key so I can power down the window a few inches. Wind and snow immediately hit me in the face, and I have to blink a few times to clear my vision. When I do, I'm surprised at who I see. It's the man from the market yesterday. His head is covered in a beanie and the way he's holding his face against the wind hides the scarred side.

"Hi. Thank you so much for stopping."

He bends and peers inside the truck, his eyes flickering from Daniel to Kelsey. He shows no surprise at seeing me.

"Why are you driving out in this?" he asks, bringing his eyes back to mine. This close, they look a dark smoky gray, instead of the black they appeared the other day. I wonder if they change according to what he's feeling.

"We were dropping off a pie at Mrs. Myers' place. It wasn't supposed to be this bad this early," I tell him.

"You learn around here to always expect the worst. It says to expect snow tonight, then you prepare for it today. This close to the mountains, there's no telling when the snow will actually get here."

"Is there any way you can pull me out?"

He straightens and looks toward the front of the truck, then the back, assessing the situation, before bending back down.

"Snow's too thick. I've got chains on my tires, but they won't do any good. You're too far down into the ditch."

I grip the steering wheel and try to stay calm. It could be worse. We could still be out here alone. Besides, I didn't really think there was a chance I'd get my truck out today anyway.

I blow out a breath. "I hate to ask, especially in this weather, but is there any way you could give us a lift to town? My cell phone isn't picking up a signal out here."

He turns his head, and in the six or so inch gap of window, his scar comes into view. The skin looks even more mangled up close. A twinge of pain pierces my chest. The pain he must have endured to have such scars.

He turns back to me, then looks over to the kids. When his eyes flick back to mine once again, his jaw tics, and I know he really doesn't want to help, but there's no way he can just leave us out here. I'm unsure if it were just me he'd leave me to fend for myself or not, but he won't do that to kids. I understand his reluctance; he doesn't know us, and I'm sure he has better things to do than lug around a woman and her two children, but it still irks me that he's so hesitant. It's not like I purposely drove my car off the road.

His voice is gruff when he says, "Grab the kids and let's go," before standing and walking away.

They're both shivering when I tell them, "Come on, let's go get warm."

Grabbing the key out of the ignition and my purse from the

floorboard, I push open the door and the kids follow me out of the truck.

"Wait, Daniel!" I say when he makes a move to walk out of the ditch. I lock my doors, grab Kelsey's hand, and help both kids out of the ditch. Together, we walk over to the running truck parked behind my Range Rover. The man is already inside waiting for us.

I open the door and let Daniel get in first, then Kelsey, before climbing in after her. I didn't realize how cold I was until the warm air from the vents hit me. The truck is old, so it has a bench seat with a seat belt in the middle. I grab the strap and hand it to Daniel. "You and Kelsey have to share a seat belt." I click mine into place once theirs is done.

I glance over at the man and find his hands gripping the steering wheel tightly as he looks ahead. I swallow and say, "Thank you for the ride. You have no idea how much I appreciate this."

A grunt is all I get in return as he puts the truck in gear and slowly starts to creep forward. I fold my hands on top of my purse and look straight out the windshield. I hate the silence, but I'm not going to force the guy to talk if he doesn't want to. He may not want to accept my gratitude, but this is the second time he's come to my rescue, and I'm grateful.

Something tugs on my jacket, and I look down to Daniel. He pulls me across Kelsey and tries to whisper, but it's still loud enough for the man to hear. "What's wrong with his face, Mom?"

"Daniel," I scold, and look up at the man in embarrassment. I know he had to have heard the question, but he shows no sign that he did. "You don't ask questions like that."

"Sorry," he mutters sullenly.

"Don't worry about it. It's alright," the man says, keeping his eyes forward and his expression neutral.

"No, it's not. It's rude and he shouldn't have asked it, especially loud enough for you to hear."

"He's just curious. At least he's honest about his curiosity."

I sit back and think about his statement, remembering back to the old ladies in the market yesterday. From what they said, he doesn't come to town a lot, so I'm sure when he does, the gossip and whispers start anew. I can't imagine everything I'm sure he's over-heard. No matter how quiet people are with their opinions and remarks, it'll still always get back to the recipient of their chatter, especially in a town as small as Cat's Valley.

"I'm sorry we're pulling you away from wherever you were going," I tell him, just to keep some form of conversation going. For some reason, I want him to talk to me.

"I saw your truck from my cabin."

"Oh," I remark. "I didn't see it from the road when I was looking for houses."

"It's hard to see from the road with all the trees, especially when you've got snow blowing in your face."

It turns quiet, then I tell him, even though he never asked, "Something ran out in front of us. I know better than to slam on the brakes in the snow, but I did it to avoid the animal before I realized what I was doing."

"Probably a fox. We get them out here a lot during the winter."

"Mom." Another tug on my jacket has me looking down at Daniel again. "I gotta go pee."

I look over at the man, then back at Daniel. "Can you wait a bit longer? We have to go slower than normal, but we'll be there soon."

All of a sudden, the truck stops, and the man lets out a deep sigh. I'm just about to tell him that Daniel will be fine until we get to town when he climbs from the truck. I look out the windshield and realize he didn't stop for Daniel, but because a tree's fallen across the road, blocking our path. The man walks to the tree, looks at it for a moment, then comes back to the truck.

He hammers his hand on the steering wheel once, mutters a curse under his breath, then looks over at me and mumbles an apology for cursing in front of the kids.

"I can't move it and that's the only road that leads to town, unless we want to go up the mountain and around, which will take hours in this weather, and there's no guarantee we'll make it."

I look from the tree in the road to him, then down to the kids and back to the tree. I talk to the windshield when I say, "I'm sorry." I bring my eyes to him. "Do you know Mrs. Myers? Could you take us to her place, and I'll call someone in town when the roads clear up and the tree's gone?"

His stormy eyes face me. "No," he says bluntly. "I'm surprised you even made it down the mountain in this weather."

He looks out the windshield, his brows narrowed into a frown. Kelsey fidgets beside me, and I look down at her. She's looking forward and most wouldn't notice it, but I see the worry on her face. She doesn't show her feelings often; the scared look on her face earlier and right now are more than I've seen in a while. I reach over and grab her hand. She looks up at me and I smile, trying to ease her worry.

The man's hand brushes my shoulder when he lays his arm on the back of the seat. He turns his head to look out the back windshield and the truck starts to move backwards slowly. A minute later, he's backing into a narrow road that looks to be access to a field, then pulls forward and drives the way we just came from.

"Where are we going?" I ask, curious.

"My place," he grunts.

My eyes widen in shock. I'm not sure what I expected his answer to be, but that certainly wasn't it.

"Do you have a landline? Maybe I can call someone—"

"And what?" he interrupts. "Have them drive over the huge tree in the road? Or have them risk themselves going over the mountain?"

I snap my mouth shut, because he's right. My only two choices are to take the kids back to the car, something I wouldn't do, or let him bring us to his house. I know nothing about this guy, but he doesn't rub me as being someone to harm us. I still hate knowing we'll be imposing on him though.

31

"Mom," Daniel says, tugging once again on my jacket. "I really have to go."

Before I get a chance to respond, the man does. "Five minutes, kid. Or I can pull over if you can't wait and you can freeze your willie off."

I sputter out a laugh and the guy looks over at me. His face is blank and the look wipes away my lingering mirth.

"Can you wait five minutes, Daniel?"

I can tell he wants to say no, but he's trying to pull off the big-boy act in front of the man. After several seconds, he nods.

I look up. "Since you're taking us to your home, can we have your name?" That's one thing that's bugged me since yesterday, not knowing his name.

He takes so long to answer that I fear he won't. We're passing by my car on the side of the road when he says gruffly, "Alexander."

For some reason, the name suits him perfectly. "Thank you for helping us, Alexander," I tell him.

He doesn't respond, just keeps his eyes pinned on the road in front of us. Several minutes pass before we turn down what I assume is his driveway. The snow is still coming down heavily, so it's hard to see what we're driving toward. Everyone stays silent as we slowly creep along, until we pull up to a small cabin. And a cabin is definitely what it is.

He pulls to a stop, shuts off the engine, then opens his door. I follow suit and get out of the truck, then turn to help the kids down. As we walk to the porch, I take stock of the cabin. It's rustic and well-used, but looks properly maintained. We follow Alexander up the steps, and I notice two wicker chairs and a small table between them. On the railing, there's a coffee mug. He notices it at the same time I do and picks it up.

"I was out here drinking coffee when I noticed your truck," he explains.

I turn and look out over the yard toward where I know my Range Rover is. I can barely see anything but a little red blip off in the distance. My eyes slide to the left, and I see a big red barn about fifty feet away. Then they land on a partially built structure.

When I turn back around, Alexander is already gone and the door is standing wide open. I walk the kids across the threshold, then close the door behind us. I take a minute to look around the place. It's just as small as it looks from the outside, but it has a homey feel to it. The floors are a dark hardwood, along with the walls. On one wall is a mounted TV with a brown leather couch and a small wooden table across from it. In the corner is a fireplace that currently holds burning logs. There's a fluffy gray rug in front of it. Very cozy. At the opposite end of the room starts a small area where it looks like a table should be. Beyond that is the kitchen. I spot Alexander standing at the stove.

A wiggling Daniel reminds me that we need the bathroom. I take off my jacket and gloves and have the kids do the same, then hang them on the hooks by the door. Grabbing his hand and with Kelsey following me, I walk us to the bar that separates the dining area and kitchen.

"Could you point us to the bathroom?" I ask Alexander's back.

He doesn't turn around as he says, "Down the hall on the left."

With one last glance at his back, I lead the kids across the living room and into the hall. The bathroom we enter is small, with only a toilet and sink. Kelsey and I wait outside while Daniel does his business. I notice a closed door across from the bathroom and another down at the end. Kelsey goes next while Daniel and I wait.

Once they're both done, we go back to the living room to the couch. "You both sit while I go talk to Mr. Alexander."

He's still standing at the stove when I walk into the kitchen. Steam rises from the pot he's stirring.

"I want to thank you again for helping us," I say. "Hopefully the roads will be clear enough tomorrow so my truck can be pulled out and we can get out of your hair."

"They won't."

He leaves the stove and grabs three mugs out of the cabinet to the left.

"What do you mean, they won't? How could you know?"

He starts pouring the contents of the pot into the mugs before turning to face me. His scars stand out in the light of the room. They're harsh, but oddly beautiful.

"Because I've lived here my whole life. They don't move fast around here. It'll be at least two or three days before the road is clear enough to pull your truck out and for them to move the tree."

He grabs two of the mugs and sets them down on the bar, then hands me one.

"Hot cocoa. Figured you and the kids could use some to warm up."

Before I get a chance to respond with a thank-you, he leaves the kitchen. I turn and watch as he walks out the front door without a backward glance. I look down at the mug in my hand, then at the ones on the bar. The man is a contradiction. At the market yesterday I got the feeling he's not a very friendly person. I got the same vibe in the truck, but then he's thoughtful enough to make my kids and me hot cocoa because he thought we may need to warm up. It was very kind of him, and I can't help the small smile that tugs at my lips at the kind gesture.

I call the kids over and they sit at the bar and drink their cocoa while I stand beside them. Holding the mug up to my lips, I look around the kitchen. The appliances seem to be newer than the rest of the house that I've seen so far. Above the bar is a rack of pots and pans, and down at the end hangs cooking utensils. The counters and cabinets are a polished wood.

Worry starts to set in when I realize that we're stuck here for God knows how long. From the rumors in town and his behavior so far, I don't take Alexander for being a people person. I'm sure having a strange woman and her two kids thrust upon him isn't something he's looking forward to. I look down at the kids. I hate to impose on him, but it's not like we have a choice in the matter. Staying in our car until the roads are clear enough for someone to help isn't a choice. We'd freeze out there.

My thoughts are interrupted when I feel something bump my leg. Looking down, I'm startled to see a pair of green eyes looking up at me. It's a medium-sized dog with longish black hair, sitting on its haunches with its tongue hanging out the side of its mouth. I almost laugh at the comical look.

"Hey," I say calmly. When Daniel makes a move to get up to see what I'm talking to, I tell him, "You stay there."

He whines, but stays put. I need to make sure this dog is safe before I allow my son to come near it. I squat and hold out my hand and the dog immediately comes over and licks it. Its tail is wagging as it butts my hand with its head.

"Hmm... are you a boy or a girl?"

It doesn't take long to figure out it's a girl, as she flops to her back, then rolls over, showing off her swollen teats.

"You've just had puppies," I murmur, rubbing along the side of her belly.

I laugh when she wiggles her back around, almost splitting herself in half sideways. I look over when Daniel walks up beside me with a big smile on his face. I can't scold him for not waiting for me to say it's safe for him to come over. Although he's plenty short enough for the dog, Daniel gets down on his knees. When the dog bounds up and starts licking his face, he laughs, bringing a smile to my face.

I get up from my crouch and face Kelsey. "Would you like to come pet her?" When she shakes her head, I try enticing her with, "She just had puppies."

Her eyes light up fractionally before she looks down at her mug still half-full of cocoa, the look disappearing. A twinge of pain hits my chest. She should be down there with her brother, enjoying playing with the dog. She should have friends. She should be doing sleepovers and pillow fights. Not sitting there looking like this is her last day alive. I want to rush to her and gather her in my arms, promise her that everything will be okay. But I don't. I baby her enough, and don't want to smother her. I have to pick and choose the times I coddle her.

I turn back and watch Daniel roll around on the floor with the dog jumping around him. I laugh when his giggles get louder. I grab Daniel's and my empty mugs and carry them over to the sink. There are a few other dirty dishes sitting in the sink, so I decide to wash them. It's the least I can do after everything Alexander's done for me and my kids.

Chapter Four

Alexander

WHEN I PULL OPEN the door an hour later, both pain and longing stop me in my tracks. Laughter rings through the cabin, both childish and feminine, something these walls haven't heard in years. Still gripping the doorknob, I track the sound and find Gwen and her son on the floor in the living room with Gigi. Her daughter is on the couch watching them with a blank face. I'm not sure what it is, but there's something not right about the young girl. She seems too quiet and withdrawn for a girl her age.

Gwen looks up at me and her grin falls away. I don't know why, but for some reason that bothers me. I don't say anything as I close the door, take off my jacket, and hang it up before walking to the kitchen. My nose picks up a smell, and I see something boiling in a pot on the stove. I frown, not sure if I like the woman going through my cabinets and fridge, then I feel like an ass because they obviously need to eat.

"I hope you don't mind," she says from behind me. "I'm making potato soup. I didn't want to plunder too much in your cabinets. I found the potatoes on the counter."

I turn and face her. "It's fine. Cook whatever you want."

She nods. "I didn't say it earlier, but thank you for the cocoa. It was thoughtful of you."

I turn from her and go to the sink to wash away the dirt on my hands from hanging out in the barn.

"It was no problem," I throw over my shoulder.

She steps further into the kitchen and leans against the bar, her hands resting beside her hips.

"I always get the cheap powdered packets of hot chocolate. I haven't had homemade cocoa in years."

I grab the dish towel and dry my hands. Hanging it back on the stove, I turn around and mimic her stance against the sink. I don't say anything. Hell, even if I wanted to say something, I wouldn't know what to say. Besides my mom and sister, I haven't had a woman here since Clara died. What surprises me is that having her here isn't as bad as I thought it would be. What surprises me more is her total lack of interest in my mangled face. Not once have her eyes lingered on the scars. Even now, she's looking directly into my eyes.

"You have a nice place here. It seems very cozy and quaint," she says idly.

"Thanks," I mutter, pushing off from the counter. "Going to grab a shower. Make yourselves at home."

My abrupt departure startles her. Her mouth parts slightly with surprise and she turns and watches me walk out of the kitchen. I need to be alone. Her being here, talking with her soft, gentle voice, smelling like vanilla, and complimenting my cabin is too much. I don't know how to act around women anymore. It's been years since I've had to.

As I pass by the living room, the little boy stops playing with Gigi and looks up at me, his smile disappearing as his eyes go to the right side of my face. I'm used to the looks, so they don't bother me anymore. When he asked what was wrong in the truck, it was no shock to me. It was actually refreshing to have someone say their thoughts out loud. The people in town, the ones I used to be friends with, always keep their concerns and thoughts to themselves or whisper behind their hands, worried they may offend me or some shit. I grew up in these parts, but the people seem like strangers to me now.

Gigi leaves the boy's side and trots over to me. I pat her head when she puts her front paws on my lower stomach.

"Hey, girl. You havin' fun?" Her tongue hanging out the side of her mouth is my answer. She jumps down, and instead of going back to the boy, she takes off for the kitchen and the doggy door separating her from her pups.

I catch sight of Gwen standing at the bar looking at me. Her eyes drop when she notices I've caught her staring. I turn on my heel and walk down the short hallway, anxious to get away for a few minutes.

I take a hot shower and push away the weird feeling of having strangers in my house.

Twenty minutes later, I emerge from my bedroom dressed in jeans, a green thermal shirt, and bare feet. The TV is on when I walk out into the living room. The boy is sitting on the floor leaning against the couch, watching a bunch of meerkats run around on the screen, while the girl has her head bent over a book she's writing in.

A pang hits me square in the chest at the sight. Once upon a time I wanted this scene to be my reality, and while this is reality, it's not *my* reality. It's fake, it's someone else's. It's the woman's who's in the kitchen cooking something on my stove.

Seeing the fire has dwindled down, I walk over, crouch, and throw a couple small logs into the fireplace. Standing, I walk into the kitchen. Gwen is scooping the potato soup into bowls. When she hears my approach, she turns with a smile on her face.

"What's that smell?" I ask.

She grabs one of the bowls and hands it to me. "Sugar cookies."

I nod and dip my spoon into the soup, bringing a chunk of potato to my mouth. She watches me eat for a moment before grabbing the other bowls and setting them on the bar.

"This is good," I mumble around a mouthful.

39

"Thank you." She fidgets for a minute. "I feel strange being in your kitchen. Like I'm imposing in someone's space. I don't feel right looking through your cabinets with you standing there." She laughs. "So, where are your glasses?"

Carrying my bowl with me, I walk over to the cabinet by the fridge and open it, showing her the shelf of glasses and cups. She smiles gratefully and grabs two glasses and two plastic cups. She sets them on the counter, then opens the fridge and takes out a jug of juice.

"Juice?" I nod.

"What are your kids' names?"

Handing me a glass, she takes the cups over to the bar and sets them down beside the bowls.

"Daniel and Kelsey."

She calls the kids, and the boy, Daniel, rushes and takes his seat, wasting no time in digging in to his food. Kelsey comes at a more sedate pace. I watch with interest as she sets the book down on the bar—I can now see it's a crossword puzzle book—sits on the stool, and starts eating. Her eyes don't show any emotion at all as she stares down at her food, just disinterest. This girl is holding something deep inside her, it's there in her eyes. I just don't know what it is. I lean back against the counter across from them as Gwen picks up her own bowl and starts eating.

Minutes later, the stove's timer goes off and she sets her bowl down to take a tray of cookies out of the oven. The smell is stronger once they're sitting on the stove, and although I'm currently eating, my stomach still rumbles. I haven't had homemade cookies in years, and these look and smell really fucking good.

"Hey, mister," Daniel says, and I turn my head to regard him. "What's your dog's name?"

"Gigi."

"What kind of dog is she?"

I lay my empty bowl in the sink, then turn back around.

"She's a Lab mix."

"What does a Lab mix mean?" He scoops up some soup and puts the spoon to his mouth.

"It means part of her breed is Labrador."

"What other part is she?"

This kid is just full of questions. I look over at Gwen, who's taking the cookies off the cookie sheet and setting them on a plate. There's a small smile playing on her lips as she keeps her head bent. I turn back to Daniel.

"I don't know what other part she is. She was a stray that showed up here a couple of years ago."

"Well, then how do you know she's part Labrador then?"

A snicker sounds behind me.

"Because she has the same features as a Lab does."

"Oh." He looks thoughtful for a minute, then says, "I really like her," before digging back into his food.

Gwen comes to stand beside me and sets down a saucer with cookies on it.

"You both finish up and then you can have some cookies," she says, then offers me one.

She looks at Kelsey, who still looks indifferent as she eats her food. A normal kid would perk up at the mention of cookies, but not this girl. She gave no indication she even heard her mother.

"Kelsey," Gwen calls. The girl looks up, nixing my thought that maybe she's deaf. "Is your dinner okay?"

Kelsey nods, then drops her head back down to her food. I frown, more than a little curious about what's wrong with her. Normally a person would think she was being bratty or ornery, but the total lack of emotion on the girl's face says it's a lot more than that.

I eat two cookies, which taste like sugar heaven, then walk into the living room. I grab the remote off the couch, take a seat, and am just getting ready to channel surf until I find something to watch, when a little body settles on the couch beside me. I look down at Daniel, to see him looking at the scars on my arm.

"Why does your arm and face look like that?"

When he looks up at me, I only see innocent curiosity. This kid won't run around town fueling gossip and telling everyone my business. Even though everyone in town knows what happened, they still feel the need to run their mouths and speculate about shit they just don't understand. Daniel only wants to know because he's a kid and kids are curious, especially about things that aren't normal. My scars are definitely not normal.

"They're burn scars."

His eyes widen, and I wonder if maybe this could be too horrifying for a kid his age, then he asks, "What happened?"

A sharp pain hits my chest, and I turn my head away from him, not wanting him to see the pain I'm sure reflects in my eyes. It takes me a minute to control my reaction.

"I was in a wreck and the car caught fire." My answer still comes out gruff.

There's obviously more than that to the story, but that's not something he needs to hear. The horror of the details is too much for even adults, let alone a young child. Not to mention, I'm not sure I could give them anyway, not without breaking down. Even the thought of what happened nearly cripples me.

He looks down at the scars again. "Do they still hurt?"

"Yes and no," I answer honestly, then elaborate when he looks at me with confusion. "They don't actually hurt, but what I lost when I got these scars hurts me in here." I point to my chest.

He frowns as he takes in my answer. It's hard to explain such a thing to someone his age, but after a minute, I see recognition dawn in his eyes. This kid is smart.

"My daddy died," he says, so quietly I barely hear him.

He keeps his head bent and plays with the edge of his shirt.

"I'm sorry," I say gruffly, because I don't know what else to say to him. I feel sorry that he lost a parent at such a young age.

"Can I...." He stops and looks up at me again. The hurt is still evident in his eyes, but it's not as strong. He's obviously had to time to grieve, but that pain will never fully go away. Biting his lip, he starts again. "Can I touch them?" He points to my arm.

Now this question takes me by surprise. Asking about my scars is one thing, but wanting to see what they feel like is different. It's not that it bothers me really, it's just no one has ever touched them before. Not even my mom. Not because she's repulsed by them, but because it's just something you don't do.

I look back toward the kitchen and see Gwen washing the dishes. I know I should offer to wash them since she made dinner and cookies, but oddly enough, I'm enjoying sitting here talking to Daniel, something I never thought I would like doing.

He waits patiently for me to answer, his eyes lacking any censor or morbid nosiness. Pulling in a deep breath, I lift my arm out in front of me. The distorted skin, even to my own eyes, looks revolting. I barely hide my flinch when Daniel puts one fingertip against the skin on my forearm and runs it down to my wrist. I don't have much feeling left on the surface, so the flinch was more of a psychological reaction. He looks at them with fascination, and I watch him with the same feeling coursing through me, because there's no disgust coming from him whatsoever.

I lift my head when Kelsey comes to stand by the couch. Her eyes are on my arm, and I drop it to my lap. Once again, her eyes show nothing as she takes a seat and opens her crossword puzzle book.

I'm just about to get up when Gigi comes around the couch, a small fur ball hanging from her mouth. She stops in front of Daniel and gently lays the pup on the floor.

"A puppy!" he squeals, sliding from the couch onto his knees on the floor. Gigi nudges the puppy with her nose and Daniel leans way over until his nose is almost touching the floor and pets the pup on the head.

Obviously Gigi feels comfortable enough to bring her babies around Daniel. His smile is miles long as he plays with the pup. Gigi gets up and ambles off, only to return a minute later with another puppy.

"How many does she have?" Daniel asks after Gigi leaves for the fifth time.

"Seven."

"Wow!"

"How old are they?" a feminine voice asks.

I look up and see Gwen standing behind the couch watching her son play with the pups, a smile curving her lips.

"Four weeks," I answer.

My eyes land on Kelsey. She still has her head bent to her book, but the hand holding the pencil isn't moving, and I see her eyes flicker to the floor every few seconds. It's clear she's interested in the puppies, and I'm confused as to why she doesn't just go visit them with her brother.

"You can go play with them," I tell her quietly.

She lifts her head, and a spark of excitement lights her face before she quickly wipes it away. Before she drops her head back down, something flashes in her eyes, and the force of the emotion hits me square in the chest. It's a look I've seen reflected back at me for the past four years.

I get up from the couch and walk to the kitchen. I feel Gwen's eyes on me, then hear her footsteps following me. I go to the cabinet holding the glasses, grab one out, then fill it with water. I gulp down the cool liquid, then take in several deep breaths, feeling like I can't draw in enough air.

The glass clatters in the sink when I drop it. I turn around to face Gwen, my chest heaving, and see her watching me with concern. I'm sure my reaction is a bit confusing for her. She has no idea that the pain I witnessed in Kelsey's eyes reminds me so much of my own.

I have no right to ask, it's none of my business, and it's an invasion of privacy. I've known this woman barely a day, and I've been less than friendly most of that time. But after seeing what I did in that girl's eyes, it's something I need to know. No kid should feel even half of what I feel on a daily basis.

I look up and meet Gwen's worried gaze. She knows what I'm going to ask. She knows I saw the absolute pain in her daughter's eyes.

"What happened to her?" I clear my throat when my question comes out hoarse.

She looks over her shoulder toward the living room for a minute before bringing her gaze back to me. Pain flashed across her face. She walks further into the kitchen and stops when she's beside me. Her back goes against the counter and she wraps her arms around her stomach like she's trying to hold herself together.

"She found her father, my husband, Will, dead in her bedroom a little over two years ago. She was six." I mutter a curse and my heart sinks to my fucking toes. She talks over me. "We didn't know it, but he had a blocked artery. She was crying for her bear and while he was in her room grabbing it, he had a heart attack. She hasn't spoken since, except at the funeral, and a year ago when she asked me if I was going to die when I had the flu." She stops and swallows thickly. "And to whisper in the dark at night, praying to God to bring her daddy back." Her voice breaks at the end.

I don't know what to say. I've been so wrapped up in my own grief that I don't know how to deal with someone else's. I hate the thought of these three going through something like that. It makes my chest ache.

I don't know what I planned to do or say when I turn to face her, but I don't get the chance before she gives me a sad smile and says, "She has selective mutism caused by a traumatic event. The doctors say she could one day all of a sudden talk, but there's a chance she may never want to again."

Her words hurt something deep inside me. My instincts tell me to reach out and comfort her, but I hold back, not really sure if I should. Her head's down, and she takes deep breaths as she tries to get a hold of her emotions. When she lifts her head, her eyes are watery, but I can tell she's forcefully pushing the tears back.

"I'm sorry," she says softly. "I shouldn't burden yo—"

"Don't," I say a bit more harshly than intended. Her eyes widen. "Don't apologize for your pain. Never be sorry for something like that."

She stares at me for a full minute before she nods. "Thank you."

I turn away from her, not wanting her gratitude for something so significant. I look out the window and am surprised to see the sun already setting. I look over when Gwen moves away from me.

"Wait," I call, and she turns back. "I'm sorry for your loss. And Kelsey...." I pause and she waits. "She'll be okay."

I don't know why I feel compelled to tell her that, but I do. It's clear Gwen still suffers from the loss of her husband, but the pain of losing part of a child is so much more.

"I know," she says quietly before turning and leaving.

I stand at the kitchen sink for several more minutes, looking out into the darkness, pushing back my own painful memories. I release a breath, push away from the sink, and walk back out into the living room. Daniel, who's still on the floor, has his head down beside one of the puppies, his eyes barely staying open. Kelsey still has her head stuck in the puzzle book. She must have carried it with her from their truck. It looks well-worn, with the pages curled, indicating she uses it a lot.

I look over at Gwen sitting beside her. "You three can have my bed."

My suggestion surprises her and she gets up from the couch.

"Alexander, we can't take your bed."

Hearing her say my name does something to me. That's the third time she's said it. It still sounds foreign coming from someone other than my family, but it's nice.

"Yes, you can. There's three of you. You can't all fit on the couch."

"The kids can have the couch. If you have extra blankets, I can sleep on the floor."

I give her a look that says she's stupid if she thinks I'm going to let her sleep on the hard floor. I may be out of practice dealing with people, but I'm not so far gone that I'll allow something like that.

"That's not happening, Gwen."

It's not until she looks at me strangely that I realize that's the first time I've said her name out loud. I wonder if she got the same weird feeling I get when she says my name.

She looks down at the couch, then back at me. "But you won't fit on the couch. Your feet will hang off the edge."

"I'll be fine. I've slept on worse, and it's only for a few days."

She bites her lip as she thinks it over. I let her believe she has a choice when she really doesn't. Luckily, she relents and nods. "Okay. Thank you."

I give a short nod, then walk around the couch and bend down to a now sleeping Daniel.

"I can—"

My stern look has her shutting her mouth. I scoop the little boy in my arms and carry him into my bedroom. Gwen follows me and pulls back the cover, and I set him down. He curls on his side. I grab some clothes for tomorrow as she pulls the covers over him. Stopping in the hallway, I pull out a pillow and a couple blankets from the small linen closet and go back out to the living room. Gwen is already rounding up Kelsey.

"Thank you." She smiles. "You have no idea how grateful I am for everything you've done for us today. I don't know what we would have done without you."

"Don't mention it," I tell her, and throw the pillow and blankets on the couch.

I turn back and she's just standing there. She shuffles on her feet for a minute before saying, "I keep an emergency bag of stuff in the back of my truck. I should have grabbed it before we left, but didn't think about it. Could we grab it tomorrow if we're still not able to leave?"

"Yeah."

"Thanks," she says, smiling. "Good night."

That same feeling from earlier hits me. "Good night, Gwen." I look to the girl. "Good night, Kelsey," I say softly to the retreating girl's back. She's doesn't turn, but she does stop walking and her spine stiffens.

We both watch as Kelsey stands there for a moment, then moves forward again. Gwen shoots me a sad smile before following her daughter. I watch until the light in the bedroom goes off.

I round up the pups and load them back into the utility room, Gigi following behind me. After, I release a tired sigh and settle down on the couch with my feet hanging off the end. I'm not sure why, but I feel a connection with Kelsey. I know how deep her pain runs. I know exactly what she's going through. I know the feeling of wanting to block people out, to push people away. The pain that grips you so tight it feels like you're suffocating. That no matter what you do, things will never be good again. And you'll do almost anything to bring back the person you lost.

I close my eyes and an image of blond hair flashes in my mind. Laughter sounds in my ears, so loud I almost open my eyes to look for the source because it sounds so real. I shove the image and sound away, not wanting it to pull me under.

Chapter Five

Gwendolyn

I OPEN MY EYES AND see a pair of gorgeous green ones staring back at me. I hold my breath and bask in the attention Kelsey is giving me by simply looking at me. To anyone else, it may be a small thing, but coming from her, it's everything. Kelsey doesn't look at people unless she has to. I think it's because she's worried her pain may shine through enough for people to see. I miss looking into my daughter's eyes. They are the prettiest green I've ever seen.

I feel a twitch on my hand and out of the corner of my eye, I see her hand lying in the palm of mine. My hand is palm up, so *she* placed her hand in *mine*. This lightens the pain in my heart. I push back the threatening tears and just lie there for several minutes, staring at her. She doesn't move her eyes from mine and gives no other sign of how she's feeling.

"Hey, beautiful," I whisper, and smile softly at her.

Her eyes flicker back and forth between mine, but she stays unmoving.

Gently, so as to not startle her, I reach up and lay my hand against her soft cheek. My love for her and my motherly instincts have me wanting to pull her forward into my arms to simply hold her. Every night while she prays for God to bring her dad back, I pray that he'll bring my daughter back.

Her hand moves in mine, and I wrap my fingers around hers, then push her hair back behind her ear.

"I love you, Kelsey. I miss hearing your sweet voice so much," I say tenderly. "Will you let me hear it?"

I hold my breath, praying with every fiber of my being that she'll open her mouth and say something. When she just lies there, her eyes still on mine but giving no indication she's going to talk, my heart sinks.

The bed moves slightly, and before I'm ready to let her go, Kelsey's rolling to her back, dislodging my hand, then sitting up. Daniel takes her place and bounces to the middle of the bed. I'm not sure how it happened; when we went to sleep last night, he was in the middle of the bed with me and Kelsey on the outsides. I'm hoping it was Kelsey that moved to the middle because she wanted to be by her momma.

"Hey, kid." I grin and ruffle his hair. He giggles, and I throw my arm around his middle and drag him to me. Dipping my head, I growl into his stomach, causing him to burst out into laughter. Hearing the sound loosens the knot in my stomach.

When I pull my head back, he leans down and gives me a kiss on the cheek. "Good morning, Mama." Not waiting on me to reciprocate, he crawls from the bed.

"Wait for me," I call when he goes to the door to open it. Since we all slept in our clothes last night, I get up from the bed and head straight to the door. Daniel's bouncing on his feet with his legs crossed in true I-have-to-pee fashion. Kelsey's already standing next to the door when I get there.

While Daniel is in the bathroom, Kelsey and I walk into the living room. My eyes immediately go to the couch to see it's empty, the blankets neatly folded at one end with the pillow on top. I look around and still don't see Alexander. I notice his boots, which were at the door last night, are gone, meaning he must be outside.

I bite my thumbnail, contemplating whether I should make something for breakfast or wait to see if he comes back. After a minute, I hear Kelsey's stomach rumble, and make my decision. I lead her to the kitchen, where she sits at the bar. I spot my purse on the counter and grab my phone from beside it. Still no signal. I blow out a breath and set the useless thing back down.

Turning to the fridge, I rummage through it and pull out a carton of eggs. Next, I go in search of ingredients for pancakes, and smile when I find them. It really does feel strange going through someone else's cabinets and fridge. I hope Alexander doesn't mind.

I turn to Kelsey. "Pancakes and eggs sound good to you?"

She gives me a barely noticeable nod, and I set to making the batter. Daniel comes bounding out from the hallway, briefly looks to the living room, then skids to a stop at the end of the bar.

"Have you seen Gigi?" he asks, excitement in his eyes.

I dump the flour in the mixing bowl and crack open an egg to do the same. "No, but I'm sure she's probably out with Mr. Alexander and will be back in a few minutes."

He looks disappointed as he walks to the barstool and takes a seat. I finish putting the rest of the ingredients in the bowl before pushing it, along with a spoon, over to Kelsey.

"Mix that for me, please?"

As her way of acknowledging my request, she grabs the spoon and slowly starts pushing it around the concoction, her eyes focused on her task. After cracking open several eggs and putting them in a bowl, and adding a bit of milk, I push that toward Daniel.

"You get to beat the eggs," I tell him. When he grabs the whisk sitting in the bowl and starts stirring too fast, I add, "Gently, or they'll slosh out the sides."

With both kids occupied for a few minutes, I take the opportunity to use the bathroom.

"I'll be right back," I let them know before heading back toward the hall.

I do my business, flush, and wash my hands. Running my tongue over my teeth, I feel the fuzz and wish for a toothbrush. I open the medicine cabinet, hoping to find at least some toothpaste or mouthwash, and come up empty. The cabinet is pretty bare, only carrying a bottle of aspirin and a comb. I wrinkle my nose. One thing I hate is having a mouth full of fuzz.

Remembering seeing a bathroom in Alexander's room, I wonder if I'm brave enough to trespass in there to look for some mouthwash. Desperate for a fresh mouth, I decide to go for it.

I feel like a thief getting ready to break into a house when I peek my head out of the bathroom. Spying the kids at the counter mixing the contents in their bowls and still no sign of Alexander, I walk on tiptoes down the hallway toward the master bedroom. I leave the door open and rush to the bathroom.

This bathroom is a lot bigger than the one in the hallway. While it's not huge, it's a lot bigger than you would think considering the size of the bedroom. But it's beautiful with its rustic look. Cream-colored walls, pedestal sink, claw-foot tub, and separate shower. It fits with the rest of the cabin.

Looking over my shoulder to make sure I'm not caught, I quickly walk over to the sink and open the small medicine cabinet. I almost shout with elation when I see a bottle of mint mouthwash. As I grab it, I spot a can of shaving cream, a razor, several bottles of prescription medicine, a bottle of cologne, a toothbrush and tooth-paste, and several other items you normally see in a medicine cabinet. My eyes linger on the medicine bottles, my curiosity piqued. Some say you can find out a lot about a person by their prescriptions. I personally think that's a load of crap. But the bottles do leave me wondering what he takes and why. Are any of them pain medica-tions? By the scars on his face and arms, the extent of his injuries had to have been extreme. I can imagine he may still have pain on occasion.

My eyes next stop on the aftershave, and I feel an unreasonable need to sniff it. Would the smell be strong and overpowering like some men wear, or subtle, just barely giving off a slight masculine scent? I personally like the latter. One of the biggest turn-offs for me is not being able to breathe because of the overwhelming scent of cologne on a man.

I chastise myself for even thinking about such a thing right now. It doesn't matter what cologne the man wears. It's not like I'll be getting close enough to choke on his scent anyway.

I grab the big bottle of mouthwash, then pour some of the minty green liquid in the cap and tip it to my lips. It burns as I swish it around, but it's a good kind of burn. I watch myself in the mirror for a good thirty seconds as my cheeks puff out. Tipping my head back, I gargle.

When I bring my head back down, it's not only me looking back in the mirror, but Alexander's dark gaze as well. He's leaning against the doorjamb with his arms crossed over his muscular chest with a firm look plastered on his face. Seeing him standing there surprises me, and I accidently swallow some of the mouthwash. I start choking, and I try to spit the mouthwash into the sink, but end up spraying the mirror in the process. I bend over the sink and hack up a lung or two.

By the time I'm done, my arms are crossing the sink with my forehead resting on them. It's then that embarrassment hits me. I stay hunched over the sink for several minutes, not only catching my breath, but avoiding looking at Alexander too. My face is hot, so I know it's red, from both coughing so much and embarrassment.

I'm such an idiot. I knew I shouldn't have come in here without asking him. I should have waited. He probably wouldn't have minded. He said to make ourselves at home last night. I'm sure he didn't mean go into his bathroom and rummage around.

Knowing I can't put it off any longer, I wipe my mouth with the back of my hand and lift my head, my eyes meeting his in the mirror. He's still standing in the same position as he was when I first noticed him. He looks relaxed, but that could be deceptive. Today he's wearing a pair of dark jeans, slightly worn at the knees, and a dark green T-shirt with a thermal underneath.

I straighten and turn to face him.

"I'm sorry," I say. I taste the mouthwash when I lick my lips, and I rush on. "I hate not brushing my teeth and you didn't have any mouthwash in your spare bathroom, so I decided to check in here. I'm sorry," I repeat.

I want to pull my eyes away from his penetrating dark ones, but I force myself to hold his stare. I do shuffle my feet though. There's no stopping that. I start to fidget when he doesn't say anything. I'm just about to blurt another apology, when he straightens.

"Don't worry about it," he says, backing out of the bathroom. He holds up a black backpack. "Got this from your truck."

I sag in relief and smile, my embarrassment forgotten. "Thank you."

I grab it from him and hold it to my chest, not even caring that he got my keys from my purse. After a minute, he turns on his heel and walks out of the bedroom, leaving me with my bag. I consider whether to follow him and use the spare bathroom to change and brush my teeth and hair, or just stay here and use this one. He seemed okay that I was in here, but I don't want to push it. After wiping down the mirror with a rag I found underneath the sink, I decide to use the spare one.

Once I'm done, I go back out into the living room and find Daniel has abandoned his mixing bowl and is lying on his back with a puppy on his chest and Gigi lying beside him. Alexander's stirring the fire. Kelsey's still at the bar, no longer mixing, but doing her crossword puzzle. I didn't realize she'd brought it with her until I saw her working on it yesterday evening. It doesn't surprise me though. She always has one with her.

I stop at the end of the couch and Alexander looks over at me. "I'm making eggs and pancakes. Would you like some?"

He gives me a nod and goes back to poking the fire with the fire iron.

"Daniel," I call. "We have a bag in the bathroom. There's a change of clothes, toothbrush, and toothpaste. Go get changed and brush your teeth, please."

"Okay, Mom," he responses, barely giving me a glance, too distracted by the puppies.

"Daniel." I say his name again when he makes no move to get up. I lift my brow at him when he finally looks at me.

"Okay, okay," he grumbles before getting up and dragging his feet as he walks to the bathroom.

When I pass by Kelsey, I tell her, "When your brother's done, it's your turn, sweetie." All I get in return is a short nod.

Fifteen minutes later, I place a plate in front of a newly changed Kelsey and call Daniel to the bar. Looking over their shoulders once he's seated, I spot Alexander on the couch and decide to make him a plate. After piling several pancakes and some eggs on one plate and a smaller portion on another, I grab them and tuck the syrup underneath my arm.

I hold the plate out to him and he takes it with a muttered, "Thanks."

"Would you like something to drink?" I ask.

"I'm good."

I go back for my cup of coffee, then sit at the other end of the couch. Seeing the weather channel playing on the TV reminds me I haven't even looked outside to see if it's still snowing. "How does it look outside?"

"Very white," he remarks.

I laugh, then look over when I feel his eyes on me. He has a weird expression on his face. His brows are pulled down low, and it almost looks like he's in pain. The look confuses me, but I decide to ignore it.

"Is it still coming down?"

"Yes," he answers, then stuffs a forkful of pancake in his mouth.

"Any chance you think they'll plow the roads today?"

After swallowing his bite, he says, "Nope. There would be no point. It'll just get covered again in thirty minutes."

We eat in silence for several minutes. The only sounds come from our utensils scraping our plates and the low voice of the meteorologist on the TV.

"I still don't have a signal on my phone," I say, when the quiet becomes awkward.

"Lines are probably down. Happens a lot around here when the weather gets bad."

I push some eggs around in my syrup before I look over at him. "I really am sorry you're stuck with us. I'm sure you don't care to have strangers invading your house."

He gives me a look that tells me he's tired of hearing me give my thanks, so I clamp my mouth shut. That is, until the quiet grates on my nerves again.

"You said you've lived here your whole life. Does that mean you grew up in this house?"

He sets his plate down on the coffee table in front of him.

"No. My parents had a house in town. This was my grandparents' place."

"Oh." I put my plate beside his and turn in my seat, bring one foot up and tucking it under me. "Do your parents still live in town?"

"They moved to Tennessee a few years ago."

He doesn't seem too bothered by my questions, so I continue.

"Do you have any siblings?"

"Just my sister."

I run my fingers along the smoothness of the couch. I hate to have idle hands. I constantly have to be doing something with them. My poor cuticles look terrible and would probably give a manicurist a heart attack.

"What kind of work do you do?"

His brows drop as he moves his eyes from me to the TV. "Why all the questions?" he asks.

Embarrassment has my cheeks turning pink, and I turn so I'm facing forward again.

"Sorry," I say softly. "I just figured since we might be stuck together for a few days, we may as well get to know each other a bit so we're not complete strangers."

I get up from the couch and pick up my plate. I guess my line of questioning is over. I understand his reluctance. He doesn't know me, why would he tell me about his life, even if we are staying here in his home. As long as he doesn't act like a psycho and is nice to my kids, there's no need for me to know more than I already do. Once the snow melts enough for them to remove the tree, clear the roads, and pull my car from the ditch, we'll be leaving. It'll probably be months before I see him again, if I do at all.

When I reach down for his plate, he stops me by placing his hand on my arm. His fingers are warm to the touch, and I feel a weird charge where's he's touching me. The hand he used is the one with the scars and my eyes linger on them for a moment before I look to his face. He's looking at his hand touching me.

After several seconds, he loosens his fingers and pulls his hand back. He slowly lifts his head and the look in his eyes conveys confusion. I just don't know what he's confused about.

"I'll get it," he says, his voice gruff.

I nod, then take my plate to the kitchen. I'm at the sink rinsing my dish when he walks up beside me. On the outside I appear calm, but on the inside, I'm reprimanding myself for pushing him with questions. I already knew just from the rumors and the way he acts that he's a private person. I should have known he wouldn't like being grilled about his life. Even though I told him we should get to know each other since we're practically living together for the next couple days, my real excuse is I'm curious about him.

He's silent for a minute as he stands there. I don't turn to look, but I feel his eyes on me.

He puts his plate in the sink, then says, "You cooked, I'll wash."

Surprised by his statement, I look at him. "It's okay. I don't mind. It's the least I can do since you've taken us in."

"You cooked, I'll wash," he repeats.

Instead of giving in to him, I counter, "How about we do it together? I'll wash and you dry and put away."

I don't wait for him to answer before I'm putting the stopper in the sink and filling it with warm soapy water. As the sink fills, I go to the bar to grab the kids' plates, and see them both in the living room.

I'm handing Alexander a washed plate when he says quietly, "I train horses."

Surprised by him answering my earlier question, but not wanting to show it, I only pause for a second before I continue washing a frying pan. I hand it over to him.

"The most I've been around horses are the ones they have at fairs." I laugh lightly. "I used to beg my mom when I was little to get me a pony. We lived in a neighborhood where the houses were practically on top of each other. Definitely not a place to bring a pony." I push the sponge in a cup and swirl it around. "Will, my husband, grew up on a farm in Nebraska. We always said that one day we would buy a lot of land somewhere. He wanted to get horses and have the kids learn to ride them."

I stop washing and just stare at the suds rolling off the side of the cup. We had started a savings account specifically for our move one day. As a sheet metal technician who worked on private jets, Will's income was good. Our savings account was substantial, and we'd only had a few more years to go before we could make our dream come true.

I push the thought away, not wanting the sadness that came with it. I finish with the cup and hand it over.

"Do you enjoy working with them?" I ask.

"I do. My grandfather raised horses, and I knew from a kid I wanted to work with them."

"That's nice," I remark and pass him a plate. "I didn't know what I wanted to do until I was in college. It was a toss-up between a guidance counselor or a teacher."

"What did you choose?"

"Teacher."

"What made you choose that one?"

I smile. "I like knowing I'll be part of shaping children's futures, that I played a big role in who they'll become."

He nods and turns quiet. We finish the rest of the dishes in silence, except this time it doesn't feel awkward. It's peaceful. After, I wipe down the stove and counters while Alexander feeds an excited Gigi.

I check on the kids. Daniel's still on the floor with the puppies, he'll probably be there all day if I let him, and Kelsey's on the couch. When she spots me, she gets up and walks over, holding the crossword puzzle book. The pages are curled and creased. Even knowing what she's trying to say, I flip through the pages. They're all done.

"You finished already?" I ask, and of course get nothing in return. "I'm sorry, Kelsey, we don't have another one with us. We'll get one when we make it back to town." Her frown is barely noticeable. "Come on, let's go to the living room and see what's on TV."

I grab her hand and lead her back to the couch. Alexander walks by and disappears down the hallway. Ten minutes later, he comes back out with a drawing pad and holds it out to Kelsey. "Maybe you could draw something," he says, sounding unsure.

She just stares at it for a moment, then looks up at him and hesitantly reaches her hand out. I watch the exchange, my heart jumping in my chest at the slight tilt of his lips.

Chapter Six

Alexander

"WHERE YA GOING?"

The question comes from behind me. I turn around as I'm zipping up my jacket and face Daniel. He's holding a black puppy to his chest as he looks up at me.

"Gotta go check on the horses," I reply.

His eyes get big and his mouth drops open. The surprise doesn't last long before he's practically bouncing on his feet. I've noticed since they've been here that the kid is hyper. The complete opposite of his sister.

"I didn't know you had horses!" he says excitedly. "I wanna see them! Can I come with you?"

I glance over to the door in the kitchen that leads to a small laundry room where Gwen's doing her and the kids' laundry, then look back down at Daniel. With the eager way he's watching me, there's no way I can deny this kid, even if I wanted to. And to my surprise, I find that I don't want to. His exuberant demeanor and honesty is refreshing.

I've rarely been around kids, except for my sister Christa's daughter, who's only two years old. I've only seen the toddler twice, and both times I've kept my distance, the painful reminder of what I almost had keeping me from bonding with her. I'm a shit uncle and have apologized to Christa for being so. She says she understands, and I'm sure she does, but I've seen the look in her eyes when she's visited those couple of times. I've seen the sadness lurking when I purposely put space between me and her daughter.

I reach for my gloves and lift my chin toward the kitchen. "Go ask your mom."

"Yah!" he yells, then turns on his foot and runs to the kitchen.

Just as he's reaching for the doorknob, the door opens and out walks Gwen. He skids to a stop in front of her.

"Whoa there, kid," she says, holding out her hands. "What's the rush?"

I slip on my hat and force back a chuckle when Daniel's words come out way too fast and sound like one long word.

"Mr.Alexanderhashorsesandhesaidcouldgoseethemwithhim."
He pauses just long enough to take a breath. "Can I, Mom? Can I?"

She looks over at me, and I give her a chin lift, letting her know it's okay. Instead of answering Daniel, she walks over to me with him following her, his head tipped back, looking at her with a pleading look.

"Are you sure it's okay? Daniel can be... quite rambunctious at times."

Daniel switches his focus to me, his lips moving as he silently says please over and over again.

"Yeah. We'll be fine," I tell her.

"Yes!" Daniel screeches. He shoves the puppy into his mother's arms and runs to grab his jacket.

"Hat and gloves too, Daniel!" Gwen says, laughing at her son's animated behavior.

Once he has both on, along with his boots, Gwen stops him when he tries to pass by her. She squats down in front of him and puts the puppy on the floor between her legs. He starts waddling away immediately.

"You listen to Mr. Alexander, you hear? And keep your hat and gloves on the whole time." He nods rapidly with a big grin, and she zips up his coat to just below his chin.

Before the puppy can get too far away, she scoops him up and stands. Facing me once again, she says, "Please keep a good eye on him."

As any mother would be, she's worried about her child being near a large animal. I can't fault her for that. I actually admire it. She cares a lot for her kids. Anyone can see it by the way she interacts with them and her expression when she looks at them.

I give her a single nod, before turning around and opening the door. A blast of snowy, cold air hits my face when Daniel and I walk down the steps, but he doesn't seem to mind. His face is still splitting in two with his happy grin.

It's put down a lot of snow since yesterday and it doesn't look to be letting up. Earlier this morning, I shoveled a path from the house to the barn and one to the truck, but it's already several inches deep again. Daniel chooses not to use the path, and instead trudges through the deep parts of the snow. It's up to his knees and he seems to be struggling a bit, but he's still determinedly moving forward. I slow my steps to keep pace with him.

"How many horses do you have?" he asks, lifting his leg high and stomping it back down.

"I've got two that are mine, but there's seven in the barn."

"Wow!" he exclaims. "That's a lot!"

"Take slow steps just in case there's something under the snow you can't see," I tell him when he stumbles and barely catches himself.

"Why do you have horse that aren't yours?"

"Because I train them."

He stops for a minute, his mouth falling open in astonishment. "Really? That's so cool!" I crack a smile at his enthusiasm.

It's not toasty warm like the house, but once we step inside the barn, there's a significant change in temperature. Soft neighs come from the horses as I close the door behind us. Daniel just stands there for several seconds, taking in the few horse heads that are poking out of the stalls.

"Can I pet one?"

I chuckle at the pure wonderment in his tone. Walking over to the basket of apples, I grab out a couple and carry them back over to Daniel.

"How about feeding them a treat?" I hold one out to him.

"Can I really?" He grabs it, looks down at it a moment, then turns his excited eyes up at me.

"Ever fed a horse an apple before?"

"No, sir."

"Come on. I'll show you how to do it."

I lead him over to June's stall. She's a black with gray spots appaloosa. I've had her for eight weeks now and she's about ready to go home to her family.

She neighs softly and tosses her head a couple times as we walk up to her stall. Daniel stops and stares up at her, his mouth hanging open in awe.

"This is June," I tell him.

June brings her head closer to Daniel, and for a minute I think he's going to take a step back, but he doesn't. Brave kid. Horses are big even to adults; to a child they're enormous.

I pet June along her neck and she lifts her head to me, nudging my shoulder. "Hey, girl."

I turn to Daniel. "Hold the apple out in your palm. Don't grip it. Just let it rest in your hand."

He does as I tell him and holds the apple out. Even for a kid I barely know, his expression is priceless as he watches the horse gently take the apple from his hand. A big smile appears on his face when the horse starts crunching on the fruit.

ALEX GRAYSON

"Good girl," I murmur to the horse, and run my hand up and down her muzzle and forehead.

"That was so neat!" He turns to me. "Can we feed another one?"

I smile down at him. "Sure."

Next, I lead him to Pepe, a solid brown American Azteca. The owners plan to use him as a competition horse. I've only had him a few weeks, but he's taking to training very well. Again, Daniel holds out the apple in his palm and the horse nabs it with his big teeth. It's amazing to watch the excitement that overcomes the boy's face. I always enjoy my time with these horses, but seeing it from a kid's point of view is something to behold.

We feed a couple more of the horses, and with each one, Daniel's eyes light up even more.

He's just given Bella an apple, when I ask, "Do you want to pet her?"

He nods so fast it's a wonder he doesn't give himself whiplash. I grab him under the arms and hoist him up on my shoulders, putting him more on level with the horse. Bella nudges Daniel's knee, bringing a giggle from him. Keeping one arm gripped on his leg, I pet Bella's head and instruct Daniel to do the same.

"She's so pretty," he remarks. "Is she one of yours?"

"Yes. Her name is Bella."

"Hey, Bella," he says, running the tip of his finger up the horse's ear.

"Can I ride her?"

I glide my hand up her forehead between her eyes. "Maybe once the weather is better."

I'm a very private person, preferring to keep company with only myself and the horses, so my answer surprises me. I don't like people encroaching on my personal space, but in the short time Gwen and her two kids have been here, I've found myself enjoying their company more and more. The thought of them possibly coming back to visit doesn't fill me with dread like it normally would, but instead makes my chest feel lighter. I like having them around, even

64

if it does still feel strange. It's not a bad strange, just different. I've been alone for so long that having them here is... nice. And the thought of training Daniel to ride feels right, like maybe it's something I'm supposed to do.

I look over to the next stall when I hear a bang. Bandit pops his head out and twists to look at us. He snorts and stomps the ground.

"What's that horse's name?" Daniel asks.

"That's Bandit. He's one of the ones that isn't very nice."

"What's wrong with him?"

"He's just making it very difficult to train him," I answer.

"What'll happen to him if he can't be trained?"

I walk over to the barrel of grain, then set Daniel on his feet. "All horses can be trained. Some are just more difficult than others and you have to spend extra time with them." I hand him a small bucket of oats and scoop out another. "Each horse is different, so you have to alter your training routine to fit each one."

"Oh." He turns and looks at Bandit, who's tossing his head and snorting. "He's pretty."

"He is."

Daniel and I walk over to the first stall, and I top off the oats feeder, then check to see if the water needs to be refilled or the hay replenished. We do this to the rest of the stalls. At each one, Daniel reaches out and touches the horses, a look of pure rapture on his face. When we come to Bandit's, I tell Daniel to stand back. I'm unsure if Bandit will play nice or not, and I'm not willing to take the chance of Daniel getting hurt.

"You ready to head back in?" I ask him once everything is back in its place.

His shoulders droop and his face loses some of its cheerfulness. "I guess."

The look of disappointment doesn't settle well with me, so I try to lighten his mood. "You can come with me when I check on them before bed." At his excited fist pump, I tack on, "As long as your mom says it's okay."

"Yes, sir." He nods and the smile reappears on his face. I check to make sure he's still bundled up well before we both walk back out into the cold. He once again chooses to walk in the feet-high snow instead of the path I shoveled.

"Maybe Kelsey will come with us next time," I suggest, and look over at him.

He grabs a handful of snow in his gloves and smashes it into a ball.

"Nah," he says, tossing the snowball at a tree. "She never does anything anymore."

The hurt in his tone is easily heard. He misses his big sister. He may act like he's not affected by the loss of his father, his young age making it easier, but deep down, he is. He not only lost his dad, but with how Kelsey's detached herself so much, he lost his sister, too. Poor kid.

"Don't give up on her, okay?" We both stop walking and he looks over at me. "She's still really hurt from losing your dad. It takes longer for some people to heal." He doesn't say anything, just keeps his eyes on me. "Do you understand what I'm saying?"

He looks down for a moment, then brings his eyes back up to me and nods. "Yeah." He sniffs and runs a snow-covered glove under his nose. "I just wish she would play with me. We used to always play games."

His tone and the wounded look in his eyes send shards of pain to my chest. I understand the heartache he's going through. I walk over to him, making my way through the deep snow, and put a hand on his shoulder.

"She'll come around. She just needs to figure out how to let go of the pain in her heart first."

We both start walking again. I stay in the deep snow with him. Once we make it to the porch, we stomp our feet, trying to get the clumps of snow off our boots.

"Can I name one of your puppies?" Daniel asks, slapping his gloves together.

"Sure," I answer. "Got any ideas yet?"

"Uh-huh. I want to name the black one with the white on his face Pepper, because he looks like a Peppermint Pattie and it's my favorite candy."

"That's a good choice."

Right as I'm reaching for the doorknob, it's pulled open and Gwen's standing there. Not expecting her sudden appearance, I take a step back. Her eyes go from Daniel to me then back down to Daniel.

"Did you have fun?" she asks, stepping back and letting us enter.

"Yes!" Daniel says exuberantly. "I got to feed the horses apples and pet them. They were so pretty, Mom!"

She smiles and sets to helping him unbundle. "I'm glad you had a good time. You about ready for some hot chocolate to warm up? Your hands are freezing."

I take my hat and gloves off and drop them in the small basket by the door, then hang my coat on the hook and start working on my boots.

"Yeah, but can Mr. Alexander make it again?" he asks, unknowingly insulting his mother's hot-chocolate-making skills.

She winks at me, then feigns shock. This playful side of Gwen is intriguing to watch. I don't tell jokes, and I don't laugh at them. My life is very stale, and it's the way I want it. Laughing and smiling isn't something I do anymore, as there's really nothing to laugh and smile about, but since she's been around, I find myself wanting to. She and her kids have brought a sliver of light back into my life in the short time I've known them. I didn't think it was possible, and I'm not entirely sure I want it to continue, but right now, I'm enjoying it too much to wish it away.

"What's wrong with my cocoa?" Gwen asks, playfully throwing her hands on her hips and narrowing her eyes at her son.

He reaches out and pats one of her hands, saying with a serious tone, "Yours is still good, Mom." He uses his pointer finger and thumb and puts them so close they're almost touching. "But I like his a tiny bit more."

Gwen laughs, and before I realize it, I'm chuckling with her. She looks over at me when I do, and I use the excuse of grabbing my phone from my coat pocket so I don't see the expression on her face. Her shock is apparent, which doesn't really surprise me. I know I put off a serious vibe, maybe even an asshole one at times. Even to my own ears, the laugh sounds weird coming from me.

"Would you mind making more of your delicious hot chocolate?" she asks, unable to hide her uncertainty.

I push away the strange feelings she's provoking in me and turn to face her.

"Yeah. I can do that."

My voice sounds rough, so I clear my throat before making my way to the kitchen. Daniel's already on the floor again with the puppies. I'm surprised but pleased to see Gigi up on the couch, her head only inches away from Kelsey. She's trying her best to ignore the dog, but her head keeps tilting toward her. Maybe Gigi can be of help with unleashing some of the pain Kelsey harbors.

I gather the necessary ingredients and set to making hot chocolate. It's a recipe my mom used when I was a kid. My mom was never the type to buy already prepared food. She made everything from scratch. She also made sure her kids knew how to cook.

Gwen steps up beside me as I heat the milk in a saucepan.

"Thank you for taking him with you. He doesn't get the chance very often to spend time with a man and he needs that."

I look at her out the corner of my eye, and see her running her finger over a scratch on the counter surface.

"It was no problem. He's a good kid."

She nods. "He is. I hate knowing he's not getting the experiences and advice he needs from his dad."

Her voice trails off, and I glance over at her. She's looking at the wall ahead of her. There's nothing there, so I know she's in her own head, probably remembering something about her husband, or maybe silently wishing he was still here. It's already painful that she lost her husband, but having to raise two kids on her own, knowing they'll never see their dad again.... I can't imagine the pain.

"Seems like he's doing okay to me," I say, attempting to make her feel better. I don't like knowing she's in pain, which is strange for me, because it's been a long time since I've really cared about how someone else feels.

"Thanks," she says.

She grabs some mugs from the cabinet as I remove the pan from the burner and set it on a cool one. She watches as I finish making the hot chocolate. Neither of us say anything. Normally the silence would be uncomfortable, but right now, it's not. I like having her by me. It doesn't feel like she's invading my space, just that she's sharing it with me.

A wave of vanilla hits my nose. It's subtle, but sweet. A strange feeling, one I haven't felt in a long time, has my stomach dipping. I frown, not entirely sure I like the new feeling. It's leaving me off-kilter. I don't like not being in control.

Daniel, as expected, bounds up to the bar, Kelsey walking placidly behind him. It hurts something deep inside me every time I look at her and see the unhidden anguish in her eyes. I feel for this girl because I go through the same pain every day.

The kids sit at the bar and enjoy their hot drinks while Gwen and I stand by and watch. Daniel chatters nonstop about the horses he saw. The pure joy on his face as he talks animatedly makes my heart hurt a little less.

My eyes stray to Gwen every few seconds, watching, but hoping she doesn't catch me. She's looking at her son with a smile on her face, genuinely enjoying his energetic rambling. When Daniel mentions coming back once the weather is warmer so he can ride a horse, her eyes stray to me for a moment before going back to him. "We'll see."

Deep down inside a place that's been dormant for years, I hope she does decide to come back. I want to be around these people more. They distract me from my own pain. Not that I'm glad they carry pain, but it reminds me that I'm not alone in the world. There are others out there suffering just as much. In less than two days, this small family has helped quiet the screams in my head, something no one has been able to do. Of course, that might be because I haven't let anyone close enough to really try. My family has been there for me, but they suffer from their own grief.

My eyes travel to Kelsey to find her looking at me. Her eyes look so sad, and when she notices I've caught her stare, she looks away. It knocks me in the chest every time I look at her. I want to take away her pain. A child her age should never look the way she does, like her life is over.

Once the kids are done with their hot chocolate, Gwen tells Daniel it's time to shower. He ambles off, while Kelsey goes back to the living room where her notebook is on the couch. Gwen goes to the laundry room to fold the few pieces of clothes she washed. She offered to wash mine earlier along with hers, but I declined. I know she's only trying to help because her and her kids are staying here a few days, but I've told her several times, there's no need. She insists on cooking though. I didn't argue. I may know how to cook but it's been a long time since I've had someone do it for me. And as much as I thought it would freak me out having another woman here doing something such as cooking, it hasn't. That doesn't mean it won't later. I keep waiting for the nerves to hit, but so far, they haven't.

I leave the kitchen and go to the living room. Kelsey's on one end of the couch, drawing pad in her lap, so I take the other end. I grab the remote from the coffee table and switch the TV on, but keep the volume low. I can feel her eyes on me, but I keep my head forward. We stay like this for a while, me seemingly ignoring her, and her looking at me out the corner of her eye every so often.

Keeping my eyes on the TV, I ask, "Do you like cartoons?"

I'm met with silence, which doesn't surprise me. However, she does turn her head my way. I turn to face her as well. Her eyes are still blank, but underneath the emptiness, I see something lurking. Something that tells me she wants to let go so badly and be part of the world again, but is afraid to.

"What are you drawing?" I ask, then look down at the drawing pad. Her hand is covering part of the paper, so I can't see it all, but it looks to be a dream catcher.

She follows my eyes down to the pad, looks back at me, then surprises me by handing it over. Her eyes hold uncertainty as I grab the pad and hold it up to take a look. I was right, it's a dream catcher, but this one's unique. It has the usual webbing in the middle where the dreams are said to fly through, and the feathers falling from the bottom, but there's also an added feature. Dripping from the webbing and falling alongside the feathers are drops of some kind of liquid. Most would probably think raindrops, but my bet is on tears. The picture is stunningly beautiful but also very devastating. It shows her pain.

"This is beautiful," I say, and hand it back to her.

For a second, her eyes reflect light instead of complete darkness, and it makes me feel ten fucking feet tall that my compliment pleased her.

Hearing a noise behind us, I look over the back of the couch and see Gwen standing at the bar watching us. Her eyes look glassy and her hand is covering her mouth. Her eyes flick back and forth between me and Kelsey before they settle on me. Her hand falls away and she's wearing a smile. I tip one side of my mouth up then face forward again, glad I could bring a smile to Gwen's face and some form of pleasure to Kelsey.

LATER THAT EVENING, after everyone has gone to bed, I'm lying on my back on the couch with a notepad in hand, working on something, when I hear murmurs coming from the hallway. I turn my head to try to listen better. The murmurs stop, but then start back up again a minute later.

I set my notepad down on the coffee table and get up from the couch. Unsure of what's going on and not wanting to wake anyone that might be asleep, I walk down the hall silently. The murmurs get louder the closer I get to the half-open door. I stop just out of view and listen, not being nosy, but making sure everything is okay.

The softly spoken words nearly bring me to my knees.

"Please, God, just let my daddy come home," Kelsey's tearful voice whispers. "And please tell him I'm sorry. I miss him so much. I just want to hug him again and tell him I love him." Her voice is lower when she finishes. "In Jesus' name, amen."

Hearing those words whispered in such an agonizing way damn near suffocates me. It's hard to pull in air because the weight on my chest is so heavy. I don't get emotional. I've cried once as an adult, but right now, this eight-year old's excruciating words have tears springing to my eyes. The need to rush in there and take her in my arms is almost overwhelming. Only knowing it's not my place keeps me on this side of the door.

Kelsey's quiet after that. No more words are whispered. Obviously, Gwen's asleep and didn't hear her, because I know I would have heard her consoling her daughter, if not crying along with her.

With one last look at the door and my heart heavy, I walk away and go back to the couch. I spend the next couple hours finishing up the project I was working on, determined to get it done quickly, then set it aside. It takes me a long time to drift off to sleep, and when I finally manage to, it's a restless sleep filled with the whispered prayers of a broken girl.

Chapter Seven

Gwendolyn

I WALK DOWN THE hallway, rubbing sleep from my eyes, when I hear Daniel laughing. When I awoke a few minutes ago, I was alone in the bed. For a split second, panic had me scrambling to get the covers off to search for them, but then I realized where I was. I may not know Alexander, but the way he's been with the kids the last couple of days, he seems like a good guy. That may be naïve of me, but I like to think my instincts are good.

As I walk by one of the living room windows, I see a thick layer of snow falling. The thought of the snow not letting up, forcing us to stay longer, doesn't fill me with the dread you'd think it would. It does the opposite, in fact. I want to be here longer. I feel comfortable here. I like being near Alexander.

I spot Daniel and Kelsey at the bar, while Alexander leans back against the counter watching them, a small smile playing on his lips. The man is already striking, despite his scars, but when he smiles, it almost knocks the breath out of me. When he laughed yesterday at Daniel's comment about Alexander's hot chocolate being better than mine, all I could do was stare. It was the first time I'd seen him smile or laugh and the look on his face was nothing but beautiful. It sent butterflies to my stomach. The surprise on his face when he realized he was laughing said he's not used to doing it.

Daniel laughs again and it pulls me from my thoughts of Alexander's beautiful face. He's always been a happy boy, but I don't remember him being quite this cheerful. For some reason, he's taken an extra liking to Alexander. I wouldn't have pegged Alexander as the type to willingly spend time with a boy Daniel's age, but I'm glad he's going out of his way to be nice to him.

Will's been gone for over two years now, and I know it's time I open myself up to the possibility of dating again, to try to find someone that would be good to both me and my kids. Daniel needs a man in his life, and I don't want to be alone forever. I know Will would want me to find someone else, to try to be happy again, to find a good man that could take on the father role that he can't, but the thought of dating terrifies me. Will was my high school sweetheart. He was my first for everything. I don't know *how* to date.

I walk into the kitchen and find out why Daniel was laughing. Gigi has her puppies on the floor trying to gently play with them, but all she's managing to do is knock them off their feet and onto their backs.

What has me surprised and my heart stopping in my chest is the almost-smile on Kelsey's face as she watches momma dog and her puppies. It's not touching her mouth, but it's definitely there in her eyes. I see more animation on her face than I've seen in years. I think Alexander plays a big role in that too. Her interest in him is unmistakable. Last night, the look on her face when he said her drawing was beautiful had me wanting to burst into tears. Thankfully, I managed to hold them back. I would be lying if I said I wasn't a bit jealous Alexander's gotten more of a reaction out of Kelsey than I have in years, but seeing her eyes showing more than just lifelessness far outweighs the emotion.

Alexander sees me approaching and whips around to stir something in a pot. I walk up beside him to find him cooking eggs and grits.

"Need any help?" I ask, then grab a mug and fill it with the coffee that's calling my name.

"I got it," he grunts.

I look over at him and see a frown on his face. "Everything okay?"

"Yeah. Just didn't sleep well last night."

Guilt tightens my chest. It's my fault he's on the couch and not in his big comfortable bed.

"I'm sorry," I tell him. "I noticed the snow still coming down. Tonight, the kids and I will take the couch and chair so you can have your bed. I know it can't be good for your back."

The glare he shoots me is sharp and says without words that my suggestion is ludicrous and pisses him off.

I hold my hands up and grumble, "Fine," and continue making my coffee.

I make the kids a plate, and once again, we all eat in the kitchen with the kids at the bar and Alexander and I standing. Afterward, I do the dishes while Kelsey sits at the bar with her drawing pad and Alexander and Daniel go out and check on the horses.

When I'm done, I walk around the bar beside Kelsey. She looks over at me, her eyes back to their previous empty state.

"Can I see?" I ask, then hold my breath. She's shown Alexander her drawing, now I hope she'll show me. I won't force the issue if she refuses, but it'll hurt. As advised by her therapists, unless it's for her well-being, I rarely push Kelsey into doing things, preferring to have her come to me on her own instead. I want her to *want* to show me, not make her. I don't think it's that she doesn't want to share stuff with me. I think it's more like she cares so little about anything she does that maybe she feels like no one else will.

I want to cry tears of joy when she hands it over. I pray she doesn't notice my hand shaking as I reach out and grab it. Forcing my eyes away from her, I look down at the drawing pad. My breath catches at what I see. It's a whole bunch of differently designed sad faces. They're simple in design, but hold so much meaning.

Looking closer, I notice something else. Hidden amongst the sad faces are a few smiley faces. Overall, there have to be about thirty sad faces and only five smiley faces. I don't know if I should cry or smile at the picture. On one hand, it's obvious the dominant emotion Kelsey feels is sadness. On the other hand, knowing she feels glimpses of happiness lightens my heart and gives me hope. Kelsey never appears happy, or at least she never shows it, but it's apparent there are times she does. I just wonder what happens during those times. What brings on those bursts of pleasure? I want to replicate them over and over and over again, so all she feels is that emotion.

I hand her back the pad and scoot closer to her. She never pulls away from me when I show her affection, and she doesn't now when I wrap my arm around her shoulders and bring her in for a hug. Her arms go around me, then tighten. I squeeze my eyes shut at the contact because it's not common for her to put effort into hugs. I don't know what's happened recently, but there've been several changes in her, ones I pray will continue and grow.

I pull back from her, but rest my forehead against hers. It's amazing how she can watch me with emotionless eyes when my own emotions are running rampant.

"I love you," I tell her softly.

Every time I say those words, I hope I get a reply back, but I never do, and today is no different. One day I will though. I refuse to believe anything other than that.

LATER THAT AFTERNOON, I step out onto the porch while the kids eat lunch. Alexander's been out here for hours, only coming in for about thirty minutes after he and Daniel were done with the horses before leaving again.

Everything is white and covered in snow. It's a beautiful sight.

Surprisingly, the temperature isn't blistering cold like you'd think it would be with all the snow. It's deceptive, making one think it's colder than what it actually is.

I'm surprised to find Alexander sitting out on the porch with his feet crossed at the ankle and propped up on the railing. He looks relaxed as he writes something in a notebook. He looks up and watches me with an unreadable expression as I approach the vacant chair closest to the door.

"Mind if I join you?" I ask in case he wants to be left alone.

He flips the notebook over and lays it on his lap, then grunts in reply. I take that an acceptance and sit.

I gaze out across the yard, mesmerized by the beauty of the place. With the snow covering everything, it looks like a snowy wonderland. It must be so peaceful living in a place like this. Cat's Valley isn't a large town with the hustle and bustle of cars, noise, and the awful smell of pollution, but there's still a big difference between there and here. That's another reason why Will and I wanted to buy land. We wanted the solitude of living away from everything as we raised our kids.

My gaze skitters across the property and lands on the partially built structure, which I assume will be a house once it's finished. All I can see are the bare walls, but it looks like it's been there for a while.

"What are you going to do with your cabin once you finish the house?" I ask, bringing my eyes to him.

His looks over at the house for a brief second before looking back out at the yard.

"Nothing," he says, a strange note in his voice. "I'm tearing it down."

My eyes widen in disbelief. "But why? Why would you partially build a house only to tear it down again? I bet it would look beautiful once you finish it."

He's quiet for so long that I think he's not going to answer. I'm about ready to forget my question, once again overstepping boundaries, when he surprises me.

"It was supposed to be for my wife and child."

His voice is so quiet, I barely make out the words. But I do, and the anguished way he utters them says a lot more than his actual words do. There's obviously more to the story, and it's apparent it's a painful one. I want to ask him about it, but it's not my place. I don't need to worry, because he tells me on his own.

"They died four years ago." He clears his throat when his voice cracks. "A drunk guy pulled out in front of us right before the bridge over Hallow's Creek. I swerved to miss hitting him head-on and ended up rolling down the embankment and landing on the passenger side under the bridge."

My stomach bottoms out and it literally feels like my heart is hurting at the tormented tone in his voice. To lose a spouse is gut-wrenching and one of the most painful experiences a person can have. Losing a child is ten times worse. To lose both would be beyond excruciating, unbearable. I can't imagine ever getting over something like that.

"I'm so sorry," I whisper. The sentiment is so lax for what he went through, but it's the only comfort I can give. There's nothing anyone can do to make it better.

He looks at me, his eyes holding a mountain of pain. "Thank you."

"That's why you want to tear it down. Because it reminds you of them?"

"Yes," he answers. "That and there's no need for it anymore. It's only me, and I don't need a house that size for just me."

"Maybe you'll find someone else to share it with," I suggest, then want to take back the words. It's clear he's still grieving for his deceased wife and child. To even suggest him finding someone new, even though it's completely reasonably, is insensitive.

His jaw tics, and I worry I've pissed him off. I tense and wait for him to tell me to go to hell, but it never comes. He turns his head my way, looks right at me, then says with conviction, "That'll never happen."

"I'm sorry," I say. "I didn't mean...." I trail off, not really knowing what I meant.

His eyes lose some of the heat and he looks past me to the house. "It's okay." He takes a deep breath, then brings his eyes back to me. "It was Clara's dream. The plans for the house... they were all her ideas. I gave input here and there, but I let her have free rein." He stops and rubs his hands down his face and looks away from me. "That house was supposed to be hers and our children's, and I wouldn't want to share it with anyone else."

I nod. "I get it."

We sit in a comfortable silence for a while. The sun is actually peeking out for the first time in days, and I wonder if it's finally over. I watch the way the sun reflects off the snow, making it look like it's sparkling.

After a while, I decide to go back inside. I've encroached on Alexander's time alone long enough. Right as I open the screen door, he calls my name, and I look at him.

"Snow's letting up. They'll probably get to the roads tomorrow."

I ignore the way his words make me feel.

"Yeah. I figured so."

He's quiet for a moment, and I think he's done, so I turn to go inside, but then he shocks me.

"It's been nice having you and the kids here," he says quietly.

Again, I ignore the way his words make me feel. Except this time, it's not sorrow, but pleasure. I'm glad to know we weren't a complete burden to him, that he enjoyed us being here. I know I've enjoyed it, and from Daniel's excited nonstop chatter, and the signs of life from Kelsey, they have too.

I smile. "Thank you for taking us in. It's been really nice. It's peaceful here."

"Yeah," he says, then looks out across the yard. "If the cell towers are back up I'll call Travis tonight to get an update about the roads."

"Okay."

I go back inside, hating the fact that we could be gone tomorrow. There's no telling when we'll see him again, and that thought doesn't settle well in my stomach. It actually twists it in knots. I've got no right to feel this way. The only reason we're here is because we had no choice, and it's only been three days, but I've gotten used to waking up and seeing him. I don't know why, but I look forward to it.

The kids are done eating when I walk back inside, so I wash the few dishes that are dirty. After, I roll some hamburger meat into meatballs and throw them in the crockpot for dinner along with some seasoning, the whole time silently wishing the snow would pick back up and keep us here a few more days.

THAT EVENING, AFTER everyone is finished with dinner and the kitchen is cleaned, we all sit in the living room watching *Lilo and Stitch*, one of Daniel's favorite movies. He's on his stomach on the floor with Gigi lying beside him. Both canine and boy have taken a strong liking to the other. Several of the puppies are curled up next to Daniel, while the rest are against their mom. I may have to talk to Alexander about getting one of the pups when they're ready to be adopted.

And no, I'm not using that as an excuse to see him again. Or that's what I tell myself anyway.

I'm sitting on one end of the couch, Alexander on the other, with Kelsey between us. I was surprised when he stopped on the movie even before Daniel had a chance to ask. I wouldn't have pegged him for watching cartoon movies, and it brings a smile to my face because I know he's doing it for Daniel. Every time Daniel laughs at something that happens, I catch Alexander looking at him. I think he likes knowing he's pleased my son.

Kelsey's sitting cross-legged watching the movie, but she doesn't laugh when something funny happens, instead just stares at the screen. I'd give anything to hear her giggle again.

Once the movie is over, I get up from the couch to put the clothes from the washer into the dryer. This is the second time I've washed clothes since being here. I can't stand wearing the same clothes more than one day.

When I walk back into the living room, Kelsey has her drawing pad in her lap again and Daniel is rolling around on the floor with squirming puppies all over him. Alexander's sitting at the bar with the same notepad he had earlier outside.

I walk to the back of the couch. "Hey, kids. I'm going to grab a shower."

"Okay, Mom," says a distracted Daniel. I get a blank stare from Kelsey.

I turn to Alexander. "Are they okay out here?"

"Yeah."

With a nod, I turn and go to Alexander's bathroom. I've gotten used to using his room to sleep in, but for some reason it still feels weird using his bathroom to shower. Maybe it's because he caught me using it without his permission yesterday. Or it might be because I smell him every time I enter the room. His smell lingers in the bedroom, but more so in the bathroom, because that's where he puts his deodorant on, washes his body, and shampoos his hair. It reminds me of when I was looking at his cologne in the medicine cabinet and wondered what it smelled like. Now I know, and I'll only ever admit to myself, it smells heavenly.

I turn the shower on and strip down, leaving my folded clothes on the edge of the sink. Before stepping in the shower, I open the medicine cabinet and pull out the disposable razor and shaving cream I spotted the other day. I know I shouldn't use it without asking first, but it's a disposable and I'm sure he has more somewhere. I haven't shaved in days, and I can't stand the little pricklies on my legs any longer. I'll tell him I used it so he knows to toss it and get another if he's grossed out by it.

I sigh in relief when I rub my hands up my now smooth legs, then wash my hair. My emergency bag didn't include shampoo, conditioner, or body wash, so the kids and I have been using Alexander's. I take a big whiff of the body soap, enjoying the smell entirely way too much, before lathering up the washcloth.

Five minutes later, I turn the shower off, grab a towel, and dry off. Somehow the curtain must have not closed all the way, because there's water on the floor. Not seeing it until it's too late, I slip, and I grab for the sink to catch myself. In doing so, I knock my clothes, then watch in slow motion as they fall from the sink and into the open toilet. When I realize what's happening, I try to grab the clothes, and end up sliding again in the water. My hip slams into the corner of the counter, and I cry out at the pain, then fall to my knees.

Tears spring to my eyes as my hip radiates a sharp pain. I try to push them back, but a couple manage to escape. I look down and see a deep purple mark already forming. That's going to leave a nasty bruise.

"Gwen!" Alexander's deep voice calls frantically from the other side of the door. "Are you okay?"

My eyes widen when I see the doorknob jiggle, like he's trying to open it. With me on my knees, buck naked.

"Yes," I say loudly. "Don't come in!" My voice cracks from the stupid tears that are still trying to make their way to the surface.

"What happened?" he demands.

"I slipped and fell and hit my hip."

I can't be sure, but I think he mutters "Fuck" before he says, "I'm coming in."

"No!" I yell, then blurt, "I don't have any clothes on!"

It's quiet, and I wonder if he's walked away. My eyes skid to the side, and I see my clothes sitting in the toilet, which reminds me I have nothing to wear.

"Alexander?" I ask, hoping he hasn't left yet. I wince in pain when I slowly get to my feet.

"Still right here."

"Umm... do you have any clothes I could borrow?" I ask. Even though he can't see me, I squeeze my eyes closed in humiliation. "I... uh... sort of knocked mine in the toilet when I was trying to catch myself." I inwardly groan. I feel so stupid right now. "And my other set are still in the dryer."

My eyes narrow when I hear a rusty chuckle on the other side of the door.

"It's not funny," I mutter.

"It kind of is," he replies. "Hang tight."

I wrap the towel around me and tuck a corner between my breasts.

A minute later, he calls my name, and I crack open the door just wide enough to peek around the wood. If I wasn't so embarrassed and in pain, I'd be captivated by the beautiful smirk lifting his lips on the unscarred side of his face. Smirks aren't supposed to be beautiful. They're normally supposed to piss people off, not stupefy them with their gorgeousness.

The look disappears when he sees the tears still swimming in my eyes. He steps up with a small pile of clothes in his hand, his eyes drawn down into a worried frown.

"Are you okay?" he asks again.

"It's going to leave a nasty bruise, but I'll manage."

His eyes flicker back and forth between mine several times, before he thrusts the pile of clothes at me. Holding the towel tighter to my chest, I step to the side just enough to reach out for the clothes. For a second, his eyes land on the hand holding my towel before he clears his throat and looks down at the floor, then takes a step back.

"They'll be big on you, but it's the best I can do," he mumbles, then turns on his heel and leaves the room.

My gaze follows him until he disappears. I close the bathroom door, then lean back against it, for some reason feeling flushed. A subtle woodsy smell has me looking down at the clothes clutched in my arms. Before I know what I'm doing, I bring them to my nose and take a whiff, then cringe when the action makes me feel like a weirdo.

I walk over to the toilet and fish out my soaked clothes, throwing them in the sink and thanking God there was no dirty business in the commode. After rinsing them out, just because I don't want toilet water in them, I wring them out and set them back in the sink to grab when I leave the bathroom. Guess I'll be washing another load tonight.

I hang the towel on the hook on the back of the door and grab the black sweatpants Alexander gave me to wear. He's right, they are big on me. Not just in length, but in the waist as well. I have to roll them four times, making sure to avoid resting them against my bruised hip, before they'll stay up, and even then, they're on the verge of slipping down.

The dark gray V-neck T-shirt comes next. It's huge as well and comes down to midthigh. I'm forced to wear it back further on my shoulders, or my cleavage will show. I turn to face the mirror and wrinkle my nose at the sight before me. I look ridiculous in this humongous outfit, but I can't help but *feel* comfortable in it. The material is surprisingly soft against my skin.

Grabbing my brush from the emergency bag, I start on the tangles in my hair, then haphazardly throw it into a bun on top of my head. Packing the few things I used back in the bag, I nab the wet clothes from the sink and open the door. I come to an abrupt stop when I see Alexander sitting on the end of the bed. His head lifts and he stands.

He takes a step toward me, then stops. "I wanted to check on you." He gestures to my hip with a tilt of his chin. "You mind if I take a look?"

"Umm... you really don't have to do that. I'm sure it's—"

"I'd prefer to be safe. You can hurt your insides and not realize it until later. It's obviously bad enough to make you cry. I know it's not the same, but I have a degree in veterinary medicine, and with some things human and animal bodies work the same."

I stand in the bathroom doorway with my wet clothes hanging from one hand and my bag clutched to my chest with the other, unsure of what to do. The concern in his eyes is apparent, but I wonder *why* he's so concerned. More than likely after tomorrow we won't be his burden anymore. I've learned over the last few days that Alexander can be a very compassionate man; the expression on his face when he looks at Kelsey sometimes proves it. I'm sure it's just that soft side he rarely lets show that's allowing him to worry, and I'm sure it's nothing personal.

The slight frown on his face is what makes my decision. Taking a step back, I drop the wet clothes on the tiled bathroom floor and set the bag down beside them, then make my way over to him.

We both stand there awkwardly for a moment before he says, "You want to... ah...." He gestures down to my waistband.

"Oh." I laugh awkwardly, feeling my cheeks heat. I grab the rolled-up waistband and bring the material down to just below my hip, making sure to keep my pubic area covered. The shirt falls in its place, so I grab that as well and lift it, exposing a small portion of my lower stomach. Stretch marks from having two kids come into view, and I force myself to not cover myself again.

Unexpectedly, Alexander drops to his knees in front of me and my eyes follow him down. He looks up and our gazes lock. For some reason, looking down at him as he gazes up at me from his knees seems strangely erotic. The hand holding my shirt up starts trembling, and I tighten my fingers around the material.

He finally breaks our stare and looks to the purple skin on my hip. I suck in a sharp breath when his fingers graze the skin. I tell myself it's because the touch hurts, and not because it sends butterflies to my stomach. His eyes briefly flicker back to mine before he gently starts prodding the sensitive area. I close my eyes when the area he touches turns warm. I haven't felt desire since Will died, and I wonder if what I'm feeling now is the same. It scares me, but his hand on me feels too good to care right now. Goose bumps appear on my skin, and I know Alexander has to see them, but he doesn't react. For that, I'm grateful. I try to push the feeling away, but it stays and grows.

At my grunt of pain, he pulls his hand away, and I miss the warmth it caused. "Shit," he mumbles. "Sorry."

He keeps his hands to himself as he examines it for a few more moments.

"It seems to have the typical bruising, showing no signs of internal damage that I can tell." He stands. "You'll be sore as shit tomorrow. After you leave here, keep an eye on it, and if a large part of the injured area turns purple, swells, or if you become dizzy, call the doctor."

I nod and release the waistband and shirt, letting them fall back into place. Stepping back, I tell him, "Thank you." His chin comes up in acknowledgement, and I clarify, "For the concern. Thank you."

"You're welcome," he grunts.

I turn and grab the clothes and bag from the bathroom door. When I turn back around, he's already gone, leaving me with an odd feeling in my stomach.

LATER THAT NIGHT, I lie in bed and listen to the soft words coming from Kelsey, my heart splintering into two, then three, then into a thousand pieces.

"Please, God, let my daddy come back home. I miss him so much. I just want him to come home. That's all I'll ever ask you, if you just let him come back to us. And please tell him I'm sorry." She sniffles, then finishes, "In Jesus' name, amen."

The last part I can barely hear. I know why she's apologizing. He was in her room getting her bear for her when he collapsed. Both her psychiatrist and I have told her multiple times that it wasn't her fault, that his heart wasn't working properly, but I know she didn't believe us. I don't know what else to do to make her believe it. She's only eight years old, but she carries around the guilt that weighs a ton. A week after the funeral, I found the bear ripped to shreds in her closet.

I want to reach out to her. I want to pull her into my arms and soothe her cries away. To tell her nothing is her fault and that I love her. That her daddy loves her even if he's not here anymore to show it. But I worry if I do that, she'll pull further away from me. She only whispers her prayers because she thinks no one else can hear them. This is her private time, her safe time to talk to the only person she feels like she can right now. I don't want to take that away from her, and I'm scared if she knows I hear her every night, that I relish hearing her voice, even if her words tear me apart, she'll stop. She needs this. I want her to come to me with her voice when she's ready for me to hear it.

So instead of comforting my daughter like I'm dying to, I silently cry into my pillow and wait for her to drift off to sleep. It's only then I turn around and wrap my arms around her, giving her in sleep what she won't allow me to give to her when she's awake.

Chapter Eight

Alexander

JUST LIKE LAST NIGHT, I walk silently down the hallway until I make out the murmured whispers from a girl begging God to bring her father back. I gently lay my hand on the door and listen as she slowly melts my heart until it's a puddle at my feet. My chest aches with the need to walk in there and take away her pain. I've never heard such tortured words before. The pain that comes from them is overwhelming and unbearable. Even my own immense pain from losing the ones I loved can't compare to this. This girl's pain is so much more.

My head falls forward, and I pull in a deep breath to steady my heartbeat. It's been quiet for several moments, and I know she's finished. I let my hand fall from the door, and I walk down the hallway back to the living room. I drop to the cushion and let my head fall in my hands.

They're leaving tomorrow. The sun is coming out and the temperatures are supposed to be in the lower fifties, much higher than it's been in days. The snow won't melt in one day, but it'll be enough to let the road crew get to the fallen tree and her truck. My call earlier tonight to Travis confirmed they'll be working on the roads tomorrow.

I'm not ready. It's unreasonable and irrational, but I don't want them to leave yet. I'm not ready to give up Daniel's buoyant behavior or Kelsey's quiet and depressed mannerisms. I'm not ready to give up Gwen's giving and resilient personality. I want to keep them here. With me. They've brought so much light into my life since they've been here, and I want to keep it for a while longer. Which means they need to leave as soon as possible, before my dark world rubs off on them. I want to be selfish and harbor that light, but I won't.

What hurts the most was the dejected look on Daniel's face when Gwen informed him and Kelsey they'll be leaving tomorrow. What surprised me was the morose look on Kelsey's. That girl and her sad eyes have me wrapped around her little finger. And the boy…. Everyone should have a Daniel in their lives. Gwen tried cheering the two up with promised visits to all their friends once the roads were clear enough for it, but I could tell it didn't work. I could also tell it wasn't working for Gwen herself. She tried to hide it, I'm not sure if it was just from the kids or from me too, but I know she doesn't want to leave either. The four of us, in a matter of days, have become close, formed a bond of a sort. And that right there is another reason they need to leave. I can't let that continue. It's not something I deserve. It's something they need to form with a man who's worthy. A man who will be there for them always. A whole man, not one who's only half of himself.

I give my hair one good pull, letting the pain push away the unwanted feelings, before releasing it with a muted growl. I'm pissed at myself for wanting something I shouldn't. This family is too good for me. I couldn't even protect my own when they needed me. How could this family be any different? I refuse to take that chance.

I lie back against the cushion and force thoughts of Gwen and her two kids away, and instead let my own demons take over. Closing my eyes, I let the screams of pain and fear flood my mind, reminding me why Gwen, Kelsey, and Daniel are better off without me in their lives.

THE CREAKING OF the floor is what wakes me. My eyes flash open, and I swing my legs over to sit up on the couch. My eyesight quickly adjusts to the darkness of the room as I look around for the source of the noise. There's a dark figure standing in the mouth of the hallway. A short figure. Much shorter than Gwen, but taller than Daniel.

"Kelsey?" I ask softly.

She takes a couple of steps into the living room, then stops.

"What's wrong, honey?" I ask, knowing I won't get a response.

I make a move to get up, but then my ass plops back down when she starts walking toward me. I hold still and she doesn't stop until she's only a foot away from me. I can't see clearly in the dark room, but I can tell she's looking at me.

"Kelsey, is everything—"

I stop and sit there stunned when she springs forward, wraps her arms around my neck, and sits down sideways on my lap. I hold my breath and don't move for several long seconds, but then slowly bring my arms around her. For as long as she's been here, I've never seen her show either her mother or brother any affection. She doesn't shy away when her mother holds her hand or kisses the top of her head, but she never initiates any contact. For her to do so now, with me, is shocking, and damn near crushes my heart. I just don't know why. Why would she pick me?

I feel wetness on my neck and heated breaths as she buries her face against me and cries softly. My arms tighten around her tiny waist, and I tug her back with me as I lean back against the couch.

"Shhh," I whisper into the darkness, rubbing circles on her upper back. "It's okay."

"I miss my dad," she whispers back, further obliterating my heart and shocking me more.

I squeeze my eyes closed to keep back the tears wanting to fall. I am so completely blessed to hear this girl's beautiful voice after years of not letting anyone hear it, but the tortured words and the pain behind them leave me feeling like I'm taking my last painful breath.

"I know you do, honey," I say softly. "I know you do."

Unsure of what to do, I adjust us both so I'm leaning back against the arm of the couch with her still lying in my arms. I debate with myself whether I should get her mother or not, and then decide against it, worried that she'll withdraw even further. Obviously, there's something about me that makes her feel comfortable enough to come to me, even though I have no clue what it is. Kelsey needs this, I know in my gut she does, and although Gwen is her mother and has a right to know, I won't break Kelsey's trust. In the short span of time they've been here, she's come to mean a lot to me, all three of them have, way more than they should.

Kelsey's cries quiet down after a while, and I feel her breathing against my neck even out. She's finally asleep. The thought of taking her back into my room where her mother is doesn't even cross my mind. It makes my heart feel lighter having her trustingly sleep against me.

I settle us down even more, grabbing the blanket I threw on the back of the couch and laying it over her. My legs hang out, but that's perfectly okay with me.

I kiss the top of her head and tighten my arms, making sure she won't fall off during the night. Leaning my head back against the armrest, I close my eyes and send up my own silent prayer that this girl and her family will find the strength to be whole again.

I WAKE WITH SNORING in my ear and something tickling my nose. Cracking my eyes open, a headful of red hair is all I can see. I tip my head to the side and brush away the few strands of hair that've gotten caught in my beard. A soft smile plays on my lips when Kelsey's nose wrinkles.

Feeling eyes on me, I look over and see Gwen sitting on one of the chairs, staring at us. My smile slips away at the intense look on her face. At first, I wonder if she's mad, because the hard slash of her mouth, downward line of her eyebrows, and the redness covering her cheeks make her appear like she's holding in anger. I'm just about to ask what's wrong, when all of a sudden she lets out a soft hiccoughing sound right before her face crumples and her eyes flood with tears. Her eyes leave mine to look down at her daughter snuggled in my arms. I look down as well and know exactly what she's feeling. My heart constricts at the pure innocence on Kelsey's face. Her face is relaxed in her sleep, not giving off the painful look she normally carries.

I look back at Gwen, and I want to get up and pull her in my arms. To comfort her, but to also let her know she's not alone. Our situations are different on many levels, but there's one thing that's the same. We both mourn the loss of someone special to us. Gwen not only mourns her husband, but her daughter as well. I mourn my wife and the family we'd barely begun to share.

I hold on to Kelsey as Gwen struggles to bring her emotions under control. Her lips tip up into a beautiful smile as she wipes away her tears. A look to the left shows the sun is already making its way over the horizon, surprising me because I never sleep this late.

"Will she stay asleep if I move her?" I ask quietly.

She gets up and comes over to us; her eyes soften even more as she peers down at her sleeping daughter.

"She should," she whispers.

Pulling back the cover, I slowly sit up and place my feet on the floor. I adjust Kelsey so she's lying sideways in my arms with one under her shoulders and the other under her knees. Gwen follows us as I walk down the hallway to the bedroom. Neither of the kids move as I lay her down next to Daniel. I slide part of the cover over

Kelsey, and before I know what I'm doing, I'm bending down and placing a kiss on her forehead, then leaning over and doing the same to Daniel. These may not be my kids, and I may not have any ties to them, but they already have a place in my heart.

When I turn to leave the room, Gwen's standing behind me, watching with a weird look on her face. She turns before I can question her on it, and we both walk down the hallway. She heads straight for the couch, grabs my blanket, and starts folding it. I go over to the fireplace and throw in a couple of logs, stirring it back to life, before turning to face her.

With her back to me, she asks in a hoarse voice, "What would you have done if I had told you she would wake up?"

"Stayed on the couch until she woke on her own," I tell her.

She lays the blanket down on the couch, then the pillow on top, before turning to face me.

"Why?"

I walk over to her and stop when I'm a foot away. The need to be close to her is too strong to ignore right now. It scares the shit out of me, but I don't have the will to push it away.

Her head tips back the closer I get to her. Her vanilla scent wafts up to me, reminding me of the cakes my grandmother used to bake us kids when we were little.

I stop when I'm only a foot away. "Why what?"

"Why would you do that for her?" Her eyes are soft but curious as she asks the question.

"To be honest, I don't know." And I really don't. I have no clue why these people have touched me so much in such a short time. But there's no denying it.

She nods, looks down for a moment, then lifts her head.

"What time did she wake you?"

"It wasn't too late."

"I'm sorry. You should have woken me."

"She was fine."

I don't say anything about Kelsey whispering to me. There's

obviously a reason she spoke to me last night. Maybe she's finally decided to start opening up, and I was the first person she was able to do it with. Maybe she senses my own heartache and feels like she can relate. Maybe she'll wake up today and start talking. Or maybe she was half asleep and vulnerable at the time and it slipped out before she realized it. No matter the reason, telling her mother doesn't seem right.

And a tiny part of me, the evil, selfish part, wants to keep it to myself for a little while. It makes me feel so damn special that she picked me to hear her voice after so long.

We both stand there, neither breaking eye contact. My hand itches to reach out and graze my fingers along her cheek. I know it would be soft. I haven't wanted to touch a woman since Clara died, and I never thought I would again. Or rather, I never thought I would want to. These feelings confuse me, because I want to feel them, but they terrify me. What could I possibly offer Gwen and her kids? A small cabin on the outskirts of town? A man that's both physically and emotionally scarred? Certainly not protection, because it's painfully obvious how well I do that. I remember that fact every single fucking day of my life. What this family could give me far exceeds anything I could ever give them, and that's not fair.

With that thought in mind, I take a step back, pushing away the need to be near her that I couldn't force back moments ago. It hurts so damn much when I see the disappointment in her eyes. I have no idea what's going on between us, but whatever it is, she feels it too. If I was a better man, a whole man without a black hole in my heart, I would snatch up the opportunity to have a woman like Gwen, and her kids. But I'm not. Instead, I put even more distance between us, and continue to hate the look she gives me.

"I'm going to go check on and feed the horses," I tell her, my voice gruff.

Her hands play with the bottom of her shirt and she nods. "Okay."

I force my feet to take me away from her before I do something

I'll regret later. My boots and jacket are on, and I'm reaching for the door when she calls my name. I only turn my head to look at her over my shoulder, afraid if I turn my whole body, I won't be able to stop myself from going to her.

She's closer to me from where I left her in the living room, like she was following me to the door, but then stopped herself. It makes me wonder if she's having as hard a time as I am with staying away.

"The kids should be up soon. Would you like breakfast?"

Her face holds a hopeful expression, and I don't have it in me to tell her no. She's leaving today, and as hard as it's going to be, I do want to spend time with her, Kelsey, and Daniel before they go. I just need to get my shit under control first. Spending time with my horses and giving myself a pep talk should do it.

Or rather, I hope like hell it does.

"Yeah," I answer.

The smile she gives me damn near knocks me on my ass.

Before my legs get a mind of their own and carries me over to her, I shove open the door and step out into the surprisingly warmer weather. I hate the heat. That's part of the reason I love Colorado so much; it never gets too hot here. It's nowhere near hot right now, but it's definitely warmer than what I want it to be. It's because of the warm weather that Gwen and her kids are leaving today.

The sun is just barely peeking over the horizon, and the white snow on the ground makes everything blinding. Drops of water are already dripping from the roof, and although there's still a lot of snow on the ground, several inches have already melted away. As the day goes on, even more will melt. It's amazing, the difference from yesterday to today.

I step off the porch and head to the barn, anxious to get the horses fed and back to the house.

HOURS LATER, I'M standing at the window with my chest feeling hollow as I watch Jeremy's forest green Blazer make its way up my driveway and park next to my truck. I grip the window seal when he gets out and looks around before walking to my porch. Seconds later, his knock sounds. I want to ignore it, or tell him to go the fuck away, that he can't take away something I want to badly.

My eyes skitter away from the door and land on Gwen, who's standing at the end of the bar with a questioning look. She heard the knock as well, and I'm sure she's confused as to why I haven't answered it yet. I'm in denial and just want to ignore it, but I know I can't. They don't belong here with me.

She takes a step toward the door to answer it, so I force my legs to move. I get there before she does, and I step in front of her to pull it open. Jeremy's standing on the other side, hands shoved into his jeans pockets. I've known him for years, and he's a nice enough man, but at the moment, I hate him. My initial reaction is to scowl at him and slam the door in his face. When he looks at me strangely with a hint of fear, I force the expression away. It's not Jeremy's fault I can't get my shit together.

He pulls one hand from his pocket and thrusts it out to me. "It's good to see you, Alexander."

I don't take his hand at first, just look down at it. It's not often I'm offered a hand to shake anymore. I know that's mainly my fault for not inserting myself in situations where I need to shake hands, but I also know it's because people are leery of me.

I grasp his hand in a firm shake. It's not lost on me that he held out his left hand so I have to shake with my left, the unscarred one. However, Jeremy's left-handed, so it could simply be that and not that he didn't want to touch the mangled skin of my right hand.

"Jeremy," I grunt.

"Hey, Jeremy," Gwen says, stepping from behind me and offering him a smile. "Thank you so much for coming to get me and the kids. I hope the roads weren't too bad."

His eyes leave mine to look at Gwen. Jeremy's in his early fifties, and while men his age are still very capable of having a sexual appetite, he looks at Gwen with respect and what looks like fatherly affection. My body relaxes at the innocent expression. It's stupid of me, and I have no right, but I don't want to think of Jeremy wanting Gwen for his own.

"They've been plowed and the salt's doing its job, so they weren't bad."

"That's good."

An awkward silence fills the air as all three of us stand there. I'm used to living in the quiet, so it doesn't really bother me much, but Gwen shifts beside me and Jeremy shoves his hand back into his pocket and rocks on his heels.

It's Gwen who speaks first. "I'll... umm... just go make sure the kids are all ready," she says before leaving Jeremy and me alone.

"Place looks good," he says lightly after several moments.

He's been out here a quite a few times. When Clara were still alive, we hosted barbeques every once in a while. Half the town would show up normally.

"Thanks," I reply.

Silence ensues once again, and fuck if I know what to do to fill it.

Unable to just stand there any longer, I turn on my heel and throw over my shoulder, "You want a cup of coffee before you go?"

"Oh... uh...." He follows me into the kitchen. "Sure."

There's already a fresh pot made, so I walk over and pour him a cup. I've gotten used to Gwen and the kids being here, but now with Jeremy, it feels strange again. Even when I have clients over, we don't come into my house. In the last four years, I've only had my family here, and a couple of old friends.

Jeremy sits at the bar, coffee cup in hand, while I lean against the counter across from him, my arms folded over my chest. I know I'm making him fidgety with my stillness, but I'm out of my element when it comes to visitors. I don't shoot the shit or joke around anymore. I'm quiet and like my space, preferring to stay away from everything and everybody as much as possible. I like this lifestyle now. It's different from what Clara and I had, but it's something I need now.

"So, how have you been?" he asks, then grimaces. "Sorry," he mutters, looking down at his coffee. "Stupid question."

I let him off the hook, because really, under normal circumstances, most people would have already let go of their grief, or at the very least learned how to deal with it and move on with their life. Asking a question such as that shouldn't be a big deal.

"I've been good."

I make sure to keep my voice neutral so I don't scare him off. I hate that people are leery to be around me, that they tiptoe and whisper behind my back. Yes, what happened destroyed me and it's fucked me up in more ways than one, and yes, I do keep away from town because I really don't care to be around people, but when I am in town it pisses me off that they act like I'm a goddamn freak or something. My scars are hideous, and every single fucking day I think about how I wasn't able to protect the two people I loved more than anything in the world, but when people pull the wary card, it reminds me even more of how much I've lost and what I've done, or rather, wasn't able to do.

"That's good." He nods and takes a sip of his coffee.

"How have you and your mother been?" I ask, because that's what people do, right? When one asks the other how they are, it's polite to reciprocate.

He seems surprised by my question, and I guess that's my fault. I haven't been the friendliest person to be around when I do show my face.

"Mom fell the other day and bruised her hip, but other than that, we've been good."

"I heard you and Gwen talking the other day about that." I pause and surprise myself by adding, "If you need help making that ramp, let me know."

His brows lift at my offer, and I can't really say I blame him.

"But I don't want to go, Mom," Daniel's voice interrupts us.

I look up and see Gwen and Daniel walking into the living room, their bag slung over her shoulder, with Kelsey behind them.

Gwen stops, glances at me, then turns Daniel by his shoulders to face her. "I know you don't, sweetie, but we have to. This is Alexander's house and we've imposed on him long enough."

I want to tell her that they haven't been an imposition at all, that I loved having them here and want them to stay, but I keep the words locked tight in my mouth.

"Can we at least come back and visit him? I really like it here."

Her eyes slide to mine for a brief second before going back to him. Her voice lowers when answers. "We'll see."

Her words send a spark to my chest. The thought of them possibly coming back has my stomach tightening in both anticipation and dread.

"You ready to go?" Jeremy asks, getting up from his chair and pulling his keys from his pocket.

Again, Gwen glances my way before looking at Jeremy. "We are."

Gigi comes trotting into the kitchen and Daniel drops to his knees and hugs her around the neck. Gigi licks his face a few times, and when he pulls back, there are tears swimming in Daniel's eyes. It makes my heart hurt, watching the exchange.

"I'm going to miss you, girl," Daniel says gloomily. "Take care of your babies."

With a sniff and a wipe to his nose, he climbs to his feet. I wait to see if Kelsey will say goodbye next, but she just keeps her head forward, not even looking at Gigi. Gwen scratches her head a few times and murmurs her own goodbye.

I push off from my perch against the counter and grab a couple of things off the bar as I pass by it. My feet feel like lead as I lead everyone to the front door. Gripping the knob with my hand, it takes me a minute to twist it and pull the door open. My jaw hurts from clenching it so tightly.

I turn around once we're off the porch, and I'm pushed backwards a couple of feet when a small body barrels into me. Looking down, I see Daniel has his face buried against my stomach. My hands settle on his shoulders.

"I'm going to miss you," he mumbles against my shirt.

I clear my throat, then say, "I'm going to miss you too."

He pulls back and looks up with sad eyes. It takes everything in me to not drop to my knees and hug him and not let go.

"We can come back, can't we?"

I glance over to Gwen to find her watching us. Unsure what to say, I repeat her words to him. "We'll see." When his face drops with disappointment, I hold out my hand to him. "I want you to have this."

He reaches out and takes the wooden horse. "Wow," he breathes. "This is so neat."

"My grandfather made it for me when I was your age."

He looks up. "Really?"

"Yeah."

"Thank you!" He wraps his arms around my waist again. "I promise I'll take good care of it."

Gwen walks up and sees the small horse. "What do you have there?"

Daniel pulls back and thrusts his hand out, looking at the horse likes it's worth a million dollars. "Alexander gave it to me. He said his granddad made it for him when he was my age."

Gwen's surprised eyes dart to mine. "Are you sure?"

I look down at Daniel and see the awe on his face as he looks at the horse. "I'm sure."

"Thank you," she says quietly.

My eyes go to Kelsey, who's standing behind Gwen. I take a step toward her and hold out a notebook. Her eyes slide to mine before going to the notebook. Hesitantly, she reaches out and grabs it. Her eyes stay glued to it as she opens it to the first page, then the second, then the third. Gwen, who's now standing beside her, gasps.

"You did this?" she asks, lifting her eyes.

I nod. "Yeah. I know her other crossword book is full, so...." I trail off.

"This must have taken you hours."

Shrugging like it's no big deal, which it really wasn't, I say, "I spent a few hours each night on it. It didn't take me too long."

Kelsey's still turning the pages of the homemade crossword puzzle book, one after the other. After several moments, her head lifts and her eyes meet mine. The look I'm so used to seeing in her eyes, the one that says she's lost and can't find her way back, isn't so prominent. Her eyes turn glassy and her bottom lip trembles. Terrified that I did something wrong, I'm just about to apologize when she launches herself into my arms. My own encircle her.

I look at Gwen over her shoulder to find her biting her lip and fighting her own tears. Kelsey hugs me for several seconds, then pulls back. Her eyes don't meet mine as she turns around and rushes away.

I understand her need to be away, to put distance between herself and what could possibly hurt her again. Not that I would ever hurt her intentionally, but the emotional aspect of letting someone in after tragically losing her father is scary as hell.

Gwen turns to Jeremy. "Can you give us a minute?"

"Sure," he answers and walks away. Gwen watches as he helps the kids into his Blazer, then turns back to me.

"I know I've already said it, but I wanted to thank you again for helping us. Not just for coming to our rescue on the side of the road and letting us stay here, but for what you did at the market the other day as well."

She's standing so close I can see black specks in her blue eyes and smell her sweet vanilla scent. A slight breeze blows a few strands of her hair across her face, and once again I have to force my hands to stay at my sides and not push away the wayward hair just to give myself the excuse to touch her.

I look to the side where the partially built house is, seeing it but not really looking at it, before bringing my eyes back at her.

"It was nothing, really."

She squints. "It was a lot to me. To us. There's no telling what would have happened had you not seen my truck and come to investigate. You didn't have to bring us back here, but you did. And you didn't have to be so nice to my kids."

I don't know what to say. I don't do well with gratitude because I'm never around people that need to offer it.

Before I get a chance to come up with a response, Gwen shocks me by stepping closer, grabbing my shoulders, and leaning up to kiss my cheek. I close my eyes when her soft lips meet the gnarled skin of my cheek. Instead of pulling away, she steps even closer.

"You're a good man, Alexander. Take care of yourself," she whispers in my ear.

Pulling back, she looks at me a moment longer, gives a small smile, then turns and walks away. I watch her and the farther away she gets from me, the harder my heart pounds.

"Gwendolyn!" I call when she's almost to the Blazer. That's the first time I've used her full name.

She turns around, and the look on her face almost has me falling to my knees and begging her to stay.

"I programmed my number in your phone last night. If you or the kids ever need anything, call me."

After a moment, she nods, and walks the rest of the distance to where her kids and Jeremy are waiting. I swear I feel a piercing pain in my heart as I watch them ride away.

I stand there for a good ten minutes after they've left, feeling like I've just lost something precious and important.

Chapter Nine

Gwendolyn

"WHAT DAY ARE YOU GETTING IN?"
I switch the phone from one ear to the other, grab the cleaner from underneath the sink, and spray the table down. I then attack it with my rag. Daniel was helping me make biscuits earlier and started playing with the leftover dough.

"The twenty-third," Emma answers. "I hate that I can only come for two days, but work's been hectic lately. I was lucky to get off what I did."

Emma's a triage nurse working in the emergency department. A few weeks ago, she complained of several nurses quitting all within a span of a month, leaving the department short-staffed.

I use my nail to scrape away some dough that's dried on the table. "We'll have to make the most of it while you're here. The kids are excited to see you."

"I've missed them. I can't wait to see them again." She pauses for a moment, then asks quietly, "How's Kelsey?"

I drop the rag on the table and plop down in a chair. This is the first time I've been able to really talk to Emma since we got back from Alexander's, and I've been dying to. Her work has been keeping her very busy.

"She was actually showing signs of improvement for a few days, but the last week she's dropped back into her depressive state. I actually saw her smile again, Emma." I whisper the last part like it's some big secret, but it's because I'm worried if I speak louder my voice will crack.

We left Alexander's place a week ago, and since that day, I haven't seen any life whatsoever from Kelsey. I know she misses him, and if I'm truthful with myself, I do as well. I miss him so damn much it makes my stomach ache. Daniel's asked about him several times over the last several days, so I know he misses him too.

"Oh, Gwen, that's wonderful!" she says happily, then remembers the sad part of my statement. "What was going on when she smiled? You said a few days.... Something's happened. What is it?"

This is the part I wanted to ask her about. I hesitate, wondering how I should go about it. She may not even have the answers I seek.

"Do you remember a guy named Alexander from when you used to visit your gram's during the summers?"

There's silence, then, "Does he have a last name?"

I shake my head, then feel foolish because she can't see me. "I don't know it. He said his grandfather raised horses and he'd go over sometimes to help him. He actually inherited the farm. It's out on Hallow's Road, only a few miles down from your gram's house."

I hear her hmming across the line as she thinks it over.

"Yes!" she shouts, then lowers her voice. "Alexander David Christenson. The reason I remember his full name is because I always liked it. I had a crush on him one summer when some boy knocked my ice-cream cone out of my hand. Alexander saw it and bought me a new one. I think I was ten at the time. Why? What does he have to do with anything?"

Guilt eats at me as I think about my next question. I know I should ask him myself, but I just can't bring myself to. Whatever the answer is, I know it's extremely devastating for him, and I don't want to see the pain I know his eyes will hold if I do ask.

"Do you know exactly what happened to his wife and child?"

Emma's quiet for several seconds before she answers, her voice sad. "I don't know much. Only that he was driving when someone pulled out in front of him. He swerved to avoid hitting him and they rolled into Hallow's Creek. I don't know how accurate it is, but from what I was told, his wife and little girl drowned."

My hand flies to my mouth and a soft sob escapes before I can stop it. "Oh my God," I whisper brokenly. "How awful."

"Yeah. It was pretty tragic."

It feels like there's a ton of bricks on my chest. Poor Alexander. It's already bad enough to lose someone, but to lose them in such a harsh way.... I can't even imagine the pain he went through. Is obviously still going through. No wonder he always looks morose. No matter how much times passes, be it four years or twenty, you never get over something like that.

"Gwen? What's going on?" Emma asks, pulling me from my thoughts. "What happened was horribly sad, but you seem more upset than a person should be that wasn't there and didn't know them."

I get up, grab my coffee from the counter, and bring it back with me to the table. Pulling one of my socked feet up to the seat, I hug my knee.

"The kids and I... uh... were sort of forced to stay with him for a few days last week."

"What do you mean, forced to stay with him?" she asks suspiciously.

"I was out visiting your gram. When we left, the snow was coming down really hard. An animal ran out in front of me, and I slid off the road when I pressed the brakes to miss it." Before she has a chance to ask, I reassure her. "We were all okay, but I couldn't get the truck out. Luckily, Alexander came by and found us. However, there was a tree in the road so he couldn't take us back to town. We had no choice but to go home with him."

"Damn it, Gwen. Why am I just now hearing about this?" she scolds.

"Because this is the first time we've really been able to talk." I tuck my bangs behind my ear. "Anyway, Alexander took us in for three days. Emma—" I stop and have to clear my throat. "Kelsey smiled. She actually smiled, and showed more of her old self than she has since Will died."

I hear a sniffle from Emma, and I know she's just as amazed as I am. She was there from the beginning of my and Will's relationship, she was there the days the kids were born, she was there through each milestone, and she was there when we all fell apart after he died. She helped pull us together. When Kelsey went quiet and withdrew, Emma was affected as well, because she loves my kids as if they were her own.

"Wow," she says. "Has she talked?"

I prop my elbow on the table and rest my head in my hand. "No. Nothing like that, but I've seen more animation on her face than I have in years. I'll take anything I can get."

"And you think Alexander had something to do with it?"

"I do," I answer. "I don't know what it is about him, maybe it's because she senses his own pain and can relate to him."

"And Daniel?"

"Daniel absolutely loves him. Alexander was so good with both of them. He portrays this hard and quiet man that obviously doesn't let people get too close, but with the kids, I guess he couldn't help but open up."

"And what about you?" she inquires quietly.

"What about me?" I play dumb. I get up from my perch on my chair and carry my coffee cup to the sink. It's cold, so I pour it down the drain.

"Has he opened up to you?"

I spin around, lean back against the counter, and look down at my socked feet. Wiggling my toes, I answer her as honestly as I can. "I don't know. He wasn't as cold when we left. But that could just be because we weren't complete strangers anymore."

"And how do you feel about him?"

It takes me a minute to answer. How do I feel about Alexander? That's both easy and hard to answer. It's also scary to think about. I've tried pushing him from my mind the last week, but no matter how hard I try, he's there. It's like he's wormed his way inside and has grown roots.

"I don't know. I like him. He's quiet and reserved, but he's also compassionate. I liked watching him with Daniel and Kelsey. It was like, although he wasn't sure what to do with them, instinctually he knew. He was so patient with them. He'd take Daniel out to the barn to help him with the horses. And when he looked at Kelsey, I swear, Emma, it was like he was trying to absorb her pain."

"Is he still as hot as he used to be?" she teases, then laughs.

"I don't know how he used to look, but the man looks damn good now."

She clears her throat before asking quietly, "He has scars, doesn't he? From the accident."

I feel bad talking about him like this, but it's Emma. There's no censure or disgust in her voice. Emma's not like that. She never judges people by their outward appearance. It's what's on the inside that counts.

"Yeah." I blow out a breath. "The right side of his face has burn scars. He has them on his right arm as well. I can't be sure, but I think there may be more. The scars wouldn't matter anyway, no matter how bad they are."

"I know. Are you going to see him again?"

Before I get a chance to answer, I hear a car door slam outside.

"I need to go. Jeremy and his mom had the kids over for lunch and they just got back."

"Okay. But I want updates on the Alexander situation," she informs me.

"There might not even be an Alexander situation to report back to you."

I walk over to the door and pull it open. Daniel, Kelsey, and Jeremy are walking up the driveway.

"True. But there might be as well."

After promising to call her in a couple days, I hang up. I smile as the kids and Jeremy walk up on the porch.

"Did you guys have fun?"

I ruffle Daniel's hair as he stops in front of me and hands over a Tupperware container. "We did and we brought you lunch back."

Bending down, I kiss the top of his head. "Thank you." I look at Kelsey next. "Did you enjoy your lunch?" I ask gently.

She gives a single nod and that's it.

After thanking Jeremy for lunch, Daniel rushes off inside, I'm sure to pull out the video game. The boy would play 24-7 if I allowed him to. Kelsey follows him at a slower pace. I turn back to Jeremy after watching the kids go inside.

I hold up the container. "You didn't have to bring me lunch, but thank you regardless."

"You know it's no problem. Since you couldn't come yourself, Mom insisted we bring lunch to you."

They invited me as well, but I had too much to do around the house. That, and I wanted to take the opportunity to have a few minutes alone. Since being snowed in with Alexander, my mind has wandered to him more times than I can count. It's very distracting.

I smile. "Well, thank you. And thank your mom as well."

"You got it." He taps the railing before turning and walking down the steps. At the bottom, he turns back. "You need anything, even if it's just for me and mom to take the kids for a bit, call us."

"Thanks, Jeremy. I really appreciate everything you and Peggy have done for me and the kids."

"It's we that thanks you, especially Mom." He looks over to his truck, then back to me, his expression mournful. "I was never able to give her any more grandchildren. Having Daniel and Kelsey around helps, since Benny's all grown up."

Pain for Jeremy and the loss he endured has me starting for the stairs to offer him comfort, but before I take three steps, he shakes his head and stops me with his words. "Don't. It's okay. It was many years ago."

I nod and hold my place.

"I better get going. I still need to stop by the pharmacy and grab Mom's meds." With a wave, he turns and gets in his Blazer.

I stand and watch as he drives away, beyond blessed to have two such wonderful people in our lives. Actually, we have quite a few people I consider very close friends. When we first moved to Cat's Valley, I was so worried it was a mistake to uproot the kids from where they began their life and where the memories of Will were, but it didn't take long to realize it was the best decision I could have ever made for us. We've gained a family since moving here.

I go back in the house and find Daniel exactly where I thought I would, stuck in front of the television with a game controller in hand.

"Hey, kid," I call.

He swings his head around to me for a split second before going back to the TV. "Yeah, Mom?"

"An hour, then I want you off to do your chores."

"Okay."

Leaving him in the living room, I walk down the hallway to Kelsey's room. I tap lightly on the partially closed door before pushing it open. I find her on her bed, with the notebook Alexander gave her on her lap.

She looks up when I sit beside her on the bed. I lean back against the headboard, mirroring her position. Although she has a ton of store-bought crossword puzzle books, she's chosen to do this partic- ular one since we've been back. The whole notebook isn't filled, but the majority is.

"Are they difficult?" I ask.

After a moment, she gives me a single head shake.

I look down at the one she's working on and see she's about halfway through it. I'm curious to know what she'll do when she finishes them all. She goes through them so fast, it's only a matter of time before she'll be done. I still can't believe Alexander took the time to do this for her, knowing her obsession with them and not wanting her to go without. It was one of the sweetest gestures anyone has made for us.

"Do you miss him?" I ask, and look back at her. There's no need to elaborate who I'm referring to. She already knows.

For a brief second, pain flashes in her eyes. She looks away from me and pins her gaze across the room. I'd bet anything she's not looking at anything in particular. She just doesn't want me to know how she feels.

"It's okay," I whisper, and drape my arm over her shoulders. "I miss him too."

Surprising me, she leans her head against my chest. Tears prick my eyes, but I force them away.

We stay this way for several minutes before she pulls back from me. Her eyes are guarded once again, and I know I'll get no more out of her.

I kiss the top of her head, then murmur, "An hour and then it's chore time, okay?"

When I look in her eyes, they tell me she heard and understood. I slide from the bed and walk to the door. I look back and see Kelsey's nose stuck back in the notebook. I quietly pull the door halfway closed before walking away.

THAT EVENING, I LOOK down at the phone in my hand. Alexander's name is pulled up. I want to push the button to call him so badly, to hear his voice, but I'm chicken. What if he doesn't want to talk to me? What if he's already forgotten about us? What if he was relieved when we left?

I toss my head back against the back of the couch and roll my eyes up to the ceiling. The kids are in bed and the house is quiet. For some reason, I feel antsy and restless, and the need to hear Alexander's voice is getting stronger by the day. I feel like a schoolgirl missing her crush. I don't know what it is exactly I feel for him, but whatever it is has grown quickly. Way too quickly to be considered rational. Feelings this strong for someone I really don't know aren't normal.

I run my fingers over the blank screen of my phone, and bite my lip. What if I just text him? It won't be the same as talking to him, but maybe it'll appease this need I feel. At least this way I can at least gauge his feelings toward me contacting him. He did put his number in my phone, after all. Of course, he told me to call him if the kids or I needed him, not just for random stuff or because I simply wanted to hear his voice. But then again, I *do* need him. Just not in the capacity he was referring to. I don't even know in what capacity I need him. I just know it's a need that keeps growing.

Blowing out a breath, I bring my phone to life. His name pops up on my screen.

Just do it, Gwen, my inner self demands.

With nervous fingers, I bring up a new text thread, hoping I'm not making a mistake.

Me: Hey. It's Gwen.

I drop the phone in my lap, refusing to watch the screen to see if he saw it. My knees bounce, and I tap my fingers against the arm of the couch. Spotting my water on the coffee table, I reach for it. Just as I'm pulling the bottle away from my mouth, my phone vibrates. I jump and a stream of water wets my shirt.

"Crap," I mutter, then cap the bottle and put it on the cushion beside me.

Ignoring the wet spot on my shirt, I grab for my phone.

Alexander: Gwen, is everything okay?

111

Of course, he automatically thinks something is wrong. After all, why else would I be messaging him? A small part of me, a part that I ignore, hurts that he apparently wasn't glad to hear from me.

Feeling like an idiot for taking advantage of his offer to contact him if I needed anything, I shoot off a quick reply.

Me: No, nothing's wrong. I just wanted to say hi.

I hit Send, then regret it when I realize the message makes me sound like a weirdo. Seriously, who messages someone just to say hi? Even though he's not here to witness it, I still feel my face burn.

My phone vibrates again, and I glance down.

Alexander: How are you doing?

Okay, so maybe he's not as appalled to hear from me as I thought. If he was, he wouldn't encourage conversation, right? Or is it simply out of courtesy? I hate being so unsure.

Me: I'm doing good.

Alexander: And the kids?

I smile, touched that he asked after them.

Me: They are both good too.

I set my phone down, then pick it back up.

Me: How have you been?

A minute later, my phone vibrates.

Alexander: Been busy with catching up on things around the house.

I look at the screen, wondering what I should say next. I don't want our silent communication to be over yet. Oddly, it's soothing knowing he's on the other side of the signal thinking about me. It makes me feel not quite so alone in my feelings for him. Which is stupid; just because he's messaging me doesn't mean he's thinking about me like I'm thinking about him.

Me: Kelsey loves the book you made her. It's the only one she works on now. And Daniel carries the wooden horse everywhere with him.

No matter what Daniel is doing, you can see a lump in his pocket from the horse. At night, when he's sleeping, he puts it on his nightstand, only to put it in his pocket the next day.

Alexander: I'm glad they're happy with them. I'll have to make

Kelsey another crossword book for when she finishes this one, and let Daniel see my grandfather's wood carving collection.

My heart warms. His words imply we'll see him again. I try not to let his message get to me, but I can't help the butterflies swarming around in my stomach. I wish we were seeing him tomorrow.

Me: They'd both love that.

It turns quiet after that, and I can't think of anything else to say without sounding like a complete fool.

Knowing my time is up for the night, I send one more quick message.

Me: I'll let you go. Have a good night, Alexander. Take care.

A minute later, he messages back.

Alexander: You too, Gwen. Sleep well.

I can't help the smile that forms on my face. It's definitely not the same as talking to him on the phone, but I'll take any form of communication I can get.

That night I do sleep well. I sleep with images of a broken man with beautiful scars.

Chapter Ten

Alexander

I SIT IN THE CANVAS chair with my arms crossed over my chest and my legs stretched out in front of me. I'm positioned in the middle of my front yard. It's freezing out, but I don't feel the blistering cold. My attention is completely consumed by the half-built house in front of me.

I've been out here hours, just staring at it, contemplating how and when I want to tear the structure down. Half of the reason I've kept it was because it was a link to Clara and Rayne. A link I wasn't ready to destroy yet. While I don't think I'll ever be ready to let them go, I know I need to stop standing in place and try to start moving forward.

The building's walls are discolored, swelling, and becoming dilapidated from lack of protection from the weather. It's become an eyesore. I always knew I would eventually tear it down, it was just finding the motivation and courage to do it.

I look down at the picture in my lap. The edges are slightly wrinkled and there are several creases. One of the nurses took it right after Rayne was born. I'm sitting on the side of the bed with my arm on the pillow behind Clara's head. Baby Rayne is snuggled up in a blanket, lying in Clara's arms. We're both looking down at her, and our smiles are so big it's a wonder our faces didn't split in two. The nurse that snapped the picture was a good friend of ours, so she took it upon herself to use my phone to capture the scene without us knowing. It's one of my favorites of the three of us together.

Immediately after that photo, the nurses rushed Rayne away to the neonatal intensive care unit. She was eight weeks early, weighing only three pounds two ounces, and needed more time to develop her lungs and continue to grow. Clara was in the hospital for five days after that. Technically, she could have left earlier, but with Rayne still there, she stayed as long as they would allow her. Once she was released, both Clara and I stayed in a nearby hotel, since the drive from home to the hospital was a good forty-five minutes. We wanted to be as close to Rayne as possible. For the first two weeks, we visited every day and stayed for as long as the nursing staff would allow us. Logan, a friend of ours, came out to the cabin every day and fed and watered the horses for us, but eventually I had to start making trips out myself. Every single day though, I was at the hospital with my wife, talking to our daughter, watching her slowly get stronger. Those days were scary, but were also the best of my life. I wore a permanent smile for seven weeks.

The crunch of tires pulls me from my memories. I turn my head and watch as a black Dodge truck comes down my driveway. I stand and put the picture in my jacket pocket. It'll go in my bedside drawer when I go back inside, along with the other two I have in there. The first year after they died, the picture was in a frame that sat on my nightstand. It was a constant reminder of what I had and then lost. A reminder of how I failed the two most important people in my life.

The truck stops and a man I haven't seen in weeks steps out. I turn back and face the half-built house, knowing he'll approach without my prompt.

James and I have been friends since grade school. After Clara and Rayne died, I pulled away from everyone, including him. He gave me my space to grieve for a while, but then started forcing his way back in, no matter how much I tried pushing him away. Besides my family and clients, he's one of only two people that ever come out here. Travis, another friend, who moved to Cat's Valley his senior year of high school, is the other.

He stops beside me and we both look at once was supposed to be Clara's dream home.

"How was your trip?" I ask after several minutes of silence.

He blows out a breath, then grumbles, "Stressful as hell. I'm damn glad to be back and away from my crazy-ass sister. God love her, but fuck, I can only take so much."

I grunt. "How was your mother?"

"Cool as a fucking cucumber. If not for her I probably would have bashed Lena's head with one of the vases used for the center-pieces. She had a bitch fit over the fuckers because they didn't match the flowers she picked for them. She picked the damn things out herself and knew from the get-go what flowers she was using."

James has been out of town for the last week for his sister, Lena's, wedding. His sister lives only two hours away, but she wanted the whole family down for the entire week. The thing with Lena is, she's a spoiled brat. She's the baby of James' five siblings and believes the entire world revolves around her. She's the only one of the bunch to turn out like that. James and I used to joke that she was switched at birth, that his sweet baby sister was out there somewhere probably with stick-up-their-ass parents.

"God help the poor bastard that's married her," I comment, only half joking.

Being the oldest of his siblings, there's a seven-year gap between James and Lena. That still didn't stop her from following us and their other siblings around and trying to boss us all into doing what she wanted. We all put up with her because Cassandra, James' mom, would have had our hides if we didn't.

"Believe it or not, she doesn't treat him that way. To her, he's her holy grail and she seems to worship the ground he walks on. They both do. He still sees her bitchy side because everyone else around her gets the you're-beneath-me treatment. I don't know." He shrugs. "It's interesting to watch a softer side of Lena."

A soft Lena. I wouldn't have thought it was possible.

"You still planning to tear it down?" he asks after several quiet moments.

I look over and find him watching me curiously, arms crossed over his massive chest. I turn back.

"Yeah. Wood's rotten, so it's only a matter of time before it starts falling apart anyway."

"Let me know if you want help when you do," he offers.

"Thanks, but I think this is something I need to do on my own."

He slaps my back. "Gotcha."

"You want a beer?" I ask, ready to get out of the cold and away from the unstable structure before me. Every time I look at it, memories I've tried to forget resurface. That's why I normally avoid looking at it like the plague. I don't need any reminders. I'm reminded of it every time I look in the mirror or close my eyes. But with Christmas coming up and the anniversary of their deaths, I was drawn to it. I failed them by not saving them, and this is my punishment.

"Sure," James says, knocking me out of my thoughts.

I turn and lead us to the house. Gigi meets us at the door, tail wagging when she sees James is with me. She's been in a slump the last several days, and I know it has to do with a certain little boy not being here. I clench my jaw and push away the unwanted emotions over not having Gwen and her kids here anymore. The house has felt too damn empty, and I wonder if it'll ever feel normal again. Empty isn't anything new to me, but now that I remember what it feels like to be filled with more than empty blackness, I don't think I want to go back to it.

I pull two beers from the fridge and hand one to James. I don't drink often, but I always keep a few in the fridge just in case I feel the need for one. I pop the top, flick the cap in the trash, and take a couple pulls.

James does the same, then sets his bottle down on the bar. Tapping his thigh, he calls, "Up, Gigi." She jumps and places her front paws on his lower stomach. "How're the babies doing, girl?" She gives her answer by licking his hand.

"How's Bandit?" he asks once Gigi drops back to four legs.

"Still a stubborn bastard," I rumble.

He chuckles. "So, he's still kicking your ass, you mean?"

I grit my teeth, beyond frustrated with the animal. "He damn near bit my hand off yesterday when I tried to feed him an apple. Then almost busted through the wood on the side wall of his stall. I had to move Bella to another stall because she was becoming agitated."

He takes another pull from his beer, and wipes his mouth with the back of his hand. "I don't know, man. It might be a lost cause with that one."

I grunt at the suggestion. "No horse is untrainable. He just needs to learn that I'm the bigger male. Mutual respect for each other is paramount when training horses. He hasn't learned to respect me yet, but he will."

I turn and open the fridge, grabbing out lunch meat, lettuce, tomato, and mayo. Dropping it on the counter, I ask, "You want?"

"I'm good." He finishes off his beer and tosses the bottle in the trash. "I just wanted to stop by and catch up. I gotta get back to town before poor Miss Mable has a fit because I haven't come by to see her."

Miss Mable is his seventy-year-old neighbor and has appointed herself his honorary second mother. His father left when he was eight years old, so his mom had to take on the role of mother and father. She worked two full-time jobs to support her five kids, meaning she wasn't around much. When we were kids, Miss Mable would have us both over for homemade cookies several times a week. Being kids, we loved cookies, so we never complained. Over the years, she still insisted James come over at least twice a week to sit with her and enjoy her delicious snack. He complains now, but I know he secretly loves the old woman. She was there for him when his mom couldn't be, and has earned a permanent place in his life.

I chuckle. "Next time you come out, bring me some of her snick-erdoodles."

"Will do." He laughs.

Any other friend would have insisted I go get them myself, trying to force me back into society. One of the many reason James and I have stayed in contact since Clara and Rayne died is because he doesn't tiptoe around me and doesn't try to force me to get over losing them. He respects that I'm a grown-ass man and can make my own damn decisions.

He also doesn't look at me any different than before the accident. My scars mean absolutely nothing to him.

"Since when do you wear earrings?" James asks, tipping his chin toward the bar.

I don't need to look to see the small hoop earrings lying on the counter. I found them on my bedside table the day Gwen left and they've been sitting on the bar ever since.

I give him a look that has his eyebrows raising.

"Who is she?" he asks, taking my look for something it's not.

"No one," I mutter, slapping some ham down on top of a slice of mayonnaise-covered bread.

"Bullshit. The only women you've had in this house have been your mother and sister, and I know they haven't been for a visit in a while now."

"Leave it." I peel off a layer of lettuce and slap that down on top of the ham. "She's no one important." The lie tastes bitter on my tongue. Gwen is definitely more than no one. I just haven't figured out what she is, and I'm scared as shit about it.

"It's okay to move on, Alexander," James says, his deep voice turning softer. "Clara would want you to."

I look up and shoot him a glare. Slamming the jar of mayonnaise down on the counter, I growl, "What if *I* don't want to move on? I don't fucking *deserve* to move on."

His expression turns hard. "That's bullshit and a cop-out if I ever heard one. Stop fucking blaming yourself for something you had no control over."

My chest heaves as both anger and grief grip me. I know in my head what he's saying is true, but my fucking heart just won't get on board. It insists that there was some way I could have saved them.

Placing my hands on the counter, I hang my head, trying to rein in the lashing I want to give James.

"Look, I get it." When I lift my head to tell him he gets nothing, he continues, as if knowing what I'm about to say. "I may not know from experience what you're going through, but I still get it. I know it has to be hard, but fuck, Alexander, you can't live with that regret for the rest of your life and never move on. I've left you be, and I'll continue to do so because I've got no right to try to push you into something you aren't ready for yet, but don't give up. Don't close down the option of building something with someone else. You'll die miserable and with a lot more regret than you carry now."

I drop my head again, wanting so damn badly to take his words and run with them. To leave the past in the past and look forward to a future. An image of Gwen pops in my head, and it causes a rush of adrenaline through my veins. If offered the chance, I'd give almost anything to have that future with her.

Gwen's gorgeous face is replaced with Clara's equally gorgeous one. Short blond hair replaces brown, and green eyes replace blue. I squeeze my eyes shut tighter when my beautiful baby girl's face appears. I miss them so fucking much. I want to reach inside my mind, snatch them out, and place them in front of me so I can touch them. Knowing that's impossible, I also want to shove them away. I want to forget them because remembering them hurts so damn much. But then the thought of doing that sends splinters of pain to my chest and stomach. It makes me physically ill.

A hand grips my shoulder tightly, and I look up to see James standing beside me, a look of empathy on his face.

"No pressure, but you really need to think about the possibility of moving on. You can't hold on to them forever."

He lets go, walks out of the kitchen, and a minute later, I hear the click of the front door closing. Gigi nudges my thigh with her nose, sensing my pain, and I absently reach down and rub her head.

Unable to stomach food at the moment, I put the sandwich in a container and place it in the fridge for later. My eyes land on the earrings on the counter, and I finger one of them.

Last night, when I saw her message, my body tensed, ready to bolt into action and race to town. When she said she just wanted to say hi, I relaxed back in bed, but adrenaline still ran through my veins. It's been a week since I saw her, and it surprised me how much I missed her. And Daniel and Kelsey. There's been several times I've caught myself grabbing for my keys to drive to town and hunt her down. I don't know where she lives, but it wouldn't take much to find out.

When she mentioned Kelsey using the crossword puzzle I made for her and Daniel carrying the horse around with him, it warmed my heart. My eyes land on the small box in the living room that carries part of my grandfather's wood carving collection. Two days after they left, I was in the barn tending to the horses when I came across the box. My mind automatically went to Daniel. Wiping off the dust, I carried the box inside. I didn't know then why I brought them into the house. There were no plans for me to see Daniel again, but something compelled me. Maybe a small glimmer of hope that I would see him again.

Picking up the earrings, I put them in my pocket and leave the kitchen. I take a seat on the couch and grab the notebook from the end table. I flip it open to about a quarter of the way through. Last night I told Gwen I'd have to make Kelsey another crossword puzzle for when she was done with her current one. What I didn't say was I had already started on one. The last one was a rush job, so I'm sure to a seasoned crossword puzzler—like Kelsey seems to be—they're easy. I'm making this one a bit more tough.

I spend the next couple hours working on the crossword puzzles, then dig through the box of wooden figurines. There are several different horses, they were my grandfather's favorite to carve, but there's also other animals. I pick up a fox, specifically remembering when he carved it. He had just gotten done with the tail when the knife slipped and cut into his finger. He didn't use the special whittling knives, but just a regular pocket knife. He said it was just a hobby to him, so he wasn't going to spend a lot of money on whittling knives.

The knife cut through and the only thing that stopped it from chopping off his finger was the bone. I was eight at the time, so when I saw the blood, I turned white and had to sit on the floor before I passed out. I watched as he grabbed several napkins, wrapped them around his finger, and taped them on with masking tape. He then proceeded to finish the fox. Later that day when my grandmother saw his bandage job, she started yelling at him for waiting too long to have it tended to. He drank a bottle of whiskey while she sewed him up. That was grandpa, stubborn and tough as they came.

I chuckle when I run my finger over the rusty bloodstain that never came out of the wood. I put it back down and pick up a carved dinosaur. Or what's supposed to be a carved dinosaur. This was my one and only attempt at wood carving and it turn out to be a disaster. I ended up cutting myself as well, but unlike my grandpa, my mom insisted I go get stitches. I was ten and it hurt like a bitch, so I told my grandpa that I'd leave the wood carving up to him.

After looking through the box a few more minutes, I close it up. If given the opportunity, I'll let Daniel pick out the ones he likes.

I call Gigi and we both go outside to close up the barn and make sure the horses are in their respective stalls for the night. The sun's already setting as we walk across the yard. As much as I enjoy winter, I hate the short days.

Once the horses are situated, Gigi and I go back inside, completely ignoring Clara's house. I've had enough of the memories for today. Gigi trots to the utility room, while I head for the bathroom for a shower. I had to put the pups back in the utility room because the little rascals were starting to tear shit apart. I normally let them out in the evenings to roam when I'm around to keep an eye on them. A couple of days ago, I started letting them out in the yard.

Stripping down, I make sure to keep my eyes away from the mirror. Although the scars cover half of my body, I've found that if I don't actually look at myself in the mirror, I can keep the haunting memories at bay easier.

My shower is quick, and I'm out and dressed in sweatpants and a T-shirt ten minutes later. Without looking at the photo, I place it back in the drawer next to the other two before going out to the living room. My phone flashes, indicating I have a notification. My heart rate picks up when I think it might be from Gwen.

I grab it off the counter, disappointment hitting when I realize it's from James. I also have an e-mail from Brice, June's owner. I sent him an e-mail earlier today letting him know that June's ready to be picked up. I pull up Brice's e-mail first, confirming the pickup for tomorrow at three. Next, I open James' message.

James: I meant to tell you earlier. Mom invited you over for Christmas. I told her I'd bring it up to you.

I type out a quick reply.

Me: Tell your mom I said thanks and Happy Holidays, but I'll be busy.

He already knew the answer and so does his mom, but he tries every year. I'm grateful to Martha for caring, but Christmas isn't a good time for me, and I'd be shitty company. I always spend Christmas alone, mentally preparing for the next day, the anniversary of their deaths. Every year, I spend the day that they died with my good friend Jameson. It's the only time of year when I get shit-faced. It's also the two days a year that no one should be around me.

The ding of my phone interrupts my thoughts. Thinking it's

James replying, I swipe my finger across the screen without looking, then pull in a deep breath when I see Gwen's name instead. I settle down in a chair before pulling open her message.

Gwen: Hey. Sorry to bother you again, but I wanted to ask when Gigi's puppies will be ready to adopt? If you're adopting them out, that is.

My lips tip up into a smile.

Me: They should be ready next week.

Her reply comes almost immediately.

Gwen: Before Christmas maybe?!

I chuckle at her excitement.

Me: Yes.

Gwen: Yah! You've just made my night. Or rather, unknowingly made the kids' night. I'd like to get one for them for Christmas.

She unknowingly made my night as well, because that means I'll get to see her again. I try to not let that thought get to me, but it does anyway.

Me: What day would you like to come over to pick one out?

I lay my phone down on the counter as I wait for her reply. The earrings once again catch my attention. I pick one up and place it in my palm. The diamond at the center of the hoop twinkles in the light from the kitchen.

My phone pings again.

Gwen: Does Christmas Eve work for you? In the evening? I'll have my friend Emma come watch the kids, that way I can surprise them with the pup on Christmas morning.

Anxiety has my stomach churning. Do I really want to chance being around her so close to the worst day of the year for me? But then I think, maybe it'll do me good to see something so beautiful before the ugly makes itself known.

Me: That works.

Gwen: Great! I'll see you then. Thank you, Alexander. Have a good night.

Me: You as well, Gwen.

I get up from my stool, grab Kelsey's notebook, and bring it back to the counter. Since Gwen will be coming by next week, I'd like to get it done before then so she can take it back with her.

Anticipation of seeing Gwen again has my blood pumping faster. We may not ever really be anything to each other, but even so, the thought leaves my chest feeling lighter.

Six days. Only six days before she'll be here. I silently pray those days go by quickly, even knowing I have no right to ask for such a thing.

Chapter Eleven

Gwendolyn

I GRIP THE STEERING wheel tightly with sweaty palms as nerves leave me shaking. I feel silly that I'm so nervous, but no matter how much I try to calm myself down, it doesn't work. I'm like a schoolgirl on her first date, waiting on that moment he leans in for the first kiss. And this isn't even a date. I'm going to pick out a puppy for my kids, for goodness sake.

Get a hold of yourself, Gwen! I chastise myself.

Pulling in a deep breath, I try to calm my racing heart as I turn down Alexander's driveway. It's been almost two weeks since I've seen him, but we've texted every night since that first message. I don't know if he's just doing it to be polite, but it's been nice. The only thing that makes me feel better is he's initiated some of our conversations. It's crazy to think about how much I've missed him, considering I've only known the guy for a little over two weeks.

As much as I missed him though, I'm just as scared to see him again. What if he's turned back into the brusque guy he was that first day? What if he just thrusts a puppy in my arms and tells me to leave? I'm not under the illusion he feels anything for me, but it would be nice if we could at least be friends. He seems like he needs friends. Remembering the old ladies at the market and what they were whispering amongst themselves, I understand why he stays away.

I pull to a stop in front of his cabin and turn off my car. I force my hands to hold steady as I reach for the door handle. Stepping out, I look around. It looks different with the snow gone. Just as pretty, but different. I notice a chair sitting in front of the half-built house and briefly wonder what he's been doing sitting out here. A soft neigh catches my attention. A couple of horses are grazing in the field. I smile as one of the horses tosses its head, its long mane blowing in the wind.

I turn when I hear a creaking sound and find Alexander on the porch watching me. He must have been sitting in the chair. He's wearing a pair of old jeans and a gray-and-red plaid shirt, sleeves rolled up his forearms and a white shirt peeking out the top where a few buttons are unbuttoned. His face appears serious and tense, the scars marring the beautiful surface in tight lines.

Nervously, I lift my hand and wave. "Hi."

He's silent for a moment, and I shuffle my feet, suddenly feeling unwelcome. Then he says something that has my chest blossoming.

"It's good to see you again, Gwen."

I can't help the smile that steals across my face or the flutters that start in my belly. Unexpected pleasure takes root inside me.

I start walking toward him, and it pleases me more to see his lips are tipped up into a small smile. The man is so breathtaking I could look at him all day. The thought has a blush creeping up my cheeks.

By the time I make it up the steps, my anxiety is getting to me again. Why in the world is this so hard? It's ridiculous, and I once again give myself an inner pep talk.

"How have you been?" he asks, once I'm standing in front of him.

It takes me a minute to ensure my voice doesn't come out breathless. "I'm fine. And you?"

He tips his head up and grunts, "Good."

"I, uh... I really appreciate you letting me adopt one of Gigi's puppies. The kids will love having one around."

Something flickers in his eyes, but before I can figure out what it is, he says, "No problem. I only plan to keep one, so I'll be looking for a place for the others anyway. You just made it a bit easier for me."

An idea comes to me. "If you'd like, I can talk to Jeremy and see if he and his mom would like one."

He nods, and after a moment of silence, asks, "Would you like to come in?"

"Sure."

I follow him into the house and immediately feel like I'm home. A pang hits my chest. Everything looks the same as it was before, but it's silly to think it would be different. It's only been two weeks. I almost laugh at myself.

"Something to drink?" Alexander asks, standing by the bar. He appears to be as nervous as I am and it lessons some of my anxiety.

"Yes, please."

He turns, and I follow him into the kitchen, taking a seat on one of the stools. There's a pot of something boiling on the stove that smells delicious. He pulls two glasses out of the cabinet, sets them down, and retrieves a pitcher of tea out of the fridge. After pouring us both a glass, he slides one across to me.

"How's business?" I ask, then want to smack my forehead.

How's business? How freaking generic is that?

As if sensing my inner foolishness, one corner of his mouth tips up into a smirk. The look renders me speechless and I duck my head in embarrassment. I'm not cut out for this. I should have gone to a pet store and gotten a puppy from there.

"It's good. Got another horse today," he answers. "Looking forward to working with her."

I lift my head, forcing myself to get past my awkwardness. "It's a girl? What's her name?"

"Nina."

A fierce pain nearly has me falling from my chair. "I've always loved that name." I look down at the glass in my hands. "Will and I... if we had another girl, had planned to name her Nina after my mother." I bring my gaze back to him and smile sadly. "Kelsey's name came from his mom."

Alexander's brows dip down in a frown. "Maybe one day you still could."

A month ago I would have thought the idea impossible, but now, looking at Alexander and thinking about what he's made me feel recently, the idea doesn't scare me as much. An image pops in my head of Alexander holding a baby girl. It's unrealistic to place him in that image, but it formed before I could stop it. I have no clue what my feelings for him are or his for me, but something deep inside has placed him in my vision for a reason. I saw the way he was with Daniel and Kelsey. Alexander would make a wonderful father. I have no doubt in my mind.

Emma's words from the other day play in my head.

I don't know how accurate it is, but from what I was told, his wife and little girl drowned.

Looking at Alexander and knowing what I know, I understand why he seemed so hard that day at the grocery store and when he found me and the kids. Anyone that went through what he did would be left bitter.

The scars on his face and arm give him even more reason. People can be so insensitive to things they haven't experienced, and I'm sure he's heard the rumors and whispers.

I give him a soft smile. "Yeah. Maybe one day."

The look that crosses his face confuses me. It's a mixture of longing and pain. He turns away before I can decipher the meaning behind it, and sets his empty glass down in the sink. When he turns back, the look is gone, and I wonder if I imagined it.

"Puppies are this way," he says, his voice coming out deeper than normal. "You wanna go pick one out?"

I get up from my stool and carry my glass to the sink, depositing it beside his before turning back to him.

"Lead the way."

He takes me through a door in the kitchen, one I hadn't gone in during my time here. It seems to be a big utility room. There are several stacks of totes in one corner with a work bench beside them, a multitude of tools littering the surface. Typical male, leaving his tools out. There's a weight machine and treadmill off to one side. Front and center is a big black motorcycle.

I look over to Alexander and raise my brow. "I didn't take you for the type of guy that rides motorcycles."

His eyes turn mischievous. "I'm sure there's a lot of stuff about me that would surprise you."

I have no idea what to be surprised about more, the playfulness of his tone, the words themselves, the humor in his eyes, or the fact that it seems as if he's flirting. I know I like all four of those reasons, especially the last one.

I'm so far out of date with how flirting works that I have no clue how to respond. Luckily, Gigi comes up with little fur balls trailing behind her, and saves me from having to form a reply.

"Oh, my goodness!" I exclaim, and squat down. "They've gotten so big!"

I scoop one pup in my arms and he immediately starts lapping at my face. I laugh and rub my hand up and down his back.

"They've turned into menaces," Alexander states, squatting beside me. He grabs one pup by the scruff of his neck and settles him against his chest. Gigi, appearing jealous of her own pups, puts her front paws on Alexander's thigh and her face right in his, as if reminding him she's there. "They've started chewing on my shoes. One found my wallet on the coffee table and chewed the corner off."

I laugh, setting down the puppy and picking up another. "They only want to play."

"Then the little shits need to play with each other and not my stuff. I've had to keep them in here when I'm not in the house.

There's no telling what the state of things would be when I came back in."

I plop down on the concrete floor, the coolness of the slab immediately chilling my butt, and a horde of puppies starts climbing on my lap. I notice one of the pups, a black one with white on its face, off to the side watching what's going on. It's the one that Daniel named and grew attached to the most.

"Is there something wrong with that one?" I ask, pointing the lone pup.

"Nope. She's the runt and quiet one of the group." He pauses. "I also think she misses a certain little boy."

I smile, finding it sweet he thinks the puppy misses Daniel.

Now that he's mentioned it, she does look smaller than the others.

I pat the floor beside me. "C'mere, Pepper," I coax her softly. Her head tilts to the side, then the other way, before she gets up from her haunches and slowly walks over to me. I pet her head and back, then pick her up. She doesn't wiggle around or try to get to my face like the others. She just looks up at me with calm eyes.

I hold her up to my face and rub my nose with the tip of hers.

"Aren't you just a sweetheart," I murmur.

I look over to find Alexander watching me. I duck my head back to the puppy, feeling warmth come over my cheeks.

"Is it okay if I take Pepper?"

"Sure," he says, a hint of gruffness in his voice.

I smile at the puppy. "You hear that? You're coming home with me. Daniel's going to be so excited to see you again!"

We both stand, me with Pepper in hand. I laugh when I look down and see both our feet covered in the rest of the puppies.

"There's no way we'll make it out of this room without at least one making it through the door."

"They'll be all right. They need to be let out for a bit anyway."

Taking careful steps so we don't squish one, we walk to the door. As soon as it's open, there's a mad dash of puppies bounding out.

Watching them tumble over their feet, I remark with a giggle, "I wish I could take them all home."

"You're more than welcome to," Alexander says with his own chuckle. The deep laugh still sounds strange coming from him, but I love hearing it.

I wrinkle my nose when I look at him. "No thanks."

He grunts, but I see a small smirk playing on his lips. "And of course you'd pick the calmest of the group, leaving me with the rambunctious ones."

I shrug, letting my laughter show in my eyes. I snuggle the puppy to my chest and her cool nose touches the underside of my chin.

"Yeah, but I think we were meant to have this one." I look down at the soft eyes of the puppy. "She was calling to me."

When he doesn't say anything, I look at him and find him watching me and the puppy with an expression I've never witnessed on his face before. The look holds me captive, and I'm stuck staring into his dark gray eyes. I saw several different emotions in those eyes in the time the kids and I were here, but never the look they hold now. Something's different in their depths. Something that both scares me and sends shivers all over my body.

"I think you may be right," he says quietly.

Feeling a warm tongue on my chin, I break our stare, give my head a shake, then look back down at the puppy again.

"You wanna play with your brothers and sisters for a few minutes before we go?"

I bend and set the pup down on the floor and her siblings rush over to check her out, as if she could possibly be different than she was a few minutes ago. I opt to watch them for a few minutes versus looking back at Alexander. Seeing him again has left me a flustered mess, and I need a moment to compose myself.

When I do lift my head, it's to find him still looking at me. I caught him doing that several times during our stay here, but he normally looked away when my eyes met his. He isn't this time, and I wonder why. What's changed about him?

Suddenly feeling the need to talk, I blurt out the first thing that comes to mind.

"What are you doing for Christmas tomorrow?"

He blinks, taken aback by my question, then turns away, but before he does, a look of pain so fierce it nearly has me stumbling back washes over his face.

"Nothing," he grunts.

Forging ahead, I say, "Why don't you come with me and the kids out to Mrs. Myers' house? She's actually my friend's grandmother, and I know she'd love to have you there as well."

Instead of answering, he walks over to the stove and a thick cloud of steam floats from the pot as he lifts the lid. Grabbing a big metal spoon from the counter, he starts stirring the contents. All I can do is stand there and watch his tense back. I want to go to him and offer whatever comfort I can, but I know he wouldn't be receptive. If it wasn't his stiff form that screamed to stay away, then the clenched fist resting on the counter certainly would.

I'm just about to apologize—for what, I have no idea—when he lifts the spoon from the pot and some of the hot liquid spills onto his scarred hand.

"Shit," he curses.

Even from several feet away, I feel his pain from the scalding liquid.

Without thought, I rush over to him, grab his forearm, and drag him over to the sink. I turn the water to cold and stuff his hand under the stream. The skin, already marred by burns, is turning an angry red. I keep my head down and make sure his hand stays in the water.

"I'm sorry," I say, barely loud enough for him to hear me.

"For what?" His question comes out gruff, and I wonder if it's from the pain of being burned or the pain he felt before. "You didn't do anything."

I look up to find his gaze locked on me once again. The pain is still there, but there's also curiosity.

"For whatever reason my question brought on your pain."

His eyes flicker away for a brief moment before coming back to me.

"I don't do well at Christmas," he comments quietly.

I hold his eyes for a moment, then dip my head back down to look at his hand. "I understand." I don't really understand, but I get the sense it has something to do with his wife and little girl, so in a way, I guess I do. This will be the kids' and my third Christmas without Will. With each holiday that passes, the pain of not having him with us comes back tenfold. There will always be that heartache, no matter how much time goes by, but there's something about the holidays that brings it to the forefront and makes it fresh again.

I look back down and see the redness of the fresh burn and the shiny taut skin of the old. I'm not sure what comes over me, but I run my finger over the tight flesh, making sure to avoid the new burn, and am surprised at how smooth it feels. I trail my finger past his wrist and slowly make my way up his arm, feeling the slight dips and rises of the scarring. The hair follicles must have been damaged because his arm is hair-free. When I reach the edge of his rolled-up sleeve, I turn his arm over. The same damage appears on this side as well.

An ache forms in my chest, right where my heart sits, at the pain this man has gone through. Both physically, but especially mentally. And I know there's no way for him to escape it. Every time he looks in the mirror, every time he uses his hands, he's reminded of that pain.

Tears prick the backs of my eyes, but I force them away. Me crying for him is the last thing he needs, and I'm sure he wouldn't appreciate it.

Suddenly realizing I've overstepped my bounds by touching him, I pull my hand away and reach for the towel on the counter. Gently, I tap the towel against the red skin.

"Does it hurt?"

His voice is deep when he answers. "No. Some of the nerves in my hand are damaged, so I don't feel everything I should."

My heart hurts for him. His life has been affected by that one accident in so many ways. And it'll continue to affect him for the rest of his life.

I put the towel down and turn off the water. I'm just about to tell him I should go, when his next words stop me.

"When you touched me...." He stops, and I look up at him. "I felt it when you touched me."

My breath catches; I'm not sure how to take his statement. The look he's giving me is intense but at the same time unsure. Like whatever he's feeling is strong, but he's unsure what that feeling is. I know just what he's going through. The feelings running through me leave me confused and, if I'm honest, a bit warm.

My legs become jelly when the look in his eyes turns to something more intimate. It's not crude or offensive, but it's definitely not innocent, and not a look he's given me before, but one that I find that I like.

I hold my breath as his eyes track down my body, and I swear every place his eyes touch, I feel a soft caress, as if it's more than his eyes perusing my body. Tingles start in my belly and make their way down my legs. I grip the counter behind me because I seriously worry they won't be able to hold me up much longer.

He's only a couple feet away from me, so when he takes a step closer, the heat of his body and his scent engulf me. It leaves me dizzy, and goose bumps appear on my arms. He reaches out with his scarred hand, and the moment his fingers go beneath my hair, cupping the side of my neck, my stomach does somersaults. I close my eyes as intense sensations race through my body, heating it up twenty, forty, sixty degrees.

I feel the slight tremble of his hand against me, and I open my eyes. His gaze is on the hand that's resting against my neck, then moves to my face. They hold both yearning and wonder.

"What is it about you that makes me want to be close to you?"

he marvels in a low voice. His thumb rubs gently against my neck. "Why do I want to touch you so badly when I haven't wanted to touch anyone in years?"

I swallow, mesmerized by both his questions and the reverence in his voice as he asks them. Not to mention the way his hand feels against my skin. I haven't let another man touch me intimately since Will died. Except this... this feels like so much more than Will's touch ever made me feel. We always had a very good physical relationship and we always found pleasure in each other's arms. Our lovemaking was sweet but passionate, and I felt that tingle of desire up until the very last time Will touched me. The feeling I get from Alexander's touch is different. Stronger.

I suck in a sharp breath when Alexander closes the small gap still separating us. My tongue slides out to wet my suddenly dry lips, and his eyes track the movement, then land back on mine with even more longing. I release the counter and lay my hands against his lower stomach, unable to keep them off him a moment longer. His eyes close for a fleeting second at the contact.

"Why is it you?" he asks, opening his eyes to reveal a tortured expression. "Someone so soft and sweet and good. Someone I don't deserve, but for some reason I desperately want more and more each day."

"Alexander," I whisper, hating the agonizing pain I hear in his voice. I want to tell him he deserves so much more than he thinks. That whatever plagues him, which I know has to do with the loss of his wife and child, doesn't prevent him from deserving love or happiness.

Before I get a chance to voice my thoughts, his head dips and he rests his forehead against mine. The scars on his face stand out from the tenseness of his expression. I lift my hand and rest it against his marred cheek, badly wanting to erase the uncertainty I see.

"I don't deserve you. I don't deserve whatever could happen between us." I want to object, but he continues before I get a chance. "But there's something I want more than my self-loathing for wanting something I shouldn't."

"What?" I rasp.

"A chance to know what it feels like to kiss you."

My response is immediate and without thought. "Please kiss me, Alexander."

His eyes flicker back and forth between mine, and when he sees the same want in my eyes, he lowers his mouth.

The second our lips touch, a soft groan leaves his throat, and a moan leaves mine. My eyes close automatically and my fingers fist his shirt. His lips are soft and velvety as he gently rubs them against mine. The kiss is innocent by many standards, but it still sends my body skyrocketing, leaving me feeling like I'm floating.

As chaste as the kiss is, I want more, and from the tightening of Alexander's hand around the back of my neck, he wants more too.

Tentatively, I open my mouth and offer my tongue, hoping I'm not being too forward. A shiver races through me when his tongue touches mine. Mint, that's what he tastes like. Fresh and cooling. I love the taste and want more of it.

Taking over the kiss, he gently invades my mouth. I accept him inside and make soft mewling sounds. Using his other hand, he tilts my head to the side, giving us both better access. His lips leave mine and he nips at my bottom lip, then they come back and tenderly take my mouth again.

The kiss doesn't last longer than a minute or two before he pulls back, resting his forehead against mine again. I keep myself from protesting and asking him to kiss me again. Even with the kiss lasting such a short time, the impact of it has both of us panting.

His eyes are closed and a small smile plays on his lips. "So sweet," he whispers, then opens his eyes. The smile disappears and the pain is back. "So much more than I thought it would be."

He pulls back, but my hands stay locked on his shirt. I'm not ready to let him go yet. The feelings he's conjured in me... I'm not ready to release them. I want to hold on to them and him and never let go. I want more from this man than I've wanted in a long time.

There's half a foot between us now, but his hands are still in my hair, the palms against my neck. His eyes close tightly, and I watch as he pulls in a deep breath before reopening them.

I dig my fingers into his shirt more, and he moves an inch closer.

Finally finding my voice, I tell him, "I know about your wife and daughter," I say gently. "I know they drowned." I want to take back the words at the profound pain on his face, but this is something I need to get out. "I can see the guilt in your eyes because you blame yourself." I take a step closer to him and lower my voice. "I'm going to tell you what I've told Kelsey many times. It wasn't your fault, Alexander."

"You don't know the whole story," he says thickly. "If you did, you wouldn't be saying that."

"I don't need to know the whole story to know it wasn't your fault. I may not know much about you, and we may have gotten off on the wrong foot, but I know you're a caring and compassionate man. I saw that when you went out of your way to help a stranger and her kids on the side of the road during a snowstorm. I saw it when you spent time with my kids. I saw it in the way you looked when I told you about my husband. I don't need to know the story to know that you would protect your family fiercely."

He's quiet for several moments, and several different emotions flash in his eyes. Anger is one of them.

"You wouldn't feel that way if you knew what happened, how I didn't protect them," he says, his tone bitter.

"Then tell me."

I want to know why he feels the way he does, because there is no doubt in my mind that his view of the events will be much different than mine. There's no way this man, this wonderfully strong man, would stand by and watch his family die and not do everything in his power to stop it. I know this deep in my gut.

"I can't." His jaw clenches and even more pain fills his face.

Moisture appears in his eyes, and he looks away for a moment, before pushing the tears away and bringing his gaze back to me. "It hurts too much to remember."

To see such a strong man on the brink of falling apart has my own tears rushing to the surface, but like him, I force them away. He needs the people in his life to be strong, not break down.

I can see in his eyes that no matter how much I tell him that it wasn't his fault, he still won't accept it. The pain is too deep and he's had years to embed the guilt inside himself. It makes my heart weep for him.

My curiosity to know exactly what happened to his family grows. What makes him think it was his fault? I'm sure I could ask just about anyone in town and they would tell me, but that doesn't feel right, and I run the risk of them not knowing all the facts. I want to hear it from Alexander, not from someone who could mix up or warp the facts.

I step up, get to my tiptoes, and press my lips against his for a soft kiss. I want to memorize the taste of him, because I get the feeling I probably won't get another chance to do it again.

I pull back and look into his eyes. "No matter how you may see yourself, I see a great and wonderful man standing in front of me right now."

His brows lower into a frown as he looks down at me. His hands flex against my scalp, and I watch a war rage in his eyes. A minute later, he gives his head a small shake and he unlocks his fingers from around the back of my head. Disappointment and a fierce burn settle in my stomach when he takes a step back, both mentally and physically putting distance between us. He's pushing himself away from me.

I'm forced to let go of his shirt, and I drop my head to hide the hurt his rejection causes. I force air into my lungs and try to compose my face before looking up at him. I can tell he doesn't like his decision any more than I do.

"I'm sorry." His Adam's apple bobs.

My smile is sad. "I know."

We stand in the kitchen silently for a moment, before I force myself to turn away from him. I grab my keys, which I dropped on the counter when I got here.

"I should go. My friend Emma has the kids and we're due to go out to Jeremy and Mrs. Peggy's house this evening. I still need to get the puppy settled in before we leave."

I feel rather than hear him walk up behind me. I hold my breath and close my eyes, hoping he'll touch me again, but he doesn't. Instead, he just stands there. I feel his breath against the back of my neck. I close my eyes, wishing he'd lean closer.

"I've got a crate on the porch you can use for the pup," he says.

Not waiting on a response from me, he walks out the front door. I look around the house one more time, hoping the pain of not being here anymore will go away soon. Seeing Pepper curled up on the floor by the couch, I walk over to her. I squat down and the rest of the puppies come bounding over, with Gigi trotting behind them. I give each a pat on the head and Gigi a rub and kiss on the tip of her nose before scooping up the runt.

Careful to not let the other puppies through the door, I slip outside and close it behind me. Alexander has the small crate sitting on the railing of the porch, and I approach him. I slip the puppy inside and he closes the latch. Without a word, he picks up the crate and we both walk to my truck. The further away from the house I get, the more it feels like I can't breathe properly. In the short time the kids and I were here, it became our home. I know it has more to do with the owner of the cabin than the cabin itself.

I open the passenger-side door and he sets the crate inside, then slides the seat belt across it to secure it better. The act makes me smile. He even worries about the puppy being safe.

Once he's done, he closes the door and turns toward me. I desperately want to reach out to him, and I know he wants to do the same. I can see it in the stiff way he's holding his body, like he's forcing himself back. I wish he would give in.

"Thank you," I say softly.

"You're welcome. Tell the kids I said hi and Merry Christmas."

"I will."

It takes everything in me to force my legs to move to the other side of the car. He doesn't follow me, and I wonder if it's because if he does he won't let me go, or he's worried he'll snatch me in his arms and kiss me one last time. I don't think I've ever wished for anything more to happen than I do that.

We stare at each other for a moment from over the top of the truck. My keys dig in my hand so hard I worry it might break the skin.

"Goodbye, Alexander."

His jaw is tense when he says, "Goodbye, Gwendolyn."

For as long as I remember, everyone has called me Gwen. This is the second time he's used my full name, and I have to admit, I love the way it sounds when he says it.

I give one last smile before opening the door and climbing inside. I breathe in through my nose and out through my mouth before starting my truck. Looking out the passenger-side window, all I can see is his torso and arms. As much as I want to see his face again, I know it's best that I don't.

"You ready to go home, girl?" I ask the puppy beside me, putting my finger through the slats and rubbing a tuft of fur.

The yard is big enough that I don't need to back up, so I put the vehicle in drive and pull away. I make the mistake of looking into the rearview mirror and see Alexander still standing there, watching me drive away.

At first, it's just one tear that falls, but it's quickly followed by several more. How is it that one man I hardly know can affect me so strongly? It's not just me though. I know he's had an impact on Daniel and Kelsey's lives as well.

As soon as his house is no longer in view, I pull over on the side of the road and let the tears fall, knowing I need to get this out of my system before I get home.

Chapter Twelve

Alexander

T HAT NIGHT, I LIE IN bed with sweat drenching my body and my muscles tensed. The sheet, covering me from the waist down, is tangled in my legs, and I kick the damp cloth away.

I just woke from a dream. One that I've had before, but still leaves me gasping for breath every fucking time. It was of me watching my wife and little girl die. I fucking watched them die and did nothing to stop it. I heard the screams and cries and pleas, but still did nothing. I remembered the heat and the smell of my flesh melting, but the pain of that doesn't compare to the pain of watching my family die right in front of me. In tonight's dream, the screams and cries were louder, filling every part of my soul. Even now, as I lie here, I hear the echo of them. Tomorrow is Christmas and the day after will mark four years they've been gone.

I shift on the bed and a wave of vanilla scent filters through the air. Without looking, I grab the second pillow beside me and bring it to my nose, then breathe in deep. I've washed the sheets but not the pillowcases yet. They smell like Gwen and I'm not ready to wash away her scent yet. It's fucking pathetic, but I don't give a damn.

Every single night, when I lie down, I grab her pillow. It helps with the dark places my mind likes to wander to as I'm trying to drift off to sleep. I don't lie on the pillow because I don't want my scent to override hers. It sounds creepy as fuck, but damned if I'll stop. I know eventually the scent will fade, and I'll have to wash the pillowcase, but until that time comes, I'll keep it right here beside me.

I cling to the pillow tighter, using it as a shield to ward off the memories wanting to force their way into my mind. For once, I don't want to remember my ultimate failure. I want them to stay hidden in the back of my mind and let the memory of touching Gwen, kissing her, feeling her warm skin against mine and the soft strands of her hair between my fingers, come forward.

I think back to earlier today when I told her I wanted to know what it felt like to kiss her. I only meant to lay my lips against hers for a brief moment, but when she opened her lips and offered me her tongue, there was no way I wasn't taking it. She tasted so damn sweet, like cotton candy and cake rolled into one. I knew before my lips even touched hers that she would taste good, feel so damn good, but fuck if I knew it would be as amazing as it was. I wanted to devour her mouth and never come up for air. I wanted to kiss her and kiss her until she begged me to stop.

I roll to my side, taking the damn pillow with me like some lovesick fool. My eyes land on my phone on the nightstand. The lateness of the hour is the only thing keeping me from grabbing it and sending her a message. Earlier, when she got out of her car and looked around, I sat on the porch and just took her in before making my presence known. She looked so pretty standing there, like something fresh and beautiful, and it took my damn breath away. I could look at her for hours.

When she heard the creak of the chair as I stood, and our eyes met, I tensed, ready to stalk to her and pull her into my arms. I was surprised at the need to touch her, taste her. When she was here during the snowstorm, the need gradually grew, but I was able to ignore it. But as she stood there staring at me, that need slammed into me like a freight train. Then, when she walked up the steps and stood before me, it took every bit of strength I had to keep away from her.

I lost the will to fight when she came to me when I burned myself. The hot soup didn't really hurt. The curse slipped past my lips more out of habit than any real pain. I'm used to not having much feeling in my hand, or the rest of the right side of my body, so when she touched me and I felt it, really *felt* it, the need to feel it again overrode my need to keep away from her. Then when she looked at me with eyes that held so many emotions, need being one of them, I knew right then I wouldn't be able to hold back. I only needed her permission, and when she gave it, I took what I had been dying to have, even knowing I had no right to want it.

It hurt so fucking much to touch her, even at the same time it felt like heaven. The kiss didn't last near as long as I wanted it to, but way longer than it should have. It's better for everyone if Gwen stays far away from me. I can't take the chance of my darkness marring her life.

Taking one last deep breath into the pillow, I let it go, and I swear my heart fractures. I sit up and swing my legs to the side. There's no way I'll be able to get to sleep again tonight unless I wear my body out to exhaustion. Getting up, I pull on a pair of jogging pants and make my way to the utility room, the click-clack of Gigi's nails on the floor following me.

I flick on the light, then head straight for the weight bench, while Gigi goes over to her pups and gives them a few sniffs, her motherly instincts forcing her to check on them. I don't use the weight bench as often as I like, getting most of my workout through working with and caring for the horses.

An hour later, my body is finally worn out and sweat drips down the sides of my face. I know I've pushed myself too far when I feel pain in my lower back. Since the accident, I can't do near as much as I could before.

I sit on the floor, my knees drawn up with my elbows resting on them. My eyes land on the motorcycle, and I remember Gwen's words from earlier.

"I didn't take you for the type of guy that rides motorcycles."

I smile. There are a lot of things Gwen doesn't know about me. But then again, there are a lot of things about me that are different than they used to be. Back when Clara was alive, and before she got pregnant, we would take at least one day a week and just ride. She'd sit behind me with her arms encircling my waist and we'd let the road take us wherever it wanted to. When she got pregnant, those trips stopped, and I haven't been back on the bike since. I was actually thinking the other day about selling it, but now that Gwen's shown interest, the thought isn't as appealing. And that's trouble, because I don't need to think about Gwen being on the back of the bike with me. I don't need to think about Gwen at all, but it's impossible to stop.

I get up and Gigi and I leave the room. The pups push their way through the door behind us, and I'm just too damn tired to fight with them. Hopefully the house won't be destroyed come morning.

I stop and grab a glass out of the cabinet for some water. Spotting the bottle of Jameson, I grab it and set it on the counter. The need to drink away the memories of Clara and Rayne and Gwen has me opening the bottle and pouring a couple inches in the glass. I turn and lean back against the counter.

I'm lifting the glass to my lips when my eyes land on the notebook with the crossword puzzles in it. I meant to give it to Gwen earlier, along with the small box of carved wooden animals and the earrings. But then I kissed her and all thoughts of anything other than the taste of her lips fled my mind.

I lower the glass, suddenly not wanting it. I pour the whiskey down the drain, rinse the glass, then refill it with water.

I run through the shower, ignoring my body when it comes to life as images of Gwen pop into my head. I glare down at my dick when it begs for attention as I lie down in bed and vanilla hits me again. I think about tossing the pillow across the room, but I know

I'll only get up to grab it again in a few minutes. It's like I've become addicted to the smell.

I grab my phone to check the time.

One thirty.

It's Christmas morning.

And just like clockwork, pain grips me in its tight fist. So it begins....

Chapter Thirteen

Gwendolyn

I WATCH WITH A SMILE as the kids open the gifts that Emma and her grandmother bought them. They opened their gifts from me and the ones that Will's parents sent this morning when they got up. Pepper was a huge hit, especially for Daniel.

Now we're at Emma's grandmother's house. Daniel squeals in delight when he tears away the paper from his last gift. It's a new video game. He jumps to his feet and rushes over to Emma, throwing his arms around her waist. Pepper follows him and sits at his feet.

"Thank you, Aunt Emma!" he says, grinning big.

"You're welcome, buddy." She ruffles his hair and winks.

I look over to Kelsey and see her opening her gifts at a much slower rate. She doesn't bounce around and hoot and holler like her brother does with each gift, but I know she's still grateful, she just doesn't show it.

I get up from the couch and sit down beside her. She's holding a new Kindle in her hand. Besides her crossword puzzles, Kelsey loves to read, something I'm glad she's into.

"Do you like it?" I ask, looking down at her.

She lifts her head and meets my eyes. Her nod is small and barely seen. She used to have a Kindle until she accidently dropped it a month ago and the screen started turning purple. She never asked for another, something I didn't expected from her because she never asks for anything like normal kids do, but I planned to buy her another one anyway. When I told Emma about it over the phone, she asked if she could get it for her instead. Of course, Emma had to go all out and get the newest model.

I wrap my arm around her shoulder and pull her to me, then kiss the top of her head. She rests her head against my shoulder for several moments before pulling away.

Releasing a sigh, I get up and start stuffing the trash into a bag, then carry it into the kitchen. Noticing a few dirty dishes on the counter and feeling the need to do something, I decide to take care of them. I'm rinsing a plate and putting it in the dishwasher when I feel a presence beside me.

"What's wrong with you today?" Emma asks, handing me another plate.

I look up, not altogether surprised by her question, but also not prepared for it either.

"Nothing." I play dumb. "Why do you ask?"

She looks at me, telling me with her eyes that she's not falling for the act.

"Come on, Gwen. You've been awfully quiet since you got here. What's going on with you?"

I grab the dish towel and dry my hands. I plop it down on the counter, then turn to face her.

"I'm worried about him," I admit quietly.

Her brow wrinkles in confusion. "Who?"

I keep my eyes on her when I say, "Alexander."

Recognition dawns and she comes to stand beside me.

"I didn't realize you cared for him this much."

"I'm not sure what I feel for him, but the thought of him out there all alone on Christmas doesn't sit well with me." I turn my head and let Emma see the pain on my face. "He blames himself for what happened to his family."

"But why would he—"

"I don't know. I've told him that it wasn't his fault and he says I would think differently if I knew the whole story." I stare off across the kitchen. "I may not know him that well and don't know exactly what happened, but Emma...." I look back at her. "A man that treats my kids the way he treated mine would *not* just let his family die without doing something."

She nods her agreement. "I've only met him a few times while visiting Gram, but he always seemed like a nice and caring guy."

I turn back to the sink and grab a rag, then start wiping down the counter.

"The kids miss him," I tell her quietly.

"I don't think it's only the kids that miss him."

A smile forms on my face. "No, not just the kids." I stop for a moment, then reveal, "We kissed yesterday."

I look over when Emma doesn't respond, to find a big grin on her face.

"I knew something had to of happened between you," she says smugly. "How was it?"

I let out a breathy sigh. "It was short, but one of the best kisses I've ever had." I drop my head, a blush forming on my face when I remember the feel of his lips against mine. "I feel like such a school-girl with her first crush. I don't know how to do the whole dating and flirting thing."

"Not much has changed since you and Will started dating. I'm pretty sure it all works the same way."

There's laughter in her tone, but the mention of Will brings on a touch of pain. I always thought he and I would be together forever. We'd have kids that we would love and watch them grow up, then watch them have kids of their own. We were supposed to grow old together.

When she sees that her words did the opposite to her intention, she takes the rag from me and tosses it in the sink. Grabbing my hand, she turns me to face her.

"Gwen, you know that Will would want you to move on, right?"

I nod. "I know. It's just...." I stop and take a deep breath. "For such a long time, it's been hard to imagine a life without him, but when I think about Alexander, it isn't as hard anymore." I blink away the tears wanting to break free, guilt gripping my chest.

Emma, knowing me all too well, knows exactly what I'm thinking. "It'll always hurt when you think about Will not being in your life anymore, but it's normal to get past that pain enough to move on. He'll always be a part of your life, you'll always love him, but you've got enough love in you to give it to someone else as well. He'd want you to find someone to take his place and make you happy, to treat his kids as if they were his own. From what you've told me so far, Alexander may be that man."

"I'm not sure he wants to be that man. I'm not even sure if I want him to be that man. We know nothing about each other."

But you do know, my mind whispers.

"Sometimes you don't need to know much about the person to know they are the one."

I think about her words for several moments. I've been drawn to Alexander from the first moment I met him. Standing in line at the grocery store, even with him being less than friendly, I felt some type of pull toward him. I didn't know what it was, I still don't, but it was definitely there, and it was strong. I wonder if he felt the same.

"Why are you still here?" Emma asks, pulling me from my thoughts.

"What do you mean?"

"Go to him, Gwen. You know you want to."

"I'm not sure if he wants us around," I tell her.

"You don't let that boy push you away."

We both turn at the sound of Mrs. Myers' raspy voice. She's standing in the doorway with her hands on her hips, the soft look in her eyes saying she heard our conversation, or at least enough of it to know what's going on.

"That boy has had enough sadness in his life to last a lifetime. It's about time he had something good come his way."

"Do you really think we should go?"

"Yes" comes from both of them.

"What if he turns us away?" I whisper my fear.

"I'm sure he'll try," Mrs. Myers says. "But you don't let him. From what I've overheard, he'll want you there, he's just scared."

It only takes me a minute to think over what I should do.

"Okay."

They both smile at me.

Mrs. Myers leaves her spot by the door and walks to the fridge. "I'll put together a couple plates of food for him."

I turn to Emma and pull her in for a hug. At her ear, I whisper, "Thank you."

I walk over to her grandmother and do the same. She pats my cheek when I pull back.

"That man deserves some happiness, just as much as you do."

I leave them both in the kitchen preparing plates for us to take to Alexander. Daniel is on the floor playing with some of his new toys. Kelsey's on the floor as well, but what has me surprised is the puppy sleeping on her lap. She's staring down at Pepper with her brows pulled down, her hand slowly stroking her back. I take a minute to watch her, pleased that she's taking a liking to the pup.

"Hey, kids," I call after a moment. "Grab all your stuff together and get ready to go."

"Aww... Mom." Daniel pouts. "Can't we stay for a bit longer?"

I smile at them both. "Nope. How do you both feel about going to see Alexander?"

That gets Daniel's attention and he jumps up from the floor. "Can we really?" he practically yells.

"Yes."

"Alright!" I laugh when he pumps his fist in the air and starts to immediately gather his toys together. If only it were always that easy getting him to clean his room.

I turn to Kelsey and am pleased to find a light of interest in her eyes. She may not show it, but I know she misses him.

"Would you like to go see Alexander, Kelsey?"

Her nod comes faster than normal and has a bit more enthusiasm to it. She gets up from her perch on the floor, carefully setting Pepper back down, and starts gathering her things as well.

Ten minutes later, the kids are bundled up and we're at the door saying our goodbyes to Emma and Mrs. Myers. The puppy, food, and presents are already packed in the car.

"I hate that I'm leaving early when you leave tomorrow," I say after pulling back from our hug.

"You'll see me tomorrow when you take me back to the airport. And as soon as the hospital hires more nurses, I'll come back for a longer visit."

"I miss you already."

"I miss you already too."

We both shed a tear or two before the kids and I walk to the car. Mrs. Myers lives on the same stretch of road that Alexander lives on, so it won't take us long to get there. Butterflies start in my belly, and I'm nervous as hell as we pull out onto the road. Doubt starts to plague me. What if he really doesn't want us around anymore? What if I've only imagined the connection we have?

I clench my jaw and push the thoughts away. There's no way I could have imagined the emotion in his eyes when he looked at me. I know he has to feel something for me.

I look in the rearview mirror and see Daniel watching out the window, a look of anticipation on his face. I look next at Kelsey, and find more than just a blank expression on her face. I amend my earlier thought. I know he has to feel something for *us*.

Five minutes later, I'm pulling up next to Alexander's truck. I take a minute to compose myself before turning to the kids.

"I want you both to stay here until I come back for you."

"Why can't we go in with you?" Daniel asks, bouncing in his seat with excitement.

"I want to make sure that it's okay that we're here first."

His brow wrinkles. "But why wouldn't it be okay?"

I smile. "Because he may have other plans."

I can tell he doesn't like my answer, but he nods anyway. I pass a brief glance at Kelsey, then face forward again. Pulling the keys from the ignition, I suck in an encouraging breath, and exit the car.

As I walk across the yard, my eyes catch on the partially built house. My heart hurts when I notice some of the walls that were standing yesterday are now lying in a pile beside the rest of the house. I know him tearing down the house had to have pained him.

My legs shake the rest of the way to the porch and my heart pounds an erratic rhythm that I can hear in my ears. I stop in front of the door and will the nerves away. I lift my hand and rap my knuckles against the wood, then realize my knock was more like a light tap, so he probably didn't hear it.

"This is stupid, Gwen," I mutter to myself. "Get a hold of yourself."

I knock harder and release a big whoosh of air as I wait for him to answer.

And I wait.

And wait some more.

I frown, wondering why he's not answering the door. I turn and look around the yard, but don't see him or Gigi. A look at the barn shows the door firmly shut. I knock again, but get the same silent response. I contemplate going back to the car and leaving, but instead, something compels me to try the doorknob.

It's unlocked.

After a moment of hesitation, I twist the knob and push open the door. The house is quiet when I peek inside.

"Alexander?" I call, and still get nothing.

I look back at the kids in the car before pushing the door the rest of the way open and stepping inside. The TV is on with the volume down and there's a light on in the kitchen, both indicating he has to be around here somewhere. Again, I wonder if I should go out to my car and call him, but decide since I'm already here, I may as well try to find him.

"Gigi!" I say loudly.

A second later, Gigi comes running out from the hallway and skids to a stop in front of me, her tail thumping against the floor.

I run my fingers through the hair on her head. "Where's your daddy, girl?"

Her tongue falling out the side of her mouth is my answer and it makes me laugh. I tilt my head to the side, listening for any sounds, but besides the whoosh of Gigi's tail against the hardwood floor and the crackle of the fire, it's silent.

Knowing I should probably just leave, but feeling an uncontrollable need to see Alexander now that I'm here, I head toward the hallway Gigi came from. She trails behind me, making me feel a fraction better about being in Alexander's house without his knowledge. At least she's there to chaperone.

The spare bathroom door is open when I pass by it, and as expected, he's not in there. Just as I reach his bedroom doorway, a creaking sound comes. I know that sound. It's the bathroom door in Alexander's room.

I stop in my tracks just outside the doorway as a billow of steam releases into the bedroom, followed by Alexander, wearing nothing but a towel wrapped around his waist. I'm completely transfixed and feel like a creeper when all I can do is stand there and stare at him. His back is to me as he opens a dresser drawer. Strong muscles flex and move as he grabs something out and closes the drawer. There's a tattoo on his upper right shoulder that looks to wrap around to the front, and another that covers his entire left side. It's a jumble of a bunch of different things, but I'm unable to tell what they are. Unconsciously, I take a step closer to get a better look.

His head snaps up when he hears the creak of the floor, and he whips around. I snap out of my daze and am just about to apologize for sneaking up on him, but my words catch in my throat. On his back, there's not one burn mark that I could see. On his chest though, it's a different story. The right side of his torso is completely covered in scars, all the way from his shoulder to below the towel. My eyes travel down past the towel that ends just above the knee and see the scars continue down.

"What are you doing here?" his gravelly voice asks, and my eyes snap up to his. He's standing there staring at me, one of his brows raised.

My tongue stays stuck to the roof of my mouth for several seconds before I can force it to start working.

"I... uh... I," I stammer. I avert my eyes away from him, hoping not looking at him will help me answer his question. "I came...." I jerk my thumb over my shoulder toward the living room. "The kids and I came to see you." I bring my eyes back to his for a brief moment, then move them away again. "No one should be alone on Christmas." Then I finish lamely, "Mrs. Myers sent food."

When he doesn't say anything, I bring my eyes back to him. He's still standing in front of his dresser, but his hands are balled into fists at his sides, clutching whatever he took from the drawer tightly, and he seems tense. I swallow past the dryness in my mouth.

"I knocked, but you didn't answer."

He still doesn't say anything, and I open my mouth to apologize, but he interrupts me.

"You and the kids shouldn't be here right now."

I ignore his near nakedness, push past my nerves, and step into the room. Tilting my head to the side, I ask, "Why?"

It's his turn to avert his eyes.

"Because today is not a good day for me."

He's already mentioned he doesn't do holidays, but I get the feeling there's more to it. Realization dawns, and I suck in a breath.

"Today's the anniversary of their deaths, isn't it?" I ask, keeping my voice quiet.

The pain he shoots my way when he brings his gaze back to me almost steals my breath.

"Tomorrow."

"I'm so sorry." I take a step closer to him, not entirely sure what I'll do once I'm close enough, but he holds his hand up to ward me off.

"No!" he says harshly, and I freeze in place. His head drops and his hands go to his hips. His chest rises and falls as he pulls in several deep breaths before lifting his head again. "Sorry," he utters. "I'm just not in a good place right now. You and the kids should leave."

His words hit me in the chest and the pain of it is staggering. I know I have no right to feel this way, but I wish so much this man would let me be there for him. I want to help make him better, even if only for a few minutes. I wish he would open up to me and tell me how he feels, so I can find a way to help him. I know there's nothing I can do to take away his pain, but if I could relieve it even just a fraction, it might help.

I think about my kids in the car, the excitement of seeing Alexander again, and I can't bring myself to give in so easily. Alexander might not want to admit it, but he needs all three of us.

"Please." I take another step toward him. "The kids really want to see you. They're waiting in the car."

My soul sings when his eyes flare with something akin to longing. I know deep in my heart my kids have touched him in some way and he's missed them too. My throat tightens with the thought. He's touched their lives as well, along with mine.

After a moment, he nods, and my body sags with relief.

"Thank you."

Now that the tenseness of the situation is over, a new awareness makes itself known. Before I can stop myself, my eyes travel back down his body. The scars covering the right side don't take away from the beauty of his chest, only add to it. Packed with muscles, the left side of his chest is covered in a thin layer of bristly hair, while the right has none. His stomach has deep ripples from his six-pack. The hair covering half his chest disappears beneath the towel.

I blush fiercely and want to slap myself when I think about what's under that towel. I haven't felt desire for another man since Will and I got together, and it's strange to do so now. I ache to run my hands over his body. My mouth waters to trace over both the hard planes of his muscles and the rigid lines of his scars. The tingle that starts in my toes travels up my body and centers between my legs, leaving my entire body feeling flushed. That feeling intensifies and my eyes widen when the towel starts to tent.

"Gwendolyn," Alexander calls roughly. Knowing my face is flame red but unable to do anything about it, I look at him. "Don't look at me like that."

I jump at the growled words and the intensity in his eyes. He looks like he's seconds away from stalking over to me and devouring me whole. The prospect of that sends my already pounding heart into overdrive. I want nothing more than to yell at him to come take me, but now's not the time, and I wonder if it ever will be.

I silently ask myself if I truly want there to be a time.

Yes, my mind screams immediately, and I know it's true.

I want this man to touch me, I want Alexander to take me. I want to feel his skin against mine and for him to kiss me again. The need for that is so strong that I wonder if I've ever wanted anything this badly before.

I take a deep breath and push down the desire. My kids are still out in the car waiting on me. Wanting Alexander is the last thing that should be on my mind at the moment. I need to focus.

"I'll, uh... go grab the kids while you get dressed," I mumble, then turn and rush down the hallway, swearing I hear his deep chuckle as I go.

Before opening the front door, I stop and rest my forehead against it. I steady my breath and my racing heart, knowing I can't have a red face when I go out to the car. Once I'm sure I'm under control, I pull the door open, and welcome the cool air that hits my face. I start across the yard, but then slow when I don't see their heads popping up over the front seats. My steps become faster and fear settles in when I don't find them inside. I spin and look across the yard.

"Daniel? Kelsey?" I call.

The only sound I hear is the light breeze blowing in my ears. I turn back to the car and check the back seat one more time, hoping I somehow missed them. I only find Pepper's empty cage. My chest starts to hurt with my heavy breathing as panic soon replaces the fear. We're practically out in the middle of nowhere with virtually no traffic, where in the world could they be? I was only in the house for a few minutes, so they couldn't have gone far. They've never run off before, so for them to do so now—I refuse to think there's another reason they aren't in the car—seems strange.

"Daniel and Kelsey!" I yell again. "Where are you?"

I stop my frantic look around the yard when I still get no answer, and pull in a deep breath. The last thing I need to do is have an anxiety attack. I need to pull myself together and think rationally. I think back to when I walked out to the living room. Could they have been in there and I didn't even realize it?

Barking comes from my right, and I turn to see Gigi bounding up to me. She stops at my feet and looks up. I absently reach out to her, but look over to the porch. As soon as I spot Alexander standing at the top of the steps, dressed in jeans and a thermal, I start toward him.

"Are the kids inside?" I ask, out of breath even though I've only walked ten feet.

His eyes look over my shoulder to the car, then back to me.

"No."

"Are you sure?"

Instead of answering, he looks out across the yard.

"Fuck," he hisses.

The next second, he's off the porch and barreling toward the barn. The door was closed when we first got here, I remember looking at it and seeing it closed, but now it's open by several feet. With my heart in my throat, I run after Alexander. From the way his feet eat up the ground and the look on his face when he saw the door open, there's something more to worry about than the kids being with the horses, even though that thought alone is enough to send terror through me. They've only been around horses a couple of times. They're so big compared to my little kids, so the damage that could be done....

I push those thoughts away, refusing to allow them entrance into my mind.

"Oh God, oh God. Please don't let anything happen to my kids."

Up ahead, Alexander skids to a stop, grabbing hold of the door so he doesn't slide past it, and rushes inside out of view.

I'm panting and my heart races when I make it to the door. The sun is shining bright outside, so when I run inside, I'm momentarily blinded by the dark interior. I widen my eyes in a hopeless attempt to see better, my breathing stuttering in fear of what I might find.

I become accustomed to the darkness and take a step forward, but an arm stops me, pulling me back against a firm chest. I know it's Alexander from his scent, but that doesn't stop me from gripping his forearm and getting ready to push it away.

"Shh," Alexander whispers.

"Huh?" I asked, confused, stopping my struggle before it begins. Why is he just standing here? It's obvious this is where the kids went. We need to find them.

"Don't make any noises or move. We don't want to spook him."

That's when I look up and see Kelsey standing in front of a huge black horse. Fear nearly has my throat closing as I try to pull much-needed air into my lungs. One stomp from that horse and the damage could be fatal. I've always thought horses were beautiful animals, and I loved the idea of owning some one day with Will, but I get the sense this horse isn't very friendly.

I force my body to lock tight so I don't run forward and snatch her away. From the tenseness of Alexander's body behind me, he's forcing himself to stay still as well. We both watch, helpless and holding our breath as Kelsey lifts her hand and holds out an apple. My heart lodges in my throat.

"Alexander," I whimper, scared for my little girl.

His arms tighten around me and his heavy breaths fan across my ear. I can also feel the thump of his heartbeat against my back, and I know it matches my own racing beat.

"Wait," he whispers.

Tears make my vision blurry, and I blink rapidly, not wanting to miss a second of what's happening.

Alexander's body gets even tighter when the horse looks down at the apple offered to him. He lowers his head and opens his mouth slowly. I want to both squeeze my eyes shut and run toward the danger, but all I can do is stand there.

The horse takes the apple from Kelsey's hand and starts chomping on it. Kelsey, seeming mesmerized by the big beast, still has her hand raised. The horse butts his nose against it, then lets out a soft neigh, and Kelsey starts rubbing the side of its head.

I'm still stiff as a board, but Alexander relaxes a bit behind me.

"Well, fuck me," he breathes gruffly in my ear.

I want to turn around and ask him what's going on, but I'm too scared to take my eyes off the horse and my girl.

Kelsey steps closer to the big animal and my body stiffens even more. My nails dig into Alexander's forearms, and I know it has to hurt him, but he doesn't react.

The horse rubs its head against the side of Kelsey's as she continues to run both her hands down its neck. She turns her head to the side, and it's the first chance I've gotten to see her face. What I see has all the air rushing from my lungs. She has one of the most gorgeous smiles on her face I've ever seen.

Out the corner of my eye, I see movement, and both Alexander and I look over. Daniel is standing in front of another stall with the puppy in his arms. This horse is white and brown and much less intimidating, but it still makes me nervous that he's so close. We don't know these horses or what they are capable of.

"Mom, why are you crying?" Daniel asks, walking over to us. I breathe a sigh of relief when he's far enough away from the stall.

I didn't even realize I was crying until he questioned me. I don't answer him, and instead detach my nails from Alexander's arm and move toward Daniel, making sure to walk slowly. Once I reach him, I haul him into my arms, the poor puppy squished between us. I lift my head and look over to where Kelsey is with the other horse.

Taking measured steps, Alexander walks closer to her. His movements seem casual, but I can see the tenseness in his back as he keeps his eye on the horse. Kelsey is no longer facing the horse, but is turned toward Alexander.

"Kelsey, honey, come over here with me please," Alexander calls in a calm voice.

She looks back at the horse with longing and pets him one last time, before turning and meeting Alexander halfway. The beautiful smile of before is gone, replaced with a look of confusion.

As soon as Kelsey is within arm's reach, Alexander drops to his knees and gathers her into his arms. I watch, more tears coming to the surface as he embraces her tightly, and I swear it's like he was just as afraid for her as I was. Like the thought of harm coming to her hurt him just as much as it did me.

Turning to Daniel, I bent down. "Stay here."

When he sees my firm look and gives me a nod, I leave him there and walk over to Alexander and Kelsey. Sensing my presence, Alexander releases her and stands. I only spare him a brief look before I'm pulling Kelsey into my arms. Now that I have her close and know she's okay, the noose around my neck loosens, and I can finally breathe properly. More tears pour down my face.

The situation wasn't that dire, but it could have been. When you have kids, the worst scenario always plagues you.

I sniff my tears away, then pull back and look at Kelsey. Her brows are pulled down into a frown as she looks at me.

"You and Daniel can't run off like that," I tell her sternly. "You both had me so worried. I had no idea where you were."

"I was just showing her the horses, Mom," Daniel says, walking up to me with Alexander at his side. He still looks bewildered. "Then I told her about feeding them apples and asked if she wanted to give it a try."

Before I get a chance to explain to him the dangers of running off, Alexander beats me to it.

"Daniel," he begins. "You're supposed to always ask your mother before you take off like that. Something bad could have happened and we wouldn't have known until it was too late. Had you waited just a few more minutes, I would have taken you and your sister to feed the horses." Alexander puts his hand on Daniel's shoulder and squeezes gently. "Remember what I told you about Bandit the other day?" He thinks for a minute, then nods. "He's not a horse you want to be around at the moment."

His words have my stomach dropping and panic wanting to take hold, but I force it down. The kids are okay, thank goodness, and hopefully have learned to not run off again. I still intend to ask Alexander later what he meant by the horse not being good to be around though. I'm not sure I like that he brought Daniel out here if he knew the horse was dangerous.

Forgetting it for now, I quickly hug Kelsey again and bend to place a kiss against the top of Daniel's head.

I look over to Alexander and find him watching me with a soft expression on his face, but there's still a hint of tension there. I give him a shaky smile, relieved and grateful he was here to help keep me calm. There's no telling what I would have done had I come in the barn and found Kelsey standing in front of that horse. I certainly wouldn't have kept still in my frantic state. He very well could be the only reason Kelsey and Daniel are still safe and unharmed.

As we walk back to the house, Daniel yapping away to Alexander about his puppy and Kelsey her normal silent self, I send up a silent prayer to God, thanking him for giving Alexander the ability to keep my kids safe.

Chapter Fourteen

Alexander

"WOW! THESE ARE SO COOL!" Daniel shouts about all the wooden figurines in the box on the floor.

Seeing his excitement over something I've always cherished makes my damn insides giddy like a girl. After what happened earlier, I'll definitely take the giddy stomach versus my heart feeling like it was being ripped from my chest.

When I ran in that barn and saw Kelsey in front of Bandit, my stomach bottomed out, and I damn near fell on my ass with the force of it. She looked so damn small compared to the huge animal. One wrong move and she would have been gone. Not wanting to spook the horse into doing something fatal, I had to force myself to stay in place, then force Gwen to do the same when she barreled into the room after me. Having no other choice but to watch Kelsey look death in the eye was one of the scariest things I've ever had to face. Knowing the love that Gwen has for her children and that she had to do the same thing, made it ten times worse.

I fucking hated just standing there, feeling like a worthless human being, as Kelsey teetered between being a healthy, beautiful girl and a dead one, but we had to be careful. Bandit is so unpredictable and has a violent streak, so using caution was a must. Dark memories of not being able to save Clara and Rayne tried pulling me under, but with iron will, I pushed the visions back. I *had* to stay focused. If I didn't, Kelsey would have suffered.

But then the damndest thing happened. It both shocked the shit out of me and left me mystified. The fucking horse, the one that damn near took off my hand the other day, took the apple out of Kelsey's hand with gentle movements. Then the bastard proceeded to *pet* her with his head. If it wasn't for the huge amount of relief I felt at Kelsey being safe, I would have been pissed. All this time, the fucking animal's been playing me.

Fucking prick.

Even so, I'm so fucking grateful he chose that moment to be mellow. I'd take him biting off all my limbs over and over again versus him attacking Kelsey.

"You make sure you take really good care of them, okay?" Gwen says firmly, bringing me back to the present.

Daniel nods solemnly. "I will."

My eyes move to Kelsey, who's sitting on the floor with several of the puppies curled up against her legs. She's not paying them any mind, but every so often I see her petting one. She has the new crossword puzzle book I made her in her lap. When I gave it to her, the smile she gave was small, but it was there nonetheless. It was her eyes that were more expressive. She was happy about the book. Coming from someone who doesn't show happiness often, the look was a big deal. Each new smile from her make my own pain lessen. I've come to realize that making Kelsey smile or even show just a hint of joy is something I enjoy doing.

It's Christmas Day, and while I was surprised to find Gwen in my house earlier and just a bit angry that she would be there on one of two days a year it's not wise to be around me, I'm glad they're here. The darkness of my regrets still lingers in the back of my mind, but having them here has been a good distraction. I know I shouldn't use them as such, but damn, I don't want them to leave.

Gwen moves from her position on the floor by Daniel and comes to sit beside me on the couch. With Kelsey leaning against the couch, she's forced to sit right beside me. Her leg brushes against mine, and I feel it behind the zipper of my jeans.

The damn woman is wreaking havoc on my emotions. I'm trying so fucking hard to keep my thoughts pure when it comes to her, but it's nearly impossible. Catching her in my room earlier after jacking off in the shower because thoughts of tasting her wouldn't leave me, left me in a befuddled state for several moments. Right after I came all over the shower floor, guilt started plaguing me. Not because I felt like I betrayed Clara because I was thinking of another woman—I know Clara would want me to move on—but because I've got no right thinking about another woman when I couldn't even take care of the one I had before. One that I loved with my whole heart. One that I had a baby with that I couldn't protect either.

I'm a heartless bastard who should have his balls kicked into his throat.

Then the anger came on when I saw her standing there. I wanted to lash out at her to make her leave. Between the anniversary of Clara and Rayne's death looming close and the guilt of what I just did in the shower, my emotions were raw and there was no telling what might happen. I'd wanted her gone at the same time my mind screamed at her to stay.

Then she had to say the kids wanted to see me, the look in her eyes silently saying she wanted to see me too. I couldn't turn them away.

Things changed when I gave my consent. The look in her eyes turned carnal as she ran them down my body. Fuck if I didn't want to march straight to her and plunder her mouth with mine. To lift her in my arms and carry her to my bed. Only pure force of will held me back.

Gwen shifts beside me and my dick starts to stiffen. I jackknife off the couch so fast that Gigi jumps up from her perch on the floor and barks once. Leaving the three in living room, I head to the kitchen for a glass of water.

It's getting harder and harder being around Gwen and holding in my emotions. The woman makes me feel things that I don't want to feel. Having her kids here makes me want things I don't want to want.

Like a family and a life filled with laughter.

My eyes land once again on the bottle of Jameson when I open the cabinet for a glass. I've never been one to drink excessively, but the urge to do so now is strong. Anything to make these unwanted feelings disappear.

I turn from the sink after filling my glass with water, and find Gwen standing in the doorway, watching me curiously.

"Would you like me to heat up some of the food Mrs. Myers sent over?" she asks, coming to stand opposite me and leaning against the counter.

I shake my head instead of answering her verbally. I'm not sure how steady my voice will be at the moment.

She glances down at her feet, then brings her head back up.

"What did you mean when you asked Daniel if he remembered what you said about Bandit?"

I take a swallow of the cool liquid, then set it down on the counter before crossing my arms over my chest. She briefly looks at my arms before flicking her gaze back up to mine.

"He's been trouble training and hasn't been the nicest horse to be around," I tell her. I've been waiting for this question.

Her eyes widen, and a hint of fear flashes across her face. Before she has a chance to respond, I reassure her.

"He was never close to him when I had him out there with me, Gwen. I wouldn't put him in danger."

It only takes a moment before she nods. "I know."

The rope around my neck loosens with her words. I don't like her thinking I would be so careless as to put either of her kids in danger. Those kids have wormed their way into my heart and I'm not sure there's a way for them to get out again. Already I know I'd put down my life for them.

"I saw that you started tearing down the house," she states softly.

The reminder of what I was doing before my shower earlier lodges a sharp pain in my chest. It seemed fitting to start tearing down the house I was supposed to share with my family on the eve of when they died. I started it, then stopped when my back suddenly gave out. Part of it was due to my total lack of finesse tearing it down, the anger I felt making me clumsy and uncaring of how my back would be affected. Now that I'd started, I wanted it done and over with.

"Yeah," I answer gruffly.

She moves away from the counter and comes toward me. The closer she gets the more tense my body gets. I left the living room to put some much-needed space between us, and here she is now closing the gap.

Once she's standing in front of me, she puts her hand on the arm with scars and looks up at me with concerned eyes. I feel the touch everywhere. It's like, now that my desire for her has slipped by my defenses, it wants to consume me. Or rather, I want to consume her. I've gone years without any form of intimate contact, I haven't *wanted* to touch anyone, but now it's damn near all I can think about when I'm around her.

My jaw tics and my hands grip the counter behind me as I fight back the urge to reach for her.

"Are you okay?"

My smile is tight when I respond. "Yes."

She frowns, and damned if it doesn't make my chest tighten. The hand she still has on my arm is warm, and I look down at it. Her fingernails are cut short and painted a soft pink color. Her hands are so small that they'd be dwarfed in mine if I were to lace them together.

She must see something on my face as I look down at her hand, because seconds later, she jerks it away. I bring my gaze back to her and see a bright flush on her cheeks, and I know she must have felt the connection too. It still amazes me that she's not affected by my scars. I'm not jaded enough to believe that all people will be repulsed by them, but it's as if she doesn't see them at all.

When she moves to take a step back, I reach out and seize her wrist before I realize what I'm doing. Our eyes lock the minute my hand touches hers and from the silent communication between us, we both know the other felt the electrical zap at contact.

"Don't," I whisper, and gently pull her toward me. "I like it when you touch me."

I'm an idiot for asking for more from her, and I have no idea why I am, but the thought of her not touching me now is something I just can't comprehend. Even the innocent touch of her hand on my arm is something I need. I'll regret it later and feel like a bastard, but right at this moment the longing is much too strong to ignore.

I lean back against the counter and widen my stance. She watches with cautious eyes as I continue to pull her toward me. With shaky hands and shallow breathing, I put my arms around her waist and pull her chest against mine. I don't know why I'm so nervous. Before Clara, I had had my fair share of women, but this feels different somehow.

With her so close, we lose eye contact. Her arms go around my waist and she rests her head against my chest.

The embrace is both innocent and intimate. Feeling the warmth of her body, her soft curves against the hard muscles of mine, sends blood rushing to my cock, but it also feels comforting. I squeeze my eyes closed at how good this feels, how *right* it feels to have her in my arms, like this is where she's supposed to be. I want that to be true so fucking much, but I know it can't be.

I hold Gwen in my arms and concentrate on memorizing the feeling of having her there. I wish we could stay like this forever, but it's not possible. Not with the guilt I still carry. Not knowing I let my family down. Gwen and her two kids are too important. I won't take that chance with them. There's too much to lose.

So instead, I'll soak up every single second I have with her and Kelsey and Daniel, and keep these moments locked away and only let them out when the pain gets to be too much.

We stand like this for several minutes, enjoying the feeling of being in each other's arms. I want to put my fist through the wall when the moment is interrupted by my phone ringing. Gwen pulls back before I'm ready for her to and looks over at my phone sitting on the counter. When I make no move to grab it and instead tighten my arms around her, she looks up at me.

"Are you going to get that?"

"No," I tell her, never moving my eyes off her.

When the phone stops ringing, her forehead lands on the center of my chest, and her hands clench the back of my shirt tighter, like she doesn't want to let me go either. A growl leaves the back of my throat when my damn phone starts ringing again. I'd love nothing more than to chuck it against the wall.

"Alexander," Gwen calls, pulling my murderous gaze from the phone. I lose the glare when my eyes land on her. "Maybe it's important."

Right now, I don't care if it's important. All I care about is keeping Gwen where she is. But I know that's not being rational.

Reluctantly, I loosen my arms and she takes a step back. I stalk over to the phone and snatch it from the counter. Looking at the screen, I release a tired sigh.

It's my mom, and I know there's no way I can put her off anymore. It's been a couple of weeks since I've spoken to her and she knows what tomorrow is. She's a mother and her natural instinct is to worry about her kids. She knows how tough the anniversary of their deaths is. If I don't answer now, she'll only continue to call back until I do. Or even worse, call the sheriff and have him come check on me. Yes, she's done that before when I went weeks without answering her calls.

Pulling in a deep breath, I swipe my finger across the screen.

"Hey, Mom," I answer.

Gwen's eyes widen when she hears who's on the phone. A moment later, she leaves the kitchen, I assume to give me privacy.

"Alexander," my mom breaths through the phone. I can tell she's surprised I answered.

"How are you?" I ask, leaning against the counter and crossing my ankles.

"Much better now that I've heard your voice."

"Mom, I'm—" I start to apologize.

"No, Alexander," she interrupts. "Your dad and I have been talking and he's made me realize something. I know I hover too much. I know I've smothered you over the years since...." She trails off, not needing to clarify. "I just worry about you. I hate knowing you're in pain," she finishes quietly.

I twist my neck from side to side, trying to relieve the tension I always get when I talk to my mom. She doesn't mean to add more stress, and I'm sure it would upset her if she realized how much she's caused me with her worrying. I haven't had the heart to tell her because I know she's only doing it out of love. That, and the fact it wasn't just me who lost Clara and Rayne. She lost a daughter and granddaughter.

"I get it. I really do, but you've got to stop worrying so much, okay?" I hear her sniffle on the other end of the line and it makes me feel like a dick, but I press forward. "I'm fine. Yes, it still hurts to breathe sometimes, but I'm getting there." I pull air in my lungs and let it out slowly, knowing this is going to hurt her, but also knowing it needs to be said. "I love you, Mom, and I know you mean well, but when you constantly call and ask how I'm doing, it helps keep that wound open."

Her hiccupping sob guts me, and I close my eyes. When I open them, they meet Gwen's over the bar. She's standing on the other side of the couch with one of the puppies in her arms, watching me.

I'm not sure if she can hear what I'm saying, but I'm sure my expression says enough.

"Oh, Alexander, I'm so, so sorry, baby," my mom cries softly, her voice tearful. "I never meant to make it harder on you."

Still keeping my eyes on Gwen, I console her. "I know. And I love you for caring so much."

She sniffs again and then there's a shuffling sound. Next comes the deep murmur of my father's voice talking to my mom before he gets on the line.

"Son."

"Hey, Dad. How is she?"

"She'll be fine." He sighs. "I heard what you told her and it was something she needed to hear. She can't keep smothering you. She needs to let you heal."

I feel like an asshole because I know my mom wants me to heal, she's just not giving me what I need to do so. I'm not entirely sure I deserve to heal after what I've done.

"How are you doing?" my dad asks.

You'd think that after upsetting my mom to explain that her constant worry wasn't helping me that having my dad ask the same thing would bother me. There's a difference between my mom asking versus my dad. I love my mom just as much as my dad, and I appreciate both of them worrying, but whereas my dad takes my answer for what it is and leaves it at that, my mom will dig and dig, thinking if she gets deep enough I'll reveal my true feelings.

Knowing he's asking because of what tomorrow is, I say honestly, "I'm doing the best I can."

He's quiet for a moment, then says quietly, "You need us, you call."

"Will do, Dad. Thanks."

He clears his throat, then changes the subject like I knew he would. It's not that he doesn't care, it's that he knows not to push.

My eyes are still glued to Gwen, who's now holding the puppy closer to her face. She watches me curiously.

"Your mom wants to come for a visit. I've put her off for as long as I can, but I'm not sure how much longer I'll be able to."

I break my gaze from Gwen and turn around. It's hard to think about anything other than Gwen when I'm looking at her. I think that's part of the reason I want to keep her here so badly. The guilt and pain don't consume me as strongly when she's here.

It's been almost a year since I've seen my parents, and I know it hurts my mom that it's been so long. As much as she bugs the hell out of me, I miss them both.

"Give me a couple weeks and tell her to plan a trip."

"You sure?" my dad asks.

"Yeah."

We talk for a few more minutes about nothing in particular before we hang up. I keep my back turned to the living room, trying to gather my thoughts before facing Gwen again. The woman has me wrapped up in feelings I haven't felt in a long time, and I have no idea what to do with them. With fear of sounding like a pansy-ass, Gwen's put me through the emotional wringer.

Instead of going back to the living room, I opt to make myself a plate of the leftovers Gwen brought with her. Mrs. Myers only lives a few miles from me and there's been several occasions she's called on me for help around the house. Both of us, along with a couple more houses, are the only people out this far from town. I don't mind the times I've had to help the little old lady out, and whenever I make one of my rare trips to town, I always call her to see if she needs anything. A couple times when I went by her place she insisted I stay for dinner. She's a really good cook, so when I bite into the home-made mashed potatoes and the oven-roasted turkey, my taste buds nearly explode with pleasure. I scarf down the plate of food in no time.

When I walk back into the living room a few minutes later, I only find Daniel and Kelsey.

"Where's your mom?" I ask Daniel.

He pauses in playing with the puppies with a couple of the

wooden figurines and looks up at me. Shrugging, he says, "She said she was going to the bathroom."

My eyes immediately move to the hallway, where I have a view of the bathroom door. It's open with the light off. Not caring that she uses the bathroom in my bedroom, but finding it weird that she would do so, I make my way down the hallway to the door down at the end.

When I step through the doorway, I'm both surprised and pissed at what I see. Gwen's sitting on the bed with the pictures from my nightstand in her hand. I don't know why it makes me angry that she's looking at them. It's not that she went through my nightstand. Yes, I'm a private guy, but with Gwen I've been more open than I have with anyone else in a long time. It's just... I don't like her looking at what's caused all my pain and heartache, knowing I'm the reason I'm going through it.

"What are you doing in here?" I ask, my tone harsher than I intended it to be.

She jumps up from the bed, startled both by my presence and tone. She looks down guiltily at the pictures still in her hand before bringing her eyes up to meet mine. I'm trying to rein in the anger, but I know some of it seeps through. I'm sure she didn't purposely come in here to snoop, I just don't know why she is in here.

"I'm sorry," she says, her face drawn down into a frown. "I was looking for my earrings I left on the nightstand. I thought maybe they fell in the drawer."

My hand, already in my jeans pocket, fingers the earrings I have in there. For some insane reason, I've been carrying them around with me since the day James saw them on the bar. Maybe it makes me feel closer to her having them so close to me. Or maybe I'm just fucking weird. For whatever reason, when I get undressed at night, I place them on the nightstand, then put them in my pocket the next morning.

I pull them from my pocket and show them to her.

"Oh," she says. She doesn't ask why I have them in my pocket, and I don't offer the information. "Thank you."

She doesn't say anything for a moment and makes no move to take the earrings from me. She simply looks down at the pictures. I grind my teeth, holding back the urge to snatch them from her hands and stuff them back in the drawer. I know exactly what she's looking at, I just don't know what she's thinking.

"She's beautiful," she says softly, rubbing her finger over one of the pictures. "They both were." She looks up at me and sadness lines her face.

My gaze drops to the photo. It's the one I was holding outside the other day. I swallow thickly, trying to push my emotions back. I don't say a word as I stand there and watch her look at the next one. It's like I'm frozen on the spot, even as my mind screams at me to take them from her and hide them. I still love my lost family, but I'm ashamed of what happened to them. What I did to them.

The next photo is of Clara and me standing in front of the fire-place. She was six months pregnant. I was holding the sonogram we had done earlier that day that finally showed us the sex of our baby against her rounded belly. The first couple times she was being stub-born and not showing her goods to the doctor, but that time we got lucky. At the bottom of the picture, Clara had printed the words Our First Family Photo.

The last image is the sonogram itself. It's not often I bring the photos out anymore—it's too painful to look at them—so to see them now and tomorrow being what it is, makes me feel like one giant pincushion with thousands of needles being pushed into it.

Her head finally lifts, and there's tears glistening in her eyes. After blinking a few times, she turns and gently sets the pictures back in the drawer and closes it. I pull in a few deep breaths while she has her back turned.

When she does turn back around, I say the first thing that comes to mind. "You should leave."

I regret the words as soon as I say them, but I don't take them back. I need to be alone. My reprieve has come to an end, and she and the kids need to leave before I completely lose it. I feel the threads of my control snapping, and I don't want them to see me like that.

The pain that crosses her face has the ache in my chest escalating. I hate myself for putting it there.

She nods, then looks down at her hands. After a moment, she walks toward me. I want to reach out to her and apologize as she passes me, but I don't. If I do, I know I won't let her go, and she needs to.

I follow her, but stay at the mouth of the hallway as she tells the kids to gather their things. Daniel grumbles and looks sad. I look at Kelsey, and the expression on her face says it all: Disappointment and despair. Between Gwen's and the kids' reactions, I want to stab myself in the chest. It'll likely hurt less than the pain I'm feeling now.

Gwen gives me a sad smile as she and the kids walk to the door. I walk behind them and step out onto the porch. After Daniel says goodbye and Kelsey looks at me blankly, Gwen tells them to go to the car.

"I'm sorry. I didn't mean to snoop," she says, hurt evident in her voice.

"I know." I stuff my hands in my pockets to keep from touching her. "I just...." I clear my throat and look out across the yard. "I need to be alone."

She lifts her hand like she's going to reach out to me, and I hold my breath, both hoping she doesn't and silently begging her to. Making her decision, she drops her hand.

"Thank you for letting the kids and me stay for a bit. They really enjoyed spending time with you."

She nods and tries to smile, but it falls away too quickly to be real. I wonder if she enjoyed it as well, or if she regrets coming. I know I'm giving her mixed signals, and I feel like shit doing that to her, but I'm so fucked-up right now, I have no idea what I'm doing. I want to grab on to her and never let her go. I want to cherish her kids and love them like they should be loved. I want to care for Gwen like she deserves. I want to be the man they need, but I'm so damn scared of failing. I so afraid my past won't allow me to be the person they should have.

Looking over to the car and seeing the kids occupied, I do what I know I shouldn't, but am unable to stop myself. I step closer to Gwen and cup the side of her face. Her skin's so soft compared to mine, and I wish I could feel it against me all the time.

I dip my head and very gently lay my lips across hers. I hear her breath hitch as she holds still, letting me do what I both want and need. I don't take the kiss far, giving us both just enough. My lips slide across hers and she tastes like vanilla, just as I remembered from yesterday. We open our mouths at the same time, and I meet her tongue with mine.

The kiss is soft and gentle, and I pull back before it can go any further. I hurt from the loss, and from the look on her face, she does too.

Without another word from either of us, she turns and walks down the steps to the truck, and I'm once again left watching what could have been drive away. My hands slide inside my pockets and brush against the earrings I never gave back to her.

I DRIVE DOWN THE small embankment and park my truck at what is the location of all my heartache. I turn the truck off, and with a pain so sharp it feels like I'm being stabbed to death, look at the two crosses hammered into the ground. It wasn't my doing. I'm not sure who did it, but they've been there for a while. I see them every time I go to town, but it never hurts so much to see them as when I'm this close. I try to avoid them as much as possible, but there's no avoiding them on this day.

Taking a deep breath, I reach over and grab the bottle of Jameson and get out of the truck. It's ironic, because normally this time of year the water is pretty low; however, the year that Clara and Rayne died, we'd had an unseasonably warm and rainy winter, so the water was pretty high. Had it not been...

I wipe the thought away, because there's no fucking sense in thinking about what-ifs. It won't change a damn thing.

I sit down and lean against the pillar. Before I can stop them, my eyes land on the spot where everything was taken from me. Every year, on the day they died, I come out here and spend the night, using only my jacket and alcohol to keep me warm.

Memory after memory flood my mind, and I try to chase them away with the Jameson. It never works, no matter how much I drink, and that's why I always end up plastered. Their ghosts haunt me the most when I'm here. This is my penance for not saving them. It's what I deserve, and the very least I can do is suffer for them.

I take a big swig from the bottle, then another, and another. It burns going down my throat, but after the first few swallows the pain fades. Raising my knees, I rest my arms on top of them and let the bottle dangle between my legs. My head clunks back against the concrete, and I close my eyes. As soon as I do, the screams of pain and the wails of my baby girl swarm me, pulling me into a dark abyss that I wonder if one day I won't be able to escape from.

Chapter Fifteen

Gwendolyn

I STARE SIGHTLESSLY across the room as I fold clothes. Memories of Alexander's face yesterday when he caught me looking at the photos plague me. He looked so broken and torn. And angry. There was a tic in his jaw and his body was tense, like he was seconds away from pouncing. I get his anger and his sorrow. I shouldn't have been in there. I should have waited until he was done with his phone call and asked. I didn't realize the ramifications of looking in his drawer. When I saw those pictures, sorrow slammed into me like a sledgehammer. I had no connection to the woman and baby, but for some reason, I still felt the loss of them as if I did. That feeling grew when I saw the pain on Alexander's face.

Although I understood his need to be alone when he told me I should leave, the rejection still hurt. His wounds were wide open because of the impending anniversary of their deaths, and I wanted nothing more than to be with him, to show him comfort and not let him be alone during his grief. No one should ever have to go through such a heavy emotion alone.

The need to see him now, to reassure myself he's okay, is strong, and the more I sit here and stew over it, the stronger it gets.

I look up when Kelsey walks into the living room. My eyes fall to the standard crossword puzzle book she has rolled up in her hand. I lift my gaze to hers, confused, because ever since Alexander gave her the one he made, she hasn't used the other ones.

I drop the towel I was folding in my lap and ask, "Did something happened to the book Alexander made you?"

She looks at me for a moment before shaking her head and looking down at the book in her hand.

"Why aren't you using that one?"

She doesn't answer, but she doesn't need to. I saw the answer in her eyes before she managed to clear it away. She's hurt from him turning us away yesterday.

"Come sit." I pat the cushion beside me.

She comes to the couch and sits down stiffly. I turn so I'm facing her and make her look at me.

"I know you're hurt from yesterday." When I get nothing from her, I forge ahead. I want her to better understand Alexander's behavior so she doesn't think it has anything to do with her, Daniel, or me. "Something happened a few years ago that hurt him terribly."

Understanding dawns on her face, and I get the sense that she already knows he's hurting, she just doesn't know why. The look doesn't surprise me. It's said that those who are going through pain recognize it in others. I've seen the way Kelsey looks at him. Even at such a young age, there was sympathy and recognition of mutual anguish.

"He lost his wife and baby, who he loved dearly." I wrap my arm around her shoulders when her eyes start to water. "I'm not saying this to hurt you. I want you to know he's in pain, and I don't want you to think his actions have anything to do with you or Daniel." I wipe away the single tear that slides down her cheek. I hate knowing this is hurting her. She's too young to be going through so much pain. Losing her father was enough, and I know hearing about Alexander hurts her even more.

She looks at me with questions in her eyes, and I hold my breath, hoping beyond hope that she'll speak. Disappointment has my shoulders sagging when the look disappears and she turns her head away.

"Hey." I call her attention back to me. Once I have her eyes again, I tell her quietly, "You know how you're really sad about losing your dad?" Although the therapist said to not shy away from bringing up Will because Kelsey needs to learn that it's okay to talk about him, it still hurts when I do. Every time he's mentioned it brings fresh pain to her face, but this is the best way to get her to understand Alexander's situation.

She nods once, though her face drops with the movement.

"Sometimes people react differently than others when they lose someone they love. Alexander's very sad for losing his family, but he's also angry because they were taken from him. Sometimes it's hard to hold that anger in and we may accidentally hurt the ones we care about."

I stop and give her time to process what I've said, and she frowns as she thinks it over.

"Do you understand what I'm saying?" I ask after a few moments.

Her head dips down, indicating she does. I tuck a piece of hair behind her ear and lean closer so our eyes are level.

"It doesn't mean he doesn't care, he just wanted us to go so he wouldn't hurt us. He needed to be alone for a while."

Leaving him behind, knowing of the heartache he was going through, was hard, but I understood. Especially when I saw his face when we pulled away. I saw the turmoil. He wanted us there, but for some reason I think it made it harder on him. I know he didn't want us to see him in the state he was headed for. I could have dealt with it, but like him, I didn't want the kids to see it either. So we left, even though it tore me apart to do so.

I lean forward and kiss Kelsey's cheek, then pull back. "I love you."

She doesn't respond, but I know she returns the feeling.

Kelsey goes back to her room, and I return to folding laundry. Or rather, I try to. I'm too distracted, so the clothes are only receiving a half-hearted attempt.

I spot my phone on the coffee table, and it only takes me seconds to come to a decision. I snag the device from the table and speed-dial Jeremy. He answers on the third ring.

"Hey, Jeremy. Can I ask a big favor?"

———

THIRTY MINUTES LATER, I'm turning down the road that leads to Alexander's land. After calling Jeremy and asking if he could watch the kids for a while, I took off, an unexplainable force driving me to see Alexander.

I make it to the bridge over Hallow's Creek, and my stomach bottoms out when I see Alexander's truck at the bottom of the embankment, almost under the bridge. Curiosity and dread have me pulling over and exiting my vehicle. As I walk down the small hill, I thank God that his truck shows no sign of an accident. My eyes catch on two crosses that have been placed in the ground, one smaller than the other, and I know they are for his wife and daughter. An ache forms in my chest, because this is the reason he's here.

Looking around, at first I don't see him, but I know he has to be here. When I do finally spot him, he's hunched over with his arms resting on his raised knees and his head hanging between his legs. The position is telling enough, but when I call his name and he looks up at me, my heart feels like it's been pierced with a serrated knife.

His face is wet with tears and his eyes are bloodshot. A bottle of alcohol dangles from one hand, and it looks to be about three-quarters empty. The temperature isn't quite freezing, but it's still cold enough and he's only wearing a light jacket. I get the feeling this isn't the first time he's done this. I'd even go so far as to say he does this every year on the same day. This is the place he lost everything. The thought brings tears to my eyes.

Cautiously, I walk over and get down on my knees in front of him. Even through my jeans, the ground is cold. He watches me with bleary eyes. When I take the bottle from his hand, he blinks at me slowly, like he's unsure of what's going on. A gust of wind swirls around us, and I feel it in my bones, but he doesn't seem to notice.

"Alexander," I say in an agonized whisper. Seeing him like this tears me up inside.

"What?" he grunts.

"What are you doing to yourself?" I ask the question that I'm pretty sure I already know the answer to.

When he answers, his voice is strong and much clearer than you'd think coming from someone who's drunk almost a full fifth of whiskey.

"Paying the price the only way I know how."

He reaches down by his hip and produces another bottle of alcohol, this one full and unopened. I contemplate taking the bottle from him, but decide against it for the moment. As much as it pains me to see him drink his sorrows away, this is his way of coping and who am I do deny him? I saw the beer in the fridge when we were staying with him, but they were pushed all the way to the back, which makes me think him drinking is a rare occurrence.

"Why are you here?" he asks before taking a big swallow of the amber liquid, then wiping his mouth with the back of his hand.

"I was worried about you. You shouldn't be alone."

He looks at me for a moment, his eyes drooping slightly, before he looks away. His jaw is tight and the hand not holding the bottle balls into a fist. "You shouldn't be here."

"I'm sorry," I tell him. "But I won't leave you here by yourself."

His eyes swing back to me and the look in them reminds me of the day we first met in the market. Despondency, regret, and anger flash in their depths.

"I don't want you here," he growls as he leans forward.

Although I know the anger is born out of guilt and pain, I still flinch at his tone. He sees it, and for a moment it looks like he's going to apologize as torment replaces the guilt and pain, but then the emotion is gone and his face goes blank. His head drops back against the concrete with a thud and he closes his eyes.

Walking on my knees until I'm on the other side of him, I settle my back against the pillar. Our shoulders touch as I wrap my arms around my knees. It's early evening in winter time, so the sun will be setting shortly. The temperature is sure to drop at least ten degrees, and I'll likely be frozen come the end of this, but there's no way I'm leaving him out here alone. He can push and shove all he wants, but it'll get him nowhere.

We sit this way for a while, neither of us saying a word. I don't want to interrupt his thoughts, I just want him to know I'm here if he needs me. Every so often, the breeze will pick up, sending a shiver through my body. I try to hold off the shakes, but they end up getting the best of me and I start shivering. His arm that's pressed against me moves occasionally when he lifts the bottle to his lips.

After thirty minutes, I feel eyes on me and look over. He's watching me with a frown and the side of his face that's scarred is pulled tight. I can smell the whiskey on his breath every time he breathes out, and it mixes with his own personal scent.

His frown turns into a scowl and he turns his head away from me with a muttered "fuck" before he clumsily climbs to his feet. I make a move to get up to help, but he shoots me a look and growls, "Stay there."

I watch as he staggers his way to his truck. His movements are sluggish, but he's still moving relatively well for having drunk so much.

He slams the truck door, and I'm surprised when he comes back with a blanket.

"Sit up," he barks when he's standing in front of me. I ignore the harsh command and do as he says. He unfolds the blanket and places it around my shoulders, making sure to tuck it around the front of me. The gesture is sweet, and I know he's doing it because he cares, even if his tone and attitude say otherwise.

"Thank you," I state once he's back to leaning on the pillar. He doesn't answer, just takes another swallow of his drink.

Again, we sit in silence. The sun is starting to set behind the trees, leaving behind a beautiful purple and pink sky, and I'm grateful for the blanket. I lean my head back against the pillar and rest my eyes. A few minutes later, I open them when Alexander starts to talk, his voice devoid of emotion. His eyes are closed.

"I met Clara the summer my family and I went to help my aunt and uncle move. They lived a few hours away from here and were moving across the country for my uncle's new job. On the second day we were there helping them pack up, the family that was buying the house came by to take measurements for a back porch they were going to add on. It was Clara's family. I had only just turned fifteen at the time, and she was fourteen, but I remember thinking she was the prettiest girl I had ever seen. We struck up a conversation, but they were only there for about thirty minutes before they left again, so I wasn't able to learn much about her. It bothered me, because I wanted to see her again. I thought I wouldn't get the chance, but on the fourth day, they came back and then again a day later, which was our last day there."

As he talks, his expression turns soft. It's a look I've never seen on his face, but one that makes him look devastatingly handsome.

"Each visit was short, but with each one, I dreaded her leaving. She was so sweet and soft-spoken, but also had a sense of humor a mile long. We'd sit outside on the porch and make each other laugh until our stomachs hurt. She was one of the easiest people to talk to. On the last day, I got her phone number and promised to call her. I did as soon as I got home, and for a year and a half, that's how we communicated."

He stops for a moment and stares off into space, as if lost in thought, then shakes his head and continues. I keep my eyes on him, not wanting to miss anything.

"The day I got my driver's license, I begged my mom to let me go see her, but she wouldn't. She said it was too far to drive with my newly earned driving status. It took me six months to convince her to let me go, and even then, I had to pull over and call her every hour."

He chuckles, but it sounds dry.

"We talked for a year and a half on the phone, but when we saw each other again in person, we were both so nervous. It was easy on the phone, because we weren't face-to-face. We finally managed to get over our awkwardness and it felt just as natural as when we first met and then when we spoke on the phone. I visited her once a month and we became really close over the years. We both dated other people, but for me, none of the girls really mattered. I knew I had feelings for Clara, but she lived so far away, so I tried pushing the feelings aside, but it never worked."

He takes a swallow of his drink, then uses his arm to wipe his mouth. I can't take my eyes off his face. It's so animated when he speaks of the girl he fell in love with as a teenager.

He drops one of his legs and rests the bottle on the top of his thigh.

"We attended the same college and it wasn't until I was a junior and she a sophomore that things changed between us. We started dating and making plans for the future. We married after college, and decided right away to start a family. Her degree was in interior design, so she was able to work from home. It was perfect for us, because she wanted to be at home with our kids. We were both so excited. We tried for months, but she never got pregnant. It took two years...."

He trails off, and I know from the look on his face whatever he's about to say will be excruciating for him. I clutch the blanket in my fists to keep from reaching out to him, worried the gesture won't be welcome. His body is tenses, as if he's barely holding himself together.

"She lost the baby when she was two months pregnant," he says, then stops to clear his throat when his voice cracks. "She was six weeks pregnant when she lost the second." I suck in a breath and my hand flies to my mouth. Immediate tears fill my eyes. But he's not done. "At four months, she miscarried our third baby, and at one month miscarried our fourth. After that, I had decided we weren't going to try for a fifth. Each miscarriage killed us a little inside, and watching Clara go through each one became too much, but she wanted to try one last time."

Unable to stand the small gap between us, I scoot closer to him. The sun is below the horizon, leaving us in shadows. I know he has to be freezing, but the warmth of the alcohol and the memories he's facing right now must be giving him the ability to ignore the cold.

I watch the hand that's not holding the bottle flex back and forth into a fist as he continues to talk, further breaking my heart for him.

"We were so careful. She made it thirty-two weeks before the baby decided to come." A smile touches his face for a brief second before it slips free. "She was so tiny and incredibly gorgeous."

He pulls a picture out of his pocket, and I recognize it as one of the ones in his nightstand drawer. It's the one of them in the hospital. He fingers the photo with reverence, likes it's one of the most precious things to him.

"Due to her being so early and her lungs not being fully developed, after a visit just long enough to snap this picture, she was rushed to the neonatal unit, where she was given the chance to grow stronger. She was there for seven weeks before she was deemed ready to go home."

The bottle drops from his hand and tips over. The amber liquid spills and runs down the embankment toward the water. My eyes swing back to Alexander to catch him dropping his head in his hands, where he fists his hair. His shoulders slump as he breaks down right in front of my eyes. I get on my knees and move closer to him. I hate seeing him in this state, and *I* need to reach out to him, but I think *he* needs me to as well. As soon as I touch his shoulder, his head whips up and he stares at me with anguished eyes. The look terrifies me. His pain has become my pain.

"Alexander." I have no idea what I want to say, but I need to say something to help wipe the immense pain from his face. Before I get a chance to come up with the right words, he stops me.

"No," he says roughly. "This is something you need to know."

I nod and sit back on my legs, but still keep my hand on his shoulder; my need to touch him, to silently let him know I'm here is too great. My heart pounds heavily in my chest. I know what he's about to say will be devastating.

He squeezes his eyes shut for a moment, then digs the heels of his hands into the sockets and rubs so hard it has to hurt.

"We were so damn happy we were able to finally bring her home," he continues, his voice so scratchy it sounds like he's been screaming for hours. "The weather was rainy and warm for that time of year. I remember looking over and seeing the smile on Clara's face, knew I had the same big grin of happiness. By the time Rayne was released, it was already dark and the lights from all the Christmas decorations we passed made Clara's face glow even more."

I tense, afraid of where he's going, and I silently pray I'm wrong. My stomach rolls when he starts talking again, his words and the sorrowful way he says them shredding my heart into tiny pieces, then crushing them into dust.

"We were coming up on Hallow's Creek when a car coming the other way swerved in front of us. I jerked the wheel to avoid hitting him head-on. I could hear Clara screaming in my ear, but I was too focused on trying to keep the car on the road. It was slick and there were puddles. I hit one and hydroplaned. We hit the shoulder sideways and the impact flipped the car over." His terror-filled eyes move to a spot close to the bridge on the side of the road, and I know he's seeing where the car started its first roll. "We rolled four times until the car stopped on Clara's side."

Tears flood my cheeks and my hand digs into his shoulder. His tone is no longer hoarse, but now blank, revealing no emotion at all. It's only the tears sliding down his face that show his pain.

"Alexander, please stop," I croak, not sure I can hear the rest.

He doesn't stop though, and I force myself to listen to him, somehow knowing he needs to do this, even if it does destroy me. My pain is nothing compared to his, so I can do this for him.

"It was the heat from the flames that brought me to. They hadn't made it to me yet, but they were close. The tiny wails of my beautiful baby girl were the first thing I heard, but they only lasted a few seconds before they abruptly stopped. I was barely conscious, but the silence scared the shit out of me. I needed to hear her cry so I knew she was okay."

He stops talking all of a sudden and looks around frantically, a look of panic on his face. I realize what he's looking for and hand him the almost empty bottle. The relief floods his face when he grabs it and downs the rest. I wish there is more I can do to help dull the pain this is causing him, but all I can do is sit here, helpless.

"My fucking legs and right arm were trapped between the seat and the steering wheel. It was dark outside, so when I looked to the back seat to find my little girl, all I could see was darkness and what looked like water. That's when Clara came to. She immediately started screaming Rayne's name and tried to get to the back seat, but she was trapped as well. The dash had crushed her legs. The flames coming from the dash were getting closer to me, but I didn't feel the heat anymore. My sole focus was to get to Rayne and Clara. Clara looked at me and begged and pleaded for me to get Rayne out. It wasn't until the water started rising and covering Clara that I realized we'd rolled down the embankment and were in the creek. Fear like I've never felt before seized me, and I started jerking as hard as I could on my arm that was trapped. I couldn't reach Clara or Rayne with my left, and no matter how hard I pulled and yanked, I couldn't fucking get my right one free.

"Clara was smashed up against her door and the water was creeping up on her fast and there was no way for her to get away from it. She was screaming and crying hysterically, while I kept trying to get free. The flames reached my leg first, and I felt and smelled as my jeans were burned away. Then it hit my flesh and it was excruciating. The pain from being burned tried to pull me under, but I fought to stay conscious. I couldn't take my eyes away from Clara as the water reached her face and swallowed her up."

He stops and his breathing becomes labored as he stares off into space. His eyes look wild, and I know he's reliving the horror of that moment. I grab hold of his wet cheeks, the blanket falling from my shoulders, and make him look at me, desperate for that look to disappear. The roughness of his beard on the left side feels so different than the smoothness of his scars on the other side.

His eyes meet mine and they appear unfocused, as if he's not seeing me.

"Alexander," I call, making sure my voice comes out strong when I feel anything but. "Look at me." I give him a shake.

I don't know if it's my tone or the fact I'm so close to him, but he seems to snap out of it. He flinches, but I don't let that affect me.

"You're not there anymore," I tell him quietly. "You're here with me right now."

His eyes flick back and forth between mine and he frowns, then gives me a nod. I'm surprised when his head drops from my hand and he lays it against my shoulder. Next, his arms wrap around my middle, and I'm forced to get back up on my knees. He's hunched over me as he seeks comfort.

His voice comes out muffled and broken when he speaks next. I already know what he's going to say, but it still hurts nonetheless.

"She begged and begged me to help Rayne up until the water covered her face, and even then, her eyes pleaded with me until she couldn't hold her breath anymore. I watched her drown, and I couldn't do a damn thing. I let my baby and wife die." I'm shaking my head no, but don't get a chance to voice my objection. "I tried so fucking hard, Gwen, I swear I did, but I couldn't get free. My arm had gouges from me pulling so hard. When the flames reached my upper body, I wanted it to devour me. I wanted to die. If they couldn't live, then neither would I. Right as it got to my face, someone yanked open my door. It was pouring outside so the rain coming in helped control the fire long enough for them to throw water on me. I already felt dead inside when they pulled me from the car. The pain of the burns was searing and unbearable, but the pain of knowing I'd lost my wife and newborn baby couldn't compare."

My shirt is soaked by the time he's done. My own face is drenched in tears as well. Even though I was the one giving him comfort, I still cling to him just as tightly as he clings to me. His weight sags against me, and I know it's not only from the alcohol, but from emotional exhaustion.

We stay this way for a while, him with his arms wrapped around my waist, his head against my shoulder, and me with my head resting on top of his. I pull the blanket around us both.

After a few minutes, he pulls back, and his tired eyes look up at me. I wipe away my own tears and sit back on my legs. My eyes feel swollen from crying and his carry so much pain. I don't know what to do to help him. There's really nothing I *can* do to help him.

"I'm sorry, Alexander." It sounds so inadequate for what he's gone through. "I'm so sorry for what you went through. For what they went through. I can't imagine...." I close my eyes and take a deep breath before opening them again. I can't even finish the thought because it's too incomprehensible.

He swallows, then nods. It looks like he wants to say more, but his eyes drop to my shirt and notices it's drenched.

"Shit," he grumbles scratchily. "Sorry."

It's a weird thing to notice at a time like this, but I think it's more of an avoidance thing. Now that he's told his story and has relived the pain, he's only too willing to push it aside and try to focus on something else. From the look in his eyes, his attempt isn't successful. I have a feeling it won't ever be successful. How does someone recover from something like that?

I shake my head, letting him know I don't care about my shirt.

"Please don't apologize." It almost comes out as begging. I feel restless because there's so much I want to say, but I know none of it will ever be good enough. "I don't know what to do," I tell him honestly. "I wish so much there was something I could do to help your pain, but I know there's not."

"You've helped me already," he responds quietly, confusing me.

He looks down at his hands and flexes his fingers. I pull the blanket tighter around my shoulders when a gust of wind sweeps over us.

He's quiet for a few minutes, then turns hazy eyes my way. He opens his mouth to speak, then closes it and shakes his head, as if mentally warring with himself. Pulling in a deep breath, he tries again. "I can't drive." He looks over to my truck, then back to me. "But we need to get you out of the cold. Can you take me home?"

Pleased that he's asked, I nod. I'd stay out here in the cold all night if I had to, but I'm glad he wants to go home. I know being here makes him feel closer to his wife and baby, but the way he's drinking his sorrows and guilt away hinders his grieving process. We'll never forget the ones we love, they'll be with us always, but we need to learn to live without them, to not let the pain of their loss rule our lives. Alexander hasn't been grieving, he's been living in his pain all these years. He's not learning to move on, he's staying in place and immersing himself in guilt.

"Yes."

I stand, still holding onto the blanket, and wait for him to follow. He doesn't at first, just sits there and looks around in the dark, as if searching for something. I give him a few minutes as I gather the two bottles of Jameson and a brown paper bag. It takes him a moment, but then he slowly gets to his feet. He's surprisingly steadier than I thought he would be, but his movements are sluggish as we make our way over to my truck. His eyes linger on the two crosses we pass, and even in the dark I can see fresh heartache on his face.

He climbs inside without saying a word. His eyes appear distant, like he's not in himself right now. I throw the blanket and trash in the back.

"Do you have your keys?" I ask.

I get a single nod in response. Walking over to his truck, I lock the doors, then go back to mine. It's cold inside, but thankfully my truck heats up quickly. Neither of us speak as we make the five-minute drive to his house.

He doesn't ask me inside, but I get out anyway. The only light that's on is the one by the barn, and it's dark enough that I have trouble seeing my way to the porch. Thankfully, he walks slowly, and I'm able to follow him. I trip when I make it to the steps, but he turns and catches me before I fall, then guides me up the rest of the way. I have no idea how he's able to move so smoothly with so much alcohol in his system. My only guess is his highly emotional state must have helped burn off some of the effects.

Keys jingle once we're standing in front of the door, and a second later, we're inside. He stops several feet away with his back to me. His head is hanging forward and the defeated posture makes me ache for him.

I walk up and place my hand on his back. Keeping my voice low, I ask, "Are you okay?"

He shakes his head, then answer verbally. "No."

"What can I do?" I'm whispering now.

He turns and regards me with bleak eyes. "Stay with me," he answers gruffly. "I don't want to be alone right now."

There's no hesitation when I nod. "Okay." Relief immediately covers his face. "I need to call Jeremy and let him know I won't be home tonight."

When Jeremy came by the house to watch the kids earlier, I told him I didn't know how long I'd be. He told me to take as long as I needed. I didn't tell him what I was doing exactly, just that I was going to check on a friend, but I think he knew anyway. The kids have mentioned Alexander a few times, and I'm sure he saw something when he picked the kids and me up after the snowstorm. He never said a word, but his eyes held understanding.

Once I get off the phone with Jeremy, who said he'd stay with the kids, I shed my jacket. I find the living room empty and the kitchen the same way. I walk down the hallway, where I see light filtering out of his bedroom. Unsure of what I'll find, I walk cautiously into his room. Gigi is on her bed sleeping soundly. I find Alexander in the bathroom, staring at his reflection in the mirror. He's looking at himself as if he's disgusted with what he sees. I understand the reaction, even if I don't agree with it. He's the most beautiful man I've ever met, on the inside and out. I just wish he saw that himself.

I walk up behind him, but stay to the side so I can keep him in view. At first, he doesn't seem to notice me, but when I stop behind him, his eyes flicker to mine. The look of revulsion disappears and something else takes its place. Reverence, maybe? Wonder? Confusion? I'm not sure.

He holds my stare, and I wonder what he's thinking. What's going through his head? Before I get a chance to dwell on it, he turns around, grabs my hand, and leads me back into his room, flipping the light off as he goes. We stop at the side of the bed. He pulls back the covers, and without asking, I slip off my shoes and climb in. He reaches back and tugs off his shirt before following me.

Under different circumstances, butterflies would be swarming in my stomach right now. Being in bed with Alexander is something I never thought would happen, but I'll admit, I've secretly wondered what it would be like, especially the last few days. Now though, after everything that's happened today, sex is the last thing on my mind. Comfort is what he needs right now.

My eyes briefly hit on the scars on his chest before I bring them up to meet his.

193

"Roll over," he says deeply.

I roll over, and as soon as I do, a wall of warm muscle meets my back. His arms band around my waist, tugging me against him, and his legs spoon mine. My arms line up against his. The embrace is tight and secure, and I get the sense he needs that right now, to feel connected to someone.

His warm breath blows across the back of my neck. "Thank you."

My arms tighten against his and tears prick the backs of my eyes at the way his words crack as they leave his throat. He buries his face in my hair, and I hear him take a deep, shaky breath.

I lie there for a long time, going over what he revealed tonight and wondering how he's coped this whole time. Not because guilt should have eaten away at him, but because of how he lost his family. His baby was only seven weeks old. He never got to have her in his home. And to watch them die right in front of your eyes, knowing there was nothing you could do; and there wasn't anything he could do, no matter how much he may think otherwise. No man, woman, or child should have to witness something so horrific. For him to do so and still manage to get by just shows how strong he is. But then I wonder how well he is managing. Watching him tonight talk about his family, he looked half dead, like a vital part of him was missing.

I close my eyes and bring one of his hands up to my mouth, kissing the back of it. Learning what he's been through makes me want to cement myself into his life even more. To love him and help bring him back to the living. To cherish the great man he is and the wonderful father he could be. Something tells me, like a soft whisper in the night, that I was meant to meet this man for a reason. My kids and I were brought into his life not by coincidence, but by fate.

His breathing against my neck has evened out, indicating he's asleep. I relax my body against him more, wanting no gaps or spaces between us.

"Good night, Alexander," I say softly into the dark, not expecting a reply.

"Good night, Gwendolyn," he whispers, surprising me, then kisses the back of my neck.

I don't know if he did it in his sleep or if he's fully conscious, but regardless of the reason, it brings comfort to my own beaten heart, solidifying that I'm exactly where I belong.

Chapter Sixteen

Alexander

I WAKE WITH A DRY mouth, pissed-off stomach, and headache from hell, but none of that matters because I have something warm and sweet in my arms. Something I know shouldn't be there, but I cherish it just the same.

The sun is bright coming in the window, so I shove my face deeper in Gwen's hair. I breathe in deep, loving the smell of her. It's amazing how right she feels in my arms. I wish I could hold her here forever.

Memories of yesterday run through my mind. I totally fucking lost it in front of her and told her everything. She had a right to know, especially because I know she feels something for me.

She didn't say much or act disgusted, but given time to think about it, that doesn't mean she won't today. Gwen's a good, loving woman, and I know she doesn't judge, but what happened to my family, what I couldn't prevent, would turn anyone's stomach. Rationally, I know there was nothing I could do to save my family, but my heart screams at me, saying there had to have been something I could have done. I could have told the doctors that since it was so late, we should wait until the morning to bring Rayne home. The only reason I didn't was because Clara and I were both so excited about finally being able to bring her home and start living our lives as a family. I could have not jerked the wheel so much or tried harder to keep control of the car. Maybe they would still be alive if I had just slammed on the brakes and hit the car head-on instead of swerving.

There are so many what-ifs. Too many for the guilt that plagues me to let it rest.

I pinch my eyes shut and force away the painful memories. I don't want them to pull me under right now. Not when I have Gwen in my arms, because I don't know how much longer that will last. I wouldn't blame her if knowing what she knows now changes her feelings toward me.

She shifts in sleep, and as inappropriate as it is under the circumstances, my body reacts. I will my growing erection to go away, but unfortunately, it has a mind of its own. The more I'm around her, the harder it gets to keep that reaction at bay. I want her so fucking bad. My body's been deprived of release, and now that it's found something it wants, it wants it now. It's more than just my body that craves Gwen, though, it's my soul as well.

And your heart, my mind whispers.

She moves again, rubbing against me harder, and I can't keep back the low groan. My arms tighten around her, trying to hold her still. Now is not the fucking time for this. I need to know how she sees me now that she knows of my inability to save my family.

I'm not sure if it's my arms tightening around her or if it was my groan, but her body stiffens, letting me know she's awake.

"I'm sorry," she says, her voice rough with sleep. I keep my arms around her when she tries to pull away.

"Don't apologize," I say gruffly. I've noticed she apologizes a lot, and I wonder if it stems from her need to please. She has that sweetness about her, and I'm sure it bothers her if she knows she's displeased someone.

In an attempt to loosen her up, I rub circles on her upper arm. I don't want her to be anxious around me, particularly over something as natural as sex. I don't see the sexual tension we have between us dissipating anytime soon, especially on my end. Luckily, she starts to relax.

As much as I want to keep us in our quiet cocoon, I need to look at her and see what's she's thinking. I pull my arm from around her waist and get up on an elbow. With my chest no longer behind her, she rolls to her back. My chest meets the side of her, and I put my free arm on the other side of her hip. She looks so beautiful lying below me. When her eyes meet mine, her expression is unsure.

"Thank you for last night," I tell her. Before anything else is said, I need her to know that no matter how she feels about me, I'm grateful for her being there with me last night. More than just under the bridge, but letting me hold her as well. Every year, I've always made sure I was alone for their anniversary, but having Gwen there last night made it a little bit easier.

She takes one of her hands and places the palm against my cheek. I close my eyes, loving the feeling of her soft skin against mine. It's the side where my scars are. She seems to do that a lot; touch my scars. I don't have feeling on that side like I do on the left. Surprisingly, when she touches me, I feel her touch as if I do.

"There was no way I could leave you alone. I was where I needed to be."

Her softly spoken words are music to my ears, but I'm still unsure how she feels about what I said last night. Insecurity is a bitch and can grip even the surest person. I don't feel particularly strong at the moment, and I need to know what she's thinking.

"Why did you stay?" I ask, unable to hold back the tone of uncertainty.

Her eyes turn sad. It's a look I want gone from her face.

Instead of answering my question, she states quietly, "Alexander, there was nothing you could do to stop what happened to them."

Part of me knows what she says is true, but a bigger part says otherwise. I've tried so fucking hard to let go of the guilt, but it's festered so much that it's a part of me now.

She sees the turmoil in my eyes and cups my other cheek. I don't think I'll ever get used to her touch.

"There was nothing you could do," she says more forcefully, but her eyes remain soft. "No matter how many ways you alter something in your mind, if it wasn't meant to be, then it wouldn't have changed anything. We don't have control over what happens to us in life. The only thing we can do is live it the best way we can."

I want to believe her so fucking bad, and maybe one day I will, but it's still too fresh to believe right now.

"Why did you stay?" I ask again, needing to know if it was only out of sympathy for someone who was in pain, or if it was something more.

Her eyes flick back and forth between mine for several seconds, as if trying to figure out how to answer my question. My heart thumps heavily against my ribs as I anxiously wait. Her eyes only give away her nervousness and show no clue as to what her answer will be.

"Because," she starts, then licks her lips. "Because I care about you a lot and seeing you in so much pain...." She closes her eyes as if she's in pain herself. I can tell she's fighting against her emotions and ultimately wins the battle when she opens them again. "It was hard seeing you like that, and I wanted to help in any way I could."

I run a finger down her face, starting at her temple and ending at the underside of her chin. This woman really is incredible. How she could feel anything for me after I exposed my deepest regrets is beyond me. She's never looked at my scars and thought them hideous. She's always looked beneath them.

"I don't deserve for you to be here with me." She opens her mouth to refute me, but I talk over her. "But I'm not strong enough to let you go either." I dip my head and place a single kiss against her lips before pulling back an inch. "There's so much I want from you, Gwen. So damn much, and it scares the shit out of me because I know this feeling isn't fleeting. It's real and so damn strong. I don't know why you came into my life, but now that you're here, I'm not sure I can ever willingly let you go."

Her eyes are wide and her breath fans across my lips as her breathing becomes labored. I'm not sure if it's due to me practically baring my soul or if it's something more carnal. It feels so fucking wrong to even slightly desire this woman in light of what yesterday was. It was a day of remembered loss and was emotionally draining. Today's a new day, but it's still the day after the anniversary of losing my wife and baby, and while that pain is still very much alive, desire and lust fight their way to the forefront of my mind. That puts another mound of guilt on my shoulders, but I shove it away for the moment.

I lower my head until my lips rest against hers. Her breath hitches when I sweep my tongue gently across her lips until she opens up to me. I meet my tongue with hers, and even though neither of us has brushed our teeth, she tastes so good. Too fucking good.

A soft moan leaves her lips and the sound heightens my desire for her. One of her hands laces through my hair and digs into my scalp, pulling me closer to her. I'm only too willing to oblige.

I trace my hand down her neck, her arm, until I reach the back of her thigh. I lift her leg and hook it over my hip. It leaves her wide open for me to settle between her legs. Through our kiss, I keep my eyes open to make sure she's okay with what's going on. Her eyes are closed, but there's no mistaking the intense pleasure on her face. It amps up my own need.

She lifts her other leg and wraps it around my waist. Both of her legs hold me in place. A deep groan leaves my throat when my hardness meets her soft center. The need to grind myself against her is too strong to resist.

Ending the kiss, I rest my forehead against hers and push my hips forward. Even through our jeans, I feel the warmth of her. Her eyes blaze hot as I start a slow grinding rhythm.

"Alexander," she moans, and digs her fingers into my shoulders.

I have no plans to let this go all the way, but the sound of her pleading voice saying my name is nearly my undoing.

"You're driving me crazy, Gwen," I growl softly. "I don't know what to do with you."

I put one hand down by her head and use the other to lift her leg higher. I'm desperate to feel her skin against mine, but I know if I shed our clothes, there's no way I would be able to stop from taking her. I have no idea what the future holds for us, but one thing I know for sure is that I want her more than my next breath.

This... thing building between us only gets stronger the more I'm around her. My mind wages a war with itself. Part of me demands I let go and allow myself the freedom to pursue a relationship with her, but another part says I'm not good enough for her and her kids. I don't know which is more dominant, but I do know which I want to win the battle. I've been alone for so long, and I don't want to be anymore. I haven't felt the softness of a woman in over four years, and I miss it. I don't want Gwen because she's the first woman I've wanted since Clara died, but because she's the first woman I've actually enjoyed being around since then. It's not just her body I desire, but her mind and soul as well.

Her nails rake down my back gently, sending goose bumps over my flesh. It spikes my need for her, and I trail my fingers up her side and under her shirt. Her hiss of pleasure shoots straight to my already rock-hard cock, causing it to pulse in my jeans. I press myself against her harder, earning myself another breathless moan.

My hand slips up higher until I reach the underside of her breasts. The soft material touches the tips of my fingers, and they itch to travel higher. I look into Gwen's eyes, silently asking for permission.

"Please," she whimpers, and I almost lose it.

Her hips shift restlessly below me, causing her pussy to rub against my aching erection.

"You gotta stop moving, Gwen," I groan against her neck, then take little nibble along the flesh.

"I need...." She trails off, but there's no need to finish her sentence. I know exactly what she needs, because it matches my own.

"I know, baby. I'll take care of you," I tell her hoarsely.

I lift the bottom of her bra and tug it upward until her breast falls free. I cup the plump softness with gentle hands and give it a squeeze. She feels so fucking perfect in my palm. She must feel the same because she releases a small cry of pleasure the second I touch her. I pinch her nipple and roll it between my fingers, keeping my eyes on her face as I do so. Her bottom lip is between her teeth and her brows are slashed downward as she drowns in sexual bliss.

My eyes drop to her breast, and the sight of her creamy flesh and rose-colored nipple makes my mouth water. Unable to deny the need to taste her, I take the tip in my mouth. Her eyes were closed, but as soon as she feels my warm tongue, they pop open and stare down at me. I hold her gaze as I suck on her and flick my tongue back and forth across the tip. Her hand goes back to my hair and gives it a tug. Not to push me away, but to pull me closer.

I drop my other arm to an elbow, laying more of my bottom half against her. I release her nipple and push up her top and bra on the other side, exposing her other breast. I give it the same treatment, the delicious taste of her making my cock even more impossibly hard.

I groan against her breast, knowing it's sending vibrations through her. Her head tips back and she releases a husky moan.

I drop her nipple from my mouth, then take her lips again. My hips start to grind harder against her. I feel like I'm going to explode at any minute, but I refuse to let myself find relief. I need to know she's found hers before I can let go.

Ending the kiss, I bury my face in the crook of her neck and rain soft kisses there, never letting up on the steady rhythm of my strokes against her pussy. Her moans become cries and her teeth sink into the flesh on my shoulder. The bite stings, but spurs me on more. I wrap my arm under her ass and lift her hips up higher.

All of a sudden, she throws her head back and releases a throaty cry. I grunt when her nails dig into my lower back as her release completely consumes her. Her body tenses below me, locking her legs even tighter around me. I feel my own release start at the base of my cock, the pleasure so intense that it leaves me dizzy.

I push my hips further into her, wishing our clothes were gone and I could feel her pussy clamping down around me.

Sparks run down my shaft and the tip of my cock tingles as the first jets of cum shoot from me, coating the insides of my jeans.

I drop my chest down to Gwen's and shove my face back into her neck. Her shirt and bra are still pulled up, so her naked breasts rub against my chest. My spent cock twitches, but I force the renewed need away.

I breathe in her delicious vanilla scent as I try to catch my breath. Her heated breath on my cheek says she's doing the same.

Now that the moment is over, reality settles back in. Shame for how I just rutted against her and guilt for the disregard of what yesterday was has my stomach sinking to my toes. Gwen deserves so much more than a dirty orgasm inside our clothes. She should be worshiped and cherished and loved properly. And Clara and Rayne's memory deserves more respect than a passing thought.

I pull back and stare down at her. There's a fine sheen of sweat on her forehead and her cheeks are flushed. She looks incredibly sexy, but still manages to appear innocent.

"Fuck," I muttered. "I'm sorry. We shouldn't have done that."

She frowns and drops her chin to her chest, effectively disconnecting us. I feel like an ass because I immediately know where her thoughts go, and it's the furthest from the truth.

I grab her chin and make her look at me again.

"I know what you're thinking. Don't," I demand. "It felt good, incredibly good, you just deserve better."

Her hands, which were clutching my back, now come to rest on my sides. I feel tingles where my nerve endings are supposed to be damaged.

"You deserve more too," she says quietly.

I give her a half smile and lean down and peck her lips before pulling back. "Thank you."

Her smile lights up her face and it makes my chest tighten. I push up from her chest and roll to the side, my feelings for her getting to be too much. I need to back away before it swallows me whole.

I catch the hurt look on her face as I sit up in bed and swing my legs to the floor, but I don't stop. I sit on the side and hunch my shoulders. My eyes land on the scars on my arm and hand. I flex the hand, watching as the skin tightens and turns white. Gwen has never paid attention to my scars, and I've never really cared what others have felt about them, but they still make me feel inadequate when it comes to her. I'm not only fucked-up on the inside, but the outside as well. It's a constant reminder of how I failed in my duty as protector. It's not fair of me to expect or even want her to settle for someone like me, even though I know she would.

I feel her hands rest on my back, and I grimace, glad she can't see my face. Her lips touch the back of my neck, and my fucking body responds. I silently curse my inability to tamp down the need coursing through my body.

"Are you okay?" she asks, rubbing her hands up and down my back, unknowingly tormenting me further.

I nod, unable to speak at the moment. My eyes slide to the partially open drawer. I just barely make out the images that are inside. The picture I had with me under the bridge feels heavy in my pocket now that reality has made its way back home. I'm a bastard for letting things go as far as they did. I should have never touched Gwen, knowing that I can't give her what she rightly needs.

I get up from the bed, and without looking back at her, mutter, "Shower."

I know I'm being an asshole, and I've probably hurt her, but I can't turn back. She needs to know that I'm not the man for her.

I force my legs forward. I don't dare to look back because I'm scared of the look I'll see on her face. Once the door is securely closed behind me, I hunch my body against the sink and pull in a deep breath. This whole thing was a huge fucking mistake. I can't regret having them in my house during the snowstorm because they would have frozen if they'd stayed out there, but I should have worked harder at keeping them at a distance. I should have put up more shields at the first sign of affection I felt toward them. My only excuse is they bombarded me without me even knowing it. It's too late now to push those feelings away, but I can work at ensuring they don't become stronger.

I slip out of my clothes, then turn and face the mirror, needing a reminder of why it can't work between Gwen and me. My jaw hardens as I stare at my fucked-up face and body. The skin puckers and looks warped in some spots. Where my beard should cover the bottom half of my face, the scars prevent it. The doctors say I was lucky because the burns on my face weren't near as bad as the other areas of my body. They're still bad enough. When the door to the car was ripped open, the fire had just reached my face and the rain helped keep it from spreading too fast, and gave the guy enough time to pour more water on the fire and douse the flames. Had I been in the car for a couple more minutes, the flames would have completely engulfed me. There are still times I wish it had.

I close my eyes, remembering the pain and smell of my flesh burning. I remember hearing the crunch of metal as the door was yanked open. My body screamed in pain but my eyes stayed pinned on Clara. Even in the dark interior of the car, I could still see her lifeless eyes open, as if they were glowing, accusing me. Judging me for not saving Rayne. My eyes stayed connected with her dead ones every second I was in that car.

It wasn't until they started pulling me out that I searched the back seat where my little girl was. It was too dark, and I couldn't fucking find her. It was just an empty black abyss. I was weak from the pain but I still fought to get free. I needed to get to Rayne. After only seconds, my strength gave out and the fiery pain took over.

Days later, I overheard the doctors tell my parents that they were amazed the pain from the burns didn't leave me incoherent, that I shouldn't have been able to focus on searching for Rayne when I was being pulled out. What they don't understand is that the pain of losing them, of being right fucking there and being unable to do a damn thing was more painful than anything else I could imagine. I'd take being burned a thousand times over going through that pain again.

Remembering that day usually makes me feel one of two things, immense pain or unrestricted anger. My expression turns into a twisted scowl, indicating the anger has won out. All at once, my hand balls into a fist, and before I know it, I swing out and punch the mirror. Shards of glass rain down on the sink and floor. I bring my hand to my face and watch as blood drips from the knuckles. Lifting my eyes back to the ruined mirror, I'm satisfied when most of the glass is gone, only leaving a few pieces behind and obscuring my reflection.

"Alexander!" Gwen calls through the door, sounding frantic.

"I'm fine," I call gruffly.

"Are you sure you're okay?"

I feel bad for the scared tone in her voice, but it's better for her to know now that I'm not completely levelheaded.

"Yes. I'll be out in a few minutes."

It wouldn't surprise me if she were gone when I'm done. It would serve me right and be better for her. But a small part of me wishes she wouldn't be. I need to push her away, but I selfishly don't want to let her go.

I turn from the shattered mirror and turn the shower on. Not waiting for it to warm up, I walk underneath the cold spray. The freezing blast of water steals my breath, but I force my body to remain still. I prop my hands on the shower wall and hang my head, letting the cold water cool off my hot temper. I may feel safe to lose it behind closed doors, but I never want Gwen to witness it.

I stay under the water for several minutes, breathing through my nose and out through my mouth before I roughly wash my body. I pick the few splinters of glass out of my hand and set them on the shelf in the shower, then scrub the cuts with soap.

Avoiding the glass on the floor, I step out of the shower and grab a towel. By the time I'm done drying myself, blood is dripping down my hand and onto the floor. I rinse the cuts again, smother them with ointment, then wrap a piece of gauze around my hand. Wrapping the towel around my waist, I pull open the door, unsure of what I'll find or what I *want* to find.

My heart drops when I find the room silent and empty.

What did you expect, Alexander? my subconscious asks. *For her to stick around and get rejected by you again?*

I shake my head, willing the thought away, and grab some jeans from the closet. I pull on a shirt and socks and go out to the living room, preparing to walk to the bridge for my truck. The thought of going back there so soon has my fists clenching at my sides. My reluctance to be around people isn't the only reason I don't like going to town. That bridge is a part of it too. If I could, I'd avoid the damn thing. Unfortunately, the only way around it to town tacks on three hours.

I come to a stop, surprised, when I find Gwen in my kitchen, her back to me as she stands in front of the stove cooking something. When she hears my approach, she turns. The wary look she gives me makes me want to hit something. Myself mainly, because I'm the source of the look.

"Hey," she says softly, her eyes guarded.

I clear my throat and walk the rest of the way into the kitchen.

"Hey." She twists her hands in front of her nervously, and I want to take her in my arms.

"I'm making eggs and bacon." She jerks her thumb over her shoulder, indicating the stove. "I figured you might be hungry."

I frown, wondering why she could still be concerned about me after I left her the way I did in the bedroom, but then I remember, this is Gwen. She's kind and giving and would push past the hurt if it meant it would somehow help others. I may not know her that well, but I know her enough to sense she's that type of person.

I shift from one foot to the other, suddenly feeling awkward. "You didn't have to do that."

She frowns and looks down, and I feel like an even bigger ass. I walk over and lift her chin. I need to fix this. She didn't ask for me to climb on top of her and rut away, although she didn't ask me to stop either and from the way she reacted, she wanted it, too. The least I can do after dry humping her is to not be a jerk.

"I'm sorry," I tell her, hoping she sees the sincerity in my eyes. "I'd love some breakfast."

Some of the hurt leaves her face and she gives me a small smile. One corner of my mouth tips up, and the act seems to satisfy her even more as her smile grows.

"Good." She runs her hands down the front of her jeans and takes a step back. I want to yank her forward again until her soft body meets my hard one, but I drop my hand and let her go. "You go have a seat. It's almost done."

Instead of doing what she says, I stand where I am and watch as she turns back to the stove and picks up a spatula. Her tight jeans mold perfectly against her ass, and I jerk my eyes away before my body can appreciate the view. Her hair is tossed up into a messy ponytail, with a few strands falling down the back. Her graceful neck is on display, and I'd love nothing more than to run my lips up the slender column.

I frown, wondering why it's so hard to keep my thoughts pure when it comes to her. I turn and take a seat at the bar, putting my balled fists on the wood surface. I try not to watch her move around the kitchen, but it's a feat I don't manage. She looks way too good and natural as she cooks. Yes, she was here for four days and cooked each day, but she looks as if she's been doing it here in *my* kitchen for years. Like this is where she belongs.

She sets a plate of food and a glass of orange juice down in front of me before making her own plate and sitting beside me. I look down at the food and my stomach twists. Nausea from too much alcohol the night before has me regretting telling her I wanted breakfast. I ignore the queasiness and pick up my fork, refusing to hurt her feelings even more by turning it away.

"When we finish eating, I can take you to pick up your truck if you'd like," she says a few minutes later.

"I can walk. It's not that far. I'm sure you need to get back to Kelsey and Daniel." I set my fork down and turn to regard her.

She shakes her head. "I've already called Jeremy this morning. He knows to expect me home in about an hour. Besides, it's on the way."

I nod, get up from my chair, and take my plate to the sink. Gigi comes sauntering around the corner and stops at my feet to look up at me.

"Okay," I agree, secretly glad it'll give me a few more minutes with her. I grab a bowl from the cabinet, pour some dog food in it, and set it on the floor for Gigi. I give her head a few rubs while she chomps down on her breakfast.

When I turn back to face Gwen, she's looking at me with watchful eyes. It unnerves because there's no telling what she's looking for and if she finds it. She drops her eyes seconds later and grabs her own plate. Instead of setting it in the sink like I did, she washes the dish, along with mine and the ones she used for cooking, and places them in the drying rack.

Five minutes later, we leave the house and make our way to my truck. Neither of us has said anything since we finished our breakfast. Before I'm ready, we're pulling along the side of the road by the Hallow's Creek Bridge.

My body tenses up and my jaw tics as we both sit in the truck silently. This place always makes me edgy.

I look over when her hand touches mine and gives it a reassuring squeeze. I find her looking at me with understanding.

"Do me a favor?" she asks in the quiet of the truck.

"What?"

"Call me if you ever want to talk."

A fierce pain wedges its way in my chest, because she knows this is goodbye for us. I know it too, but I still fucking hate it. It's for the best though.

I nod, even knowing I'll never call. If I do, I won't be able to stop, and then talking on the phone won't be good enough.

"Thank you."

I cup the side of her face and lean over the console, placing my lips over hers in a soft kiss. Pulling back, I rest my forehead against hers. Closing my eyes, I wish so much that I could be more for her. I kiss her forehead, then pull away and open my door.

She doesn't get out, and I don't look back as I walk over to my truck, unlock it, and climb inside. I ignore the two crosses as they come into view.

Gwen is still at the top of the embankment when I pull out. Through the windshield, I can barely make out her expression, and the sad look she's wearing almost has me pulling over and stalking back to her. I pull away, and I try to keep my eyes on the road and not the rearview mirror, but they slide there before I can stop them.

Why in the hell does it feel so wrong to see her driving away in the opposite direction.

Chapter Seventeen

Gwendolyn

THE BELL RINGS, AND as typical with kids, they immediately start rising from their seats and are quiet no more. I clap my hands three times to get their attention.

"Before you go, stop by my desk and grab a field trip permission form," I tell them sternly. "It needs to be signed and returned to me no later than Friday or you won't be allowed to come along with us to the zoo."

I get "yes ma'ams" and "okays" from several of the students before they continue stuffing papers and books in their bags. I stand by my desk with the stack of forms in my hand.

"Good job on that test, Joey." I smile and hand a form to the black-haired boy in front of me. "I knew you could do it."

"Thanks, Mrs. Crews." He beams at me.

"I expect all your tests to be just as good." I laugh when he wrinkles his nose. "You did great on this one, so you know it's possible now. You just have to work at it."

He looks doubtful, but gives me a nod as he walks away. When I first came here, Joey's grades were horrible. I've been working closely with him, and I'm pleased to see they're improving.

I watch as the last student leaves, and start straightening my desk. I slide a stack of papers I'll be taking home to grade in my messenger bag, and shut down my laptop, placing that on top of the papers.

After looking over the room and making sure everything is in its place, I sling the strap of the bag over my shoulder, grab my keys from the top drawer of my desk, and leave the classroom. I make the short trek down the hallway to Valerie's room, Daniel's teacher. Kelsey is already sitting at a desk doing her homework, with Daniel doing the same at the desk beside her. Valerie stays after school every day because her husband is the principal and they drive in together. When she found out I had two kids in the same school, she insisted on watching them during the few minutes it takes me to close down my classroom.

"Hey, Val." She also insisted I call her Val, saying all her friends do. "Any plans for the weekend?"

This is the first week back to school after the holidays, and as much as I love my students and my job, I'm ready for the weekend to begin. The first week back after a holiday or summer break is always stressful because the kids are hyper.

"Michael's taking me to the movies tonight, but other than that, my butt is staying home and relaxing." She huffs, rolls her chair back, and stands. She looks as tired as I feel. "What about you?"

"Grading papers tonight." I cross my eyes, causing Val to laugh. "Then I was thinking about taking the kids for ice cream tomorrow. And I mustn't forget the dreaded grocery shopping."

"Yes," I hear Daniel hiss. "Ice cream." I grin, and don't need to look over to know he fist-pumped the air.

"Any word yet from the realtor?" I ask, and lean a hip on the edge of her desk.

"No," she grumbles. "She told me it might be a few days and to not hold my breath, as the owners can be quite stubborn."

I frown. Val and Michael have been looking for months for the perfect house, since the owner of the one they are renting recently notified them he's decided to sell. Although their current rental is perfect for them now, Val said it's not ideal for the future because it's only a two bedroom. They decided not to buy their current place, but look for something bigger because they've just started trying for a baby. Val needs an office because she writes part-time, and they want at least two children.

"How long has it been on the market?"

"Two years and counting," she answers, exasperated.

"If they were smart, they'd take your offer."

"Yeah, well, the realtor said they've declined multiple other offers. They are stuck on their figure, even though they've been advised it's way over the value."

"I've got my fingers crossed for you. But if they don't accept it, don't get discouraged. It took me and Will a year to find the right house."

She sighs. "Yeah, I know you're right, but Gwen, this house is perfect. It felt like home the minute I stepped inside."

I smile and reach over to squeeze her hand. "Then I'm sure it will all work out."

She returns my smile, her eyes lighting with confidence. "I sure hope so."

I turn to the kids. "You guys ready?"

Daniel jumps up from his seat, carelessly stuffing papers in his book bag. "Yep."

Kelsey demurely gets up from the desk and is a lot more careful with putting things away. Sometimes I catch myself looking at her and it hurts how withdrawn she is and how adult-like she seems. She should to be hanging out with friends and pointing out how gross boys are.

We bid Val goodbye and head for the door. As we walk down the hallway, Daniel looks up at me. "I made a good grade on my reading test."

"That's good, sweetie. I'm proud of you."

His look turns coy, and I wait for what's coming next.

"Since I did good on my test, could we go get ice cream today?"

I laugh, not at all surprised.

"Nice try, kid, but we've got chores to do, and I've got papers to grade." I ruffle his hair to lighten the refusal, but his face still falls. I hate when they get disappointed. They've both been in a down mood lately. I know why, but I ignore the reason behind the behavior. Because I'm a sucker, I retract my answer and offer instead, "How about this, you and your sister get your chores done in record time, and I may take you out for barbeque at Blu's. And ice cream is still on for tomorrow."

"Really?" he asks, jumping up and down.

"Yep."

My grin is so big it hurts my face. I haven't seen enough of Daniel's smiles lately, and Kelsey's been even more withdrawn than usual.

"You hear that, Kels?" Daniel says, running over to his sister. "If we get our chores done quickly, we get barbeque!"

She watches him with a blank expression, but gives him a single nod, her usual reply. He doesn't let the lack of response take away from his exuberant happiness, although, deep down I know it bothers him that Kelsey never speaks or plays with him anymore. Before Will died, Kelsey took her role as a big sister seriously. She was constantly by his side, making sure he never got hurt and stayed happy. She played with him anytime he asked. When he was a baby, she insisted on helping care for him. She was like a mini momma. Because of that, they were very close. After Will passed away, she stopped. She stopped everything. I've explained to Daniel several times why, and he says he understands, but I know it still hurts him.

The sky is cloudy when we walk out of the school doors, and I wonder what the chances are it'll rain. I hope it holds off until we get back from Blu's. Surprisingly, the weather is warmer than normal for this time of year. The weatherman says we're having a very warm winter, despite the harsh beginning.

We only live a couple miles from the school, so the trip is short. Daniel bounces in his seat the entire time, singing along to the music I have playing on the radio. He has a knack for remembering songs after only hearing them a few times.

When I turn the corner to our street, I unconsciously let up on the gas pedal when I see the familiar old blue truck sitting in our driveway. My palms immediately start to sweat against the steering wheel and my heart rate picks up.

It's been three weeks since I've seen Alexander, and every day of those weeks, I've felt the loss of him like a sledgehammer has been slammed into my stomach. I've done pretty well ignoring the constant pain, but seeing him sitting on our porch steps as I pull into the driveway brings it back full force.

I miss him so much. Much more than I should for only knowing him a few short weeks. And the kids, I know they've missed him too. It's been apparent in the way they've been moping around the house. Daniel's asked after him several times, and the only thing I can tell him is Alexander's been busy with work. I hate lying to my kids, but I hate hurting them more, and I know it'll hurt him if I were to tell him Alexander doesn't want to see us anymore.

His absence has affected Kelsey too. She rarely comes out of her room, and when she does, it's only to eat, shower, or when I make her. It's not healthy for her to stay locked up in her room all the time, so I make her come out at least for a couple hours each day. I was in her room a week ago putting clothes away and found the two notebooks Alexander made her at the bottom of her sock drawer. The sight of her hiding them away brought tears to my eyes.

I've caught myself several times reaching for my phone to call and see how he's doing. I know he cares about us, but I refuse to push our presence on him.

"Look!" Daniel shouts as I put the car in park. "It's Alexander!"

Before I have the chance to turn off the truck, Daniel throws open his door and is running toward him. Kelsey and I get out at a slower pace. I look over at Kelsey across the hood of the car and find her looking at Alexander, her expression showing her vulnerability.

I grab my messenger bag and purse and lock my car. I know I'm stalling for time, but I have no idea what to expect. He made it clear without really saying anything that whatever was transpiring between us was over.

Alexander stands when Kelsey and I make our way toward him. Daniel stands beside him talking animatedly, but his eyes remain on mine. They hold something deep, but I'm not sure what the emotion is.

"Hey," he says, his voice deep and gruff. "Jeremy gave me your address."

It didn't dawn on me until then to question how he knew where we lived.

"Hi." I shift from one foot to the other, waiting for him to continue.

His looks away from me and faces Kelsey, who currently has her head down.

"Hey, Kelsey," he rumbles.

She lifts her head and doesn't hide her hurt. I look back at Alexander and find his face a mask of pain.

Instead of acknowledging his greeting, she moves past him. We both watch as she slides the emergency key from underneath the rug, unlocks the door, and walks inside. He faces me once she disappears.

"I'm sorry," I tell him, because even if she felt it was warranted, she was still very rude just now. "She's not been having good days lately."

He nods. Guilt and shame flash in his eyes, and he looks to the side. Daniel's still standing between us, looking from one person to the other. I'm just about to tell him to go inside and give Alexander and me a minute to talk, but Alexander talks before I get a chance.

He holds out his hand, my earrings in his palm. "You forgot these the other day."

I look down at them and wonder if that's the only reason he

came by today or if it was something more. It's something I hope with all my heart, but am scared to wish for. He could have simply messaged me for my address and slipped them in the mail. He didn't have to come all the way here.

Could it be possible that he's missed us as much as we've missed him?

I hold out my hand and he drops them in my palm. I wrap my fingers around them, and though the metal is thin, they're still warm from being in his hand.

"Would you like to come in for a few minutes? I could make you a glass of tea."

I hold my breath, silently hoping he'll accept. He looks down at Daniel and sees the hopeful face staring back at him. His brows draw down into a frown before he lifts his eyes back up to me.

"Sure," he says, and it makes my heart soar.

I know I should forget about the idea of something more happening between us, but for some reason I just can't. It feels natural to be in his company, like it's where I'm supposed to be. As if something keeps forcing us together.

Daniel squeals in delight and rushes up the steps to open the door. He gushes nonstop about what's happened the last couple of weeks. Alexander listens with a smile playing on his face. It's nice to see his smile again. Kelsey is nowhere to be seen as we walk into the kitchen. I tell Daniel to let Pepper out in the fenced-in backyard while I grab glasses for tea, fill them, and hand one over to Alexander. I give Daniel a juice box when he comes rushing back inside. He rips the plastic from the straw, pokes it through the hole, then closed his mouth around it to take a drink.

Alexander chuckles at the way Daniel quickly sucks the juice through the straw, pulling his cheeks in dramatically. I laugh too because I'm happy. Happy that Alexander is standing in my house enjoying the entertainment of my son.

"Thank you for bringing the earrings back. I can't believe I forgot them again." I take a sip of my drink and set the glass on the counter before turning to Daniel. "Hey, you, aren't you supposed to be doing something?" I ask pointedly.

Disappointment has his face losing some of its merriment. He nods, looks at Alexander with bereaved eyes, then slinks off toward his room. Right as he gets to the doorway, he spins back around and rushes back to us. He stops at Alexander's feet with a look of hope.

"We're going to Blu's later," he says jubilantly. "Can you come?" He holds his hands up in prayer style, and I can't help but laugh, but I sober quickly when I realize he's put Alexander on the spot.

I dare a look at Alexander and find him looking down at Daniel. There's a wrinkle between his brows as he thinks on how to answer. I wish I knew what he was thinking right now. Is he trying to find a way to let Daniel down easy? Or is he fighting with himself because he wants to go but feels he shouldn't? I know he thinks he not good enough for us, that he feels his scars, physical and emotional, make him less of a man. I know he holds immense guilt for not saving his wife and baby, and that makes him feel like he's not worthy. That it scares him because he worries should anything happen to the kids or me, he wouldn't be able to help us either.

I understand his fears, but it's utter crap. Alexander is one of the strongest men I know, one of the most caring and generous and kindhearted. I just wished he knew it too, or at least would give me the opportunity to make him believe it.

I watch as he fights with what to tell Daniel, and I decide to let him off the hook.

Walking over to Daniel, I place my hand on his shoulder. "Daniel, sweetie, I don't think—"

"Yes," Alexander interrupts me, and I look up at him in surprise. "I'd love to go."

After smiling down at Daniel, who runs off with a shouted "Yes," he lifts his eyes to mine. His jaw is hard, but determined.

"You don't have to," I tell him, not wanting to force him into doing something he won't feel comfortable doing. "I can talk to Daniel and make him understand."

"I want to." He takes a step closer. "If it's okay with you, I'd like to have dinner with you and the kids."

My heart leaps in my chest, because I want him to have dinner with us too. Even more, I want *him* to want to have dinner with us.

I can't help the big smile that takes over my face. "We'd really like that, too."

"Good," he states, then adds, "It's settled then."

He takes another step toward me, then another, until there's only an inch between us. I suck in a breath when he lifts his scarred hand and settles it against my cheek, his thumb swiping back and forth against the skin.

His eyes close and he lays his forehead against mine. Butterflies flutter in my belly when his lips touch mine in a soft kiss before he pulls them away. I fist my hands in his shirt at his sides to keep from pulling his head back down.

"I've missed you." He whispers the words against my lips.

The agonized tone causes my throat to close up, but I still manage to get out, "I've missed you too."

"I'm sorry for being an ass a few weeks ago."

I shake my head against his. "I understand. It was a tough time for you."

"That's still no excuse," he states.

We stay this way for several moments, both quiet as our minds race with thoughts. I keep my eyes closed, afraid of what I'll find in his if I open them.

Daniel comes racing out of his room a few minutes later, out of breath and looking flushed from exertion. Alexander and I both pull back quickly.

"I'm done!" he yells, skidding to a stop beside us. "Can we go now?"

I plaster on a stern look. "There's no way you got all your chores done that quickly, young man."

His eyes widen. "I did, Mama! I promise!"

I narrow my eyes. "And if I go check, I won't find any toys stuffed under your bed or in your closet?"

He drops his gaze and shuffles his feet. "Maybe only three or two," he mutters, keeping his eyes away from mine.

"Daniel," I scold.

"Aww, Mom," he whines in response. "It's only like nine or ten, I swear."

I hold in my laugh at the earnest look in his eyes. "Daniel Liam. You march your butt right back in there and clean your room the right way."

His face falls, but I steel myself from giving in to him. He turns and grumbles as he walks away.

"Stop by your sister's room and let her know we'll be leaving soon," I call after him. There's no point in checking to see if her room is clean. It always is, and any chores I give her are done as soon as she gets home, before I even have to remind her.

ALEXANDER OPENS THE door to Blu's BBQ Pit and the kids and I file in before him. We take a seat at one of the booths in the back corner.

"Sit with me!" Daniel says to Alexander, a little too loudly.

He slides in beside Daniel while Kelsey and I sit across from them. When I peek across the table to Alexander, his jaw is hard. I look around the room. My heart lurches when I see several pairs of eyes looking our way. It makes me angry they are staring so blatantly.

I reach across the table and lay my hand over his to grab his attention. "We don't have to stay," I tell him. I hate to think he's uncomfortable.

"No," he grunts, then clears his throat. "I'm fine."

I pull my hand away and smile at him, hoping it'll help settle his nerves.

After we've browsed the menu for a few minutes, an older lady by the name of Sadie walks over, order pad in hand.

"Gwen, right?" she asks with a smile. I nod and give her my own smile. She turns to the kids next. "And Daniel and Kelsey?"

"Hi," Daniel says excitedly. Kelsey nods once.

She turns next to Alexander. "Hey, Alexander. It's nice to see you." I'm pleased to see no intrusiveness in her gaze. She also doesn't stare at his scars. She's simply talking to an old friend.

"Hey, Sade," he offers. "How have you been?" He seems to be at ease as well.

"Good." She nods. "Can't complain." After giving him another smile, she pulls the pen from behind her ear. "Now, what can I get you all?"

She leaves after taking our order, and I relax back against my seat, happy to be sitting here with the kids and Alexander. Out the corner of my eye, I see most of the eyes that were on us are no longer paying us any attention. I hope it stays that way.

Every so often, I see Alexander look at Kelsey, and remorse flashes in his eyes each time. She's completely ignored him since we pulled up to the house, and I know it plagues him.

"You wanna look at my car collection when we get home? I got a lot," Daniel asks, forcing Alexander's eyes away from Kelsey.

He turns to regard him. "Sure."

Daniel climbs to his knees on the seat. "Can we come ride a horse soon? It hasn't been really cold anymore."

Alexander's eyes bounce to mine. "That's up to your mom."

Daniel's hopeful eyes come to me for an answer, and I don't have the heart to tell him no. I also don't give him a yes either. I still haven't gotten over the day they ran off to the barn by themselves.

"We'll see."

Some of the light dims in Daniel's eyes, but he bounces back quickly. He starts regaling Alexander with questions on how to care for horses and what he does to train them. Alexander answers patiently and Daniel listens intently.

While they're occupied, I turn to Kelsey. "You okay?"

She shrugs and continues to look down at the paper menu she's been fiddling with.

"It's okay to be upset with him, but maybe you can try to cut him some slack?" I lower my voice and tilt my head toward her. "Remember what I told you the other day?" She nods, and guilt and sorrow line her face. I grab her hand under the table and squeeze. "Just keep that in mind, okay?"

A few minutes later, Sadie brings out our food and we sit in silence as we eat. Other than when we first walked in and the few minutes of awkwardness, things have settled down, thankfully. People seems to have lost their interest in Alexander being out in public. I've heard some of the whispered rumors the townspeople like to think others can't hear, and while I don't condone that behavior—it actually disgusts me—I understand their surprise when they do see him. He's become a recluse. I understand his need to come to town so rarely, but in a sense, it's just as much Alexander's fault as it is theirs, because he's purposely secluded himself from the town.

We're just finishing up when a handsome blond man about Alexander's age and a blond lady come up to our table.

"Alexander," the guy says, surprise written on his face. He recovers quickly and holds out his hand for a shake.

"James." Alexander clasps his hand with a half smile. I get the sense that James is a friend of his.

James moves his eyes to me and his lips tip up into a crooked grin.

"Who's this?" he asks, tipping his chin at me and looking back at Alexander.

"James, meet Gwen. Gwen, this is an old friend of mine, James."

"It's good to meet you, James," I say, and hold out my hand.

He grabs it gently with his bigger one. "It's very nice to meet you, too, Gwen." His eyes twinkle as he lets my hand go, and I wonder what he's thinking.

I don't get a chance to ask before he turns his attention to Daniel and Kelsey. "And who might these fine kids be?"

Daniel introduces himself before anyone else can. "I'm Daniel." He tries his best to act like the two adult men by throwing his hand out to be shaken, almost knocking Alexander in the face with his elbow.

"Daniel." I point my finger at him then point it downward. "Sit."

"It's okay," Alexander comments, then picks Daniel up and settles him on his lap so James can safely reach his hand.

"Hey, Daniel."

Daniel beams when James shakes his hand firmly.

"That's my sister, Kelsey." He points his thumb over his shoulder at her.

"Hello, Kelsey," James says, his voice turning soft.

Of course, Kelsey neither talks nor offers a smile. I see the question in James' eyes, so I offer a smile and give him a brief explanation. "She doesn't talk. Please don't take it personally."

He smiles and nods. The girl beside him moves from one foot to the other, and James' eyes snap to hers.

"I'm sorry, baby." He wraps his arm around her waist and kisses her cheek. "Lydia, I'd like you to meet Alexander, Gwen, Daniel, and Kelsey."

We all say hello and she echoes our greeting.

Alexander and James chat for a few minutes, and I end up fidgeting in my seat because every few seconds, James looks my way. His eyes hold questions and curiosity. As a distraction, I start up a conversation with Lydia. I learn that she lives in the next town over and works as a dispatcher for a big trucking company. This surprises me as she doesn't appear the type to communicate with big, burly truck drivers on a daily basis. She's beautiful in the traditional way, with thick gorgeous blond hair, green eyes, and a slim body with curves in all the right places. She also seems very sweet and innocent.

"You ready?" James asks Lydia, stopping our conversation.

She smiles at him and the love she obviously feels for him is plain to see. If I'm being honest, I feel a bit jealous at their open affection toward each other. I want that with Alexander.

Once they leave, Alexander stands to go pay for our food, after adamantly refusing my offer to pay for mine and the kids'. The kids and I gather our coats and meet Alexander at the door. He gets a few more glances, but he ignores it, seemingly not bothered by it anymore.

When we pull up to the house a few minutes later. Daniel drags Alexander to his room to show him his car collection the minute they step inside. I tell Kelsey to grab a shower, and I sit at the kitchen table to start grading papers. Every few minutes, I hear Daniel giggle and it makes me smile.

I'm flipping over the last paper and just about to go check on Daniel and Alexander when Daniel comes to my side. Looking at my watch, I'm surprised to see two hours have already passed.

"I'm tired, Mom," he says, rubbing his eyes. He already has his pajamas on, showing he really is tired.

I look behind him, expecting to see Alexander, but don't.

"Come on, kid. Let's go brush your teeth, and I'll tuck you in."

"Can Alexander do it?" He yawns as he walks sleepily beside me to the bathroom.

"How about I send him in to tell you good night?"

He nods, then grabs his toothbrush and smothers it with toothpaste.

Curiosity has me looking down the hall as Daniel brushes his teeth. Kelsey's light is on with the door open halfway, but I can't tell if he's in there or not.

Once in bed, Pepper tucked against his side, I pull the covers over him and kiss him good night.

"Love you."

"Love you too, Mom. Don't forget to send Alexander in here."

I smile. "I won't." I flip the light off and pull his door to.

For some reason, my heart starts to pound heavily in my chest as

I walk quietly to Kelsey's room. I know before I reach her door that Alexander's inside. I creep along until I'm just outside her door. His deep voice stops me from going further.

"I had a little girl," he says quietly, and even out here I can hear the torment in his voice. I hold my breath as he continues. "But I lost her a few years ago. She and my wife drowned."

Tears threaten to form in my eyes at the memory of him recounting what happened to his wife and baby when we were sitting under the bridge. I know how painful that was for him, so for him to be talking about it now with Kelsey means a lot. I hope he doesn't go into detail. It would be too much for someone Kelsey's age to handle. Hell, it's too much for an adult to handle.

I peek around the doorframe, making sure to stay out of sight. I've seen the tortured expression on his face tonight when Kelsey wouldn't look at him. I know this is something he needs to do to try to make amends with her. I think Kelsey needs it as well. She's was very hurt by his rejection a few weeks ago. I just hope she gives him a chance to explain and make it right.

When they come in view, I find Kelsey sitting against the head-board with her legs crossed, her blanket tucked around her. Alexander sits about midway up the bed, his hands clasped firmly in his lap. His knuckles are white, so I know he's clenching his fingers tightly. He's looking down at his hands, but she has her eyes on him. Pain etches her face.

"The day you, your brother, and your mom came to the house, Christmas Day, was the day before the anniversary of when they died." He lifts his head. From where I'm standing, I can't see his face, but I know it carries hurt as well. "I wasn't in a very good place at the time because I miss them so much, especially during Christmas."

He stops talking and Kelsey just stares at him. Looking down, I see her gripping the blanket in her lap. I hate to see two people I care about in so much pain.

I'm just about to make my presence known, when Kelsey opens

her mouth and completely destroys me by whispering, "I'm sorry you lost your baby and wife."

My heart freezes in my chest, and I struggle to pull air in my lungs. Tears force their way from my eyes, and I throw my hand over my mouth to keep in the sob.

My daughter just spoke.

I can't believe it. My daughter actually just spoke. It doesn't even matter that her first words weren't for me. I'm just so elated that I got to hear them, and they weren't the tortured words to God to bring her father back home.

I close my eyes and tip my head back, replaying the sound of her voice over and over in my head. I want to rush in and beg her to say something else.

When I open my eyes again, I just barely get a side view of Alexander's face. He's gone quiet, and I know he's shocked as well.

He pulls himself together a lot faster than I have and says, "Thank you."

Sending my heart soaring even higher, Kelsey speaks again. "How old was your little girl?"

It takes Alexander a minute to answer as he tries to rein in his emotions.

"Seven weeks."

Kelsey sucks in a breath and heaves it out on a whoosh. "I bet she was so pretty," she says softly.

"She was gorgeous," Alexander remarks.

"What were their names?"

His voice is pained when he answers. "Clara was my wife and Rayne my little girl."

"Rayne," she breathes. "So pretty."

Kelsey gets up and comes to sit beside Alexander, then leans her head against his arm. It only takes him a split second before he puts his arm around her shoulders and she then lays her head against his chest. The action brings even more tears to my eyes. They look like what a father and daughter would look like when consoling his baby girl.

Kelsey's next words cause my heart to slam in my chest painfully.

"Please don't tell my mom I'm talking," she says, lifting her head and pleading with her eyes.

"Why?" He tucks a piece of hair behind her ear.

She drops her eyes to the floor and murmurs so low I barely hear her.

"Because it's my fault my daddy died."

Alexander and I both jerk. I grip the doorjamb to keep myself from falling. I've always known she blames herself, but to hear her actually say it, hurts so much worse.

I watch as Alexander turns to Kelsey and grabs her chin to force her to look at him.

"Why would you think it's your fault, Kelsey?"

Her voice is a tearful whisper, and I have to lean closer to hear her. "Because I made him go get my bear and that's when he died."

"Sweetie, it wasn't your fault," Alexander says, his voice strained. "You were six years old. There was no way you could know that would happen. Even your mom and dad didn't know it would happen."

She looks at him with tears flooding down her face, and my heart feels like it's being beaten with a bat coated in spikes.

"But maybe if I hadn't—"

He doesn't let her finish. "No, honey. It still would have happened."

She sniffles and leans against Alexander again.

"What if she blames me?" Kelsey whispers brokenly, and it's that question that kills me. I lean back against the wall and slide down, my legs unable to hold my weight anymore.

I can no longer see them, but I can still hear them.

"She doesn't," he tells her, his tone more forceful that it has been the entire time I've been standing there.

"How do you know?"

"Because she loves you," he answers simply.

It's quiet for a few minutes before Alexander speaks again.

"You need to talk to your mom about this," he tells her softly. "She misses you so much."

"I miss her too," she confesses, and I want to run inside and tell her I'm right here, but I don't. She needs to do this on her own. I don't want to take the chance of pushing her away by rushing her.

They stop talking, and I lean my head back and listen to the silence, hoping with everything I am that Kelsey's silence has come to an end.

I'm so lost in thought that I don't realize Alexander's standing in front of me. I look up at him with swollen eyes, feeling lost and exposed. He doesn't say a word as he scoops me up into his arms. My eyes linger on Kelsey's door, which is closed most of the way, a sliver of light pouring out, indicating she's still awake.

My heart aches with the need to go to her, but as much as it hurts to do so, I let him carry me further away from her.

Alexander stops at the couch and takes a seat with me in his lap. I bury my head in the crook of his neck and let tears soak the collar of his shirt. He doesn't try to calm me down, just gently rubs my back and murmurs soft words in my ear. He knows I heard Kelsey speak, and he knows how much it hurts to hear her say her father's death is her fault and she worries I blame her. She couldn't be further from the truth.

LATER THAT EVENING, after Alexander has left, I walk quietly down the hallway and stop at Kelsey's door. This is my nightly routine. I always sneak back to her door five minutes after I've tucked her in, and every night I catch her whispered prayers to bring her daddy home.

Tonight is different though, for a couple reasons. One being that she spoke to Alexander tonight and my emotions are already raw from overhearing it.

The second comes when I stop at the door and hear that Kelsey's prayers have changed. If it wasn't for the fact that I watched her crawl to her knees, I'd think she just added onto the old one, but this prayer is all on its own. The new one is even more heartbreaking than the old.

"Please, God, help make Alexander better," she whispers, her hands clasped in front of her. "Please don't make him hurt anymore. I really like him, and I know my mama and brother like him too. I wish he could be with us always. And please let his wife and baby be okay in heaven with you." She pauses before finishing. "In Jesus' name, amen."

I clutch my hands over my chest, trying to calm my pounding heart. Her prayers have been the same every night for over two years. For her to change them now.... I send up a silent prayer that this change is good. I also pray that God answers my daughter's prayers.

I rest my forehead against the doorframe and whisper low enough that she can't hear me, "I love you, Kelsey. Please come back to me."

With one last glance to see her in bed with the covers tucked up under her chin once again, I walk away with my heart heavy.

Chapter Eighteen

Alexander

I LIE IN BED WITH MY hands under my head, thinking about today. I think about how I was supposed to simply drop off the earrings and then leave again. I think about Gwen's face when she saw me on her porch steps, the longing and hope present, but also the shadow of vulnerability. I think about how I had to force myself to not yank her in my arms and beg her to forgive me for being a dick.

I think about Daniel rushing up to me and the pure elation on his face as he talked nonstop. Then I think about Kelsey and the wary way she eyed me. The apparent hurt I've caused her. It made me sick to my stomach to know I've caused her more pain.

I should have refused to go inside for tea. I should have told them I couldn't go to dinner. I should have come up with an excuse as to why I couldn't go back inside to look at Daniel's car collection. But I just couldn't. Gwen and her kids have me wrapped around their fingers. I'd do anything to bring smiles to their faces and make them happy. Walking into Blu's last night and feeling all the eyes on me was uncomfortable and had my anger spiking, but I pushed through it. I wasn't going to let the nosy people of town ruin what I didn't realize at the time was something I wanted so bad. Being out with them, acting like a family, a normal family, felt so damn good. I wanted to do it again. I wanted to be a part of their lives every day.

I also think about walking out of Daniel's room and seeing Kelsey in hers. Her eyes were pinned on the door as if she were waiting for me or something. Before I could stop myself, I was walking in her room and sitting on the end of her bed. Both kids draw me in, but Kelsey more so. I know it's because of the pain we share.

She held her body stiff and her eyes were almost accusing as she watched me for several seconds. It wasn't enough, there would never be an excuse good enough for my shitty behavior, but I tried to explain it to her. I didn't want to hurt her further, but I saw the pain in her eyes when I told her about Clara and Rayne. I know of her pain, she deserves to know the reason behind mine.

Even though she said those few words to me the night before they left, I never expected her to talk again. To say my heart skipped a beat when she whispered those first words is an understatement. It was more like skipping ten beats. My stomach felt hollow and it took me several tries to pull in air. She has one of the sweetest and most delicate voices I've ever heard. It took me a moment to gather myself enough to respond. When she kept talking, even if what she asked hurt to think about, it was music to my ears.

Hearing her say her dad dying was her fault and she thought her mom might blame her was too much. I turned to her and made her look at me. I wanted her to hear me clearly when I told her it wasn't her fault and there was no way her mom blamed her. I'm not sure if she believed me, but I hope she did. There're only so many ways we can tell others how we feel. It's up to them whether or not to believe it.

My chest hurt when I left her a few minutes later. It hurt even more when I saw Gwen slumped against the wall on her ass. I knew she heard. She was there when her daughter talked, and it broke her heart to hear the devastating words leave her daughter's lips.

Without a word, I picked her up and carried her to the couch, where I sat her on my lap and just held her as she cried against my neck. No words needed to be said, as she heard it all, so we just sat there. I tried to give her the comfort she so desperately needed.

Afterward, she lifted herself from my lap, and I immediately stood, then told her I needed to go. That Gigi and the puppies were waiting for me. It was a shit excuse, but I needed to get out of there. I needed to rein in my scattered emotions and regroup. It's so easy to get sucked in when I'm around them. It's so easy to forget why I shouldn't want Gwen and her two kids. And once again, I had to watch pain line her face as I walked out the door. I should be shot dead for all the mixed feelings and actions I'm giving her.

Instead of going home when I left, I ended up at Clara and Rayne's graves. It was dark and cold out, but it didn't matter. I sat my ass down between their two graves and did nothing but look out into the darkened cemetery. I didn't talk to them, and I didn't cry, but I did listen, and I swear I heard Clara whispering to me to let go of the guilt. To move on and be happy. I want to. I want to so fucking badly. I just don't know if it's possible for me.

After, I left their graves with my heart even heavier.

Hours later, as I lie in bed, an image of the wounded look on Gwen's face as I left her pops into my mind. I grab my phone and check the time. It's after midnight. She'll be in bed, but the need to make sure she's okay is overwhelming.

I unlock the screen and type out a message.

Me: Hey.

I'm surprised when I receive a reply seconds later. I wonder if she's having as much trouble finding sleep as me.

Gwen: Hey.

Before I can stop myself, I'm typing out another message.

Me: How are you?

It takes her a minute to reply.

Gwen: I'm okay. Are you?

Okay. Not good, not great. Just okay. I don't like that she's just okay.

Me: I'm sorry for leaving so quickly earlier.

Gwen: It's fine. I understand.

She understands, but she lets me back inside every time we're together, knowing I may withdraw again. I'm an asshole for putting her through that.

Me: How's Kelsey?

Gwen: She's good. Sleeping.

I drop my phone on my chest and stare up at the ceiling for several moments, wondering how in the hell I got to this point. How I went from having everything, to nothing, then back on the verge of having everything again if I allow it.

My phone vibrates against my chest, and I look at the screen.

Gwen: I didn't tell you, but thank you for talking to her. For telling her I don't blame her and it wasn't her fault about her father.

I picture Gwen on the other end of the line, fighting back her tears. I know having her silent daughter talk to me instead of her had to hurt, but I also know that she's glad that she talked, period.

I silently accept her gratitude and tell her something else. Something I hope helps.

Me: She'll come to you. She wants to, she misses you.

Gwen: I know. It's just hard waiting.

Me: Try to get some sleep.

Gwen: Okay. Good night, Alexander. And thank you again.

Me: Good night, Gwendolyn. Sleep well.

I put my phone back on the nightstand, the tightness in my chest somewhat abated now that I know she's okay.

I roll to my side and try do what I told her to do and get some sleep. It's not until several hours later that I manage.

I STAND AT THE OPENED barn door and look out at the torrential downpour. It's been this way off and on for over a week. Work has been put on hold because of it and the horses are becoming restless. Horses are huge animals, so I need as much room as possible to work with them. I use the pasture when the weather permits, but that's been out lately, so we've been stuck in the barn. Luckily, the rain's coming from the south, which means the temperature is higher, and today is supposed to be the last day of the shitty weather.

I look over to Bandit and see him eyeing me. Surprisingly, since the day Kelsey was in here, he's calmed down, even going so far as letting me pet him a few times. He actually took an apple from my hand a few weeks ago without trying to bite it off, and has let me do it a couple times since. I got the saddle on his back two days ago before he started bucking. He still gets in his moods at times, but for the most part, he tolerates me now. It'll still be a while before he lets me sit him, but we're definitely moving in the right direction. I'll be glad to have him off my hands when the time comes.

I hear a car door slam and walk over to the barn doors, wondering who it could be. I don't get unannounced visitors very often. I'm surprised to see Gwen's red Range Rover. Squinting against the rain, I barely see her form already on the porch. It's been a month since I've seen her. A month that's been pure fucking hell. A month that's tested my restraints beyond anything I've ever had to do. We've talked or texted each night since I left her crying on her couch and that's the only reason I haven't gone to her. They kept my need barely at ease. We've learned a lot about each other in that month, and the more I learn, the more I want her and her kids in my life. My strength to keep away from her is waning and her being here doesn't help one fucking bit. Already my body is tensing, preparing to rush to her.

I look up at the sky and an unreasonable flare of anger hits me in the stomach. What in the hell is she doing driving in this kind of weather? Doesn't she know how dangerous it is?

I take a closer look at the truck and thankfully don't see the kids inside.

I take off out of the barn and run across the yard. By the time I make it to the porch, I'm completely drenched. I shake the water from my face and stalk up the steps to her. She turns when she hears the thump of my boots.

Her graceful smile falls flat and is replaced with worry when she sees the look in my eye.

"What's wrong?" she has the nerve to ask.

Instead of answering, I bark, "What in the hell were you thinking, driving in this weather?"

My question takes her by surprise and she stumbles back a step. I stalk closer to her.

"E-excuse me?" The rain pelting down on the roof is so loud I barely hear her.

Her back hits the door, but I don't stop until my chest is so close that each time she breathes in the tips of her breasts rub against the cotton of my shirt.

"You know how dangerous it is to drive when it's raining like this. Why in the fuck would you take a chance like that?"

I know my anger is irrational and extreme, but fuck if I can control it right now. All I can see is Gwen sliding off the road or flipping her car in the ditch or hitting a tree head-on because she can't stop in time. I imagine her on the side of the road, bleeding and in pain with no one around to help.

This shit right here is why I should have never gotten involved with her. Visualizing these scenarios will eat me alive. I can't take the chance of losing someone else, and I can't bear the thought that I couldn't be there if they ever needed me.

My hands rest on either side of her head, and I let my head hang forward. I pull in huge gulps of air and try to calm the raging inferno in my blood. I flinch when Gwen lays her hand against my chest. Her touch burns, and I can't get away fast enough. I throw myself away from her, and her eyes widen, then darken with pain.

"Alexander?" she questions softly and takes a step closer.

I know my eyes must look wild when I pin her with my glare. "Don't," I growl.

She stops and frowns. "I don't understand. Why are you so angry?"

I spin around, hands clenched at my sides. I can't believe she has the nerve to ask me that.

"Why am I so angry? Really, Gwen? You're seriously fucking asking me that after I told you what happened to Clara and Rayne?"

Realization dawns, and I want to fucking laugh as her eyes widen again. I turn away from her and walk to the porch railing, leaning my hands on it and staring out into the rain. My heart's pounding so hard, I hear it in my ears. I feel the throb at my temple and the start of a headache.

I hiss when I feel Gwen's hand on my back, then her heat at my side. I don't look at her, but I feel her eyes on me.

"Alexander, you can't control everything," she says gently, trying to console me, but it does the opposite. Her soft tone grates on my nerves because I love the sound of her voice so much, and whether she means to or not, she's using it against me right now. "You can't protect people from every little thing. You can't prevent them from living or doing things that are natural for fear of something happening. If it's meant to happen, then it'll happen whether you try to prevent it or not."

I hate myself so much right now because I know she's right, but I still can't get over my fear. Gwen has come to mean more to me than I ever imagined possible. I'm not sure what would happen to me if something were to happen to her or the kids. It scares the shit out of me to think about it. It scares me so much that my damn hands are shaking now with just the thought.

And what's even more fucked-up is I turn to her and tell her to leave, even though I just bitched about her driving in the pouring rain in the first place. I need her to leave like I need air to breathe. I can't be around her right now because I worry my resolve will crumble, and I'll drop to my knees and beg her to stay. And she can't fucking stay because I'm fucked in the head.

"You need to fucking leave," I grate. "Get in your fucking car and go back home, Gwen."

I ignore the flash of pain on her face and leave her on my porch as my need to be away from her grows. My hands itch to grab her. My arms ache to hold her. My lips tingle with the need to caress hers with them. My body vibrates with need to feel her against me. And my damn heart hurts because it wants to belong to her. It already does belong to her, she just doesn't know it.

I storm down the steps, ignoring her calling my name. The rain hits me in the face, but I ignore it as I stalk toward the barn and the safety it'll offer me.

"Alexander," she cries, sounding as though she's coming after me.

Water splashes up over my jeans as I stomp in puddles. I know I'm being an ass, but in my jumbled mind, there is no explanation for her putting herself in danger. There is no reason at all she should have driven in the rain like this.

I'm halfway across the yard, about ten feet away from her truck, when her wretched sobs finally get to me, and I can't take it anymore.

"Please, Alexander," she sobs brokenly.

I stop in my tracks, put my hands on my hips, and drop my head. My eyes focus on my muddy boots, but I don't really see them. All I can see is a crushed Gwen in my mind's eye, and I just can't do it. I pull in a deep breath, turn, and nearly fall to my knees at what I see.

Gwen's standing by her car, only feet away from me. She stares at me with red eyes, looking heartbroken, silently begging me to do something. I'm not sure what, but the silent plea is more than I can handle.

"What do you want from me?" I roar across the few feet separating us.

Her flinch isn't missed and the tiny movement slices my insides. She stares at me for several seconds without answering. She's completely drenched and her hair is flat against the sides of her face. The light green button-up shirt she's wearing under her open coat molds to her chest and the white outline of her bra is clearly visible. My treacherous body responds, even though this really isn't the time.

Her next words have my heart stopping in my chest and taking every bit of air from my lungs.

"You," she whispers, just loud enough for me to hear over the rain. "I only want you."

One minute I'm standing five feet from her, and the next I have her back against the passenger side door. My chest is plastered against her heaving one and her sweet breaths fan across my face. I hover my lips over hers, still fighting with myself, but know it's a losing battle.

"I don't know what the fuck to do with you," I groan.

"Anything. You can do anything," she breathes.

I do lose it after that. I lose it because there's no way I can stay away from her. It's a feat that I was never meant to win.

I slam my lips down on hers with an agonized moan. She opens immediately and my tongue sweeps inside to meet her eager one. This kiss is different than the ones we've shared before. It's not sweet and soft and innocent. It's carnal, pure and simple. I don't ask for permission, I just take, and she gives willingly.

My hands grip her hips tightly, and I hoist her up the car. Her legs wrap around my waist and her warm center meets my painfully hard cock. My scalp burns in the most erotic way when she fists my hair and tugs me closer.

We're both soaking wet from the rain, and there's a chill in the air, but neither notices. We're both too focused on the other to care.

I grind myself against her, then swallow her answering moan. My hands go to her ass, gripping it tight. I release her lips, only to trail kisses down her neck. Rain and Gwen meets my lips and it's a heady combination that has my dick growing even harder.

This woman has driven me past the point of crazy. I'm precariously close to delirious.

Her moans become whimpers when I lick across her collarbone, then slide them down to the partially open collar of her shirt, barely giving off a hint of cleavage. I dip my tongue in the hidden valley between her breasts, and I hear her head thump against the car. Needing more of her, I take one hand from her ass, push her coat aside, and yank open her shirt, not giving a fuck that several buttons fly off.

The cups of her bra come down next, and the sight of her bare breasts, soaking wet from the rain pouring down on us, is something I'll never forget if I live a thousand lifetimes.

I dip my head and take the pretty pink nipple in my mouth. I suck greedily at it and receive a cry of pleasure in reward. I flick the sensitive nub with my tongue, then tug it gently between my teeth. I release her, then give the same treatment to her other nipple.

I lift my head and look up. Sensing my eyes on her, she lifts her head from the truck and peers down at me. She looks so fucking beautiful with rain sliding down her flushed face, her hair stuck to her cheeks, and her eyes glistening with desire. I could look at her all day and never get enough.

Her hands leave my hair and she cups my face. I'm floored, and if I'm honest, scared, when I see the love shining in her eyes as she stares down at me. I feel it too, even if I shouldn't, even if it's not right. With everything I am, with every breath I take, and every beat of my heart. That's how much I love this woman. I don't know when or how it happened, but it's undeniable, indescribable, and unbreakable.

"Take me inside," she whispers.

My decision is made before the words fully leave her mouth. There's no way I can deny her, or me, for that matter. I want her too much, and from the look in her eyes, she wants me just as badly. But not against a fucking car with rain pelting down around us and her lips turning blue from the cold. I'll take her like she deserves. In a warm bed with soft sheets and a gentle touch.

"Hold on tight to me, baby, and don't let go." The words mean so much more than her legs gripping my waist. I never want her to let me go, because I'll never be able to let her go. I'm still scared shitless that I'll let her down somehow, that I'll not be there when she needs me the most, but my heart demands I take the chance.

Her legs tighten around me, and with my hands on her ass, I turn and walk us toward the house, up the steps, and through the door. I don't stop until my knees hit the bed, and I gently set her down. Her gorgeous blue eyes stare up at me as I reach back and pull off my soaked shirt. Her gaze travels down and it's not revulsion I see when she looks at my scarred chest, but blatant desire. It still amazes me that she's never seen my scars as hideous.

I slide her coat and ruined shirt down her arms. Her stomach isn't perfectly flat like some women strive for. It has a slight curve, but it's firm. When I unclasp her bra and the cups fall away from her breasts, they look perfect, even though some would say they aren't, because they sag slightly due to her carrying babies. I think she looks completely fucking flawless.

She watches me with lusty eyes as I take in her beauty for a minute. Her hands are at her sides, and I love that she doesn't try to cover herself. She shouldn't and it would be a shame if she tried.

I drop to my knees in front of her and wedge my hips between her legs. I scoot her closer to the edge of the bed until her warm pussy meets my stomach. I kiss her soft lips and wrap my arms around her tight. She does the same by putting her arms around my neck. Her breasts feel cool against my chest and it sends a shiver through me. Not from the coolness, but from simply having her bare skin against mine.

I pull back and rain kisses across her cheek, down her neck, and over her breasts, until I reach one nipple. I take the tip in my mouth and suck gently. I not only hear her moan, but feel the vibrations of it against my mouth.

After paying the same attention to her other nipple, I release her and slide my hands to the front of her jeans. Lifting my eyes, I ask, "Are you sure?"

She nods. "I've never been more sure," she says breathlessly.

I don't take my eyes off her as I unbutton and unzip her jeans. Gripping the waistband, she lifts her hips. With the material wet, it takes a minute to slide the denim down her legs. She runs her fingers through my hair when I kiss the tops of her thighs, moving closer to her center. I can smell her and it drives me crazy. The need to taste her is almost uncontrollable, but it'll have to come later. I need inside her too much. I need to take her and make her mine.

I grip the edge of her panties and pull them down her legs. Her pretty pussy is right there in front of my eyes, and I want to devour it whole. With my fingers, my tongue, and my cock.

My shaft jerks in my jeans, begging to be the first. I stand and make quick work of my pants and briefs. The heat of Gwen's stare and the uncertainty of what she'll think once I show her the rest of my scars, has me holding still once I'm completely naked. My leg is more damaged than the rest of my body. I've had multiple surgeries and skin grafts. With the amount of my body burned and the limited skin that was left to use for grafting, the doctors felt it was best to work on my face, chest, and arm first, then see if it was still possible to do my leg. Once my face and chest were done, there wasn't much available flesh left to use, so my leg got the shit end of the deal.

I have my hands balled into fists when Gwen sees the brutal scars running up and down my leg. The gruesome sight would make even the strongest sick to their stomach.

Not Gwen though. She looks at the gnarled flesh and her eyes fill with tears, not disgust. She looks up at me for a brief second, then reaches out with a shaky hand and places her palm on my thigh. Again, it surprises me when I feel her touch the instant her hand lands on me. The feeling in my thigh is more limited than in my arm, so the shock has me sucking in a sharp breath.

When she hears my hiss of breath, she snatches her hand away and looks up at me.

"Please," I growl. "Touch me."

Her eyes go back to my leg and her hand reaches out again. She starts at my hip, and with a look of deep concentration, slowly runs her hand down my thigh to my knee. Her eyes follow the movement and her brow puckers when she comes across a particularly ugly patch of skin. Not once do her eyes tell me she's appalled by the sight.

I hold my breath and lock my knees when she leans forward and rests her lips against the nasty-looking scars, then starts kissing them. Something as beautiful as her should never be so close to something as abhorrent as my scars, but I can't pull her away. I'm mesmerized by the sight of her worshipping them, and it feels so fucking good.

When she moves closer to my hip, I can't help my body's reaction. My cock jumps and a bead of precum forms on the tip.

"Fuck, Gwen," I groan. My hands lace through her thick locks of hair and force her face up. "I can't wait anymore."

She scoots back on the bed, her legs bent, but open, showing off the part of her I want so damn much.

"Make love to me, Alexander," she whispers, lifting one hand toward me.

Putting a knee on the bed, I twine my fingers with hers and lift her wrist to my mouth, kissing the soft skin. I settle my weight over her and her smooth legs wrap around my waist. With her hand still in mine, I set my hands on each side of her head. My chest meets hers, and her pointy nipples graze my pecs. I gaze down at her and see nothing but adoration in her eyes. The tip of my shaft slides against her wet pussy, and I force myself not to surge forward.

"I don't have protection," I tell her regretfully.

She shakes her head. "I'm on the pill, and I haven't...." She stops and swallows hard. "I haven't been with anyone since Will."

I didn't realize until now how much I want to take her without anything between us. I want to feel her against me, in the most natural way possible.

It's no surprise she hasn't been with anyone since her husband died. I learned from our talks recently that she hasn't dated since Will died. Why she chose me to end her celibacy, I'll never understand.

"I haven't been with anyone either."

I refuse to say her name. She doesn't belong here with us right now. I'm not sure I could get it past my lips even if I tried anyway.

"Are you sure?" I ask, needing Gwen to be completely certain. It's a big step to trust someone enough to have sex without protection.

She nods and emphasizes her answer by lifting her hips, rubbing her wetness against my hard cock. I bare my teeth and hiss at the contact.

Lifting my body, I look down as I grip the base of my cock and line up the tip. As soon as the head breaches her tight heat, my balls draw up, and I'm on the verge of exploding. I grit my teeth and force back my orgasm as I slowly sink inside her, unwilling to let it end so quickly.

I drop my head in the crook of her neck and give myself a moment to calm the fuck down. Her muscles clamp around me, and I groan.

"Shit, Gwen, you can't do that," I growl at her.

"Please move," she moans in response, shifting her legs against my hips. "I need you to move."

Pulling in a deep breath for restraint, I get to my elbows. I keep my eyes locked on her as I slowly pull my hips back, then rock forward again. Dropping my lips to hers, I kiss her as I keep a steady rhythm with my hips. Her whimpers against my mouth and the tightening of her pussy tell me she's already close, and I thank fuck for that, because I don't know how much longer I can hold on. We've barely begun, but with us both going so long without, it's impossible for either to last.

I speed up my thrusts and she cries against my lips as I hit a particularly sensitive spot. I home in on it and lift my head so I can see the pure rapture on her face. Her eyes are bright and unfocused, her cheeks a beautiful shade of pink, and her lips are swollen from my kisses and form an O as she pants.

When she tips over the edge and strangles my dick with her channel, I swear I've reached heaven. Starting in the base of my shaft, my orgasm hits me hard and fast and has me yelling to the ceiling. My thrusts become frantic as we both ride waves of orgasmic pleasure.

I drop my chest back to hers, making sure my weight doesn't crush her. We lie there silently, simply trying to catch our breath. Her hands lazily rub up and down my slick back.

After a moment, I lift my chest a few inches and gaze down at her. Sweat dampens her forehead and I push the wet strands away from her cheeks.

"Hi," she whispers with a shy smile.

The look warms my heart, and I smile. "Hey."

I kiss her lips, then roll to my side and turn her to face me. Tangling my legs with hers, I put my arm around her waist and tug her a bit closer to me. I know my cum must be leaking out of her, and I'm sure it probably feels awkward, but I'm not ready to let her go just yet. I'll grab a rag and clean her in a few minutes.

As I lie there in the aftermath of one of the best moments of my life, I wonder how I got so lucky as to meet this incredible woman. This feeling I have deep in my gut is something I never want to relinquish. It's not the sex talking. It's something I felt the first moment I saw her, something I didn't recognize at the time and still have a hard time naming even now.

Love isn't a strong enough word for what I feel for Gwen. It doesn't even come close. What I feel for her is soul-deep and everlasting, a feeling that scares the ever-lovin' hell out of me, but something I can't deny any longer and will hold on to forever.

Chapter Nineteen

Gwendolyn

"WILL YOU TELL ME about her?" I ask nervously.

The hand caressing my hip stops, and I want to suck the words back in my mouth. I shouldn't have asked. Now isn't the time, and even if it was, he may not be ready. Although it's been four years since they passed, the pain is still very raw. And for all I know, he may not ever want to talk to me about her.

We're still in bed after our lovemaking. The rain's still pouring down and the wind has picked up, the former making a soothing rhythm against the roof. I've always loved the sound of rain hitting the roof.

I lie with my head on his chest and my hand under my cheek. It's been thirty minutes since we made love, and I'm still feeling the effects of pure bliss.

I open my mouth to apologize and tell him he doesn't need to talk about her, but he stops me before I can. His hand starts languidly rubbing circles on my hip again when he starts talking.

"Clara was one of the sweetest women I've ever met. She was kindhearted and giving, and so beautiful."

I remember the picture from his drawer. She wasn't beautiful, she was gorgeous.

"She had these quirks. Like twirling her hair around her finger. Sometimes I'd find it annoying. Like when we were watching a movie. Her hand would keep going in and out of view, which was distracting. Other times, it would be endearing. She'd be doing it and for some reason, my eyes would catch on it, and I'd sit there for several minutes watching. She could do this thing where she could tie a strand of hair into a knot with just three fingers on the same hand."

My eyes drift up to him and I see a small smile playing on his face. His expression says he's far away, lost in memories.

"It was a habit she picked up from her mom and hoped our daughter would pick up as well."

The smile slowly drops from his face.

"She was cold all the time and always had to have something on her feet. You'd never catch her without at least socks, but most times she had on some form of shoes. She and her family were from Florida, so it was a big adjustment for her when they moved here. I don't think her body ever adjusted. She hated to be cold. At night, in bed, she'd always warm her icy feet by laying them flat against my calves." He laughs at the memory.

I love hearing him talking about her. She was such a big part of his life for so long. And I love that their love was so strong.

"She loved cherry filling, like in a pie, but hated real cherries. It was the opposite with coconut. She hated anything with the flavor coconut, but loved coconut itself. She loved altering words. Instead of potato, she'd say tater, and for spaghetti, it was sketti." His chuckle is quiet when he continues. "She'd get her words mixed up in the funniest of ways too. Like, she would try to say, I'm going to wash the car, and it would come out as I'm going to car the wash. Some were pretty entertaining."

I laugh lightly and tip my head back so I can see him. "She seems like she'd be fun to be around."

He looks down, then tucks a piece of hair behind my ear, letting his finger linger on my cheek.

"She would have liked you," he says warmly.

"I'm sure I would have liked her too," I tell him honestly.

As much as it pains me to think I wouldn't have Alexander in my life if Clara and Rayne were still here, it hurts even more knowing the pain he went through when he lost them. I'd rather give up my own happiness to ensure he still had his. I just hope one day he gives me the chance to make him as happy as Clara did.

I kiss the center of his chest before flipping over and resting my arm across his stomach and laying my head on it. His arm hangs over my waist and he rests his hand against the base of my spine.

"I'm sorry for scaring you earlier," I say while running my fingers over the smooth scars on his chest. As gruesome as they may appear to some, I think they're beautiful. It shows his strength and the story of his heartbreaking past.

"What was so important that you would drive in such bad weather?"

He stares down at me, and I can tell he's still bothered. It warms my insides to know he cares enough that he worried about me. But then, I hate that he went through that reminded pain.

"I wanted to see you." I shift so I'm sitting up more, taking the sheet with me. "After talking with you on the phone for so long, I just felt a strong need to see you."

I drop my eyes, suddenly feeling exposed. Not physically, but mentally.

He grabs my chin and forces my eyes back to his.

"I know I overreacted, but the thought...." He closes his eyes for a moment, looking pained, before opening them again. "I can't do it again, Gwen," he finishes in an agonized whisper.

I scoot closer to him. I know what he's thinking, and I want to wipe the thought from his mind.

"Nothing will happen to me."

"There's no way you can promise that," he argues.

Cupping his damaged cheek, I lean up and kiss his lips. "I can't, but I can guarantee that I'll be as careful as I can, and I know you'll protect me as best as you can."

His eyes turn tortured as he takes in my words. I can tell he wants to believe me, but past experiences and his guilt over not saving his wife and baby prevent him from doing so. I hold his gaze, wanting him to see the truth. His eyes stay guarded, and it makes me even more determined to show him he's a good and honorable man, and that what happened was in no way his fault.

As much as I don't want to, I need to get back to the kids.

I kiss his lips once more before pulling back. "I have to go get the kids. They're at Jeremy's and his mom's having lunch. I'm sure they're probably wondering where I am."

He lifts his arm from my waist, and I slide to the edge of the bed. I feel the heat of him following me. I try to take the sheet with me because somehow my underwear ended up on the other side of the room, and I'm not yet at the stage of shamelessly traipsing across the room naked. When I stand and tug on the sheet, it doesn't move. I turn and look at what's stopping it, and see a grinning Alexander with the sheet gripped in his fist.

I arch an eyebrow. "You gonna let go anytime soon?"

His grin grows. "I'll think I'll keep ahold of it for a while."

"Alexander," I beg.

"Nah-uh." He shakes his head, then tips his chin toward where my panties are on the floor. "You gonna get dressed?"

I narrow my eyes and hold his stare for several seconds before an idea pops in my head. Two can play this game. Turning on my heel, I make sure to sashay my hips as I walk over to my panties. With my cheeks pink, and with more boldness than I thought I was capable of, I bend with my ass facing him and scoop up my panties from the floor.

Hearing a groan behind me, I turn back to face him with my own smirk.

"Fuck me," he mutters. "That shit backfired."

I laugh and slip my legs through the holes and pull them up my hips. I still feel self-conscious as I walk over to my bra by the end of the bed, especially since my breasts aren't as firm as they used to be. His appreciative gaze says I have nothing to worry about.

He climbs from the bed, and my eyes move to the hardness swaying between his legs. Earlier, when he first pulled off his jeans and briefs, my concentration was stuck on the scars running up and down his leg, so even though it was pretty much in my face, I didn't get a good look at his erection. And afterwards, he was covered by the sheet. Now though, I can't take my eyes off it. He's huge, so huge that it's a wonder it fit inside me without ripping me in two.

My eyes go wide, and although his size is very intimidating, my body heats at the reminder of how good he felt sliding in and out of me.

His chuckle has my eyes snapping up to his, and I feel a blush creep up my cheeks at being caught ogling him.

"You keep looking at me like that and you'll be calling Jeremy to let him know he's got the kids for another couple of hours."

His laugh is deep when I drop my eyes from him and turn around. Spying my shirt a couple feet away, I grab it and my jeans beside it and put them on. I shiver when the cold and wet material touches my skin. My shirt has no buttons. I turn around to ask him for a shirt, and thankfully see he's dressed in the same jeans and thermal shirt he had on before, even though they are obviously wet. Silently, he holds out a shirt for me. I slip it on and stealthily smell the soft material.

I snag my jacket off the floor and we leave the bedroom. Gigi comes trotting out of the kitchen and meets us at the front door. I give her a few rubs before he opens the door and we step outside. The rain has stopped and there're a few rays of sunlight filtering through the clouds.

Before I can walk down the steps, he turns me around to face him, loosely putting his arms around my waist and resting his hands on my lower back.

"How about you and the kids come over for dinner tomorrow night?" he suggests.

I smile, because, well, I can't *not* smile. I love that he wants us to come back. I love that he wants to spend time with the kids. And I love that he seems to be working past his issues. We've never actually talked about what's going on between us, but we both know there is something there.

"I'd love to, and I know the kids would too."

"Good."

He drops his head and sweeps his lips across mine before settling them more firmly against my mouth. I love the way he tastes and the way he kisses me. His arms tighten around me, bringing me closer to him, and I dig my fingers into his sides as we tangle our tongues together. My core begins to pulse with renewed need, and I wish we had more time. My body is pleasantly sore, but it doesn't stop me from wanting him again. From his deep groan, he wouldn't be opposed to the idea either.

The crunch of tires on the driveway is what pulls us apart. We break away and turn our heads to see a white car driving up to the house.

"Shit," Alexander mutters when the car pulls to a stop. He drops his arms and takes a step back.

"Who is it?" I ask, turning to him.

His eyes leave the car long enough for him to look back at me and say, "My parents," before looking back.

Surprise has my mouth dropping open, then nerves start to take over.

"Wait! What?" I squeak.

Alexander turns back to me, sees my anxiety, and reaches for my hand. "Hey," he says, bending his knees to look directly into my eyes. "There's nothing to be worried about."

A car door slams behind us. I've got no choice but to nod. I've got no time to freak out or get used to the idea of meeting his parents. It's not that I don't want to; actually, I really *do* want to. It's just that I would have liked more time to prepare.

A tall man with weathered skin, dark brown hair, and kind eyes comes walking up, a petite woman with sandy-blond hair tucked into his side. As soon as the woman sees Alexander and me standing on the porch, she pushes away from the man and rushes forward, her hand flying to her mouth. Alexander releases my hand and walks down the steps, meeting her at the bottom. When he engulfs her in his arms, she's so small compared to him that the only thing I can see is her arms wrapped around his waist.

Murmured words come from her, but they're so low, I can't hear them. I look past them and see the man looking up at me curiously. I offer an unsure smile and one corner of his mouth lifts.

A moment later, Alexander and his mother break apart, and I hear his softly spoken, "Hey, Mom."

She puts her hands on either side of his face and pulls his head down to kiss his cheek before stepping back to let the man step forward. They embrace tightly, clap each other on the back, then step back.

"I've got someone I want you to meet," Alexander says, then steps back so his mother can see me.

I wring my hands nervously as they take the few steps to the porch where I'm still standing. Alexander comes to my side and wraps an arm around my waist.

"Mom, Dad, this is Gwendolyn." He squeezes me. "Gwendolyn, this is Helen, my mother, and David, my father."

"It's nice to meet you both," I say, holding out my hand to Helen.

She looks just as startled as me, but recovers quickly. I expect to shake her hand, but she surprises me when she pulls me into her arms. I'm stiff for a split second before wrapping my arms around her. Helen's head only comes to my nose. She's such a tiny thing, but her arms are tight around me.

When she steps back, David comes forward and hugs me as well.

"It's so good to meet you, darlin'," he says after pulling back.

"Gwendolyn," Helen remarks. "That's such a pretty name."

"Please, call me Gwen. Most everyone does."

She shakes her head and smiles. "I'll stick with Gwendolyn, if that's okay."

I nod and give her my own smile. "That's fine."

Helen turns toward Alexander. "I didn't know you were seeing anyone," she scolds lightly, but there's a light in her eyes.

He gives her a half smile, looks down at me, then replies, "I wasn't until recently."

She stands in front of us, her hands folded prayer style below her mouth. Her eyes glisten with tears as she looks at us. "Well, this is good news."

Although we've only just met and Alexander and I haven't known each other long, I get the feeling Helen sees something Alexander and I haven't even talked about; the seriousness of our relationship and where it's going. I know where I want it to go, and I'm pretty sure he does too. Helen though, looks as if she's already picturing our wedding day. I'd laugh if it wasn't for the fact that deep down inside, I've pictured it too and want it to come true so much.

"What are you guys doing here?" Alexander asks, slipping his arm back around me.

David gives him a sympathetic look. "Once you gave the okay, I held her off as long as I could."

Helen slaps her husband's stomach, but says to Alexander, "I couldn't wait any longer. I missed you and it's been too long."

Alexander clears his throat, looking bothered for some reason, but simply nods.

"I'm glad you're here."

Something feels strange, almost tense, and I wonder if something happened between Alexander and his family. It's good that I can't stay, because I think they need time alone together.

"I hate to be so rude, but I've got to be going." I turn to Alexander. "The kids are waiting on me."

Before he can respond, I hear his mother ask, "You have kids?"

I turn back to her. "I do. Kelsey, my girl, is eight. And my boy, Daniel, is six."

Her eyes move to Alexander. Both elation and a hint of sadness flashes across her face.

"Can we meet them?" she asks with undisguised hope. The look on her face and knowing she's lost a granddaughter have my throat clogging up.

I grab her hand and give it a firm squeeze. With my eyes, I tell her I understand her pain. She smiles sadly at me.

I'm fine with the kids meeting his parents, but I still leave the decision up to Alexander, as they are *his* parents, and I worry this may be something he's not ready for yet.

I needn't have worried. He glances at me, and I give him a subtle nod.

"They're coming over for dinner tomorrow evening. You can meet them then."

The smile that comes across Helen's face makes her appear ten years younger.

We leave them on the porch and Alexander walks me to my truck. Once I'm at the driver-side door, he puts his arms around me. I feel weird with his parents on the porch with a clear view of us, but I wrap my arms around his waist anyway.

"Sorry about that. I had no idea they were coming for a visit."

"It's fine," I assure him. "They seem like wonderful people."

He nods. "They are. Are you sure you don't mind bringing the kids tomorrow to meet them? We can do it some other time."

I'm shaking my head before he finishes. "As long as you're okay with it, so am I."

He dips his head and places a light kiss on my lips.

"See you tomorrow," he murmurs, then reaches behind me and opens my door.

Not wanting to leave him, but knowing I have to, I step back and get behind the wheel. As soon as the door is closed and I start the truck, I roll down my window. He bends and gives me another kiss before stepping back.

I drive away with a big smile on my face, feeling happier and more hopeful than I have in a long time.

Chapter Twenty

Gwendolyn

ME: *WE'RE LEAVING. Be there in twenty.*
I hit Send, then call for the kids, letting them know it's time to go.

To say they are excited to meet Alexander's parents was a big understatement. Well, Daniel shows his excitement, but I can tell the idea is pleasing to Kelsey as well from the look in her eyes. I don't have any family left and it's not often they get to see Will's parents because they travel a lot. Besides me, Emma, Will's parents, and now the few people in town we've grown close with, they have no one else.

And now Alexander and his parents. I smile at the thought.

Daniel comes running out of his room, several of the figurines Alexander gave him clutched in his hand. He informed me earlier that he wanted to take some with him to show Alexander that he was taking good care of them like he promised.

Kelsey comes out at a more sedate pace, and I'm pleased to see she's using the homemade crossword puzzle books again. She has been since Alexander talked to her. That talk has done a world of good for my little girl. She's still hasn't spoken to me, but I do catch glimpses of her looking happier than she's been since Will died. It's been a month since I heard her talking to Alexander, but I'm hoping, given time, she'll talk to me. Every night since I heard her asking God to help Alexander, she's prayed the same thing. I don't believe she's forgotten about her father; it's more she's finally accepting he's not coming home. I think she's found peace with that.

"Are you both ready?" I ask.

Daniel shouts his yes, while Kelsey nods, a ghost of a smile playing on her face. It's so hard for me to look at her when I see a happier emotion on her face, because I want to gather her in my arms and hug her so tightly.

We decided not to bring Pepper on this trip since we recently had her spayed and she needs the rest, so Daniel says goodbye as I grab the casserole dish with cheesy baked shells and broccoli. Jitters form in my belly as I pull out of the driveway. Even though I've already met his parents, I'm both anxious and nervous. I know it's stupid, because they seemed like really nice people, but what if they don't like me? What if they don't understand Kelsey's mutism and think awful things about her? What if Daniel's spirited disposition is too much for them?

If that's the case, obviously I wouldn't want my kids or me to have anything do with them, but I know it'll hurt Alexander if we couldn't be around his parents. My kids come first and always will, no matter what, but I hate to think about anything negative between Alexander and me.

I pull to a stop at the stop sign and flip on my blinker to turn down the long road that leads to Alexander's house. Making sure there's no one coming either way, I press the gas pedal and pull forward.

It happens before I know it. There's a loud blaring sound seconds before the hard hit comes from behind us. Something crunches, and the impact of the hit flings my head to the side, where it smashes against the window. Pain instantly bursts in my head, but I don't have time to really feel it before I'm flung to the other side as the car rolls to its side. The only thing keeping me in place is the seat belt digging into my shoulder and stomach.

I hear Daniel screaming from the back seat and Kelsey wailing my name as the car comes to a stop on its roof.

My head pounds an erratic beat and my vision starts to cloud. I try blinking the fuzziness away, but each time I close my eyes, it's harder for me to open them again.

"Mama!" Kelsey yells again, and the only thing I can think as my visions fills with black spots is how long I've waited to hear Kelsey call me mama again. Before the darkness consumes me, I send up a silent prayer begging God to let my kids be okay.

Alexander

I GLANCE DOWN AT my phone for what seems like the hundredth time, and the screen still shows no missed notifications. I get up from the couch and start pacing the floor. My dad, who's been watching an old football game, mutes the TV.

"What's wrong with you?" he asks.

My feet carry me back and forth over the brown carpet, and I barely spare him a glance when I answer him.

"Gwen. She messaged me thirty minutes ago saying she was on her way." I look down at my phone again, only for it look the same as it did ten seconds ago. "She should have been here by now."

"Sit down, son. I'm sure she just had to stop somewhere or there was a bit of traffic."

I shoot him a look that says his suggestions are ridiculous. "Have you forgotten you used to live here? We don't have traffic in Cat's Valley."

"True, but she probably stopped by the store and grabbed something to go with dinner."

A loud banging coming from the kitchen has my body jerking. My mom yells out "Sorry!" before going back to cooking the dinner she insisted on making.

Dread forms in my stomach for no apparent reason. It's just a gut feeling that something isn't right. Something's not fucking right.

One of the puppies, which my mother fell in love with and informed my father she was taking one home, starts barking. Thinking, no *hoping*, it's Gwen and the kids pulling up the driveway, I walk briskly to the door and snatch it open. I check the yard, I check the driveway, and I check the road in front of my property and don't see her car.

One of the puppies rushes past me out the door, and I bend down and scoop it back up, taking it back inside with me.

I bring my phone screen to life and curse under my breath when it reveals nothing.

My mom walks out of the kitchen, wiping her hands on a dish towel, and sees me standing by the door. I'm sure my face reveals my worry.

"What's wrong, dear?" she asks, walking over to me.

"Gwen was supposed to be here ten minutes ago."

Understanding dawns on her face and she places a hand on my arm. The gesture is for comfort, but it does nothing for me.

"I'm sure they're fine."

I nod and try to force a smile, but I know it comes out flat. Something tells me they aren't fine. My mind screams that something happened to them.

"Come on," she says, gesturing to the kitchen behind her. "You can help me with the salad."

"I don't—"

The ringing of my phone stops me, and I immediately bring it up to look at the screen.

Gwen calling.

Instant relief hits me.

I swipe my finger across the screen and bring it to my ear.

"Gwen, where—"

"A-alexander," Kelsey's tearful voice interrupts me.

Ice replaces the blood in my veins at the sound of her frightful tone. The hand on my phone clenches, and I have to force it to relax before it crushes the device.

"Kelsey, what's wrong, sweetie?" My voice comes out strained.

"W-we got into a-a wreck and t-the c-car's upside d-down," she sputters out.

My heart feels like it's trying to beat out of my chest, so I pull in a deep breath and try to calm myself down before I lose it. Kelsey's upset enough, so I need to keep my cool for her, even though every-fucking-thing inside me tries to pull me down a dark hole. Memories try to surface and it takes every bit of strength I have to push them back. I keep my head down and my eyes pinned on my feet, forcing myself to focus.

"Where's Daniel and your mom? Are you all okay?" I ask Kelsey hoarsely.

"Y-es. Dan-daniel's right here. M-me and him are o-okay." At the mention of his name, I hear him cry in the background.

Some of my worry lessens at knowing he's alive, but she still hasn't fully answered my question.

"Kelsey, where's your mom?"

Instead of answering, she starts crying into the phone, and I swear my heart stops and drops to my fucking toes.

I hear my mom talking to me and see my dad walking over, but I zone them both out.

"Kelsey," I say more forcefully, but try my best to keep my tone calm. "Your mom... where is she?"

She sniffles a couple times, then finally says, "S-she's s-still in the f-front seat. We keep calling h-her n-name, but s-she's not w-waking up and s-she has b-blood on her h-head."

That's all it takes for my legs to give out, and I sink to my knees, right there in front of my mom and dad. A churning starts in my stomach, and I feel like I'm going to puke. A buzzing starts in my ears and the outside edges of my vision start to blur. My chest heaves rapidly and tingles form at the tips of my fingers. I know I'm on the verge of a panic attack and there's not a damn thing I can do about it.

The only thing that brings me back is the hard grip on my shoulder and Kelsey's whimpered, "I'm scared, Alexander."

I focus my gaze and see my mother's tear-filled eyes looking at me. She's on the floor in front of me, with my dad beside her, his hand on my shoulder.

To my father, I say, "Grab my keys from the bar. Gwen and the kids have been in an accident." I don't have time to explain more, and thankfully they don't ask.

He stands and pulls keys from his pocket. "We'll take mine."

"Do you know where you are, Kelsey?" I barely get out through my thick throat.

I push past the sick feeling in my stomach and stand on shaky legs. We're already heading out the door when Kelsey answers.

"We were j-just turning on the r-road that leads to y-your h-house."

I relay the information to my mother and tell her to call 911. She whips out her phone and immediately starts dialing.

Feeling like someone's reached inside my chest and is squeezing my heart with needle-lined gloves, I run toward my parents' car. Sensing my urgency, they both run behind me, getting in the car only seconds after me.

"We're coming, Kelsey," I promise hoarsely. "Just stay on the phone with me, okay?"

Her "Okay" sounds so small and fragile.

I hear my mom in the back seat talking to a dispatcher, explaining as much as she can without having any details except for the location and that there's an unconscious woman and two children. My dad speeds out of the driveway, and I'm glad he decided to drive. I'm not sure I would be able to at the moment. My phone repeatedly taps against my ear from my hand shaking so much.

It's only about five minutes from my house, but it takes us less than two. There are two cars sitting haphazardly on the side of the road. One has the front end totally smashed in with the front windshield shattered. Even through the shattered glass, you can see the blood splattered on the inside.

As sad as it is that it appears the driver is probably dead, my only concern is the other car, which is flipped over. I climb from the car, my eyes never leaving Gwen's. My legs feel numb as I walk closer to it. Through the busted-out window, I can see Gwen's dark brown hair. Not her face, not her body, just her fucking hair.

My legs freezing in place about twenty feet away. My chest feels likes there's a ten-ton boulder sitting on it. The phone I still have clutched in my hand falls from my fingers. I don't hear it hit the ground. I don't hear my father calling my name or see him running toward Gwen's truck while my mom goes to check on the occupants of the other car. I don't see him helping Kelsey and Daniel out or hear their hysterical cries. I don't hear when Daniel notices me and starts screaming my name. I don't hear the far-off sounds of sirens that are still too fucking far away.

My eyes are focused on the matted brown hair. It's like I have tunnel vision and that's all I can see; nothing else exists. Then the vision changes, and it's Clara's pleading eyes that I see. It's her hoarse screams begging me to save Rayne that I hear. It's Clara's contorted face after the water swallowed her up, and the black abyss in the back seat as I looked for Rayne when I was pulled from the car. It's Rayne's cries, and the resounding silence when they abruptly stopped.

Then it changes again. Clara is replaced with Gwen. It's Gwen's brown hair that floats in the water, almost giving her an ethereal appearance. It's Gwen's terrified blue gaze that silently begs me. It's Gwen's hand that tries to reach for me, that I'm unable to grab hold of.

Something in me snaps, and I'm hurtled back into the here and now. Everything crashes back into focus all at once. My heart slams against my rib cage when I realize I've been standing here way too long while Gwen's been in the car, maybe dying. That thought has my feet beating against the pavement as I run toward the truck.

Ten feet away, a hysterical cry has me looking to the left. My dad has a distraught Kelsey in his arms. She's screaming "Mama" over and over again as she struggles with everything she has, trying to break free and run back to the truck. Her arms are stretched out, her fingers opening and closing pathetically, as if trying to grab for her mom. I can see my dad is having a hard time keeping hold of her. If it wasn't for the urgency of the situation, I'd be amazed at her strength.

Looking back at Gwen's ruined car and her brown hair, I take a chance and run the few feet to Kelsey and my dad. She needs to calm down before she hurts herself. I would never be able to live with myself if something happened to her.

I come to a stop in front of them, but it's as though Kelsey doesn't even see me. Her eyes are frantic as she strains to look around me at the truck and screams for her mother. I grab her cheeks and step fully in front of her, blocking her view of the truck. The sight of her red and swollen eyes, tear-soaked cheeks, heaving chest, and trembling body has my throat clogging. I quickly take stock of the rest of her and am glad when I only see a small scratch on her cheek.

Her eyes are on me now, but they stay unfocused, the pupils dilated, and I know she still doesn't see me. Her struggles have slowed now that she's not able to see the car, but haven't died down completely. My dad is still bent with one arm wrapped tightly around her waist and one around her upper body.

"Kelsey," I call. When she still looks through me, I say her name more forcefully and shake her lightly, needing to get her attention quickly so I can get to Gwen. "Kelsey!" Her pupils finally shrink and her eyes focus on me. The plea in them reminds me of Clara's when she begged me to save Rayne. I have to grit my teeth and force myself to not go back down that dark hole of remembrance.

"I need you to calm down for me, okay? I'm going to go get your mom, but I need you to stay here with David. He's my dad and will take care of you." I stop, making sure she hears me, then ask, "Can you do that for me?"

It only takes her a couple of seconds before she nods. "Okay," she croaks.

I lean forward and kiss her forehead, then pull back. My eyes briefly lift to my dad's. He gives me a nod, and I know he'll care for her. I look around quickly and am satisfied when I see a crying Daniel in my mom's arms a few feet away.

My stomach bottoms out as I turn back to the car.

You can't fucking have her, I demand silently to God. *You've taken enough from me. I barely survived last time. I know I won't be able to a second time. She's mine, and I need her. I refuse to let you take her!*

When I skid to a stop at her side of the car, I still don't see her face. It's turned slightly to the side and her mane of thick hair falls down, hiding her from view. I can see her body though, as it hangs upside down from the still buckled seat belt. The steering wheel keeps her legs from hanging down, but her arms hang lifelessly, her hands resting against the roof.

I drop to my knees, not only because I need to be on the ground to be able to get to her, but because my knees will no longer hold me up.

"Gwen," I whisper hoarsely. Not expecting an answer, I'm not surprised when I don't get one. Tears blur my vision, but I blink them away. I can't afford to lose it right now. That can come later.

The door doesn't budge when I try opening it. There's glass on the pavement, but I don't feel it as it cuts into my hands when I push my upper body through the window and gently push back her hair.

My heart stops, and I break out into a cold sweat when I see the big gash on her head, starting at her hairline and stopping at the outside edge of her eyebrow. A steady drip of blood falls from the deep cut, and when I look down, I see the small pool of blood. Icy fear slithers deeper into my gut.

I amend my earlier thought.

Please don't take her from me. Please, let her be okay. I can't lose her too. Kelsey and Daniel can't lose her. We all need her too damn much. She's too important.

I slide my fingers along her neck until I reach the spot where a pulse should be. At first I don't feel it, and I die inside, but then a faint bump hits the tip of my fingers. Then another a second later. It's weak. Too fucking weak, but it's there, and it gives me hope. I just pray it's not false hope.

Needing to get her free of the seat belt, but not wanting to jar her too much for fear of doing more damage, I angle my body beneath hers and lie on my back so I'm looking up at her. Her hair drapes against my chest, just below my face, and the blood dripping from the cut starts soaking my shirt.

"I'm going to get you out of here, baby," I tell her silent form. "Just hold on for me, okay? The ambulance is almost here. I just need you to hold on."

I know she's unconscious and probably doesn't hear me, but it helps to talk to her. It makes the possibility of losing her seem less real. I can't think of that right now, because I'll freeze again. I wasn't able to save Clara and Rayne. I'll be damned if I won't save Gwen.

Spreading my fingers as far apart as I can, I place my palm against her chest and lift my body slightly. When I release the seat belt, with my hand on her chest and my body only about a foot away from hers, I slowly lower her to me. I move her legs so they fall from behind the steering wheel.

Immediate relief hits me when I feel her warm body against mine, but it's short lived, because I know she's not out of danger. The gash on her forehead is deep and there's a chance there could be internal bleeding in her brain. Not to mention there could damage to other parts of her body. From the brief glance I got when I first stuck my head in the cab, I didn't see anything else wrong with her on the outside, but that doesn't mean there couldn't be something wrong on the inside.

I push past the panic that thought tries to bring forward.

I wrap one arm around her upper body and try to keep it as still as possible so I don't jolt her as I start shifting both of us out of the window inch by inch.

I have her out about halfway, when the space becomes too small. I'm about to call out to my dad when I feel hands on the arm I have wrapped around her. I lift my head and look out the window to see my dad down on his knees, ready to help.

"Be careful. She's got a big gash on her forehead and we don't know what other injuries she has."

He nods and slips his arms beneath her shoulders while I lift her upper thighs as best as I can with my upper body still in the truck. Once her legs are out, I scoot as fast as I can until I'm out. My dad has her laid out on her back, and I crawl until I'm hovering over her. Her face is ghostly white and it scares the shit out of me. Although I just felt her pulse a moment ago, the need to feel it again has my fingers going back to her throat.

Right as I feel the slight thump again, a voice comes from behind me.

"Sir, we need you to step back."

A second later, a medical bag is set down beside me, then a paramedic gets down on his knees on her other side, while the other waits for me to get out of the way.

I want to insist that I'm not going anywhere, that I can't leave her side, but I know I have to move in order for them to do their work.

I don't stand, I just scoot back several feet and sit on my heels. My breath comes in pants as I watch helplessly while they take her vitals and slip on a neck brace. My body feels completely numb, all except for my heart. Each heavy beat sends a sharp pain through my chest. I ball my hands into fists so tight that my knuckles scream at me. Tears leak from my eyes, scalding my cheeks.

I feel a hand on my shoulder and look up. My dad's standing there watching them work on Gwen as well, a look of deep sadness marring his face. My eyes drift past him to my mom, who has Daniel and Kelsey in her arms. Both are crying and have their eyes pinned on Gwen lying still on the pavement.

Kelsey's eyes leave her mom long enough to look at me, and I lift my arm toward her, indicating I want them to come to me. I need them in my arms right now, and I know they need me too. My mom sees my lifted arm and lets the kids go. Kelsey, with her brother's hand in hers, runs them both over to me.

I open my arms and they crash against my chest. I close my eyes and thank God they're both okay, then beg God in the same breath that their mother will be as well. I open my eyes and see Gwen now on a spinal board.

The kids cry against my shoulders, and I want to keep them against me until I know Gwen is okay, but they need to be checked out too.

As if sensing my thoughts, another paramedic comes to kneel beside us, medical bag in hand. I release the kids and try to pull back, but they cling to me. I allow their arms to stay around me, but I lean my head back so I can look at them. Their lips tremble as their tear-filled eyes meet mine.

My voice is scratchy when I tell them, "The paramedics need to check you both over, okay?" Fear enters their face, so I reassure them. "I'll be right here with you."

"Is M-mama going to be o-okay?" Kelsey asks in a terrified voice.

I have no fucking clue what to tell her because I don't know the answer. I don't want to lie to her, but I also don't want to scare her any further than she already is. I look over and see the paramedics lifting Gwen onto the gurney.

I look back to Kelsey, and I hope like fuck that I'm not lying to her when I say, "Your mom is going to be fine."

It takes her a minute, but she nods, taking my words for the truth I pray they are. She releases me and turns to the paramedic, and Daniel follows suit.

As he looks the kids over, my eyes go back to Gwen, who still hasn't woken up. It's scares me shitless that she's still unconscious. I need her to wake up and show me she's going to be okay. I need to hear her beautiful voice and see her stunning blue eyes. I won't be able to fully breathe again until I do. The only thing keeping me together at the moment is the two kids that need me to stay strong. Gwen would want me to be strong for them. If it weren't for them, there's no telling the state I'd be in.

The paramedic deems the kids fine, just a few bumps and bruises, but still wants them to be checked out at the hospital. I'm torn when he asks me if I want to ride in the back of the ambulance with the kids, because I want to be with Gwen. The thought of having her out of my sight has panic trying to take over. What if she dies on the way to the hospital? What if we get there and the paramedic says she didn't make it?

I look to the kids' scared and pain-filled faces and know I can't leave them alone. I know my mom or dad would ride with them, but it's me they want, and I can't deny them. There's nothing I can do for Gwen at the moment. She's in the hands of the paramedics, and I have to trust them to keep her safe. The kids need me more than her right now.

Gwen is loaded up and when the door's closed and I can no longer see her, I swear my heart drops to my stomach. Vomit threatens.

The ambulance speeds away with its siren blaring, and I pray once again that she'll be okay.

She has to be.

As the kids and I are loaded into the back of the other ambulance, my dad promises that he and my mom will be right behind us. I nod as the doors close behind us, and seconds later we're moving as well, at a slower speed. I grit my teeth to keep from demanding we go faster.

The kids are sitting on the gurney, and I've got each of my hands holding one of theirs. I try to smile at them to keep up the façade of Gwen being okay. I don't want them to see the worry and pain I'm currently feeling. They don't need to know that I'm slowly dying inside, and I won't be resurrected until I know Gwen will make it out of this alive.

Until I get a chance to tell her what I haven't told her yet. That I love her.

Chapter Twenty-One

Gwendolyn

I WAKE TO THE MOST beautiful sound I've heard in years. It warms my belly and makes me want to smile. I want to open my eyes and look for the wonderful sound, but I'm scared if I do, it'll only be a dream. It's something I've wanted to hear for such a long time and feared would never happen. I don't think I'll survive it if it's just a dream.

Something warm and soft is pressed to my side, and I want to snuggle into it further. A sweet and innocent floral scent hits my nose, and I love the smell. I feel pressure on my hand, and it's only then I realize there are small fingers laced with mine. I give a tiny squeeze, checking to see if it's real or just my imagination.

"Mama?" a soft voice says in my ear, and it's that sound again that I love so much. The sweet way it's said has tears forming under my closed eyes.

Unable to hold off any longer, I squint my eyes open, ready to slam them shut again and pray I can pull the dream back if what I hope is happening isn't true. I feel the pull of a bandage and a slow throb on my forehead. Bright light blinds me and the throb becomes a piercing pain. Ignoring it, I try to focus. I *need* to know if it's real. My vision is blurry, so I blink a few times.

When the world comes into focus, I'm met with eyes so green and beautiful it takes my breath away.

"Mama?" the voice says again.

My heart hurts so much at hearing this particular voice call me mama. But it's a beautiful kind of pain. It's a pain I'll not only endure, I'll beg to feel it every single day for the rest of my life.

Tears start leaking down my cheeks, and I let them, because there's no way I could force them back.

"Hey, baby," I croak, and lift my hand to lay it on my baby girl's cheek.

Her eyes turn glassy, and I know she's going to cry too. Seconds later, the first tear falls and her lips start to tremble. Her eyes flicker back and forth between mine, as if searching for something. She has a small bandage on her right cheek. Before I get a chance to worry that she's hurt, she launches herself at me and wraps her arms tightly around my neck. Mine go around her small waist, and I hold on for dear life. My body aches where she's lying on me, but I don't care. I've got my girl in my arms and she said mama.

"I was so scared you died," Kelsey cries against my neck. Her small body shakes in my arms

Tears track down my cheeks in rivers as I run my hand through her hair and down her back. As much as I hate knowing she was worried, I can't help but be grateful that it's caused her to start speaking.

"Shh," I murmur against her hair. "I'm okay."

She clings to me so tightly that it makes it hard to breathe, but she could cut off all the blood to my head and I wouldn't care, as long as I have her in my arms and talking.

Something catches my attention, and I look to the right. My eyes land on Alexander with Daniel on his lap. There's a small bandage on my son's chin and my heart hurts knowing he was hurt. I run my eyes over the rest of him, feeling relief when I don't see any other injuries.

Daniel looks at me with wide green eyes, so much like Will's. There's fear in them and it breaks my heart to know he was scared as well. They've both lost so much already.

The IV line in my hand pulls when I lift my arm toward him. "Come here, sweetie," I croak out.

He scrambles off Alexander's lap and attempts to climb onto my bed. Alexander gets up, and before helping him the rest of the way, he grabs a cup on the bedside table and lets me take several swallows. The blessedly cool water feels like heaven against my dry throat. I notice him pushing the call button on the side of the bed before he lifts the line to my IV, then lifts Daniel onto the bed. As soon as his knees hit the mattress he buries his face against my shoulder and starts crying just as hard as his sister. My free arm closes tightly around him, and I close my eyes and kiss the tops of my babies' heads.

When I open them again, my eyes go to Alexander, who's back to sitting on the edge of his chair, his hands gripping the arms so tight his knuckles are white. A whole slew of emotions crosses his face and it makes my chest ache when I realize he was worried as well.

I can't imagine the pain he went through and what was going through his head when he found out about the wreck. He's already lost his wife and baby in a car accident. I know he cares for me deeply, that's apparent at the pain in his eyes now, so to know he could have lost even more people to the same fate had to have been torture for him. I hate that he went through that.

I hold his gaze and hope he sees the silent words coming from me. The words I have yet to tell him, but desperately want to. I love this man more than I thought was possible, and I need him to know that.

A moment later, a doctor walks into the room carrying a chart. I hate it when the kids are forced to get down so the doctor can check me over. I'm impatient as he asks me questions and explains the extend of my injuries, but am glad when he says I can go home tomorrow, as long as there are no complications throughout the rest of the day and night.

As soon as he's gone, the kids are back on the bed with me. My eyes stay connected with Alexander while they cry into my shoulder. After a few minutes, their cries turn to sniffles. I break my stare with Alexander and pull both kids back so I can get a better look at them. I notice the bandage on Kelsey's cheek again and the one on Daniel's chin. More tears come to my eyes and my chest burns. It's apparent they aren't serious injuries, but they should never feel even the smallest of scratches.

"Are you both okay?" I ask them, needing them to say they're fine.

Daniel nods, and I turn to look at Kelsey. "We're okay, Mama. We're just glad you're okay too."

I close my eyes and relish in the sound of her voice. It's going to take a long time to get used to hearing it again, but I'll soak up every second and never take it for granted.

"I love you both."

They return the sentiment, and I kiss their cheeks.

I keep my arms around them both, but my eyes move back to Kelsey. I can't stop looking at her.

"You're talking." I state the obvious, because it's still so unbelievable.

She nods and drops her head. I place my hand under her chin and gently lift it back up. Utter devastation shows on her face, and it makes me want to cry all over again.

"Kelsey, sweetie—"

"I'm sorry!" she blurts, interrupting me.

"There's absolutely nothing for you to be sorry for," I tell her, my heart in my throat making it tight.

She nods vehemently. "There is, Mama. I'm sorry I made you so worried because I didn't talk. I'm sorry I hurt you." She stops, and I watch her throat bob as she tries to hold back her tears. Her voice is a whisper when she finishes, breaking my heart in the process. "I'm sorry Daddy died."

I lean my head close to her. "I want you to listen to me very carefully, Kelsey. I know I've said this before, and I'll continue to say it until you finally believe me. You are in no way responsible for what happened to your father." I stop, letting her process my words before continuing. "Your daddy wasn't getting all the blood he needed for his heart to work properly." I swallow past the lump in my throat. "He would have died either way, because no one knew of the problem. It wasn't because he went to go get your bear. His heart gave out because it was too weak to work anymore. He would have died whether he got your bear or not."

I can see in her eyes that she still doesn't completely believe me, but I also see undeniable hope that what I'm saying is true. Since we moved to Cat's Valley, I haven't put her back in counseling, hoping that the move would be a big enough change to help her open up and release some of the grief. I can see that was a big mistake.

"I miss him so much," she whispers brokenly.

"I do too. We'll always miss him and that's okay." I turn to look at Daniel and see the sadness in his eyes. I pull him closer and speak to them both. "But it's also okay to move on. Your daddy will always be a part of our lives, no matter what."

"I'll try," Kelsey says after several moments.

Although this is a very painful subject for all three of us, it feels right that we're discussing it. I've never tried keeping the subject closed, I've always been open to talking about Will to them, but Kelsey's never shown interest, or her face contorts in pain when his name is brought up, and I think Daniel likes to avoid it because it always hurts Kelsey and me. It doesn't feel forced, and I know it was time. Hopefully we can all properly heal now, most especially Kelsey.

Alexander still hasn't said anything, and I look over at him. He looks tired, with bags beneath his red-rimmed eyes. He looks strange wearing the dark blue scrub shirt. He's bent over with his elbows on his knees and his hands clasped together tightly, watching me and the kids with an intense look. Something painful lurks in his eyes.

I'm just about to ask him if he's okay, when the door whooshes open and his parents step into the room. They come to a stop when they notice I'm awake. Immediate relief has their shoulders sagging. It warms my insides to know that they care enough to worry, even if it is because I'm important to Alexander.

The kids lift their heads to look at the door, and his parents' eyes soften when they see them huddled on the bed with me. It's Helen who steps forward first, stopping briefly by Alexander and squeezing his shoulder. She comes to a stop beside the bed. David goes to stand behind Alexander.

"How are you feeling, dear?" she asks with kind eyes.

I give her a timid smile. "My head's hurting a little, and a few minor aches, but I'll be okay."

"That's good. You gave us a scare. Thank goodness you three were okay."

"How are the people in the other car?" I ask.

It's David that answers. He shakes his head, and I know the answer. A sharp pain stabs my chest at the loss of life.

"Her brakes went out in her car. Reports show she tried swerving to miss you, but she clipped the back corner of your truck."

"How many people?" I croak.

"Just her."

We all share a moment of solemn silence at the poor woman that lost her life. I send up a silent prayer for her family.

Helen looks at Alexander's still hunched form, then back at the kids.

"Why don't David and I take the munchkins down to the cafeteria for a snack?

I know what she's doing; giving Alexander and me a few minutes alone. I don't want the kids away from me, but he and I need to talk, and I know they'll be safe with his parents.

"You wanna go grab a snack with Alexander's parents?" I ask them.

Daniel nods, but it takes Kelsey several seconds to agree. She doesn't want to leave me.

"It's okay. It's only for a few minutes, then you can come right back up here."

Finally, she nods, and Helen helps Kelsey down as David helps Daniel. I give the kids a smile before the four leave the room.

I look at Alexander as soon as the door whooshes closed behind them. He's still bent over, but his head is now hanging, hiding my view of his face.

"Alexander," I call.

He slowly lifts his head, and I suck in a sharp breath at the tortured look on his haggard face. And what makes the pain rapidly forming in my chest unbearable is I don't know how to make the look go away. I don't know what to say to reassure him that I'm okay besides telling him just that, but I don't think that will suffice. I'm so damn scared that this will set our relationship back.

"I froze," he croaks. I frown, not understand what he's saying. "When we pulled up, and I saw you in the flipped truck, I fucking froze."

He drops his head again as if ashamed. My stomach drops, and I feel sick. I had no idea he was there. That he was the one to find us and had to practically relive the worst moment in his life. How cruel could fate be?

He lifts his head again and when he speaks next, his voice is raw.

"All I could see and hear was Clara and Rayne that night," he says, confirming my fears. "It was like I was there again. I couldn't do anything. I was fucking stuck, helpless once again. But then something changed. I saw you in Clara's place and the pain from that was too much. I couldn't take it. I couldn't take losing you too. Seeing you there, dying in Clara's place, snapped me out of it."

He roughly runs his hands through his hair several times, then scrubs them down his face before he looks back at me. There're tears leaking out of his eyes. I can't stand to see the pain on his face or the space between us. I reach my hand out. As if he's been waiting, he springs from his seat and sits as close to me as he can get on the bed. His hands cup either side of my face gently and he bends until his forehead meets the uninjured side of mine.

I keep my eyes on him and see him squeezing his closed. A single tear lands on my cheek. I lift my hands and mirror his. One side of his face feels prickly from his beard while the other side is more smooth from his scars.

"I'm fine," I whisper. He keeps his eyes closed, but jerks his head once, acknowledging he heard me.

His eyes open and he lifts his head an inch away. After running his eyes all over my face, staying on the bandage on my forehead for several seconds, he drops his lips to mine. He keeps the kiss to a simple meeting of lips before pulling away.

"I can't lose you, Gwen," he tells me. His tone is sure, but still laced with vulnerability. "You or the kids. I can't. I won't make it a second time. I need you three too much."

"Hey. We're not going anywhere. We're here and as long as you want us, that's where we'll always be."

"Forever," he says, no doubts or hesitation in his voice. "I want you three forever."

I look deep into his eyes and know he means it.

"I love you, Gwendolyn, and it scares me so fucking much that I almost didn't get a chance to tell you. I never want to go a day without saying those words to you."

Tears threaten again, but I don't want them to ruin our moment. With my hands still on his cheeks, I pull him down for another kiss.

Against his lips, I tell him what I've felt for weeks now.

"I love you too, Alexander. And I want to hear them from you just as much as I want to repeat them back. Every day, forever."

He closes his eyes again, like he's simply soaking up my words.

The look that comes over his face can't be mistaken for anything other than pure love.

The dull ache in my head starts to pound harder, and I can't help the wince that slips free. I don't want him to know I'm in pain, especially right now after confessing our love. I want to bask in it for a while longer before reality sets in.

I'm out of luck though, because Alexander pulls back, but grabs my hand.

"You need to rest," he says, kissing the back of my hand.

I shake my head and immediately regret it. I take a deep breath, hoping to alleviate the pain.

"I don't want to rest. I want to stay awake and see you and the kids." I smile. "And hear Kelsey talk again."

He smiles back at me. "We'll be here when you wake again. And I'm sure Kelsey will be talking your head off in no time."

"I'll never get tired of hearing her speak," I refute his claim.

He nods in understanding. "You still need to rest. You hit your head pretty hard and needed stitches. The sooner you get better, then sooner you can come home." He gives me a stern look. "But in order to do that, you need rest."

I can't help the smile that's trying to slip out. Despite the dire situation we were just in, I'm happy. More happy than I have been in years. Both of my kids are safe, my beautiful daughter is talking again, and I think on the mend, and I have Alexander. There's nothing more I could ask for.

Alexander chuckles, and the sound sends pleasure coursing through me. My head may be pounding at the moment and my body may feel like I've been hit by a Mack truck, but my heart feels so light and carefree and *full*.

He kisses me again, and this time, he lingers a bit longer, but doesn't make it too intimate.

"Lie back, baby," he says gently after pulling back.

I do as he says, and as soon as my head hits the pillow, my eyes become heavy. The pounding in my head lessens fractionally when I close my eyes. I feel a light kiss on my forehead, and my lips tip up into a smile.

I feel such a huge relief now that I know everything will be okay. There's still a small part of my heart that hurts knowing that Will's no longer around to see his kids flourish and grow, but I know he's watching us with a smile. He knows the man taking his place will love and protect us just as fiercely as he ever would. And I like to believe that Clara and Rayne are sitting beside him with the same smile and knowledge that the kids and I will do the same for Alexander.

"I love you." I feel the warmth of the whispered words against my cheek.

"I love you," I whisper back, then let my mind drift off to the stunning vision of the future. One filled with lots of laughter and love. A love so strong that nothing could ever take it away or break it.

Epilogue

Alexander
TWO AND A HALF YEARS LATER...

I PULL THE RAG from my back pocket and wipe the sweat from my forehead, then take a minute to look around and admire my surroundings. It's done. It's finally fucking done. The excitement and anticipation of seeing the pleasure on Gwen's and the kids' faces once I show them brings a smile to my face.

As soon as I step out onto the porch, I hear girly giggles and boyish laughter. I chuckle when I see Daniel chasing after Kelsey with a water gun. Gigi, Charlie, and Molly, the two pups from her litter when I first met Gwen, run after them. Every few steps he gives it a few pumps, then pulls the trigger, hitting her in the back.

It took a while for Kelsey to fully get past her mutism and start talking regularly. She still went through phases where she wouldn't speak for a few days, but the time between those episodes grew until they no longer existed.

Two days after Gwen was released from the hospital after the accident, she made an appointment for Kelsey with a psychiatrist Jeremy recommended. Kelsey went once a week, and even Gwen and

Daniel went to a few sessions with her. When Gwen told the doctor about what happened to Clara and Rayne, she asked if I would consider coming in for private sessions. I didn't really care to open myself up to a complete stranger, but I did it for Gwen and the kids. Surprisingly, it did help. Pain still grips me at times, but I'm able to manage it better.

Gwen and I both have caught Kelsey and Daniel sitting alone several times while Kelsey quietly talks about Will, their father. Daniel's recollection of him is slim, so it's good that Kelsey wants to share her memories with Daniel. It helps keep his memory alive for them both. It's also good therapy for Kelsey.

I walk down the steps and across the yard toward the house. A delicious smell hits my nose when I walk in the door. I head straight for the kitchen where I know Gwen is. She's at the counter, chopping something, and I walk up behind her, wrapping my arms around her heavily pregnant belly, and kiss the back of her neck.

"Hey, you," she says, turning her head so I can get to her lips.

I moan when she opens up to me and meets my tongue with hers. She tastes like strawberries, her pregnancy craving. She says she never liked strawberries until then.

Just like every time I kiss her, my cock turns hard and body yearns for hers. Only knowing that the kids could come inside at any minute keeps me from making love to her right here in the kitchen.

I pull back and she turns in my arms, leaning back against the counter.

My stomach meets hers, preventing me from getting close.

I smile down at her. "It's done," I say simply.

Her eyes open wide and exhilaration washes over her face. Her fingers dig into my arms.

"Really?" she asks.

I nod, then kiss the tip of her nose. "Really."

She squeals in excitement and it makes me laugh. I love seeing the pure bliss on her face.

I feel a nudge against my stomach and look down, running my hands over the sides of her swollen belly.

"I think someone else is excited too," I remark with a chuckle.

She giggles.

"I wanna see it."

I kiss her one more time before scooping her up into my arms and heading out the door. She's used to me carrying her, so she doesn't complain, just wraps her arms around me and snuggles her face against my neck. I walk across the yard and into the new house I've built for my family. I opt to wait to show the kids until after Gwen sees it. All the rooms are empty. We just need to move everything in and buy what still needs to be bought. I've had a lot of help from a few of the local people, friends that I've reacquainted with in Cat's Valley, and James and Jeremy. My parents have even made several trips so my dad could help.

James wanted to come over today to help me finish up the house, but I declined his offer. I knew today I would be done, and I wanted to be the person to put the finishing touches on it.

I lead Gwen through every room, letting her take in the white walls I'll let her pick the paint for, the hardwood floors and the shag carpet in the bedrooms, the kitchen with the granite countertops, the master bathroom with the huge garden tub and separate shower, the big family room we plan to fill during holidays. I watch Gwen's face as we go through each room, and every time her smile grows, my heart feels fuller.

Gwen and I married two years ago and we've all been living in my cramped cabin. I ended up converting the utility room into two small separate rooms for the kids. I wanted them with me, and I couldn't leave the cabin because of the horses. It was to tide us over until I could build a house for us.

When we stop at the room that's connected with ours, tears form in her eyes. It's the nursery our baby will sleep and grow up in. When we first talked about building a house, Gwen asked if she could see the designs for the one I was going to build for Clara and

Rayne. She fell in love with the design, and with a few tweaks here and there, we decided to go with it. At first it was painful to think about building something that was meant for Clara and know she'd never get to see it, but over time I realized she would want me to still build it. Besides, I have a feeling she can see it from where she is.

"This is perfect," Gwen says, her voice full of emotion. She looks around the room. "The whole house is perfect." She walks over to me, gets to her tiptoes, and gives me a sweet kiss. "Thank you," she murmurs against my lips.

I wrap my arms around her and bring her in as close as I can. I love feeling her belly against mine. When she first told me she was pregnant, my first reaction was to be scared out of my mind. Memories of the many times Clara fell pregnant only to miscarry gripped me tight and started suffocating me. It took Gwen several times calling my name to snap me out of it. Immediately afterwards, I had her doctor on the phone, demanding an appointment for the next day. He was a local doctor and the same one that treated Clara, so he knew my history with Clara and saw the fear on my face. After going over Gwen's past medical records and assessing her himself, he reassured me that she was perfectly healthy and should have no reason for concern. He said she should have a completely normal and healthy pregnancy. His reassurance helped, but didn't take away the worry completely. She's got a month and a half left, and I don't think the worry will go away until she delivers. It's just ingrained in me.

"When can we move in?" she asks.

I lace my fingers together loosely and rest them against the small of her back. Her hair is so long now that I feel the ends tickle my fingers.

"All that's left now is for you to pick a color for the walls, have the furniture and appliances delivered, then pack up the cabin and move everything over here." I give her a stern look. "And when I say pack up the cabin, I mean anyone other than you."

She laughs and pinches my sides. "Shush. I can do a little."

I narrow my eyes at her, but she doesn't back down. I give in only because when it comes time for it, I'll get my way anyway and not let her lift a finger. I've already got packers and movers lined up to help.

I scoop her back into my arms and carry her back down to the living room. As soon as I set her on her feet, we hear the pitter-patter of small feet on the porch seconds before the front door is thrown open and Daniel and Kelsey rush through the door.

"Can we see?" Kelsey asks excitedly.

I catch sight of my wife's expression. It's been two and a half years and she still gets a soft look when Kelsey speaks and shows her happiness.

I watch as Gwen takes both of the kids' hands and waddles as she leads them around the house. I follow them with a smile on my face. I look at Daniel as he eagerly points out how he wants his new room to be set up. My eyes next move to Kelsey and admire the many changes in her over the last couple of years. The once quiet girl that held so much pain in her eyes is now vibrant and outgoing. I then look at Gwen and feel my chest swell.

These three people have become my life, and with them, I've moved past the pain of losing Clara and Rayne. Through their love I've become stronger, and through me, I like to think they've become stronger. I no longer fear the loneliness of the future but embrace it with both hands, because I know it's one that I'll cherish living for the rest of my life....

For more information on selective mutism please visit the link below.

http://selectivemutismcenter.org/whatisselectivemutism/

Other Books By Alex

JADED HOLLOW SERIES

Beautifully Broken

Wickedly Betrayed

Wildly Captivated

Perfectly Tragic

Jaded Hollow: The Complete Collection

THE CONSUMED SERIES

Endless Obsession

Sex Junkie

Shamelessly Bare

Hungry Eyes

The Consumed Series: The Complete Collection

HELL NIGHT SERIES

Trouble in Hell

Bitter Sweet Hell

Judge of Hell

Key to Hell

The Hell Night Series: Complete Collection

WESTBRIDGE SERIES

Pitch Dark

Broad Daylight

About the Author

Alex Grayson is a USA Today bestselling author of heart pounding, emotionally gripping contemporary romances including the Jaded Series, the Consumed Series, The Hell Night Series, and several standalone novels. Her passion for books was reignited by a gift from her sister-in-law. After spending several years as a devoted reader and blogger, Alex decided to write and independently publish her first novel in 2014 (an endeavor that took a little longer than expected). The rest, as they say, is history.

Originally a southern girl, Alex now lives in Ohio with her husband, two children, two cats and dog. She loves the color blue, homemade lasagna, casually browsing real estate, and interacting with her readers. Visit her website, www.alexgraysonbooks.com, or find her on social media!